ZORA

ZORA

A Cruel Tale

Philippe Arseneault

Translated by Fred A. Reed and David Homel

Talonbooks

Talonbooks
278 East First Avenue, Vancouver, British Columbia, Canada V5T 1A6
talonbooks.com

First printing: 2017

Typeset in Arno
Printed and bound in Canada on 100% post-consumer recycled paper

Interior and cover design by Typesmith
Cover and inside cover illustrations by Alan Hindle

Talonbooks acknowledges the financial support of the Canada Council
for the Arts, the Government of Canada through the Canada Book Fund,
and the Province of British Columbia through the British Columbia Arts
Council and the Book Publishing Tax Credit.

This work was originally published in French as *Zora, un conte cruel* by VLB
éditeur, Montreal, Quebec, in 2013. We acknowledge the financial support of
the Government of Canada through the National Translation Program for
Book Publishing, an initiative of the *Roadmap for Canada's Official Languages
2013–2018: Education, Immigration, Communities*, for our translation activities.

LIBRARY AND ARCHIVES CANADA CATALOGUING IN PUBLICATION

Arsenault, Philippe, 1976–
[Zora, un conte cruel. English]
     Zora : a cruel tale : a novel / Philippe Arseneault ; translated
by Fred A. Reel and David Homel.

Translation of: Zora: un conte cruel.
ISBN 978-1-77201-175-3 (SOFTCOVER) – ISBN 978-1-77201-191-3 (EPUB). –
ISBN 978-1-77201-192-0 (KINDLE). – ISBN 978-1-77201-193-7 (PDF EBOOK).

     I. Homel, David, translator II. Reed, Fred A., 1939–, translator
III. Title. IV. Title: Zora, un conte cruel. English

PS8601.R758Z4513 2017   C843'.6   C2017-901887-6

Part One

Part Two *Six Years Later ...*

Part Three

PART ONE

CHAPTER
1

The Very Rich Hours of Seppo Petteri Lavanko, Master Tripe Butcher and Cutter of Virgin Throats

I n the far reaches of verdant Finland lies a forest inhabited by strange and singularly repulsive creatures. Known as Fredavians, they possess two legs and two arms attached to a torso. But they resemble human beings in no other way, the differences between them being substantial and in many ways terrifying. Judge for yourself. To begin with, measured from foot to neck, the Fredavians are little larger than certain vases used to display flowers (rather large vases, one might add, of the kind often encountered in the vestibules of Chinese restaurants in our larger cities). Their heads, however, are gigantic, like those of elephants! How their frail necks manage to support such monstrous heads without snapping defies rational explanation and can be said to border on the supernatural. In an attempt to explain the phenomenon, anatomists, not to mention naturalists and weekend dissectors, have advanced several hypotheses. Some claim that the outsized heads of the Fredavians contain several air pockets, making them lighter than their great volume would lead one to believe. Others, among whom we find the celebrated French osteologist Valentin Balancine, author of a scholarly work on the subject, have theorized that the bone structure of the Fredavians is far denser than that of humans, a material denser than diamonds! That idea, for a certain period of time, excited the curiosity of numerous alchemists, whose feverish imagination contrived a series of incongruous experiments to be carried out on these most unusual bones. In the postface to his essay on Fredavian morphology, Valentin Balancine made a touching appeal to those singular creatures, calling upon one of them to allow itself to be dissected for the greater glory of science and the advancement of human knowledge.

If the only way to communicate with the Fredavians has been through postfaces of learned treatises, it is because they remain hidden in the dark and threatening depths of their lands, in the Fredavian Forest. We do, however, possess some historical evidence of their existence. Innumerable travellers' accounts have described these peculiar dwarf-like creatures with their stubby limbs and monstrous heads as living in a "forest in the east of Finland." The museum in Grigol, a town situated a good dozen kilometres to the southeast of the forest, displays the tibia and shoulder blade of a Fredavian whose corpse local farmers discovered in 1851. The bones, clean and well preserved, lie atop a red velvet cushion beneath a bell jar. An anatomical study in ochre representing a Fredavian is displayed on the wall behind it.

Certain accounts are more ancient still, and even more startling. In China, the official historiographers of the Ming dynasty relate, in *The Annals of Xu Wengong*, that a European missionary presented the emperor Longqing with a "monstrous dwarf, no taller than a stork's wing to which was affixed an ovoid head the size of a giant panda torso." According to this account, the sight of the grotesque gnome so terrified the emperor that he fainted, and regained consciousness only after having been briskly rubbed with a decoction of camel sputum and lemon peel. For having thrown the son of heaven into such a stupor, the European missionary was torn limb from limb without the generosity of being killed prior to the act. As for the frightful creature, it was dispatched to Japan, where it too was dismembered before being cast into the mouth of a volcano.

But the chattiest witnesses to the factual existence of the Fredavians are the very humans who, until several decades ago, made their homes in the forest of the same name. They were poor and uncultured people for the most part, rustics and primitives who lived by hunting, fishing, and gathering berries, herding reindeer, and performing abortions with rusty farm implements, working as prostitutes, being periodically expelled from the forest by the tsar's surveyors, and fattening pigs that they then sold at the public markets of nearby villages. They lived distant from one another, scattered throughout the vastness of the forest. Their log cabins were filthy and damp. The Fredavian Forest engendered ill-tempered men and women of brutal mores.

The forest dwellers had laid down, over the centuries, a network of narrow tracks that allowed them to make their way from one dwelling to the next. These pathways opened in turn onto broader trails that converged on a dimly lit clearing at the heart of the forest.

In our time, hikers in the Fredavian Forest are barely aware of the almost imperceptible thinning of the dense woods. If, for whatever reason, they decided to linger in that place, their thick-soled boots might well stumble over curious ruins: foundations of disintegrating bricks, wood and building stones, planks, even the blades of axes and knives that have become so friable over time that the slightest pressure would cause them to snap or disintegrate. Our hikers might well come upon the vestiges of a lumber camp or a peasant's hut of yore, and would pay them no heed. How could they realize that in this very improbable place, a mere century before, stood the inn known as the Farting Bear, the theatre of the events we will relate in the pages that follow.

Be then informed that even during its prime, the inn, constructed of long, irregular planks, was so crooked that it seemed to tilt to one side, as if some strange forest blight had sapped its very foundations. So decrepit did it appear, in fact, that it seemed altogether abandoned. Yet a large signboard nailed to the outside wall proclaimed the specialties of the house:

AT THE SIGN OF THE FARTING BEAR
Tripe and Organ Meats
SEPPO PETTERI LAVANKO, master tripe butcher

"Everything is consumed; nothing is discarded"

Squirrel-brain purée with tomato trimmings
Boiled wolf heart with minced turnips
Lynx liver with pan juices served on aged lettuce
Wolverine sweetbreads flambéed in cod-liver liqueur
Potted badger kidneys with forest mushrooms
Roasted bear's head (2 persons)
Toad spawn with red beans in a yellow sauce
Reindeer tripe in sow butter à la Seppo,
served on Amanita mushroom caps

Dessert
Babas au jus de polecat

Seppo Petteri Lavanko, the innkeeper, was a man of unmatched nastiness. The tale that follows will surely persuade you of the truth of our assertion.

Though certain right-thinking people may claim that a person's character must never be judged by his appearance, let us examine more closely our scoundrel of an innkeeper's physique. Paunchy, low slung, and pear shaped, Seppo's bloated face and narrowly spaced pale-blue eyes were enough to make any person hideous, even had all the rest been grace and harmony. The long, droopy hairs of his moustache dangled over his lips and a bristly diadem wreathed his baldpate. In his youth a tuft of dense and curly red hair had covered his head like a mushroom cap. But by age seventeen, his hair had begun to fall out. At twenty-five he had already lost the battle against advancing baldness. By forty-two, the disfigurement of strawberry marks covered his bare scalp.

In the great lottery of intelligence, the luck of the draw had deserted Seppo, the great dispenser of judgment having allotted him hardly more discernment than a turkey. And the dispenser of judgment's elder sister, she who dispenses goodness, had proven to be meaner still, completely depriving Seppo of her favours. So quarrelsome and foul-mouthed was the innkeeper that anyone who by some misfortune crossed his path would immediately detest him. Even had he been polite, it would have made little difference; he was simply too ugly to be loved. Let us look more closely: his flaccid jowls hung from each side of his mouth like shrivelled grapes; his breasts, swollen like leather flasks, bloated his blood-stained apron; his thick and stubby legs seemed connected by railway crossties, so that he walked with a perpetual limp. It was as though nature had tattooed the features of a dead fish upon his face, a sterile mask that only hatred and resentment could bring alive. Seppo was known for no other emotion but anger.

The state of his lodgings faithfully reflected his personality. Butcher knives dripping with blood lay strewn here and there, all about the building. In winter, the chimney spat thick black smoke, day and night. The dining room boasted a dozen round tables, and in place of chairs, thick square-cut logs with hollowed-out extremities. At one end of the hall stood a small stage, upon which musicians would occasionally perform, playing the accordion and the violin. Often, during drinking binges, dancing, shouting whores and drunks crowded onto the stage, each trying to throw the other to the floor below. And when one person was left, he would break into the dirty ditty that everyone knew, transforming the inn into a bellowing gallery that would cause all plants within hearing distance to shrivel and die.

Huge barrels stacked behind the bar contained every possible variety of repugnant alcohol: polecat juice, green beer, a muddy aquavit, viscous hydromels, and aged eau-de-vie … Seppo himself distilled all the beverages, the premise being that there was nothing that could not be transformed into alcohol. Algae, mushrooms, kidneys, and even excrement: there existed for Seppo no animal or vegetable substance that did not hold within it the secret of one particular eau-de-vie or another. By perfecting the distillation of cabbage and mother's milk he created a kind of homebrew, which he called patantine, highly prized by some of the inn's older habitués, who ascribed to it antitussive properties. Seppo picked the cabbage from his own garden and drew the mother's milk directly from the breasts of the Stroller, the resident prostitute of the forest who in return could drink all she wanted at the inn.

The kitchen was located in a cramped space off the dining room. That was where Seppo spent most of his time. Eviscerated tripe lay everywhere, on the floor and the counter. The tripe macerating in jars, as it had not been stored in acidulated water, would become discoloured. A large lard pot covered by a thick crust of hardened fat stood abandoned in the corner where the counter met the wall.

The inn's only three rooms were located on the second floor. The first one, on the left, was reserved for Seppo. The other two could be reached by following an L-shaped corridor. Those two rooms were for the customers. The mattresses were covered with damp, cold, coarse animal pelts that stunk of mildew. In both rooms the humidity was enough to chill one to the bone.

Decrepit and shaky, the inn was built of long, vertical planks. Its purple paint had begun to blister and crack. As everything had been thrown together in haste, long cracks opened up between the planks, and the frigid winds of winter experienced no difficulty in finding their way inside. Three crooked steps led up to the entrance, which gave onto a narrow covered porch that made the building look as if it had a square mouth that unrolled its tongue like a concertina. It was high time for renovations, but repairs would have thrown Seppo into debt, which the innkeeper refused to consider. With the passage of years, the tall fir trees that marked the edges of the clearing had begun to cast their dark shadows over the inn, until finally their branches obscured it completely. The firs seemed to say, "Why did you come to live here, Seppo Petteri Lavanko? Why did you inflict your own ugliness and that of this building of yours on our closed universe of peace and quiet?" So it was that with their branches, the trees intentionally blocked out the light of the sky, better to maintain the clearing in a permanent penumbra. The effect could hardly have been more depressing!

Behind the main building stood another that resembled a barn but was, in fact, a knacker's shed. Here, Seppo scalded and skinned his game. Here, he would hang meat and kidneys on large hooks to age. The entire room was filled with animal carcasses, dangling between ceiling and floor. Translucent bottles full of black blood and bile sealed with pork bladders and covered with dust lined the base of the wall.

For Seppo Petteri Lavanko, nothing could be more satisfying, more relaxing, than making his way among these masses of muscle tissue, tripe, and the kinds of cuts that no normal human being would touch. The knacker's shed was King Seppo's private domain. Here he would come every evening to stroll indolently among the cuts of meat, hands behind his back. Now and then he would pluck off a piece of raw flesh and stuff it into his mouth, chewing it slowly until it surrendered its juices. How he enjoyed the sensation of being alone in his private labyrinth, among the carcasses marbled with fat and oozing blood. And if of an evening he felt in a poetic mood, with his imagination he transformed the huge quarters of meat into enormous pecans or the bodies of lubricious nymphs hanging on hooks.

Between the larger pieces, smaller morsels, such as heads, feet, and ears, hung on more delicate hooks. When the wind found its way through the cracks in the plank walls, these tidbits danced in the shadows, inducing a sense of enchantment in Seppo that would cause him to shed tears of delight, then sink to the floor among the cuts of soft meat to masturbate, with heaves and gasps.

Having pulled up his trousers, he would continue to the far reaches of the knacker's shed. There he kept even stranger cured meats, sides whose curves invited Seppo to even more loving caresses. The innkeeper could spend rich hours observing and touching, and when the damp chill of the shed finally penetrated his limbs, he abandoned his pleasing place of refuge with regret, and returned to the hustle and bustle of the inn.

For astonishing though it may seem, especially considering the sordid nature of his commerce, Seppo could boast of a clientele as numerous as it was faithful. The little community of the Fredavian

Forest, made up for the most part of the idle and the ne'er-do-well, gathered there every evening to drink polecat juice, eat pork scrota prepared in the Ukrainian manner, sing, dance, and laugh.

But the reputation of the Farting Bear had long spread beyond the bounds of the forest. People flocked from throughout the region to consume dog's-blood pudding and otter offal. Seppo looked on with folded arms as people of all kinds paraded past his counters: poverty-stricken families, lonely men, even wandering boys. There were also fortune seekers, the anathematized, dwarf breeders, professional anonymographers, itinerant salt merchants, prostitutes driven from the towns by the guardians of virtue, the sex crazed in search of a cheap whore, conspirators whom Seppo suspected of hatching dark plots against the person of the tsar, soothsayers who, in exchange for a bowl of stew and a beer, would examine the innards of game or burn chicken livers, drawing happy presages for Seppo's progeny ("may they be numerous and refined," one of them ventured, pressing one nostril closed and snorting a gleaming turquoise gob of snot from the other). There were also, as everywhere, men who had fled the towns because of their excessive consumption of garlic.

Once a legless and armless man had come calling, carried in a rucksack by his wife.

And one day, a jovial poet from Turku came for a meal of grilled bear tripe stuffed with salted turnip purée. He knew ancient Greek. For Seppo, he composed a few touching dactylic hexameters to the glory of the Farting Bear, whose picturesque charms he praised. The work would be published by a friend of friends once he returned to Turku, he assured Seppo, and would include a special dedication to the innkeeper. "*Caveat emptor!*" he added. As misfortune would have it, no sooner had the poet set off along the path northward than he perished of food poisoning. A regular at the inn, Kalle Normio, came upon the man's cold corpse the following day, his head lying in a pool of upchuck.

Another day, a homunculus arrived at the inn. If Seppo would allow him to enter his ears, he would cleanse them with a dandelion petal and a cat's whisker. Delighted at his good fortune, Seppo allowed the tiny man to climb into his right ear. The homunculus slid down the chute of wax till he reached the far end of the ear canal; there, he pierced the eardrum with the tip of his sharp slipper ("Ouch!" Seppo had cried out), and slipped into the hole, never to reappear. Seppo never found out what had become of the Lilliputian.

Many of these migratory fowl were fugitives from justice. The Fredavian Forest promised them safe refuge; never would the authorities pursue them. The sheriff's men feared the forest, those immense dark woods that were spoken of with horror in the region's villages. Even the soldiers of the tsar had been given strict orders never to venture there. More modest functionaries from lesser departments had on one occasion attempted to enter the forest on a mission and thus enforce royal claims. Never were they seen again.

Travellers were more frequent, of course, come spring and summer. The woodcutters who had cleared the land to the north during the winter headed south to spend time with their wives and children. They were stout, bearded, ill-smelling, rough-and-ready men who ambled along the forest paths, singing songs about shepherdesses and petticoats, telling spicy stories and laughing lustily. Families of settlers headed in the opposite direction, going north to occupy the lands cleared by the woodcutters and open them up for farming. One slow-moving procession after another made its way along the forest tracks, horses drawing sledges loaded high with household belongings. Enormous bales bulging with clothing, bedding, and everyday objects were heaped along with furniture in ill-fitting piles several metres high. Plump children perched atop the loads, swaying from one side to the other with the gait of the horses.

The return of fine weather held out the promise of excellent business for Seppo. From dawn to dusk, the inn hummed with customers. Travellers bivouacked outside, or fought tooth and nail as they waited for a room to come free inside. When evening fell, it was time for the regulars, the inhabitants of the forest, to take possession of the place, to drink and carouse. At first daylight, after a boisterous night, they set off toward their homes, stumbling over protruding roots as they went and vomiting in the underbrush.

As has by now become apparent, Seppo was rarely alone in his sordid little realm, surrounded as he was by woodcutters, settlers, bon vivants, and every other kind of poacher and felon on the run. Escapees from prison cells in the Grand Duchy converged on the Farting Bear, where Seppo provided nourishment without distinction to the builders and the dregs of society alike.

Inside the inn, happy wayfarers, low-lifes, and women of easy virtue gorged themselves on tripe and emptied their tankards while Seppo came and went, from the kitchen to the customers. The regulars, who were well acquainted with the innkeeper's bilious temperament, cast aspersions on his cooking in raucous voices and made sport of his rages.

"Damn your eyes, Seppo, is that kidney soup you served me, or hog piss?"

"Ha ha ha!"

"Seppo! We ordered rabbit lung potage and look what we get – leavings from your chamber pot!"

"Ho ho ho!"

"Hey! You call this fresh tripe, innkeeper? Tastes like you dug it out of your mother's corpse and served it to us roasted!"

"Hee hee hee!"

As Seppo was both imbecilic and quick tempered, the raillery never failed to infuriate him. He intended to be master of his inn, and here he was treated as though he were some comical busboy, some second-rate dishwasher! In fury he smashed plates and saucers and cursed his customers, and the more his fat, red face swelled with anger, the louder the customers laughed. But in the end, everyone in attendance raised their glasses to the health of the gross innkeeper, whose misadventures and abrasive character had long made him the laughingstock of the Fredavian Forest.

But after several fat years came the lean. A terrible famine stalked the lands to the north. Driven by hunger, entire families headed south. Starving paupers soon thronged the forest paths.

Poverty-stricken, famished visitors congregated in front of the Farting Bear, entering in silence when a table became available. Seppo, who scrutinized them angrily, more often than not felt he was witnessing funeral processions. Swarms of emaciated children followed their parents. "Better they should have thought twice before spawning these slimy shits when they don't even have a leek to chew on!" he philosophized.

How pathetic the children were, how emaciated and filthy their parents. Sometimes they were accompanied by the very old. These poor people, sometimes four generations of the same family, ate in silence, wrinkled foreheads bent low over their bowls of tadpole soup, their plates of intestines, or their goblets of cold tea. To the poor, Seppo always served the least fresh; after all, they were customers who would never complain. Often the head of a destitute family, without as much as a cent to pay for their meal, offered to wash the dishes, or perform odd jobs, or chop wood in exchange for a plate of grease or a skillet of kidneys. Seppo, who was avaricious and had no love for the destitute, despised this kind of trade. He would fly into a rage and, waving his arms, banish the penniless. Their faces drawn by hunger and fatigue, men, women, and children would file out of the inn without a word and continue along their way toward destinations unknown, never to be seen again.

*
* *

On the day that is of particular concern to us, a man and a young woman walked into the inn. It was a cold January afternoon, and the dining room was empty. Seppo was busy slicing the cheeks from hares' heads. He nodded grumpily to the visitors.

The man would have been about sixty, but in these hard times, when hunger could transform a forty-year-old into a fossil, how could one be sure? The cold had changed the flesh of his face into a brittle crust streaked with long, pink crevices. A bushy white moustache dominated his square jaw. He was husky and broad shouldered, but you could tell from his weakened state that he had not eaten in some time. His clothing was worn, but smooth and well fitted. Over his shoulder he carried a large jute sack that seemed very heavy. With every stride, he laboured under the weight of his burden, and pushed off weakly with his legs to keep the sack balanced. A broad-brimmed hat shaded half his face.

The young woman who followed him could not have been more than twenty, yet she walked hunched over as though she were a hundred. Beneath her worn dress, her bare calves were striated with frostbite. All she had to protect herself with from the cold was a shawl and a worn sweater dotted with holes.

Seppo approached the man.

"Woodcutter?"

"Yes."

His voice was hoarse. Seppo was like certain animals: he lowered his head and lost his dominant air when confronted by someone taller and more muscular. He suddenly felt intimidated by the old man.

"Heading south looking for work, are you? I thought only the peasants were suffering from famine ..."

"Everyone is suffering. There are no more peasants to feed the woodcutters, so they are leaving too."

A lengthy silence fell. The man and the young woman stood motionless. Seppo was increasingly nervous.

Finally, in an irritated voice, he said, "Got money, vagabond? No money, no kidneys."

The old man dropped the sack he was carrying over his shoulder, and it struck the floor with a solid thud, as though it contained a corpse. He spoke again, and his voice was no more than a murmur.

"I have no money. But I've got this sack of bear grease. That's what my daughter and me have been living on for days. There's nothing else to eat, not in the woods and not in the fields. Have you seen what's been going on in the forest lately, innkeeper? The settlers coming back from the north are eating tree bark. They gnaw on spruce pitch and end up with balls of shit as hard as rocks. Their family members have to clear out their assholes with birch twigs. Between the Archangel plains and here, my daughter and me counted at least fifteen dead bodies, rotting under the branches. Everything stinks to high heaven. I'm hungry. I'll give you this sack of grease if you give us something to eat."

The man was exhausted from speaking, and his voice was no more than a death rattle. Though his feverish eyes were fixed on Seppo, he seemed to be talking not so much to the innkeeper as to himself. Seppo felt cold sweat running down his back.

"It's good bear grease," said the man. "Take it, the whole sack. Just give us something to eat, something to drink."

Seppo hunched over, opened the sack, and sniffed. It was quality bear grease; that, he couldn't deny. He thrust his hand into the sack, pulled out a lump, and pushed it into his mouth. Mmmh … tasty! He took some more, fashioned it into a ball, and tossed it from one hand to the other, feigning indecision. Then the miscreant lifted the sack with both hands as if to weigh it; it contained enough grease to cook with for two months. But the evil Seppo concealed his delight and complained loudly that the grease had a bad taste, it was too runny, it had an off colour.

He stood up and wiped his hands on his apron.

"Well, grease is hard to come by these days, and even if yours isn't worth two pennies, I'll have to make do because I have nothing left to fry my kidneys with. Sit down with your daughter … What's her name?"

"Hambone."

"Take a seat. I'll serve you today's leftovers. Eat your fill, then sweep the floor."

Seppo went into the kitchen and came out a few minutes later with a skillet full of cold dog's-blood pudding and a small wooden platter that held two soggy onions, a crust of bread, and a carafe of water.

No sooner had the innkeeper placed the food on the table than the old man was stuffing the scraps of blood pudding into his mouth. He had intended to chew carefully, but his hands were faster than his jaws, and little flecks of gristle dribbled down his chin in rivulets of yellow spit. So rapidly did he eat that his Adam's apple rose and fell like the swells of an angry ocean.

"Ho there! Don't eat so fast, old numbskull!" Seppo cautioned him. "I'm warning you, if you vomit your pittance all over my floor, I'll make you wipe up the mess with the rags you're wearing! That happens a lot around here!"

The customer raised his head as if to size up what remained to eat. He picked up the carafe in both hands and drank deeply.

Seppo, standing over the table, was more interested in Hambone. She watched her father eat from her spot across the table. The skin of her face was like papyrus, and her large eyeballs protruded grotesquely from her angular visage. How old could she be? Fifteen? Twenty? He could not tell. All she wore to protect her tiny feet were thin, jute leggings held up by knotted thread around her calves.

Her father had been stuffing himself for a good two minutes when she reached out her hand to pick up a morsel of white fat that had stuck to the side of the pan. *Thump!* The old man's fist came down like a sledgehammer on the poor thing's wrist. Seppo heard her brittle bones crack. The girl yelped with pain and thrust her hand into her armpit. A tear rolled down her cheek.

As for her father, he barely lifted his head. He began trying to stuff an onion into his mouth. But the old man was toothless! He chewed frenetically, trying to break down the recalcitrant vegetable with his gums. The effort made him salivate all the more, and his spit became foam on his lips. He finally managed to break off a chunk of onion, too big, in fact, for it lodged in his gullet.

The old man straightened up. His face turned purple and he began to wheeze as he clutched his throat. This time, Seppo really lost his temper.

"Well, I'll be damned! The old dog! What did I tell you, eh? Look at 'im, can't even breathe!"

The man staggered a few steps, then fell heavily to the ground. Seppo hurried behind the counter. There hung a rack of carving knives, each one equidistant from the next. He grabbed a fish knife and turned back to the gagging man who was now wriggling like a perch at the bottom of a canoe.

You guessed it! Seppo, the man of many wiles, fully intended to make an incision in the old man's trachea and extract the chunk of onion trapped therein. But as he had spent his whole life dismembering reindeer, bears, and wild pigs, Seppo had developed a heavy hand, and delicate work wasn't his specialty! Pursuing his task with an excess of ardour, he plunged the knife so deeply into the old man's throat that its point came out the other side and even pried up a splinter from the floor – damnation!

In short order, a torrent of blood poured from the woodcutter's throat. The girl threw herself to the floor, shrieking, lacerating her cheeks, and ripping out tufts of hair. Seppo untied his apron and put it under the woodcutter's neck to absorb the blood. But there was nothing he could do but watch as the expiring man's lifeblood drained away.

One final spasm wracked the body before it gave up the ghost in a spray of tiny red globules. Seppo got to his feet and observed the scene.

"Well, look at that! What a mess!" he exclaimed, waving his hands in the air.

Whenever a customer died at the Farting Bear (something that happened more often than you would have thought), Seppo exclaimed, "Ah! If only I had an assistant!" or "Ah! If only I had another pair of strong arms to help me with the heavy jobs!" On and on he wailed, for hours on end, which finally got on his customers' nerves. But that evening, except for the new orphan who was tearing out her hair over the still-warm body of her father, there was no one to hear Seppo's complaints.

Hambone wept abundantly. Seppo, infuriated at first, calmed down as he watched her. Was it the girl's distress or the weight of his solitude that most affected the innkeeper? Gazing at the weeping girl, Seppo's heart grew danker by the minute. The poor thing, exhausted, finally fell silent but her hands, like a raptor's talons, went on clutching the dead man. She laid her head on her father's chest, and the blood that continued to bubble up from the wound coated her face and gummed her hair. Her sobs were muffled now. Seppo watched her, licking his moustache with the tip of his tongue. The image of the blood-spattered girl gave way to a vision of hefty quarters of oozing meat, and that in turn inflamed his lower abdomen. "Devil take it!" he exclaimed, "Our little sparrow has fallen from the sky, done to a turn!"

Poor, poor maiden! Now you'll be all alone! What misfortune to become an orphan at the Farting Bear on a winter's evening and to have no one but the innkeeper to console you! Better to have seen your father drown in Fox's Pond, or better still, succumb to a seizure in some charnel house in town. At least you would have escaped the clutches of that swine Seppo!

The mourning girl was still bent over her father, but her embrace had loosened. The evil innkeeper grabbed her by the hair and forced her to raise her head. The maiden's cheeks were smeared with the dead man's blood.

"I like you this way," hissed Seppo with a nasty smirk.

Hambone immediately intuited the shameful designs of Seppo Petteri Lavanko. Summoning all her strength, she shouted and struggled to escape. In frustration, Seppo the butcher grabbed her neck with one hand while the other clutched at her drawers. Lifting her up, he carried her to the staircase and climbed the steps, holding her like a sheep. Roughly, he lugged the girl upstairs, and her head and knees banged against the walls. By time he had reached the landing, her legs were covered with bruises and she had three lumps on her forehead. She gasped with horror as Seppo, beside himself now and seething with fury, heaped insults on her. When they reached the second floor, the innkeeper kicked open the door to his room. As they crossed the threshold, Hambone made one last desperate attempt to save herself: after a moment of limpness intended to distract him, she surprised her assailant by violently twisting her torso. All for naught! Not only did Seppo maintain his grip, but he also smashed his victim's head against the door jamb. Hambone let out a croak and stopped wriggling.

Fifteen minutes later, Seppo stepped out of his room wearing nothing but long underwear. When he reached the ground floor he nearly tripped over the woodcutter's cadaver.

"Ah! What a pity! The old glutton! I forgot all about him!"

Into the kitchen he went, then re-emerged carrying a bowl of sausage trimmings flavoured with wolf jism, poured himself a glass of throat-rasping red wine from the Plabet region, sat down on a stool in front of the counter, and ate his trimmings and drank his wine as he stared at the dead body. Then an idea dawned on him. He returned to the mourning damsel on the second floor, where the poor thing had just stepped out of the room and collapsed in the corridor, her skirts every which way. Seppo gave her a kick in the ribs.

"Make yourself useful, you snivelling dustbin. Mop the dining-room floor while I burn your father's body in the yard."

Alas, the task of swabbing up her father's blood fell to the poor orphan maiden.

*

* *

And so it was that Hambone added her emaciated face to the gallery of personages who populated the theatre of abomination that was the Farting Bear. By dint of treating her violently at all hours of the day and night, Seppo had ripped her garments to shreds, but the girl held on fiercely to what remained, seeing as she had nothing else to wear in any event. Her scarf, which she now wore like a spectre over her hood, obscured her visage. All day long she toiled like an ox. She swept the floor, washed the dishes, chopped wood to feed the stove, and went to the river for water. And every night she made her way back to Seppo's bed, mute and exhausted.

At first, her presence at the inn was a source of merriment for the customers. No one had ever seen Seppo Petteri Lavanko with a woman, and, come to think of it, it was not that remarkable that the repulsive innkeeper, now in his middle years, had encountered no one else on his path before this orphan, who was uglier than a toad. The regulars called Hambone "Seppo's little slut." For the first few days, she was the main subject of conversation, but they slowly lost interest. "Just make sure you don't get in my way when I'm serving customers," Seppo told her. "If you do, I'll whip you within an inch of your life!" How wretchedly treated she was, the poor child! But the worst was yet to come, as this account of a cold night in March will prove.

That evening, after a hard day's work, Hambone was seated in a rocking chair close to the stove. Seppo had come to tolerate her spending her late evenings there, once the day's chores had been completed. The inhabitants of the Fredavian Forest had all left their huts and converged on the inn to drink. Ella the Angel Maker, with a carbuncle in the same spot on each cheek, was playing her miniature bandoneon and grinning with her yellow teeth. Her husband was sitting beside her, arms dangling on either side of his body like motionless pendulums, head stuck in a plate of badger bladder next to an empty vodka bottle. Farther on, a man whose face was shaped like an onion – he was nicknamed Footpad – was dancing bare chested on a table, swaying his gaunt body covered with round, red scars that resembled bullet holes in a most disgraceful way, while the customers urged him on. Sometimes he would stop dancing and break into gesticulations and incoherent charades: thrusting his hand into his armpit he would make farting noises, or mock military salutes, or kangaroo jumps and pirouettes, one finger atop his bald cranium. He had an inelegant walrus moustache, and tufts of thick hair protruded from each side of his pumpkin-shaped head.

In a dark corner of the room Sagadat Leino, who was also Ella the Angel Maker's nephew and apprentice, was guzzling a tankard of grog, seated next to his beau Jarkko Saarinen, whom everybody called Little Lulu because he liked to dress in women's clothing and piss sitting down.

A woman stepped up to the counter, a tired-looking forty-year-old wearing a black crepe georgette dress with white polka dots, the décolleté of which exposed a flat, bony chest. The woman exchanged a few words with Seppo, who was busy behind the counter. Her skinny legs, spread wide open, hung from each side of the bar stool, and now and again she fanned her pudendum with her skirt. When she did, she emitted little sighs of relief: "Oooh!" "Ohh!" "Ahh!" She was known as the Stroller and made her living selling herself in the slums of Aveline, the poor district of Grigol. Two or three times a year she returned to the forest of her birth, to be beaten by her father and to recover from her latest dose of the clap. In the evening she would drop in at the Farting Bear, down a drink or two at the bar and, when she was well and thoroughly drunk, clamber onto the landing and swing her rear end to and fro to attract customers. She made less from a trick here than she did in town, but considering that she was at home in the forest of her childhood, she let it pass.

Altogether, that evening, there must have been a good fifty nobodies and she-mules dancing in the close confines of the inn. In the middle of a frenetic jig, the man they called Footpad began to leap from table to table. It was bound to happen: his foot slipped on a spill of godaille and he went crashing to the floor. The other customers burst out laughing, clapped each other on the back, and danced around the unfortunate man, singing:

Ride the bottle
With a bright-red ass
Ride the hop barrel
With a fine round ass!

Wake up the next day
Ass like a gooseberry
One blow to the head
The asshole's dead!

Everybody was shouting boisterously when suddenly the Stroller cried out.

"Oh! The piglet! Ah, the little sow!"

All heads turned toward the whore, who was grinning and pointing her finger at Hambone, sitting by the stove.

"Seppo's little slut is pregnant! A little snot-nose is on the way!"

The customers turned toward Hambone.

"Spotted it three days ago!" shouted the Stroller. Why, just the day before yesterday I was pretty sure of my hunch, but tonight there's no doubt. Look at her belly button, the cheapie! Her tummy's all round and her breasts are swelling! She's got a bun in the oven for sure!"

The customers gathered around Hambone, squeezing her breasts and prodding her belly. The simple-minded little girl let them without a word of protest. As was her habit, her head hung down and her eyes were half-closed. A mild fever coloured her cheeks and her lips wove the words of a mysterious litany.

"So, that's how it is," said one of the customers, straddling her. "Limp-prick Seppo has given her a little brat! Now I've seen everything!"

"Where do you think it'll pop out, the little shit?" said a woman as fat as a ruminant. "She's nothing but skin and bones. Know what I think? Seppo ought to slice her belly open with a butcher knife."

"Could be a piglet. She's carrying it real low … most likely a girl," said Ella the Angel Maker. "In any case, she doesn't look any too healthy to me, this skinny youngster. Hard as I look, I just can't figure out what Seppo saw in her to make him stick it in."

"Come now! One night when he had too much to drink he must have mistaken her for one of his sows," said the man they called Timo Korkeavuori, and everybody burst into laughter.

"I'm not surprised. Seppo's always walking around with a hard-on."

"Poor child! Now that Seppo's worked her over, that pussy of hers must stink like pickled kidneys!"

How everybody laughed and laughed! Knaves and country low-lifes enjoyed a few more moments, one dancing on a chair pointing his finger at Seppo, another taking advantage of the innkeeper's dumbfounded attitude to steal a few hefty chunks of the mouldy greenish sausage that hung from the ceiling.

But Seppo, who usually flew off the handle when customers made fun of him, didn't seem to hear the mockery flying every which way. There he stood in the middle of the dining room, petrified by the unexpected revelation. Was Hambone really going to have a child? He got a hold of himself and headed in her direction with a mean look.

"It's true you're knocked up?"

Hambone the sickly, from whose mouth a word never issued, went on rocking herself, eyes on the floor. Her pale lips formed a tight, uncomprehending circle, and no one could tell if it was a sign of madness or a mute appeal. The girl's silence made the confrontation intolerable for Seppo. He lost all patience.

"So you're knocked up, is that it? Knocked up?"

The poor child reacted not at all.

"Sow!"

And Seppo, *ab irato*, lashed out so violently at Hambone that her chair rocked backwards and tipped over. Poor child, there she lay, legs in the air, crotch exposed. The customers exploded into guffaws at the sight. "Hurrah!" they shouted, jumping up and down in mirth.

The pleasure his customers derived from his discomfiture only increased Seppo's humiliation. He started to roar and ran through the dining room, arms flailing, driving the riff-raff out of his establishment.

"Come back tomorrow! That's all for tonight. Closed! Tomorrow there'll be hashed muzzle and grilled piglet's intestine! I'll open a barrel of bear's bile! We'll play cards, I'll auction off my sow and I'll auction off my wife too, and whoever wins will be doing me a great favour! Go on now! Off with you! Tonight I've got to rough up my sullied little flower, so get back to your pigsties! Off you go! Make yourselves scarce!"

He bellowed those last words so powerfully that the customers clapped their hands over their ears. They gathered up their coats and hats and filed out of the inn, laughing. It was past midnight, and you couldn't see two steps in front of you. The merrymakers scattered along the forest paths like roaches fleeing the light. And as for Seppo, he rolled up his sleeves and laid a thrashing on Hambone to end all thrashings.

You had to feel for Seppo. He'd never been to school and even though he'd lost almost all his hair, and wrinkles had begun to line his face, he still did not know where children came from. A vinegar salesman explained to him one day that women got pregnant when a particular kind of mushroom took root in their bowels. Another time, a corpulent razor vendor who'd stopped at the inn claimed, in front of Seppo, that women made their own babies by performing strange cabalistic procedures on their navels, the secret of which they had transmitted by word of female mouth since the beginning of time. To Seppo, who asked for more information, the vendor replied that he knew nothing more than any other man on the face of the earth, for females carefully guarded their secret. It would have been useful to know the science of baby making, because then men could also make them under their belly buttons or – who knows? – in sow rumen or watermelons.

And so Seppo determined that Hambone shared the two characteristics that made women so difficult to bear: their indolence and their constant need to make themselves interesting. To draw attention to herself, so she might be taken seriously, Hambone had secretly fashioned a fetus in her spare time. Truth to tell, the whole story was a matter of indifference for Seppo, proof that deep down he was a man of magnanimity. After all, he could very well show the little bitch the door, and her fetus along with her, just as soon as it had hatched. On the other hand, he could not tolerate that the cheeky girl had humiliated him in front of his customers in the midst of a drinking session by displaying her swollen belly and making them believe that, through some mysterious connection, he had something to do with her pregnancy. That was what infuriated him and drove him to beat her. Some would say that Hambone deserved what she got because, well, children, when you don't need them, what a headache they are!

Seppo so often and so viciously mistreated Hambone that,

a few months later, when the time came for her to drop her load, her body was still covered with bruises and scars.

As it happened, on that evening the regulars were carousing at the inn. Outside, the sky was streaked with broad swaths of honey.

The customers were playing Butter the Toast, a game of singular simplicity. Seated around a table with a thick chunk of bread placed in the middle, the players, one after the other, drew a bead on it and then tried to spit on the bread. The first to miss the target had to eat the slice.

That evening the customers were extraordinarily boisterous. Around the table, a chorus of twisted mouths full of blackened teeth projected fine streams of spittle onto the slice of bread in the centre of the table. A night watchman by the name of Kalle Normio, a rapist and violinist in his spare time, was standing on a chair, interpreting a rigadoon from the New World. The customers who weren't playing the game were dancing, drinking, shouting, and singing... At one point, Footpad spat wide of the mark, and it was as if a lightning bolt of joy had struck the inn. Footpad was a low-life who spent most of his time telling anyone who would listen that he had the stomach of an ostrich, and people liked nothing more than to make him prove it. Even the violinist stopped playing to watch him stuff the bread into his gullet and when, a few mouthfuls later, the pathetic wretch spewed everything over the table, the customers were in seventh heaven. It was at that very moment that a great moaning filled the inn, a moan so deep and desperate that everyone fell silent.

It was Hambone. She slid slowly from her rocking chair and collapsed to the floor, ashen of face.

Ella the Angel Maker chortled. "Woman in childbirth! Woman in childbirth!" She was the first to rush over to the parturient to appraise the situation.

Imagine her astonishment when, lifting up the poor girl's skirts, she realized the baby was already born! A girl! The newborn lay there wriggling and sticky in the folds of her mother's dress.

"Well, I'll be! Our little Hambone has dropped her piglet! And now she doesn't know what to do, seeing as how it wasn't supposed to come for two, three more weeks, the little brat. Worse yet, it's a girl! Just look, broody hen, and you too, Seppo the simpleton. Now you're stuck with one big pain in the ass! Ah! People are going to laugh their heads off when they hear the news!"

Seppo stood motionless in the middle of the room. In one hand he held two tankards of polecat juice; in the other, a deep bowl of boiled badger scrota. He stared at the tiny smear of wet, white flesh shivering in the abortionist's hands. Cackling, she held the baby out to him.

"Seppo, you idiot, don't deprive us of the pleasure of seeing you hold a tadpole! Come on! Take it, it's yours."

It was as though Seppo had awakened from a dream. He blushed like a youngster caught stealing candy and shouted at Ella the Angel Maker.

"What are you talking about, you old hag? Take that thing in my arms? Do I have teats, maybe? Give Hambone the little gasbag! I've got work to do! Got to serve the polecat juice and the appetizers."

"Wait a second. You're the one who knocked her up. Do your duty and quit whining. Rock the child a bit to put her to sleep and use one of your butcher knives to slice off that bit of intestine that's sticking out of her belly button."

And at that, all present chimed in with loud voices, encouraging Seppo to pick up the baby. The mocking abortionist harangued the innkeeper louder still.

"Make up your mind, will you, Seppo? And if you don't, we'll use the baby as the bread for Butter the Toast!"

Seppo erupted in fury; you'd have sworn blue flames flashed from his eyes and nose. A terrifying sight, to be sure!

"Leave me alone with the little snot-nose," he finally cried out. "Is it my fault if that little monkey Hambone got a bun in her oven, even though I generously kept her under my roof because her old man croaked right here on my floor and left her fatherless?"

"But it's entirely your fault! It's your bun in her oven, beet head," Ella snapped.

"My bun? What are you saying, you stinky codfish?"

"You stuck it into her, didn't you?"

"So …"

There were three seconds of stupefied silence in the dining room, followed by a huge outburst of laughter. Footpad tore the infant, still squirming from the shock of birth, from the abortionist's hands.

"Let's play Butter the Toast! Who can spit in the little piglet's mouth?"

Footpad set the tone by spitting high into the air, a gob of sputum landing on the black fuzz that covered the babe's head. With an outcry, the customers plopped the newborn down in the middle of the table. Footpad, the Stroller, a moustachioed young blood called Anssi, and a pockmarked mushroom trafficker who appeared occasionally at the inn, Marko Sahlstedt, rushed to the table, clamouring to be the first to play. Which upset some customers, who began to grumble and push and shove. The Stroller and Little Lulu started to pull each other's hair. A few seconds later the whore grabbed an empty mug and broke it over the queer's head, lacerating his temple and slicing through one of his eyebrows.

There were a good three dozen half-wits of both sexes at the inn, and all of them with at least five pints of strong beer in their veins. They began to pick on one another, heading toward the usual violence, but as the saying goes, *a drizzle can stop a cyclone*: Butter the Toast quickly reconciled the belligerents. After they had almost come to blows, the he- and she-asses gathered around the table and, ignoring the basic rules of the game, started spitting in unison on the baby, aiming for her mouth. Seppo took refuge in the kitchen. He would have nothing to do with the proceedings.

Meanwhile, Hambone lay on the floor, gasping. With immense effort, she managed to roll over on her side and assume the fetal position. There she remained, knees drawn up, while the cannibals traded insults and blows above her baby's head. When harmony was restored, since everyone was caught up in the joy of spitting on the baby, the new mother managed to squat, and then, painfully, get to her feet and execute a few steps. She threw a brief and empty glance at the customers who formed a compact mass around her spittle-covered infant. No one saw her slip out and close the door behind her.

Outside, the poor girl steadied herself for a moment on one of the porch posts. Her legs were like rubber; gusts of wind whipped her skirts, hardened her cheeks, and numbed her calves. She gathered her strength and let loose the porch post. In a final act of coquetry, she adjusted her scarf and shawl. Poor, poor ugly duckling, be gone!

With tiny steps, like a weasel, Hambone set off down the narrow trail that led north from the inn and vanished into the night.

They found her body several days later, some five kilometres north of the inn. A trapper, Elijah Saariaho, was checking his snares along the Serpeille River. At the foot of Pöysti Falls, in the surging undercurrent shadowed by birches, the trapper came upon Hambone's lifeless body, floating on her stomach, limbs outstretched. Her formless skirts and dress undulated in the water and formed a floral diadem around her frozen silhouette. Elijah was a good-hearted man, and he pulled her from the water and shed real tears over her lifeless corpse. If indeed there is another life after this one, we would like to imagine Hambone, seated high somewhere above, on a cloud, looking on as the burly trapper wept over her dead body, replaced her scarf atop her head, kissed her frigid forehead, and then, shivering, burned the corpse before casting her ashes into the river, in full respect for the last wishes of the young woman, who had herself made the decision to end her days there. How moved we are to think that the goodness of Elijah Saariaho could open, flower, and perfume the rarely trodden path that led to little Hambone's heart, and cause it to smile ever so slightly, high up in heaven.

CHAPTER
2

The Extraordinary Pipe Tobacco of Tuomas Juhani Korteniemi

Seppo Petteri Lavanko, as we have seen, was as gross as he was coarse. From cradle to grave, his lot was ridicule. His whole life long, no one listened to or understood him, with the exception of a single human being, and even then, in his deviousness, he contrived to squander the favours of that grand heart. The meeting between the two men, several years before the singular birth that we have just related, fully merits recounting, preceded as it was by a visit to the inn by a most unusual messenger.

In the dining room that afternoon, two retired watchmen were chatting indolently with three old men from Grigol. From time to time, Seppo passed by to pour them another shot of patantine and collect their empty glasses. The rest of the time he spent in a hammock hung from the ceiling just behind the bar, stuffing his face.

Seppo and his customers turned their heads lazily when they heard the latch click on the outside door. They saw a man's shadow fall across the floor before the open doorway, a man of average height, slender of physique, and well muscled. On his back he bore a heavily laden sack, whose weight he supported with a strap around his forehead. A small pot, a skillet, and a hatchet hung from the sack.

Seppo found his appearance suspicious.

"Where are you from, wanderer?" he asked the visitor.

The man nodded and stepped up to the bar. Seppo turned to the drinkers' table and threw them an inquisitive glance. The elderly pensioners, whose long days of sloth had sapped their alertness, and who were surprised by nothing, observed the scene with indifference. Erik Loppi, an offal merchant from Grigol, and the only one of the group under sixty, shrugged his shoulders and raised his forearms in perplexity. Seppo turned once more to the stranger, for a stranger he was indeed, since he understood not a word of Finnish. And what a curious complexion! He was slender, but of the high-strung type. With every movement, his sun-darkened skin rippled across the muscles of his neck and shoulders like some precious leather rubbing against fine stones. The collar of his khaki shirt was open to form a broad V that revealed a hairless, deeply tanned chest and a wolf's tooth hanging from a leather lanyard. Seppo was quick to react.

"That wolf's tooth, is it for cleaning out the hole in your prick before bedtime?"

No response, except for a nod of the head that meant, "Yes, yes." An outburst of laughter in the inn; the old drunks found the idea hilarious and slapped their thighs in merriment. The success of his comment put Seppo Petteri Lavanko in a positive mood, since he had always wanted to be funny. He was weary of being the butt of the assembly's jokes. He beckoned the visitor to draw near, thinking he might find further ways to mock him.

The man came forward with deliberate steps. Seppo noticed he had an eagle feather behind his ear, sticking out of his long, dark hair. The innkeeper's eyes met the traveller's. Ah! He had black eyes, something Seppo didn't like one bit … His two powerful forearms strained at the rolled-up sleeves of his huntsman's shirt. That troubled Seppo, who suddenly felt intimidated and lost a good deal of his haughtiness.

Then the man reached behind his back and from one of the side pockets of his sack pulled a small package wrapped in birchbark and tied with threads of hemp. He handed the package to Seppo, pointing with the tip of his index finger at a small piece of paper slipped beneath the ties. It was a message written in tall, elegant script. Seppo took the package and shook it next to his ear, attentive to any suspect sound. Nothing. As he could not read, he rose and showed the package to Teemu Kakko, a flayer of ruminants from Ballottine, the only one present among the customers that day who knew a few letters. Holding the package at arm's length, Teemu Kakko brayed out these few sentences.

"To Mr. Seppo Petteri Lavanko, master tripe butcher and proprietor of the Inn at the Sign of the Farting Bear, in the Fredavian Forest. We would be grateful were you to take possession of this packet and retain it on consignment until such time as its designated owner, Mr. Tuomas Juhani Korteniemi, claims it, which, please be assured, should occur between now and the end of winter. The packet, should you be so kind as to certify, contains only a small quantity of tobacco of inferior quality. As compensation for your kind services and for any inconvenience you may suffer, the aforementioned Tuomas Juhani Korteniemi, upon taking possession of said packet, undertakes to pay you the sum of twenty marks."

It bore the signature *Tuomas Juhani Korteniemi*. Startled, Seppo exclaimed, "Twenty marks! Is this some kind of joke?"

Suddenly the matter had taken a much more interesting turn than expected. Teemu Kakko looked at him.

"Just who is this Tuomas Juhani Korteniemi?"

"No idea," answered Seppo. "That's all it says?"

"Wait a minute. There's a post-scriptum: 'The bearer of the present has travelled far before reaching your lands: he has made his way through forests, across an ocean, and through still more forests. Should you be so kind as to provide him with food and drink, Mr. Tuomas Juhani Korteniemi, upon reception of the present packet, will reward your kindness by reimbursing you the full price of a meal and a tankard of beer, by adding to the total the sum of ten marks. In compensation for your trouble.'"

Teemu the flayer scratched his head.

"What is it?" asked Seppo.

"That's strange, isn't it? The guy who signed the note is the same one who will come to pick up the tobacco. The same chap ... Tuomas Juhani Korteniemi."

"So?"

31

"Well, if he's the one who signed the note and who left the tobacco in a packet, why did he not simply take the packet with him? Why is he causing someone else to deliver it, and promising to pick it up later? Why all this song and dance?"

Seppo scratched his scalp and stuck a finger into his mouth. The whole thing was indeed mysterious!

"And just when will he come to pick up the tobacco, this schemer?"

Teemu reread the few lines and muttered, "No idea. There's no date, nothing."

"Well, then," Seppo burst out, "we'll just have to wait. For thirty marks I'm quite prepared to keep his tobacco warm in the crack of my fat ass until next winter comes."

Seppo whipped up a plate of warm sweetbreads and a pint of beer and placed it on the counter, pulled up a stump, and motioned the messenger to sit down and eat. The man didn't move an inch. There he stood, staring ambiguously at Seppo. The innkeeper was beginning to lose patience.

"What do you have for brains, an omelette? Sit down, you shifty fellow, and eat your portion, or else clear out and never set foot here again!"

Then something very curious happened: the visitor stuck his middle finger in his mouth and sucked on it for a few seconds. Then he briefly raised the finger, as if to see which way the wind was blowing, but then brought it forward slowly in a single motion and stuck it in Seppo's left ear. He carefully deposited his saliva in the fat innkeeper's ear canal.

"What the hell is …? Arrrggh!"

The other customers burst out laughing; Seppo minced about like a goat, trying to wipe out his ear with his sleeve. Livid, he heaped insults upon the visitor who was simply content to smile.

Then the man turned to the customers and waved his hand, as if to bid them farewell. With his joyous mood he succeeded in winning over the public, and as he made his way across the dining room toward the door, the drinkers got to their feet, lifting their tankards high and wishing him a safe journey in a language that, for all intents and purposes, he did not understand. He waved once more before going through the door, then vanished into the forest, never to be seen again at the Farting Bear. Seppo, who felt sullied, even violated, thrust his head into a barrel of meat and wept.

*
* *

The men and women of the inn had to wait until springtime for the mysterious Tuomas Juhani Korteniemi to appear and claim his tobacco.

That afternoon, Seppo was amusing himself by insulting the invisible customers in the inn, as he was wont to do when no one was present. He imagined that the dining room was full of people, and that he was engaged in scintillating conversation with them, in which he displayed the acumen of his opinions and his humour. In his splendid daydream, everyone saw in him a font of wisdom and complimented him on his well-considered views on the best way to slaughter a reindeer, lard a roast of dog, or simply wash his ass in Devil's Creek.

When he stepped into the inn, did Tuomas Juhani Korteniemi spot Seppo addressing an imaginary throng? Had that been the case, he seemed to have taken no notice. Seppo was gesticulating and talking out loud to himself when the visitor's footfalls tore him from his imaginary world. He turned about, scarlet with shame.

Our innkeeper, who was jealous of anyone with a finer appearance than his own, and there were many such people, took an immediate dislike to this elegant gentleman with delicate features, alabaster hair, a courtly bearing, and a reserved demeanour. "Looks like a queer," thought Seppo. The well-dressed man was wearing a suit – trousers, coat *and* vest – cut from a fabric as soft as raw chicken skin. Seppo tried to imagine how he must feel, his body draped in such soft, elegant fabric ... He pictured himself parading through the inn, a finely dressed dandy, basking in the envious gaze of his customers ... When the visitor approached him, he snapped out of his torpor. "Feh!" he said to himself. "Best I treat this precious fellow with caution." Not every day did a customer cross the threshold of the Farting Bear so nattily attired.

When the man extended his hand, the motion of his arm disturbed the air ever so slightly and Seppo's nostrils picked up the captivating scent of a perfume that pleased him greatly. Realizing he had been moved by the fragrance of another man, the innkeeper blushed. To hide his embarrassment, he hurriedly accepted the outstretched hand.

"My compliments, sir. My name is Tuomas Juhani Korteniemi."

"Well, I never," exclaimed Seppo. "So, it is you? We were wondering when you would stop by to pick up your consignment. This is not some post office, you know, eh?"

Seppo feigned irritation, but his cherry-coloured face poorly concealed the admiration this polished, perfumed older man awakened in him. Tuomas Juhani Korteniemi smiled politely.

"A thousand pardons. You must be Seppo Petteri Lavanko ..."

"Exactly!"

"Mr. Lavanko, my apologies. You must have far better things to do than to act as an intermediary for someone else's commerce. And, what is worse, I placed you in a difficult situation by sending my supplier directly to you, without so much as having sought your permission beforehand. Such behaviour is unseemly in a gentleman and even if the modest pecuniary indemnity I am now prepared to pay you will be insufficient to compensate you for the considerable distress all this must have caused you" – as he spoke, the older man withdrew from his pocket a sheaf of marks – "please accept, I most humbly implore, these meagre bills as testimony to my boundless gratitude."

Seppo the ill-mannered, who lacked all consideration for the niceties, seized the banknotes and began to count them in front of his benefactor. Fifty marks. Fifty marks! Seppo almost fainted! And still, better he conceal his joy, wasn't that so? Otherwise the pigeon would have strutted about in pride ... So, had the old geezer miscounted? Was it possible to be so stupid and so well dressed?

Fifty marks! To part with such a sum ... And who knows, perhaps there was more where that came from.

Why bother? Why wrack his brain? Seppo thrust the banknotes into the front pouch of his apron, took a deep breath of the perfumed air the old man exuded, and offered him tea, smiling with his rotten teeth.

Tuomas Juhani Korteniemi took a seat at a table. Seppo poured him tea, glancing at him surreptitiously.

"I trust that you took care to place the packet in a place where it would not interfere excessively with your work ..."

"Ah yes, the packet ..."

Seppo had kept it all this time on a small shelf beneath the bar. He reached down, picked it up, and handed it to the visitor.

Tuomas Juhani Korteniemi stood there, turning the packet over in his hands. Finally, growing impatient, Seppo coughed to attract the older man's attention.

"Your tea is getting cold."

Tuomas Juhani Korteniemi swallowed a draught of tea and glanced at Seppo. The whiteness of his hair seemed to accentuate the glint that shone from the blue-grey of his eyes.

"Please excuse me. You must be curious to find out what is so interesting about this tobacco that I have disturbed the peace and quiet of your forest in order to obtain it."

"You're damned right! For all the trouble I've gone to, the least you could do is show your appreciation with a wad of hard cash."

As he spoke, two words echoed in Seppo's head: "Fifty marks! Fifty marks!"

"On this date last year, I was in America, I – You have heard of America, I take it, Mr. Lavanko?"

"It's near to France, isn't it? A few Frenchmen have passed through here, must have been five or ten years ago. Ah, the scoundrels! They –"

"No, not at all," interrupted Tuomas. "It's much farther away than France. You must cross an ocean. That is where I purchased this tobacco. As I had intended to remain in America for some time,

I entrusted the packet to an American friend who was leaving to explore Europe. We agreed he would take advantage of his travels to visit Finland and that he would make a point of venturing as far as the Fredavian Forest, where he would deposit the tobacco until I returned. For I am also a resident of the forest, you see. My home is only half a league from Pöysti Falls."

"Ah, so that's who you are! You must know you are a legend of sorts in the forest. Just like the Fredavians, in fact! Everyone talks about you, but no one has ever met you. Visiting you is no laughing matter, judging by what people say!"

Tuomas Juhani Korteniemi's cottage, tidy and nicely decorated, lay in the centre of a dense spruce grove in the northern sector of the forest. In front there was a garden, and behind, a sauna. Situated on the north-south axis, the cottage lay at the halfway point between the Asswiper Bridge that spanned the Serpeille River and the Drunkard Hills. Only with great difficulty could it be reached; one had to leave the main trail and trek through brambles for more than a kilometre. Spruce branches would slash the face of the traveller, scratch the skin of his arms and legs, and rip his clothing. And so the inhabitants of the forest – thieves, rippers, and drunkards for the most part – would never disturb the resident of the cottage. But people had long wondered how someone who lived in such an inaccessible place could come and go as he pleased from his clearing, visit the nearby villages every three days to purchase supplies, and travel all the way to Grigol (for even those who did not know Tuomas knew that the resident of the forest cottage was an erudite of some kind who spent a portion of the year in town). How was it possible for this individual, who was said to be well over fifty, to leave and then return to his house several times a week?

"True enough, it is difficult indeed to reach my house, considering there is no path. That is why I chose to send my friend to you rather than to my cottage, especially since there was no one at home at the time. And I see that I did well to rely on your reputation as an honest man, for here I stand, tobacco in hand."

Seppo was almost purring with satisfaction. It had been a long time since anyone had spoken well of him! Still, he put on an irritated air.

"Fine, but the guy you sent, really! What a rascal! Just imagine, he sucked his middle finger, then stuck it in my ear! Me and the other forest guys, we gave him the bum's rush, but all the same … I'm as ready as the next guy for a good prank, really! But if you want to know what I think, that particular prank wasn't very hygienic, and there you have it."

"I never heard about that incident. I'm so sorry. Here, to expiate the fault of that rogue Romuald …"

So saying, Tuomas Juhani Korteniemi slid a one-mark note toward Seppo, who scooped it up and stuffed it into his apron pocket.

"Well, all right … but no matter what, that darkie of yours is not welcome at the inn. Give him the message if you see him."

"I certainly will."

"And what's more, why go looking for tobacco so far away, among those savages? You don't like the good tobacco from Karelia, maybe?"

"Believe me, there is no connection. You see, I am a kind of … how can I put it? Bah! Let's say a kind of old retired professor who uses his free time for curious experiments of all sorts. I'm particularly interested in tobacco. To tell you the truth, I am writing, among other things, a major treatise on tobacconology …"

"What could possibly be so interesting about tobacco? What can you do with tobacco but put it in your pipe and smoke it?"

"You'd be surprised! But in any case, it's only one of my little foibles. I'm also interested in mushrooms, rainwater, the stars … Where were we again? Ah yes, speaking of tobacco …"

And so saying, Tuomas Juhani Korteniemi slipped his hand inside his vest and pulled out a pipe, and what a pipe it was! The stem was made of polished wood, and the bowl of brushed porcelain on which were depicted, in midnight blue, strange scenes of country life against a white mother-of-pearl background. It was gently curved, rising at the end to describe a delicate corolla that encircled the flue. An extraordinary pipe it was indeed, one of a kind that Seppo, who counted many pipe smokers among his customers, had never seen before. He himself had made do with a miserable sheet-metal cutty for the past twenty years. Every day, at sundown, before the customers arrived, he would sit on the porch, congratulating himself on the day's work and huffing and puffing on his pipe. But the magnificent appendage displayed by Tuomas Juhani Korteniemi drew more admiring glances from Seppo than his surprising visitor himself. If Tuomas, in the seedy hall of the Farting Bear, could light such a pipe with the assurance and nonchalance Seppo displayed when he picked his nose, what other fine and rare pleasures must fill the life of this most excellent older gentleman? He then produced from his pocket a small leather pouch filled with very dark tobacco and, in three copious pinches, filled that admirable pipe of his.

As he puffed on it, Tuomas Juhani Korteniemi looked around the room in which he found himself. There was nothing affected about his mannerisms, which instead conveyed a certain majestic masculinity. His features were harmonious, his eyes intelligent and calm. He was, beyond a doubt, a gentleman, and sitting there in the dining room of the Farting Bear, he seemed as out of place as a ballerina in a butcher shop. If Seppo's establishment disgusted him, he showed no such sign.

He spoke in a carefully modulated voice, without condescension. Everything about him mesmerized Seppo. Curious, for all his life the innkeeper had shown nothing but contempt for the strutting peacocks of the town. Why then did this gentle-mannered gentleman who daubed at his brow with a handkerchief not kindle in him the hatred that more than once had moved him to hustle out the door any rich man so imprudent as to set foot in his inn?

"I find your establishment quite cozy, my friend!" exclaimed the visitor. "And this tea … it is certainly soothing to the throat."

The steam that rose from the teapot reeked of fish, but the smoke that issued from Tuomas's pipe had the odour of enchantment, one Seppo had never smelled before. All at once the innkeeper felt as though his heart were in a cook pot whose vapours soothed and excited, and he was almost overcome with tears of joy! It was as though he had suddenly fallen under some extraordinary spell. "Truly, today is my lucky day, to have come upon a man of such temperament!" Tuomas, as if nothing could be simpler, gently fingered the multicoloured embossed curlicues that decorated his teacup. He spoke, but Seppo, captivated by the heady charm of the visitor's tobacco, heard nothing.

"Pardon, what were you saying?"

"How sad it is that your inn is so far from Grigol. An establishment like yours, in town, would become a gathering place for men of many circumstances."

Though the remark was harmless enough, it tore Seppo from the ether-induced stupor into which the tobacco smoke had thrust him. To the elderly gentleman's surprise, the tripe butcher's face turned blue with anger and he began to vociferate.

"You don't think I know, for a whore's sake, that I'm too far from Grigol! It's those pen-pushers at town hall that refused me the permit to set up my watering hole in town!"

"Really! What a singular decision on the part of our administration!"

"Single what? A gang of bed shitters, that's what you mean! Let me tell you! One fine morning I show up at the Grigol town hall and there I meet a little turd merchant dressed up like a big shot in a three-piece suit – just like the one you've got on – and I explain to him how I want to open an inn so I can practise the innkeeper's trade. He looks me over like smoke is coming out of my ears and grins, the asshole. And he says to me, he says, 'And you want us to give you a permit to run a restaurant, is that it? But pray tell, my dear friend, what manner of cuisine do you intend to serve your customers? Perhaps the kinds of dishes typical of the land in which you grew up, if I'm not mistaken?' All the other pen-pushers start laughing at his smart-ass remarks. So I tell him I know how to prepare wolverine intestines, lemming-brain puddings, bitch's-blood sausage, and pâté of wild sow uterus, and all those men in their starched shirts are laughing insolently, as though I'd just told a good story. So the guy says to me, he says, 'According to regulations, we are authorized to judge the culinary aptitudes of an applicant before issuing a permit. Why don't you go home and prepare one of those specialty dishes of yours, then bring it here … We'll smell it and taste it, and if it passes the test, we will grant you a permit on the spot. And when we have duly authorized you to do business in Grigol, with the proper permits and all, then you may open your inn, my fine fellow!' So I hurry home and right then and there I slaughter my ass, Adalbert. Adalbert, my sole possession, can you imagine! He wasn't one of those three-penny donkeys that crawl when they should pull, who slow down when they should speed up! Not on your life! He was a monster of an ass, the hardest worker in the forest, in the whole Duchy, in fact! Why, he could haul a ton of manure for kilometres, and I barely needed to twist his balls to get him going! But those Grigol badgers were insisting I cook something, and me, penniless as I was at the time, how was I supposed to afford fresh bear tripe or even pig offal? So I slaughtered my dear old Adalbert with tears in my eyes – that's exactly what I said, sir, with tears in my eyes! – and · then I disembowelled him just to rustle up a pot of ass intestines stuffed with algae and fish heads for those slanderers. I boiled 'em for a few minutes – not too long, they should still be full of juice – then I decided not to cook the fish heads so they had a nice smell of dead pike and river slime. Aroma is my middle name! If it doesn't smell strong enough to wake the dead, throw in some more algae, I always say. I sprinkled a bit of hay over the whole thing, to make it look nice, and garnished it with some big green-and-brown mushrooms that I gathered by the municipal dump – you know, the ones that smell a little like the stinky pellets that you find in fox assholes. I stuffed it all into a big, lidded pot and hurried off to the town hall so I could get my inn in town. No sooner did I lift off the lid than the whole office filled with the fine smell of gamy fish and rotten hay!"

Seppo clenched his fists and flexed the little muscles of his flabby biceps. His blue eyes were bloodshot. He was panting again, as if by reliving those events, the dining room had suddenly become the office at the town hall, and the amused faces of the municipal functionaries were now staring at him.

"But those wretches, the kind of people that wash their faces in mother's milk every morning, they know nothing about fine cuisine, so how do you expect them to appreciate the delicate odours of a hearty dish of tripe? So I plop my pot down on the desk of the chap I spoke to earlier. He's still grinning, the insolent bumpkin, and he asks me just what I've cooked up for them. 'Good, juicy donkey tripe just barely cleaned, stuffed with fresh algae and fish heads. Smell it, then taste it,' I say, and that half-a-man shoots back, 'As for smelling, that's done already. I bet they can smell the rotten fish from here to Japan!' And the other scalawags burst out laughing. 'As for tasting, my fine fellow, you won't hold it against me if I take a pass, I trust! Even a pack of famished wolves wouldn't touch that revolting purée of yours! We asked you to cook something because we wanted to have a good laugh. Administrative work can be so boring... On your way, now! Now go back to being a pig herder and give up this outlandish idea of opening a restaurant to poison the good people of our town with sickening stews.'"

Just describing the scene made Seppo lose all self-control. He brought his fist down on the table.

"So there I was, in such a rage that I grabbed the little queer by the hair before he could finish laughing at me and stuck his head up to his neck in hot intestines! And there I held it until the other pipsqueaks, a good ten of them at least, forced me to let go. A creep slathered like a barn door was vomiting into a wastebasket. Tripe juice was dripping from everywhere thanks to the fat pigeon that was starting to smother. I was giving him a wailing he'd never forget when I felt a blow on the head from a hard object, and it was only under duress that I let go of the guy's scalded skull. While they were all figuring out what hit them, I made good my escape."

Seppo was breathing easier now. He picked up a goblet and poured himself some tea.

41

"I was afraid those pen-pushers, those louts, would complain to the sheriff's office, so I took to the woods and set up shop here, in the Fredavian Forest."

Tuomas Juhani Korteniemi listened to the innkeeper's tale, eyes narrowed with fascination, legs comfortably crossed under the table. With one hand he stroked his chin; with the other, he held his pipe.

"And the sheriff's deputies never bothered you here?"

"Of course they did." Seppo had declaimed his story loudly, but now his voice was calm and terrifying. "Agents from the police station showed up, thinking they could arrest me …"

A malignant gleam shone in the tripe butcher's eyes. His phrase hung unfinished and he fell silent. Tuomas Juhani Korteniemi would remember that silence his whole life long. He squirmed in his chair. He didn't feel well. Not well at all.

"Well, sir," he spoke once he'd recovered his countenance, "how delighted I am that your original cuisine was able to find a place where it could flourish free of constraint. Nor would I like you to have an over-optimistic view of the situation of the town's restaurant owners. Life is difficult for everyone these days … Here, in the woods, your establishment appears to me to be a warm and homey refuge for all those who seek such a place, looking for nourishment and a fire to warm their feet."

"I don't have any ass tripe on hand right now, but I would gladly stuff some badger bowels with fish and river slime if you like. Give me one hour's time to boil up the whole business. Badger's bowels aren't as juicy as ass tripe, but when you prepare them properly, they melt in your mouth, just like snot!"

Once again the admirable countenance of the visitor wavered. His blue-grey eyes widened and he stared at his host with stunned astonishment. It lasted only a second, and he quickly concluded in a perfectly amicable tone.

"Nothing would give me greater pleasure than to sample some of the specialties of your establishment. But to tell you the truth – I don't see any reason why I should conceal it from you, we're friends after all, aren't we? You do permit me to consider you a friend – I'm a bit finicky. Surely you'll understand, organ meats are not exactly my –"

"As you wish."

"But I'm touched by your invitation and utterly charmed by your bucolic little inn. Would you be inconvenienced were I to drop by from time to time for a little chat? I'm nothing but a poor pensioner, and the days are long."

His words were music to Seppo's ears; at long last he had found a brilliant, wealthy, and sociable friend. That evening, after Tuomas Juhani Korteniemi left, Seppo rejoiced three times over at the conversation he'd had with the gentleman. He could not explain why, but he felt he had grown in the presence of such an exceptional being, as though the soft light that seemed to radiate from the distinguished face of Tuomas transfigured all those who entered his orbit.

Tuomas Juhani Korteniemi kept his word. He made it a point of honour to visit the inn two or three times a month. He would generally arrive in the afternoon, when the inn was nearly empty. He always knocked before entering, which never ceased to surprise Seppo – who knocks before entering an inn? He always began by asking Seppo if he was causing him inconvenience by arriving at an awkward time. "I insist. If you are busy, I'll come back another time," to which Seppo gave an improbable response: "Not at all … As you can see, I was cleaning out my mucus membranes with cod alcohol." Only then would Tuomas agree to take a seat. But he never stayed for longer than one hour.

Of his guest, Seppo learned nothing, primarily because he never had the courtesy to question him. Tuomas would not drink alcohol when he visited the inn. He also declined the tea and food that Seppo offered. He was content to sit next to the bar and examine the decor and chat with his host. In that magnificent pipe of his, he smoked the magical tobacco that sent Seppo into flights of rapture. Exchanges between the two men were always one-way affairs: Seppo took advantage of his guest's interest in everything involving the tiny society of the forest to monopolize the conversation. He would fly off the handle for singular reasons – so-and-so had stolen his sickle, someone else had raped his sow. Seppo boasted. Seppo moaned. Seppo raved. And Tuomas listened to it all with benevolence. To such an extent that the innkeeper began to look forward impatiently to Tuomas Juhani Korteniemi's visits, for his conversations with the sympathetic gentleman had an effect on him that was both liberating and purgative.

In its complexity and finesse, the language Tuomas employed was far superior to Seppo's vulgar dialect. In fact, the innkeeper was often hard-pressed to understand what his friend was saying. Perhaps that explains why the elegant erudite magnanimously preferred to let Seppo babble on, limiting himself to asking simple questions from time to time to get him started again. Tuomas's visits to the inn seemed more motivated by anthropological interest than by the pleasures of conversation. He appeared to be studying Seppo as a biologist would a new and fabulous creature. Nothing about the inn left Tuomas Juhani Korteniemi indifferent. Seppo was amazed on occasion to find his elderly friend absorbed in contemplation of a meat grinder dripping with blood, a barrel full of raw muscle fibres, or an oil lamp into which tired moths fluttered, burning their wings. Tuomas always found an excuse not to drink the kelp tea that Seppo continued to serve him, and not touch the appetizers that the innkeeper would place on the table just for him. On occasion he would risk a word or two, when he offered some considered advice, with great diplomacy, to his host.

"My dear Seppo, I cannot help but notice all the rotted sausages hanging from the ceiling there, just above the bar. You would be judiciously investing your capital by constructing a cold room in your inn. That way, you could keep the meat longer. Add up the losses you incur by allowing some of your stock to rot, and the necessity of a cold room will quickly become apparent."

"Losses? What losses? Well-aged sausage is exactly what my customers prefer."

Tuomas, in short, was thoughtful and generous in his attentions.

He avoided preciousness, gave no sign of superiority, and maintained toward his host an amenity of which Seppo had never before been a recipient. With his well-spoken tone, his well-measured manners and calm demeanour, his unfailing though never overstated amiability, he gave Seppo the impression of being replete with the very dignity he felt he deserved. And, as though it were not sufficiently pleasant that such a gentleman would keep him company in his cold, damp grotto, each time Tuomas shared with him the enchanting tobacco that sent him into raptures.

Some two years before the birth of Seppo's daughter, Tuomas Juhani Korteniemi's visits to the inn came to an abrupt halt, without Seppo ever learning why. For the innkeeper, the blow was a harsh and heavy one. Tuomas had always found his visits to the inn of great interest, or so it seemed. All the same, Seppo noted a mysterious concomitance between the disappearance of the older man and a singular event that perturbed the daily routine of the inhabitants of the Fredavian Forest for some time.

It all began with the surprising declaration of Jarkko Saarinen, the one they called Little Lulu, during a drinking session one night at the inn (an activity in which, it goes without saying, Tuomas did not participate).

"A Fredavian attacked me!"

The singing, the outcry, and the dancing came to a screeching halt. Everyone's head turned toward the entrance. Little Lulu was standing in the doorway, face covered with nasty red gashes, his long hair tangled, forehead beaded with sweat. His dress was torn in several places.

How long had it been, seven or eight years, since anyone reported seeing a Fredavian? If Jarkko's story were true, it would be capital news indeed. Nothing fascinated the inhabitants of the forest quite like stories – proven or made-up – of the misdeeds of those evanescent Fredavians.

Since time immemorial, the Fredavians had excited the imagination of the forest dwellers. When in their humble huts they congregated of an evening, storytellers declaimed ballads, verses, proverbs, sayings, riddles, laments, fables, and poems of the country-side, and for the most part, they were the self-same ballads, verses, proverbs, sayings, riddles, laments, fables, and poems recited in the rest of Karelia. They were all about fairies, about the *menninkäinens* and the *maahinens*, about the River of Tuonela, and the best-known personages and gods of Finnish mythology. But the storytellers of the Fredavian Forest kept for the very end the most terrifying and most anticipated of all, the ones that featured the Fredavians and their master, Gladd the Argus, the Black Bard. Those stories were unknown to all who lived outside the forest. Better indeed that it be so, for the stories told of things so horrifying that no civilized man could endure the hearing of them.

The merrymakers at the inn that evening welcomed Jarkko Saarinen's tale with a healthy dose of skepticism, but also with an undercurrent of tantalizing fear. They sat him down and gathered around him. Seppo poured the transvestite a large goblet of fresh homebrew. Jarkko sipped the alcohol and told his story. Here we will report only the highlights, for Jarkko was slow-witted, a dunce if you like, with a slurred and disagreeable voice. Most of the time he spoke little, but when he wanted to tell a story, he was painful to listen to.

On that day, in the morning, he had gone down to the banks of the Serpeille River to fish. By noon he'd filled his creel with seven trout, including a "nice fat one that weighed a good three, three and a half kilos."

His nose alerted him to danger.

"All of a sudden, there it was! I'd just cast my line into the water, and the smell overcame me … Not just a smell, mind you, it was as if all the air in the forest had begun to stink of ten thousand dead polecats … It stank, stank to high heaven! Came in through my nose, my skin, my ears … I was stinking from head to toe!"

Little Lulu was afraid he would faint dead away. He turned to see where the smell was coming from.

There she was, right behind him. How long had she been rummaging through his creel full of trout? It was a female, a dirty, scruffy female. She was holding one of Jarkko's trout in her hand, not the big one, and was about to slide the head of the fish into her mouth, as if to suck on it. Jarkko's first impulse was to back up slowly, as you would when confronted by a bear, never taking his eyes off the Fredavian. "I'll just ease myself into the water, just so, backing up," he told himself, "then I'll make my escape swimming. A creature with such a huge head and such small arms surely can't swim." Then he remembered he was wearing a voluminous peasant's dress made of heavy fabric, and it would make swimming difficult. What to do? And besides, who could be sure that the Fredavian meant him ill? But what of the knife she had just drawn from a small leather sheath attached to her belt? Now her wide, feverish eyes were staring at Jarkko, and in them the transvestite saw tiny yellowish worms squirming. (Devil take it – that must be uncomfortable!) And what of the grimace of hatred that bared her blackened, toothless gums?

Bah! Nothing, most likely. After all, Jarkko had often found himself in situations in which…

AAARRGGHH!

The Fredavian went on the attack! She flung her tiny body and immense head at Jarkko, and the poor man fell over backwards. He writhed and wriggled but the Fredavian was too quick for him, and with her pocket knife she lacerated his face nastily.

"There I was, pinned to the ground! A Fredavian is heavier than you think, a lot heavier! If you listen to what people say, you wouldn't believe it … I thought I was going to die then and there," said Jarkko, as warm tears streamed down his face. "And you'll never guess who saved my life! Elijah Saariaho!"

"Whaa!"

The customers, in unison, let out a cry of stupefaction.

"Elijah Saariaho?" repeated Seppo, incredulous. "That useless hulk? That stinking pea brain? That gentleman-who-is-too-nice-to-come-to-the-inn-to-make-merry-with-us?"

Let us recall that Elijah Saariaho was the trapper who discovered the drowned body of Hambone in the river waters following the birth of her daughter.

"Yes," Little Lulu continued. "That's not surprising. I know he comes to fish in the river from time to time. In winter he hunts partridge around Asswiper Bridge. Sometimes I even cross his path, but he doesn't like company, so, when he spots me, he goes fishing somewhere else, upstream from the falls most of the time. But in any event, the Fredavian has got me pinned down, and all of a sudden Elijah pops up, out of nowhere – what he was doing there I don't have a clue – and begins kicking the Fredavian for all he's worth. The harpy picks herself up, but that takes time – when you've got a head like that and you're flat on the ground on your stomach, you need to work your shoulders to get back on your feet. While she's lying there Elijah pulls out his hunting knife, raises his arm, and *splat!* he drives the knife into the Fredavian's head."

"Oh!" exclaimed the customers, in one voice.

"The Fredavian lets out an *ooooohh!*" – Jarkko simulated her shriek in falsetto – "and leaps to her feet and heads for the woods with Elijah Saariaho's big hunting knife stuck in her head! Meanwhile, I get to my feet. For a second I think: I didn't want to go home right away, because I would have had to take the same path the Fredavian took when she ran. So I followed the river to the north and crossed the Asswiper Bridge, in the direction of Kalle Normio's. At first he didn't even want to let me in the door, I really stunk, he said! That bitch of a Fredavian had really given me a perfume job! Finally, I went down to the river and scrubbed myself with some mustard. Sure, I still stank but at least it was bearable. Kalle agreed to keep me for the night. We shared my trout."

"And Elijah Saariaho?" asked Footpad.

"No idea. No sooner did he stab the Fredavian than he left. He watched me get to my feet, straighten my dress, smooth my hair. When he saw I could stand, he went off without a word."

Not a soul at the inn was in the least surprised. Elijah Saariaho was a solitary, taciturn man who never mingled with the little forest community.

The customers bombarded Jarkko with questions. Exactly what did the Fredavian look like? Was she after his trout or did she try to molest him? What language did she speak? Was there such a thing as a Fredavian language? Was her head as big as they say in the legends? Did she wear a hat, which would match the description of the old storytellers of the forest? Did she mince and sashay before the altercation or did she attack him straightaway?

To these rapid-fire questions Jarkko could offer only the usual answers. Yes, the Fredavian had a gigantic head out of all proportion to the rest of her body. Her features were striking, with enormous eyes, a nose shaped like an apple (and runny, what's more), and a small mouth in relation to her face. Aside from her huge face, Jarkko had to admit he'd mostly seen her dirty hands and the pocket knife with which she tried to disfigure him.

All in all, people concluded that Jarkko's story was terrifying, because it was believable. Little Lulu was too dim-witted to make up that kind of a tale.

It was not long before his misadventure became the talk of the forest, and people discussed it for weeks. Not a day went by that X or Y didn't claim to have seen the Fredavian with the knife still protruding from her enormous head. Ancient legends about the Fredavians long buried in the collective imagination resurfaced. People related how, in the depths of the forest, on moonless nights, hundreds of them would congregate in clearings lit by armies of fireflies and surrender to demonic Sabbaths. They would shout out the name of their master and when, at the climax of their revelry, the Black Bard Gladd the Argus would descend from Mount Bolochel, atop whose summit he dwelled, the Fredavians celebrated his arrival with self-mutilation and the eating of raw reindeer flesh.

The excitement began to abate some two months later, when the story of the Fredavian was pushed aside by a new occurrence that was all too real (Tavasti Takala, a moonstruck young galosh-maker from the north of the forest, had buried his father and mother alive after an argument over inheritance – a story whose sordid details are of no concern to the present narrative).

But a few days after the incident, Tuomas dropped by the inn on one of his regular calls. Seppo related the story of Jarkko and the

Fredavian to the handsome gentleman. Seppo was certain that Tuomas would find the story of that extraordinary encounter captivating; imagine his surprise when his guest closed up like an oyster and took on an expression of astonishment and deepest preoccupation.

When Seppo finished relating the story, Tuomas mumbled a few polite words and left the inn precipitously. After that, his visits to the Farting Bear ceased entirely!

The absence of his only friend and confidant sapped Seppo's morale. At first, he clung to the hope that Tuomas would come again soon. Perhaps he was ill, or occupied in the town? He often spoke about his lengthy sojourns in Grigol, and even in the capital. But six months later, Seppo had no alternative but to face the facts: Tuomas was not going to return. The realization struck him like a bullet to the heart. What now? No more scent of vanilla that emanated from the freshly shaven cheeks of the elderly aristocrat? Never more, wafting between the morsels of viscera hanging from the ceiling, that extraordinary blue smoke that issued from his pipe? And now that Tuomas had vanished, who would listen to Seppo's inanities?

The seasons came and went. Seppo did not forget his friend.

Then, one day, two years after his last visit, Tuomas reappeared. One afternoon he entered the inn quietly, with muffled steps, as he always did. At the sight of him, Seppo, who was taking a sitz bath in a tub of nettle soup, let out an exclamation of joy. "Ah!" He accidentally farted in the soup, then got to his feet, pants around his ankles. He held out his hand; Tuomas withdrew his politely, declining, but smiled at the same time. Seppo blushed, muttered an apology, and pulled up his trousers. Tuomas nodded politely and spoke.

"Dear, dear friend! How happy I am to see you again! It's been a long while, has it not?"

"It sure has," exclaimed Seppo with a toothy smile. "I still remember the last time you came. I was hanging those big reindeer quarters that you see there from the ceiling. I generally leave them up two Christmases before I take them down and serve them to my customers ... How many do you see there now, Mr. Tuomas?

How have you been since the last time we saw each other? And if I'm not being indiscreet, where were you that we haven't seen hide nor hair of you for two Christmases? Off again to look for tobacco in France?"

And Seppo burst into laughter, not so much because he found himself funny, but to conceal the tempest of explosive happiness that the old gentleman's appearance brought forth in him.

As for Tuomas's comings and goings, Seppo might have received an answer had he not, as he made his way slowly toward the table at which he had been wont to sit during his first visits, been brought to a halt, as though petrified, at the sight of a barrel set beside the bar.

"My God..."

In the barrel, an infant that could not have been more than a few months old was squirming languidly among the fat quarters of tepid, yellowing meat. As it rotted, the meat exuded fluids that, when mixed together, emitted a viscous matter in which the baby seemed to be macerating. The newborn was completed naked.

Seppo hastened into the kitchen to prepare tea. When he reappeared with the teapot and two cups, in front of him sat a Tuomas he did not recognize. The gentleman's face had turned pale, his features frozen. He turned his steely gaze on the innkeeper and whispered.

"What in the world is that?"

And Seppo, who hadn't exactly invented the wheel, replied, "That? Well, that's ... those are my muskrat carcasses that I age for a few months before turning them into sausages. Tripe is my specialty, but for the fastidious souls who don't eat organ meats and insist on muscle, I always keep some fine aged muskrat meat on hand."

"No, I mean ... that child, what's she doing there?"

"What? Oh, that?"

The question startled Seppo, who did not believe that some baby could be of more interest than muskrat meat. He proceeded to relate, with more than a few shortcuts (and several omissions), the circumstances that had led to the birth of a little girl right here, between the four walls of the Farting Bear.

51

As we have seen earlier, Hambone gave birth to a child before drowning herself in the Serpeille. Meaning that Seppo, that gallows bird, suddenly found himself with a baby on his hands. The first night, after the guests had gone home, and with nary a thought to her mother's fate, he deposited the newborn in the sow's pen behind the inn. The idea being that Swingy – that was the sow's name – would devour the child before morning, meaning his nightmare would be over and done with. For Swingy was a particularly voracious sow. But to the innkeeper's amazement, come morning he found the infant gurgling away, lying in the empty trough where he'd laid her the night before. Meanwhile, the sow was rolling in her shit. "Well, I'll be," grumbled Seppo. "Swingy is getting picky. Or else the little shit disturber was yelling too loud."

Angered, he resolved to make his way to the Serpeille River, there to drown the newborn, not knowing that the previous night the infant's mother had ended her life by diving into the rushing waters of Pöysti Falls. Taking the baby under his arm, he thrust a marinated pork snout into his pocket in the event he became hungry on the trail that led to the Serpeille. What a bother, really ... The river was five kilometres from the inn, and it would take Seppo a good one and a half hours to get there, and a little more to return, as he would be tired. "What of it!" he said to himself. "When I get there, I'll do a little fishing." Before setting out down the forest path, he grabbed the fishing gear he kept hanging in a corner of the knacker's shed.

He'd been walking for three-quarters of an hour when he ran into Ella the Angel Maker, who was coming in the opposite direction, carrying a big canning jar.

"Well, well, if it isn't Seppo and his little slut! What a coincidence! I was on my way to your place. But where are you going, lugging the child like that?"

"I'm going to drown the little squirt in Pöysti Falls."

Ella's face lit up.

"You don't mean it!"

"I certainly do! What's so exceptional about that?"

The abortionist grinned.

"I'll spare you the trouble, my friend! Give me the child, I'll make good use of her."

Seppo recoiled in surprise.

"Really?"

"For sure," Ella shot back.

"Ah, if that's all it takes to please you, angel maker, here, take her!"

And with an enthusiastic gesture he handed the baby to Ella, who seemed to find the whole scene too good to be true.

"Oh, Seppo, you're not serious? You're giving me the child?"

"And how, here, take her! She's been howling since last night! I couldn't sleep a wink with the little pest making such a racket. Not to mention that she pisses every which way ... Look at the spot on my apron."

Ella gave a dry chuckle.

"Poor Seppo! Don't you know that newborn-baby piss is the best tenderizer? Do you think I'd even take a second look at your little piece of shit if there wasn't something in it for me? I've got seven children, Seppo, seven girls, and each one of them spent the first months of her life hung out to dry over a big bowl. They'd piss in the bowl and I'd collect the liquid in jars. Then I'd use it to tenderize my meat, and brew beer, and for bread, and omelettes ... I'll do the same thing with your little one, Seppo, and in a few months, when she gets too old and starts to piss vinegar, I'll have my old man go and drown her himself in the Serpeille. Off you go, Seppo, and don't worry your head about the little whiner!"

Seppo listened to the abortionist's account with great interest. "Wait a minute! I'm the innkeeper," he said to himself. "My job is preparing meals for my customers! I'm the one who has to put up with people grumbling that my meat and my kidneys are tasteless." Now that he'd received a lesson in the virtues of newborn urine, he regretted handing over the baby.

He swallowed his pride and asked Ella, "Come on, give me back the child. I changed my mind. The little girl will be more useful to me than to you."

"Not on your life, Seppo. You gave her to me, I'm holding her now, there's no going back. The deal is sealed."

"Zounds! She's my little shitstress, after all. She popped out of her mother's piggy bank in my inn, she did, then bleated like a lamb the whole night long in my sow's pen. Either you give her back or I'll take her away from you by main force!"

But Ella spat in Seppo's face and skittered off like a rabbit.

Ella the Angel Maker was a frail old woman, but she ran with surprising speed for someone of her age. Seppo was, as we have noted, squat and short legged. He dashed off after the fetus scraper but soon was gasping like an ass. The chase lasted several minutes. Ella's age and her nine pregnancies (seven children, two miscarriages) finally caught up with her. Realizing that Seppo was gaining on her, in panic she let the baby fall to the ground. Maybe the tripe butcher would recognize his progeny and let her be? No such luck! Seppo passed right by the infant without so much as a glance and picked up the pace to overtake the slaughterer of female virtue. How ugly he was, Seppo, the butt of insults! Hatred twisted his face!

When he was close enough to the old hag, he leaped on her back and threw her to the ground.

"No! Seppo, have pity! Spare a defenceless woman!" shouted the abortionist.

"Thief!" roared Seppo, smacking her square in the chops.

And, right there on the trail, Seppo perpetrated the ultimate infamy with a toothless old angel maker. Even after he shot his wad, the old witch was still writhing between his legs. He grabbed her by the hair and thrice smashed her head against a large rock. Only then did he pull up his pants, drag the corpse into the underbrush, and return home, child under his arm.

He spent the afternoon playing dominoes with his customers.

*
* *

So it was that Seppo became guardian of a little girl. The infant spent the better part of her time resting on cuts of raw meat stored

54

in barrels. She pissed and shat freely, and that was what kept her alive, for what other reason did Seppo Petteri Lavanko have to look after that little lump of chalky gristle?

It goes without saying that Seppo recounted none of this to Tuomas. He limited himself to the actual birth of the child, the mere recollection of which continued to enrage him, and strove to induce in his interlocutor a sense of sympathy by heaping one accusation after another upon the unfortunate Hambone, whose crime was to have borne a child behind his back. He ended his tale with a philosophical reflection.

"Believe you me, women, they know how to grab you by the balls. As if they weren't good for anything else."

Tuomas's face turned crimson.

"And the mother, how is she?"

"The mother … Well, uh … if you really want to know, I heard she drowned herself taking a bath in the Serpeille."

Tuomas blanched, as though all the blood that had rushed to his face during Seppo's recitation had suddenly drained away. He put his hand to his sweat-beaded forehead.

"I see … So that's the poor little girl I heard speak of."

Seppo had never seen the elderly gentleman in such a state. Abruptly, Tuomas Juhani Korteniemi lost all the equanimity he generally displayed in the company of the innkeeper; he became curt, and grave. His handsome blue-grey eyes now stared like two bottomless pits.

Tuomas thrust his bare hands into the barrel and delicately removed the child. First he laid the little girl on one of the round dining tables. Then, without so much as a glance at Seppo, he ordered in a voice that brooked no reply, "Water. Bring me a basin of hot water. Fast!"

Seppo hurried off to the kitchen and returned with a pot of warm water.

Tuomas removed his Prince of Wales jacket, spread it out on the table, and placed the infant atop it. Shirt sleeves rolled up, he dipped his fine red kerchief in the hot water and gently cleansed the little girl of the filth. He should have used soap, but where was such a thing to be found in a house where bits of innards lay scattered everywhere and where the master himself was encrusted with scum? By the time the little girl had been washed, the water in the basin was no more than a thick and gummy broth of goose shit. Tuomas used his jacket to dry and wrap the infant.

"Do you have any milk?"

"I could always milk the sow, but ..."

"No, she needs cow's milk."

"A cow? Where am I supposed to find a cow?"

"What do you feed her with normally?"

"What? The sow?"

"No, numbskull! The little girl!"

"Oh, her? I feed her sow's milk ... and when fat Helena Hiksu shows up at night to drink, she pulls out her teats and lets the child suck. She says her teats itch and it relieves her ..."

"Good enough, do what you usually do. Go fetch some sow's milk. What are you waiting for?"

Seppo could hardly wait to escape the proximity of this new Tuomas, who ordered him around without a second thought and did so, here, in his own inn! He swallowed his shame and went out to milk the sow.

He was only half-surprised when, on his return, he found Tuomas seated in the same rocking chair that Hambone, the mother of the little girl, had occupied during the last months of her life. The elderly gentleman was cradling the child in his arms and humming an old country lullaby. He sang in perfect tune, and anyone else but Seppo would have been moved to tears by the melodious words of the patriarch-protector. The child, at any rate, was cooing and gurgling happily now, her tiny red mouth dancing in the middle of her face like a freshly washed radish.

Finally the baby fell asleep. Tuomas, who had been absorbed in contemplation of the infant and the sweetness of the lullaby, shook himself from his apparent reverie. He raised his head toward Seppo and his eyes brimmed with hatred.

"You cannot look after a child. Devil take you! No one would entrust you with a pig. She is coming with me."

So that was it! Seppo was a rascal, cowardly, and wilful, but his honour had been challenged! He mustered the courage to confront Tuomas.

"Not on your life! She's mine, the little minx! I was there when she popped out of her mother's belly, I even took her in my arms, and then her mother, that heiress of a mongrel dog, went to wash her hair in Pöysti Falls and drowned herself, and I've had to feed the child and give her milk from my sow and bread from my table, and I've had to put up with her gurgling all day long, and her bawling too! She belongs to me and I won't hand her over to anyone!"

The innkeeper's lips turned purple and dry. Tuomas stood up and handed him the infant.

"So be it," he said.

Surprised, Seppo took the little girl in his arms. Clearly Tuomas was not of the quarrelsome sort! And besides, there he stood in front of Seppo, as though he couldn't care less about the child, the same person who had made such a scene that Seppo wondered if he would have to come to blows with the old man. Then calmly, Tuomas sat down in the rocking chair. He pulled out his pipe and his tobacco pouch.

Tuomas filled his pipe, and that simple gesture was enough to put Seppo at ease. He drew a match along the sole of his shoe and touched it to the pipe bowl.

Oh! The smell of Tuomas's pipe tobacco! Seppo could not draw in enough through his two nostrils to fill his head!

Tuomas got to his feet. As stiff as a stilt a hand's breadth from Seppo, he sent a thick cloud of smoke into the face of the innkeeper. Seppo blushed and his eyes clouded over. Tuomas exhaled three more puffs of blue smoke, then emptied his pipe by knocking the bowl delicately against the arm of the rocking chair.

"Give me the child," he ordered Seppo.

Seppo handed him the child with a smile.

The little girl awoke. With her black eyes, she scrutinized the face of Tuomas Juhani Korteniemi, the first benevolent countenance she had beheld since her arrival in this world.

*
* *

There were to be found in Finland those places – forests, fields, dark manor houses ruled by unscrupulous fallen members of the minor nobility – where good people would bring their daughters made great with child prior to marriage so they might carry their pregnancies to term and bear their offspring far from inquisitive eyes. The Fredavian Forest was not such a place. There, young girls came to abort. For centuries in the forest there reigned a dynasty of angel makers, the Porthen family in which the fine art of uterine curettage had been handed down from mother to daughter. It was to this lineage that Ella the Angel Maker belonged. Her whole life long, Ella, like the abortionists who preceded her, had swept (and more often than not infected) the chimneys of young townswomen from Grigol and beyond who had fallen into dishonour. Seppo had on occasion allowed Ella to perform abortions in his inn after hours and make use of certain of his butcher's implements for that purpose. In exchange, Ella would give him a percentage of the fees paid by the girls' parents.

It was a sad spectacle indeed to witness the honourable families of the town, those fathers of serious mien, faces shaded by their top hats, those anxiety-wrought mothers who arrived in the dead of night, their gaze darting around the dining room but, in resignation, offering their daughters up to Ella so that she might rid them of the infamy that had infected them. And when the abortionist had terminated her task, the young girls, wracked with pain, feverish and gasping, hurried off into the night with their parents. Often they would die in the days that followed, either because the forceps had pierced their life sac, or because they'd been contaminated by filthy instruments.

Now, as we have seen, Seppo dispatched Ella by smashing her head against a rock. He had hidden his hideous deed by concealing his victim's corpse between two fallen trees, deep in the woods. In the days that followed, Ella's family became greatly concerned over her disappearance. It seemed unthinkable that the matriarch of more than seventy years would have left the forest without telling anyone. After a week, they began to accept the idea that perhaps she was dead. Drowned, for instance, after having walked too close to the Serpeille when drunk. Or perhaps devoured by a bear. Who could know?

But the absence of that powdered and quarrelsome drunk was not the main concern for her family members. The most serious problem was that, in losing Ella, the Porthens lost their sole source of revenue.

Ella had a husband, an alcoholic who had never worked a day in his life. Between them they had seven daughters, but all seven were born deeply disadvantaged because Ella and her husband were blood relatives.

During her lifetime, Ella clearly understood that when retirement age came, she would not be able to count on a single one of her daughters to maintain the abortionist's trade. To hell with them! All were over twenty, yet so retarded she had to feed them like baby birds to get them to eat! To safeguard tradition without leaving the sacred family circle, Ella made up her mind to train her nephew, Sagadat Leino, as an angel maker.

She took it upon herself to instruct the young man once he reached the age of fourteen. It rapidly became apparent that Sagadat would never be a successful abortionist. Leaky holes terrified him, along with everything else about female anatomy, and he was so drawn to the bottle that, when clients would arrive, in the middle of the night as a rule, Sagadat could often be found in his hut along with another lad, making mischief.

Thrice alack! Sagadat was all that remained to perpetuate the abortionist legacy among the Porthens. But Sagadat found the practice repugnant, and he had squeaked by on the meagre pittance and emoluments that Ella, whose disciple he was, had passed on to him. But now that she had disappeared, where was he to find money for drink? Sagadat had no choice but to don his godmother's boots.

It was in his capacity as abortionist in chief of the Fredavian Forest that he found himself one night at the inn. The knock had come at his door earlier that evening, Seppo having summoned him. A diligence from Grigol had just pulled up at his front door, carrying a Russian couple and their daughter. They wanted Sagadat to officiate at the altar of forceps and dilators.

The forest lay immersed in inky darkness, but the light that emanated from the windows of the inn cast a sickly glow over the building and its surroundings. The customers were members of the minor Russian nobility. The young girl, no more than fifteen, had been playing hide-and-seek with a hairy garbageman who had whispered sweet nothings in her ear in a park in the old quarter, and had taken her virginity in the municipal dump. The parents had first made an appointment with an abortionist in Grigol, but when he ascertained their identity, he refused to go ahead with the procedure. Once they reached the inn, and he'd examined the little snipe, Sagadat's reaction was the same as the Grigol abortionist.

"But you must be mad! She's about to drop it! You can't abort a baby when it's reached that point. You wait, you deliver on the quietus, and you dump the little snot into the icy river!"

But the parents would have none of it; they wanted to be rid of the shameful excrescence. For his trouble, they were prepared to part with forty marks, twice the going price.

Sagadat placed his satchel full of rusty surgical implements, herbal remedies, and potions on the table and insisted he be paid first. The father would only agree to pay half the promised sum. The other half would be paid on completion, providing everything turned out for the best. Sagadat took the twenty marks, stuffed it into his waistband, and motioned to the girl to lie down on the table. The poor thing did as she was told, but since she was large and the table was small, her head hung over the edge while her legs were bent double so she could keep her feet flat on the surface of the table. She was very much ill at ease, to say the least. Sagadat felt her forehead; she was burning with fever. He looked inquisitively at the father. In broken Finnish, the latter explained that during the journey, his daughter had become greatly agitated. A few hours before taking the diligence for the Fredavian Forest, his wife had asked a doorman at the hotel where they had spent the previous night if he knew a place in Grigol where a discreet chemist could sell them a sedative. The lad recommended a sorceress who lived in the Aveline district, to whom he was eternally grateful for having removed a carbuncle from his back. The Russians hurried off to find the sorceress who, for a substantial fee, agreed to numb the child through fumigation. The family then mounted the diligence, and the father ordered the coachman to drive them to the Inn at the Sign of the Farting Bear. It was in the carriage that fever overcame her.

In truth, the girl was not well at all. Who knows what the sorceress made her inhale? Her eyes were glazed over and her breath came in faint, sharp rasps. Sagadat motioned to the father to leave the premises. He protested, since he had not foreseen that the abortionist would be a man, and refused to leave his daughter alone with him.

Seppo, hovering nearby, put in a good word.

"Have no fear, my dear sir! Our Sagadat doesn't beat around in the bushes. He gets right to the point!"

The innkeeper laughed at his own jest. But the Russian repeated in a low voice that he would not leave the room where his daughter was having her abortion.

"Well, if such is your wish ..." muttered Sagadat.

And the invert went ahead with the abortion, putting all his incompetence to the test. First, he had his victim swallow two full glasses of Seppo's patantine homebrew ("to calm her down a little") and knocked back a glass himself while he was at it. He was having a hard time keeping the liquor down, since he'd spent the better part of the evening drinking vodka with Little Lulu. It was not long before refluxes of alcohol and bile bubbled up in his esophagus, causing him to belch abundantly. Meanwhile, the young girl vomited up the rotgut. That angered Sagadat, who had to allow her time to recover before giving her the abortive decoction to drink. While her colour slowly returned, in a large pot he infused hyssop leaves, sage, rue, artemisia, and juniper, mixed with long stalks of timothy. He administered the odoriferous bouillon to the patient, and injected more of the same through her nether lips with a rubber squeeze bulb. Then he began to stimulate her twat with his fingers. "What a drag this job is," he said to himself, wiping his hands on his shirt. "If only old Ella were here, how much easier everything would be!" And, so saying, he downed another glass of homebrew.

A certain time passed, during which the adolescent digested her abortive bouillon while Sagadat swallowed shot after shot of homebrew. By then he was completely sloshed, and when the fetus failed to appear, he flew into a rage and attempted to scrape out the uterus with a long, pointed piece of metal. But instead he pierced the wall of the organ – "OOOOYYY!" wailed the girl, and "Arrgghhh," raged Sagadat as blood bubbled out onto the floor.

It wasn't long before the girl expired. The fumigation combined with the ingestion of too much abortive decoction numbed her to death – you got what was coming to you, little girl. As she heard her daughter breathe her last, the mother collapsed onto the floor. The father broke into sobs and rushed out of the inn.

Sagadat was able to fish out the yellowish head of a baby from the dead girl's entrails. "Might as well finish what they paid me for," he said as he yanked out the fetus. It was a baby that had nearly reached term, a large-sized female.

"Ah, what a disgusting sight!" groaned Sagadat, averting his gaze from the wrinkled face of the stillborn runt that looked more like a custard pie.

Pointing to the girl, Sagadat asked Seppo, "Pull down her skirts. Her piggy bank revolts me."

Seppo poured himself a glass of homebrew, emptied it in one gulp, and looked at the girl and the infant lying on the table.

"The dead child," he thought to himself, "I'll take it and leave it to pickle along with the herring. It's always tasty with –"

He never completed his thought. Everything happened too fast.

The door of the inn swung open with a crash. The first thing Seppo and Sagadat saw was the body of the Russian father rushing backwards through the door frame, bent over forward. It took them a moment to size up the situation: the man's feet hung a good metre off the floor and the tip of a pike protruded through his back. He'd been skewered from the front and, lifted off his feet, was being carried slowly back into the inn.

But even more than this funereal scene, the rush of hot, putrid air into the inn terrified Seppo and Sagadat. It was as though, much like garments turned inside out, a large invisible hand had replaced the ambient odours of animal blood and sweat with the overpowering stench of decomposing bodies. The cold air had suddenly turned warm and moist, to the point that Sagadat feared he would faint dead away.

What was that infernal consignment that bore, along with the dead body, such an odour of death and decay? Seppo pissed in his apron.

Four Fredavians burst into the inn. The first brandished the dead body of the Russian at the end of the pike. What a terrifying banner! When he stood a couple of metres from Seppo, the Fredavian standard-bearer gave his weapon a sudden shake: *shlack!* and the corpse dropped with a plop.

The Russian's wife, who had thrown herself to the floor when she saw her daughter give up her soul, and had not yet gotten to her feet, screamed when she saw her husband fall beside her like a sack of flour. The Fredavian that held the pike, with a movement of its tiny arm, pierced the breast of the mourning mother. And thus perished, in less than five minutes, three generations of Tretyakovs. If that has caused you heartache, remember they were Russians, and you will feel better straight away.

Then the four Fredavians drew nearer still and, elbow-to-elbow, formed a line, their tiny fists on their hips. It was Seppo they had come to see.

*
* *

Who neither belches nor farts is fated to explode.

Tuomas Juhani Korteniemi whispered those words of Laozi at least a hundred times into the ears of the child whose tutor he had become one week earlier. He performed the little rite with a smile, never failing to deposit a gentle kiss on the baby's forehead.

Friends referred him to a wet nurse in Grigol, Mrs. Heikkinen. The husband of the young woman – she would turn thirty that winter – spent eleven months of the year in the capital, where he worked on a scow for an inland navigation company. The couple had two boys, both apprentices in a pastry shop in Nurmes. Alone in her apartment in Grigol, Liisa Heikkinen found that time passed slowly indeed. Seeing the generous salary that Tuomas was prepared to pay her, and having received written permission from her husband, she agreed to go to work for the elderly eccentric, but for a few weeks only, "to help out in a pinch." Come spring she would return to town. "Life in the forest is not for me," she said.

From the new house he'd had built on the loftiest summit of the Drunkard Hills, kilometres from any other dwelling, Tuomas enjoyed an unobstructed view over a wide panorama of the Fredavian Forest. He took care, however, not to place his house directly atop the hill, but off to one side, on the north slope. The southwest wing of the house led to a tower built upon the summit, where Tuomas installed an astronomical observatory. There, he placed his well-upholstered burgundy armchair close to the window. From the top of the observation tower, Tuomas could gaze upon the forest at leisure, without being seen. On the ground floor, next to the laboratory where he carried out his experiments in alchemy, there was a free room. That was where Mrs. Heikkinen slept. She was comfortable enough, even though she felt a bit lonely, "far from everybody," atop these isolated hills.

At night, when the little one cried out for milk, Tuomas would awaken to watch Mrs. Heikkinen give her the breast, and that eventually convinced the wet nurse that Mr. Tuomas was indeed "a fine man, in spite of his curious ways." For she found some of his ways curious indeed – why did he have to climb up to his tower thirty or fifty times a day to scan the earth and sky with his telescope, even during daylight hours? – but, generally speaking, she noticed no trait that one would consider unusual for an elderly bachelor whom no woman had ever had an opportunity to correctly train.

While Mrs. Heikkinen gave suck to the infant, Tuomas, seated close by, observed the scene with a smile of emotion. But one thing worried the gentleman and the wet nurse: the child neither burped nor farted, ever. Mrs. Heikkinen employed every trick, and Tuomas held the infant to his chest for hours, patting her back, but the baby girl would not burp. It was a curious phenomenon, especially since, when he held the baby to his chest, Tuomas could feel the gas circulating beneath her tiny navel. It soon became a matter of serious concern. They feared that the baby would soon expand like a balloon, explode, and confirm the claims of the Chinese philosopher.

Finally, what was bound to happen happened: the little girl, for never having burped nor farted, began to swell up slowly, more so with each feeding. Her tiny tummy was stretched taut as a drumhead, and her navel seemed about to burst. Tuomas was in a panic. Baby in his arms, he travelled to Grigol to consult a physician of his acquaintance. His friend examined the infant and chided Tuomas gently.

"Is that all? Don't worry your head, my old friend. This child looks perfectly normal to me. Let nature take its course. She'll burp, you can be sure of it. It's only a matter of time."

Tuomas returned home, reassured not in the slightest.

The next day, the little one finally burped …

At half past midnight, she awoke, as she did three times a night, to suckle. Mrs. Heikkinen and Tuomas roused themselves. When the baby had drunk her fill, Tuomas instructed the wet nurse to go back to bed. He wanted to rock the little one for a while longer.

Holding the baby in his arms, Tuomas climbed to the top of his tower. He slumped down in the burgundy armchair and held the infant against his chest, patting her back. Eyes closed, he whispered in her ear.

"Now, now, why are you giving old Tuomas such trouble? I was looking forward to peace and quiet as I grow old. Indeed! At my age, to be awakened in the middle of the night by a crying baby! Do you know how old I am? I wager you wouldn't believe me if I told you! Adults don't believe me, in any event. If you only knew, you'd give me a bit of rest at night!"

Those were mild reproaches, of course. Truth to tell, in the days that she had spent under Tuomas's roof, with her charming peeps and gurgles, the little girl had embroidered a rainbow upon the heart of the venerable alchemist.

Tuomas planted a kiss on her forehead. Then he leaned back in his well-stuffed armchair and looked out the window. The sky, vast and pitch-black, was studded with stars. The muted happiness of the old man was submersed in the night like a smooth-worn stone swallowed by a gentle, enveloping misty tidal swell whose waters whispered with the regular breathing of the child. Tuomas closed his eyes … How happy he was … how well he would sleep now … sleep …

Smoke. There, in the distance. Smoke.

Tuomas shook himself from his sweet torpor. Did he see smoke? No … his vision was blurred from being awakened in the middle of the night, that was all. An optical illusion … a smudge on the window, it could only be that …

He held the baby tightly to his chest and leaned forward, better to look through the window.

A bright spot, in the heart of the forest, like a purulent pimple on ebony skin.

He stood up, laid the baby down on the armchair, picked up his spyglass, and whispered a prayer before looking into the distance.

The house he had lived in for thirteen years in the Fredavian Forest was burning. In and of itself, there was nothing tragic about that. He had not set foot there for quite some time and had taken pains, when he moved to the hills, not to leave anything behind: no furniture, no books, no precious objects, no compromising documents. The violent blaze would destroy no more than a large empty structure of wood and stone. Tuomas had not even left many memories in that ill-lighted house where, to tell the truth, he had spent many long and uneventful years. But he was aware, having observed the place no fewer than fifty times a day with his spyglass for the past several weeks, that some poor soul, doubtless having come upon the uninhabited dwelling, had sought shelter there and was growing mushrooms in the clearing that surrounded the residence.

Even the spectacle of that terrifying cabal that had surrounded the house and was watching it burn did not unduly upset him. Seven … eight … no, nine Fredavians, a full nine. Never in his lifetime had Tuomas seen so many gathered in one place. In the gleam of the flames he could even make out the grimaces on their faces. In vain he searched for a hint of disappointment or anger in the vacant eyes of the little creatures. For it was him, Tuomas Juhani Korteniemi, whom the Fredavians had come to seek out in that remote corner of the deep woods. They had not found him, of course, and it was unlikely they realized he was spying on them from afar …

The sight of the Fredavians concerned Tuomas, certainly, but he was able to stay calm. He had never doubted they would eventually find him. You could deal with the Fredavians; they were ferocious, but slow and dull-witted. He found himself wondering what had happened to the poor man who was growing mushrooms there.

He shifted his spyglass. Not far behind the group of gremlins he spotted Seppo Petteri Lavanko. "So that's it," thought Tuomas. The tripe butcher was just far enough from the flames to avoid being singed. An ill-clad young man was standing beside him.

No … the blaze, the Fredavians, Seppo … If it had been only

that, he could have managed. But things could not be that simple ... Slowly he shifted his spyglass and came upon what he was looking for. The blunt fear he'd felt in the depths of his stomach was transformed into horror.

To the south of the flame-ravaged house, at the edge of the pine forest that he had so loved for the heady perfume that filled the clearing, Tuomas saw *it*. At such a great distance, under the pine branches, it seemed so innocent, so weak ... a dwarf draped in animal skins, face smeared with blood.

As he shifted his lens to focus on the fur-covered figure, Tuomas spotted, lying on a bed of boughs, the eviscerated body of the mushroom picker who had taken possession of his former house. His torso was sliced open from top to bottom, and it looked for all the world like a fully opened purse. It was as if a huge, sharp claw had ripped him open, from throat to navel. A section of intestine hung from the cavity and lay draped across his stomach. The dead man's eyes were still open.

Feeling faint, Tuomas laid the spyglass on the arm of his chair and leaned against the windowsill, breathing deeply. The air in the room smelled of the dry wood with which he'd fed the stove. His mouth filled with thick, bitter saliva. He picked up the glass again only when he felt better.

Tuomas did not know it at the time, but as he would later relate the events of that night to a young man named Tero Sihvonen, he swore on the heads of all the gods of the ancestral Finnish pantheon that, when he refocused his spyglass on the tiny blood-smeared face that had terrified him, that face had looked right back at him, yes, looked him right in the eye, despite the kilometres that lay between him and the elderly gentleman, despite the patent optical impossibility that he could actually have seen him, so great was the distance and the night, so opaque. *He* knew that Tuomas was there, concealed behind the summit of the Drunkard Hills. *He* knew it, and *he* would dispatch the Fredavians to pursue the elderly alchemist.

Tuomas's arms fell to his side. He dropped the apparatus and did not even hear the glass shatter inside the metal and leather cylinder. "God help me!" He was bathed in sweat and felt as if his blood were pumping into his head in large, hard globules. Why now? He had just moved into his new dwelling a few months earlier ... and for the past eight days, he had been the guardian of a baby girl. Did he not deserve a few months, a few years of respite? Breathe ... breathe deeply ... "I have to leave, it's that simple. Just leave, immediately."

On the seat of the armchair, the little girl awoke. She was gurgling with contentment. Tuomas whispered comforting words in her ear. "Don't worry, my little one. I'm the one they're looking for. They are no more interested in you than a blind man in a pair of glasses."

Tuomas was one of those refined older bachelors who loved objects the ways others love their children or their wives. He truly adored certain of his books, his artworks, certain mementoes of his travels. But Tuomas was also an alchemist, and he had developed a powerful attachment to a substantial number of small laboratory instruments, several of which had been in his possession for more than forty years. And as he had neither wife nor child nor domestic animal, with the exception of the horse that would in any event help him escape, having decided to leave at the earliest opportunity, he thought first of the material possessions he loved so well. An entire lifetime of objects, be they of value or baubles, passed through his mind. In the end, he resolved to take nothing with him. What immense sadness he felt!

He considered the long telescope that stood in one corner, a gift from the personal alchemist of the Chinese emperor Guangxu, the good-natured Li Song. Then his eyes came to rest on an etching that hung on the wall above the telescope. In gratitude to his old friend Tuomas for having relieved him of an ulcer, the Parisian painter-engraver Irénée Peduncle had created for him a work that depicted a Finnish winter landscape: spruce boughs heavy with snow, a chimney emerging from the drifts, a wooden sauna ... Tuomas's heart twisted in his chest. No time to waste, no time ...

Heart pounding, he rushed downstairs, the baby in his arms. He hurried to Mrs. Heikkinen's bedroom. The good lady had fallen asleep immediately after going back to bed. Tuomas placed the infant in her cradle, then shook the wet nurse. When he was certain that she was fully awake, he spoke to her.

"Listen to me carefully, Liisa Heikkinen. And above all, ask no questions. We have no time for small talk. You have five minutes, do you hear me? Five minutes to collect your belongings, pack your bags, and meet me outside. Most of all, do not forget the little one, she is in her cradle. I will be waiting for you in the britzka. We are leaving. But, in God's name, make haste!"

In the kitchen, Tuomas found a large lump of cheese, an apple, and a sausage. He thrust them all into one of the deep pockets of his housecoat. He was about to leave the house when he stopped stock-still on the threshold. He turned about and moved up the stairs to the watchtower, four at a time. There, in his little observatory, next to his armchair, he found his pipe and matches.

He returned to the ground floor and hurried into his laboratory. A large commode made of mountain ash stood against the wall in one corner. He opened the bottom drawer. Tiny packets of tobacco were carefully arranged there, each of a different colour. Some carried explicatory notes, most in Finnish but in other languages as well. With trembling hands, Tuomas emptied the entire drawer, throwing the multicoloured packets onto the floor around him. When no more remained, he picked up a ruler from the desk across from the bed and pried open the false bottom of the drawer. One last packet of tobacco lay there, a single one, turquoise in colour. Tuomas thrust it into his pocket along with his pipe and matches. Only then did he exit the house.

From her room, Mrs. Heikkinen heard the door slam. Panic-stricken, overwhelmed with the wildest suppositions (how could she have possibly imagined that her most grotesque hypotheses would appear reasonable in comparison with what awaited her outside?), Mrs. Heikkinen hurriedly packed her bags. The task took her a good ten minutes, perhaps longer, and even then, she had no time to remove her nightdress and put on something more appropriate. But Mr. Tuomas's tone of voice when he awakened her ... The poor man was horrified. Something terrible must have happened. She was certain of one thing: this was no time for playing the coquette! Clutching a bundle of clothing in one hand, her valise in the other, and the infant under her arm, she rushed out of the house.

With a wave of his hand, Tuomas motioned to the wet nurse to throw her belongings into the baggage compartment of the britzka and take a seat on the driver's bench with the child. While he was outside waiting, Tuomas had dragged several bales of hay from the stable and placed them in the parlour and the kitchen. Once Mrs. Heikkinen had safely taken her seat on the britzka, he hurried back inside and set fire to the bales. By the time he came out, the windows of the ground floor were alive with flames.

Tuomas climbed onto the britzka and took the reins. He dared not look back on this new house where he would have wished to spend several more happy years. Even had he done so, he would have seen nothing, for tears filled his eyes. He lashed the horse and the britzka rushed across the hills. By now the house was ablaze, lighting up the night.

First they hurtled down the north face of the tallest hill, the one opposite the forest. There was no road on that side. As it was necessary to spare the horse grades that were too steep, they lost time zigzagging about in search of more gentle slopes. The rough ride made Mrs. Heikkinen sick to her stomach. A half-hour later they reached the valley. For another half-hour they drove through meadows thick with bushes, before finally reaching the denuded Plains of Archelle. Before setting out across the flats, Tuomas halted the britzka and took Mrs. Heikkinen's hand in his.

"Liisa, my dear, my good Liisa, you must dismount here. Follow the hills toward the east" – and in so saying, he pointed out the direction with his index finger – "and make sure you choose a path between bushes and shrubs. If you hear suspicious noises, hold tight to a tree trunk and do not move until you are sure the danger has passed. All the same, do not tarry. If you keep a brisk pace, before daybreak you should reach the edges of a deep, dark forest. Follow the trees but keep to the open country. Under no circumstances must you venture into the forest!"

"I know, the Fredavian Forest ..."

"Yes, the Fredavian Forest. It's too dangerous. Follow the edge of the forest, head due east. Keep on in that direction even when the line of trees veers off toward the south, and you find yourself in the swamp.

"The Ritva Swamp?"

"Exactly. From there, walking straight ahead, you should reach the high road. With a bit of good fortune you will encounter some kind soul who will carry you to Grigol in his cart. Be courageous, my good Liisa. You have a full day's march ahead of you, perhaps more."

So saying, Tuomas rummaged through the pockets of his housecoat and pulled out the sausage, cheese, and apple he had brought with him. He handed them to the wet nurse.

"How I regret having nothing else to give you, my good woman, my kind and good Liisa Heikkinen! And how long will I begrudge myself for abandoning you this way, by night, in these wild lands? I promise that one day I will travel to Grigol to provide you with the explanations you deserve, and above all to pay you the sums I owe you, with interest. I have brought no money with me ..."

The astonished wet nurse could make no sense of anything. But Mr. Tuomas was a knowledgeable man, a good and reasonable man. For a week she had observed the way in which he lived, and had never once noted the slightest sign of ill intent.

"Have no fear for me, Mr. Tuomas. But you, wearing only a housecoat, in this wind ..."

"Think nothing of it. Take care."

"And what of the little girl?"

"She will stay with me."

Tuomas Juhani Korteniemi would regret those five words for the rest of his life.

Once Liisa Heikkinen had stepped down from the britzka, Tuomas deposited a peck on the plump woman's cheek, whipped his horse, and rushed off at full gallop. Of the wet nurse we will not speak again.

The immensity of the firmament that shone far above the green carpet of the Plains of Archelle filled Tuomas's heart with a semblance of peace. The alchemist lifted his head; it were as if the universe, amused by his nocturnal pursuit across the land of mortal man, was employing its full panoply of artifice to lend it a poetic, dreamlike veneer. The galaxies whirled about for Tuomas; they waltzed for him in the autumn night, their ever-shifting contours shaped by the black liquor of intergalactic space. And the billions of stars seemed to shine their silvery light upon the alchemist and his horse like so many tiny beams.

He shook his head, like someone rousing himself from incipient sleep. He halted the britzka and looked behind.

In the distance, a vibrating black dot was growing larger by the minute.

Tuomas felt a new wave of terror sweep over him.

Against the horses of the Fredavians, urged on swift as the wind by the magical chants of Gladd the Argus, Tuomas knew the race was lost. Before him the Plains of Archelle stretched for a good fifty kilometres before turning into the wild and uninhabited woods that were simply known as the Northern Lands, a broad ribbon of forest he would have to cross through on the diagonal, in a northwesterly direction, if he wanted to reach the Sailio family hamlet. A half-hour earlier, as he fled his house, it was there that he had thought of seeking refuge with the little girl. It was a large village, with more than a thousand inhabitants. He knew people there. Gladd the Argus and the Fredavians would never dare pursue him into the village proper. But he had not expected his pursuers to pick up his tracks so quickly. By now he could see them. There was no doubt: on flat terrain, Tuomas stood not a chance.

He trained his eyes on the distant black dot. Soon the forms of a carriage with baroque ornaments hove into view. Tuomas had stopped for no more than thirty seconds, but that was enough for the Fredavians to cover three kilometres in their sorcerer's diligence! The elderly gentleman could hear the clattering harnesses of the team of horses drawing the vehicle. From the pocket of his housecoat, he withdrew his pipe and tobacco pouch.

Once more he looked behind him. Now Tuomas could make out three grotesque shapes on the driver's bench of the diligence, three enormous heads nodding in unison, three huge crania topped with misshapen headpieces, perched on children's bodies.

Tuomas's heart was pounding. His hands fluttered. He took two deep breaths. When he felt he had regained control of his fingers, he made an attempt to stuff his pipe. His movements were neither sure nor accurate; he spilled a large quantity of tobacco. The bowl three-quarters full, Tuomas put the pouch back into his pocket and brought out his matches. Then he took the child in his arms. She was awake now, and looked at Tuomas with tired eyes. The old man placed her on his lap, and with both hands free, lit his pipe and began to puff strongly. When he and the child were completely enveloped in a cloud of thick purple smoke, Tuomas filled his lungs with fumes by sucking at the pipe through tightened lips.

Immediately, a feeling of calm settled over him, as though a powerful but gentle wave were transporting him far from the Plains of Archelle. Very much at ease, he glanced once more behind him. For Tuomas, everything was happening in slow motion ... The black diligence seemed to be advancing at a deliberate pace (while in reality it raced toward him at infernal speed). The four huge, snorting black geldings that drew it spouted icy vapour from their nostrils. From high atop the coachman's seat, the three Fredavians cast carnivorous glances at Tuomas.

As we have explained, the Fredavians are thick-headed creatures. Of the three seated on the coachman's bench (there were six others in the passenger compartment), only the one to the far left was surprised to see that Tuomas, pipe in his mouth, had halted the britzka when he should have been in headlong flight. And when the elderly gentleman turned toward the diligence, the Fredavian noticed in the alchemist's eye a mischievous twinkle that startled him. What now? Alert the others and stop the diligence to avoid an unpleasant surprise? Or follow his Fredavian instincts, leap onto his prey, rip open his belly, and tear out his liver?

He turned to his two partners as if to warn them that something was amiss. At that very moment, Tuomas turned his back on his pursuers. The diligence covered the remaining few metres that separated it from the britzka. Then it hit a stone and bounced into the air. The Fredavians lost sight of Tuomas for a second, the time it took for the diligence to regain its equilibrium, and then the monstrous elves beheld a sight that took their breath away. The elderly gentleman was rising into the air.

Slowly, easily, unhurriedly … floating on a puffy cloud of purplish smoke. The smoke carried him aloft as he rose up into the night on a perfectly vertical axis, holding the baby in his arms. A soft breeze rocked him gently. Hanging there between heaven and earth, he worked to hold on to the tiny bundle that you might well have mistaken for a loaf of bread had you not known it was a baby.

From fifteen metres aloft, Tuomas looked down upon what had become of his pursuers.

The four black horses had come to a halt directly below the spot where the elderly gentleman now floated. The three Fredavians seated on the coachman's bench were the first to leap to the ground, followed immediately by six others, and Seppo Petteri Lavanko. The nine Fredavians lifted their heads. Tuomas could observe on each of their faces the look of empty-headed astonishment that was attributed to them in so many tales and legends. No longer was there the slightest hint of murderous hatred in their eyes, simply the dim-witted placidity of the dog that looks on as the stick it had been chasing for the past quarter-hour moves away in its master's hands. Standing slightly off to the side, Seppo observed Tuomas with an expression of incredulity identical to that of the trolls.

The knowledge that he was out of the Fredavians' reach relieved Tuomas, a feeling of relief that quickly turned to hate, and the elderly gentleman spat thrice into the wind, in the hopes of hitting the wretched gnomes. With one foot he tried to remove the slipper from his other foot to send it flying in the direction of the Fredavians, a gesture of puerile bravado that Tuomas found amusing given the circumstances. Then, just as he was about to put his plan into action, a catastrophe occurred that would forever change his life.

The baby burped.

It was a belch of elephantine proportions, the mother of all belches, a detonation more deafening than the volley of ten thousand cannons. There lived not a human on earth whose very being was not shaken by the shock waves. From the pygmies of Africa to the Eskimos of the Arctic wastes, via the horsemen of the steppes of central Asia and those strange-looking, brown-skinned, squint-eyed folk of the lofty mountains of South America, the men and the women of all continents, for three seconds that seemed like an eternity on that fateful evening of November 11, 1892, experienced the baby's belch. The moon shuddered in its quadrant of heaven. One of Saturn's rings shifted slightly from its orbit but quickly returned to its original location; the great celestial computer continued to function in spite of everything.

Remember! The little lass had not burped for an entire week.

Like everybody else, Tuomas's ears ached so badly that he feared his eardrums would implode against his brain. Instinctively he brought his hands to his ears to cover them.

And as he did so, he let drop, of course, the baby.

For all that time, Tuomas had been slowly ascending, and now he was a good thirty metres off the ground. At the very moment he clapped his hands to each side of his head, he realized what he had done and let out a moan of despair. He looked down: the infant vanished into the void, and with Tuomas too high, he could make out only indistinctly what was happening on the ground below. Was the baby dead? Splattered by her fall, flesh and viscera spread across the green grass of the Plains of Archelle? Tuomas, an old man with a weak heart, fainted. The purple smoke that held him aloft began to lose its welcome consistency.

On the ground, the baby's galactic burp had killed two of the Fredavians (one suffered from a cardiac malformation; the other choked on its own saliva). The two dead elves lay there, stretched out on the ground, while the seven others, having understood the worst was over, lifted their hands from their ears and opened their eyes wide to scan the sky. The Fredavians, despite their out-sized eyes, suffered from extremely poor vision, far worse than that of human beings. When they raised their heads, Tuomas was still well outside their field of vision. But Seppo, who stood close to them, could make out the black shape of the old man. He was the only one to see the small swaddled package fall from the sky, and immediately understood it was his daughter.

He took a few steps to the right to position himself in the baby's path. The child fell directly into his arms.

He walked toward the diligence. Someone was inside, someone who, during the monstrous belch, was the sole inhabitant of the Grand Duchy not to have covered his ears, the supreme eructation having been to him no more significant than the hum of a wasp's wing. The tiny personage was content to look on, expressionless, through the window of the diligence, as Tuomas continued to rise into the sky. Seppo paid this being no attention. He went up to one of the Fredavians, the largest of the group, at whose side he had been seated during the chase. He spoke in a voice that dripped obsequiousness.

"Well, uh ... so, thanks a lot, eh? I'll make it up to you one day when I can – tell me, would you mind driving me back home? We've been racing across the plains for a good hour, and I can't even imagine how long it would take me to walk back, especially with this little piece of shit on my hands ..."

The Fredavian did not deign to turn its head toward the corpulent innkeeper. In a language strange and disagreeable, it shouted out injunctions to the six of its companions that were still standing. Their response was immediate. Two took their places on the coachman's bench while the others piled into the passenger compartment. No one paid any attention to Seppo, who stood there observing the scene. As the diligence sped off into the night and vanished in the distance, the tripe butcher wondered if he should mourn or rejoice at being excluded from that mortifying cabal.

CHAPTER
3

The Sinister Baptism of
Zora Marjanna Lavanko

Tuomas Juhani Korteniemi never set foot in the Fredavian Forest again. In the days that followed that singular manhunt across the Plains of Archelle, Seppo, needless to say, would bend the ear of anyone who paid heed to his story. People listened with a mixture of skepticism and bemusement. The whole tale was an invention, from start to finish: Seppo, wandering on the Plains of Archelle with the *Fredavians*? Chasing an old eccentric no one had ever met, who could float in the air thanks to the magical effects of purple smoke? What would be next? And yet... Seppo was far too dull-witted to invent such an improbable, not to say mind-boggling story... Considering that he had about as much imagination as an elm branch, there had to be something to his story, some fragment of truth. You could, at most, suspect Seppo of embellishing a little, but even the threads that hung from his yarn had to be connected to factual account. What's more, Sagadat Leino had been at the Farting Bear that evening and could corroborate a portion of the story. And so, as they had done for Jarkko's story, the inhabitants of the forest adopted an interested but wary attitude toward Seppo's tale.

Our innkeeper asked some of his establishment's customers who regularly travelled in the region if they'd heard of a certain Tuomas Juhani Korteniemi who might have been found, dead or alive, not far from the Plains of Archelle, or in the environs of the Misty Woods. No one had heard speak of the old man.

With Tuomas having vanished into the clouds, Seppo was the only eyewitness to that phantasmagorical chase. The experience had deeply troubled him. He had difficulty recovering from the three hours spent in the company of the Fredavians. Who was that dirty little boy, dressed from head to toe in animal furs, who was in the diligence when the Fredavians had forced him to climb aboard with them? Throughout the voyage, at first as far as Tuomas's house near the river – where they had not, by the way, found the owner but instead Marko Sahlstedt, whom the Fredavians had with nary a forethought dispatched to Horna, among the lower deities – and then, during the hot pursuit across the Plains of Archelle, the little boy stayed inside the diligence, saying not a word, his blood-spattered face partially concealed by a hood likewise made of animal skins. The Fredavians did not even seem to notice his presence.

For the first few weeks, the particularly horrible memories of the night ride haunted Seppo. Then, time went its way. Seppo, to make himself interesting, often told the tale to wayfarers who stopped at the inn.

He finally established exclusive paternal guardianship. As the months passed, and despite her poor care, the little girl grew into a curiously robust child. The nomad families that stopped off at the Farting Bear on their journeys often boasted children of the same age. By comparison, it was clear that Seppo's daughter, though suffering from the same wretched living conditions as those poverty-stricken waifs, enjoyed a far more vigorous constitution. This became especially apparent when she began to walk.

She was, it goes without saying, revoltingly filthy. When she grew old enough that it began to seem immodest to allow her to wander around naked in the dining room, Helena Hiksu, who dropped by the inn to suckle the child whenever her teats itched, fitted out the child with the drawers made from jute and bleached gabardine that her own offspring had worn years before. All she asked from Seppo in return was a jar full of heron stew and a crock of patantine.

The infant spent her days strolling barefoot about the inn, to the indifference of the customers and her father. Her eyes were black and slanted like those of Asians, her cheeks were puffy and pink, her mouth nearly square, and people would certainly have found her ugly if the look in her eyes didn't shout out, "I'm two years old and I don't give a shit about you." There was a glint of malice and independence that adults found frightening. She would tolerate no caresses. Except for Seppo, who treated her like a low-life, no one spoke to her. Sharp and emotionless were the features of her tiny countenance. But on the positive side, she had extraordinary blond hair that danced lightly in the greasy air of the inn. When she made her way through the dining hall at mealtime, customers amused themselves by running their sticky fingers through her hair. Over time her blond locks became thick and black with dirt and ended up forming a hard crust on the little girl's head, and it was certainly one of the most ignoble crimes of that agglomeration of barbarians to treat in such a manner hair so beautiful it would have been the envy of cherubs.

The little girl had entered her third winter in this world when, one day, a particularly quaint group of nomads appeared at the inn. The family was made up of three men in their forties and as many women, all fat and loud mouthed. A swarm of snot-nosed, emaciated infants trailed after them, along with a snaggle-toothed hag who reeked of vodka.

Before they could sit down at a table, Seppo grabbed one of the beggars by the shirt sleeve.

"Do you have anything in your bundle? We don't hand out charity here."

"Whoa! Calm down, Mr. Innkeeper."

"Show me the butter."

The man pulled several pitiful coins from a pouch attached to his belt.

"What can we get for three pennies?" he asked.

"A whack in the chops," Seppo answered.

"Take it easy, no need to fly off the handle like that! There's more where that came from!" said the man with a guffaw.

The character rummaged around in a secret pocket sewn into his pants and pulled out a wad of dog-eared banknotes. Seppo backed off and allowed the rag pickers to take a seat. One of the fat women ordered food and drink for the whole party.

"We could eat a horse, Mr. Impresario. Bring us a big roast of reindeer with a garnish of whortleberries, some Plabet wine, and cockroach soup! We've been on the road for nine hours and we're ravenous."

Seppo poured them wine and then went into the kitchen to prepare the soup and the meat.

They were querulous and boisterous, and no sooner had the wine been served than they began to chatter. The conversation rose and fell like sea swells. Discreet exchanges turned into sudden crescendos, and the whole inn filled with shouted insults and vicious imprecations. To end their disputes, they would break into guffaws and lower their voices. Soon enough, the argument would resume. The children, nattering away, ran hither and thither. Seppo served the soup while the cuts of reindeer larded with bear fat were roasting. The three men hailed from a village located fifty kilometres north of Nurmes. People were already starting to starve up that way, so they set out with their wives – three sisters – for the capital where a brother-in-law owned an inn and could give them work for a time. They were carrying all their worldly possessions in three wretched horse carts.

Seppo plied them for news of the outside world. But at a certain moment he noticed out of the corner of his eye that the old woman accompanying the travellers had begun to remove her garments scrupulously, one by one. It didn't bother him at first. With the ovens pumping out heat and the fire blazing on the hearth, it was sweltering in the dining room. But after she took off her two heavy knit sweaters and only a shift full of holes was left on her back, the old woman – she could have been a good eighty years old, at least! – tugged at the collar of same, thrust her hand into the opening, pulled out an atrophied teat, and proceeded to stroke it absent-mindedly. Then, without having so much as stuffed her teat back in her clothing, her hand fell onto her lap, and she thrust it under her skirts and showily began itching her nether parts. Seppo tapped one of the men on the shoulder, pointing at the old lady with his chin.

"Oh, her? She's our wives' mother," he answered. "She's totally bonkers, don't pay her any heed. She's been like that forever. She shits in her skirts, and as if that wasn't enough, her ticker is running down. I wouldn't be surprised if she croaks before we get to Lappeenranta."

The old woman, with vacant eyes, pulled her hand out of her secret garden. With that same hand she snatched some of the tiny fried fish that Seppo had placed in the middle of the table to accompany the soup and wine.

At that very moment, the little girl made her entrance. There she came, tripping down the staircase that led to the ground floor just as fast as her short, stubby legs could carry her. She'd been keeping herself busy all afternoon trying to catch a mouse in the upstairs rooms. The little pug face could not yet speak, but she would frequently bray like a donkey as she cavorted around the inn. You could tell she was happy from her expression, and that was good to know, because if you went by her cries, you'd swear she were being beaten. When she was in an exceptionally fine mood, as she was that afternoon, she warbled and grunted in a particularly singular manner; you'd have thought you were hearing a calf with a bee caught in its throat.

Since she'd not seen the mouse for several minutes, she came downstairs to see whether the rodent had made its way into the dining room and hidden there. And so the light-footed child made her entrance into the overheated dining room of the inn and began to poke her nose under every table.

When she reached the table where the nomad family was seated, a broad smile rent the face of the toothless hag. With nary a forethought, and without regard to the breast that still dangled from her shift, the old woman grabbed the little girl by the arm and yanked her close.

"Oh, what a sweet little piglet! Hair as fine as a horse's mane, and pretty as sheaves of wheat ... hair so pretty you could wipe your ass with it! What's your name, sweetie?"

She ran her spittle-soaked fingers through the child's gorgeous blond hair. The child grimaced.

"Well, let's have it then! What's your name, my picky little sparrow?"

In an arthritic spasm, the tough old boiling fowl yanked at the child's hair. It hurt, and her reflex – the wrong one, it turned out – was to recoil. Caught as she was by her hair, the pain got worse as she threw her head backwards. She let out a scream, and the old shrew angered.

"So that's what you're like, miserable little numbskull! All I'm asking is your name. What's with you, all you can do is screech? Can't you talk like everybody else, or do we have to croak like frogs to get something out of you?"

The child was bawling lustily, shrieking at the top of her lungs and irritating the other customers. Seppo stepped forward.

"Take it easy, old lady. It's not 'cause she's spiteful that she doesn't answer. It's on account of she doesn't have a name."

Startled, the old woman shot back, "What do you mean, no name? By God, how can a child already be walking and not have a name? This is your child, this little minx?"

"Yes."

"So, it was too much to ask, fat ass, when your child popped out of its mother's belly, to stick a couple of syllables together, or just choose one, to give your child a name?"

The old woman was still holding fast to a thick tuft of the tearful blond's hair. The ancient ancestress waved her arms as she argued with Seppo, and put the little girl in a precarious position. She had to hop back and forth like a puppet to keep up with the hag's gestures, and avoid having her hair ripped out by the roots.

And then, because she was half-crazy and prone to sudden mood swings, the old harpy began to moan and weep. No one seated at the table paid the slightest heed; they had all returned to their bowls of soup, their drink, and their talk. Seppo had just plopped down a salad bowl brimming with aged pork vesicles glutinous with bile. The evil crone began wringing her twisted hands as though delirious memories had brought back unendurable pain.

"Oh, what an adorable little piglet, with that piss-coloured hair ... Oh, my little piglet with skin tender as white bread ... just like my Zora, my little one, my beloved Zora, isn't that so? The one that stubborn ass Gregor used as bait to trap bears ... Drunkard, craven coward! Using a child as bear bait! If I had him in front of me now, I'd rip out his chest with meat hooks! And then the bear appears, a big one at that ... and he tears my little Zora to shreds, my little one, my darling!"

The old hag let out a long, guttural groan. Her son-in-law, sitting next to her, turned to her, irritated.

"Tell us another story, Mother Hen, you've been busting our ears with this one for twenty-five years."

Everyone else was chattering away, paying the madwoman no mind. Kalle Normio, the fiddling rapist, had arrived at the inn a minute earlier and was settling in by the heater at the far end of the hall to start playing. To make yourself heard, you had to shout. The old woman turned up the volume too.

"My darling little Zora, with her pretty red cheeks, so red you'd think them cherries ... and that numbskull, that loafer, Gregor, watching the whole scene from a safe distance, chewing his tobacco, the chickenshit! Ah! So drunk he couldn't see that a bear was devouring his own flesh and blood! Let him rot in Horna, in the boiling soup of Lempo and Turja!"

By now she was spitting on the floor and shrieking as loud as her tired voice would let her, but it wasn't enough to overcome the scraping of Kalle Normio's fiddle that filled the whole room. The other members of the family were shouting and laughing as they listened to his hellish jig. Seppo's daughter was the only one who could hear the old hag's plaint. But did she understand the words that poured from the old biddy's toothless maw?

"How I wept for my Zora ... I wept so hard I'm surprised I didn't just shrivel up like a leech in coarse salt. That dog, Gregor ... that dog that ended up croaking on a wad of chewing tobacco one night when he got his breathing tube crossed up with his swallowing tube ... What a numbskull! To die from a wad of tobacco! If anyone else told me that story, I wouldn't believe a word! Serves him right! May the dogs of Tuonela devour him, that miserable wretch, that whoreson!"

On and on she went, sobbing and snivelling. At one point during her recitation, her claw-like hand loosened its grip on the little girl's hair. With her free hand, she wiped her face with the cloth of her dress, and only then did she seem to remember that the child was still at her side. The hand that clutched the girl's hair released its grasp, and the old woman slid the callused tips of her first and second fingers across the toddler's dewy-fresh cheeks.

"So, you've got no name, have you? Well, then, I give you the name of my daughter, the one heaven gave me, forty-two years ago, and that heaven saw fit to take back seven years later."

The grandmother's eyes grew big as saucers, dilated by a sudden episode of dementia, and the same slimy hand whose fingers had tripped down the little girl's cheeks snapped back to the top of her head and seized her blond hair again. With her other hand, extraordinarily agile suddenly, the old woman pulled a bone-handled knife from under her skirt. When she caught sight of the glint of the blade in the milky light of the inn, the little girl began to wriggle and to cry. "Be still, you little devil!" And so saying, the old hag gave her a resounding slap! Then, with her knife she cut off a tuft of the girl's hair. She removed the leather necklace from around her neck from which hung a small pouch, and into it, she inserted the lock of hair.

"You shall be called Zora Marjanna."

Then she hung the necklace around the little blond's neck and tightened the knot.

"Hold fast to that lock of hair, to remember the day you received a name."

And to Seppo, who was passing close by with a tray of tankards of patantine, she called, "Ho, innkeeper! Henceforth this little girl will be called Zora Marjanna."

"I couldn't give a shit," he shot back without turning his head. "I would call her Gurgle if that's what it took to shut your trap."

The ancient woman turned her wrinkled face to the girl.

"Above all, beware of men your whole life long. They are not to be trusted. They kill little girls by feeding them to bears. They clap their eyes on you, they marry you, they carry you off to their family, they mount you, they churn the butter, they knock you up and grab your child to use as bait to kill the bear that comes prowling at night around the pigpen."

Then the old bag fell silent, as if turning inward in contemplation. What happened to the child was no longer of interest to her.

CHAPTER
4

A Middle-Aged Fredavian

Little Zora Marjanna Lavanko realized early in life that to escape the humiliation and the blows, she had to keep as far away from her father as possible. Seppo neglected his daughter to the point that unless he was looking directly at her, she did not even exist for him. On the other hand, when she would no more than stray into the dining room or, worse, into the kitchen, Seppo, still furious at Hambone for having a baby behind his back, would give her a thumping. As soon as Zora climbed out of bed, she would sneak out of the inn and wander into the mist-shrouded woods. Moving along the rocky shores of male society, she became a loner, hard bitten and indifferent. When she felt the pangs of hunger, she returned to skulk around the inn, slipping into the dining room on cat's feet to gather leavings from the tables, then going back outside to eat her loot. At times she was bold enough to dart into the kitchen when she saw that Seppo was busy in the dining room, and there she stole porridge and milk. Sometimes she was caught red-handed by her brutish father, and he would thrash her within an inch of her life.

In short, she ate far too little for what her quickly developing body needed. But by the strange mechanism of resilience, she reacted to the hunger, cold, and constant beatings by growing with astonishing vigour. Zora, who often had no more to sustain her all day than boiled cabbage, who walked barefoot through the bloody leavings strewn across the floor of the inn, and who spent most of her time in the forest to avoid her father's punishments, that Zora was pink cheeked and quite big for her age. Spending the long winters outdoors kept her cheeks rosy all year round. She may have lacked some fat around the flanks, but she had broad shoulders and her arms were stout.

Around her neck she wore the necklace the old woman had given her three years before. More than once she almost lost it because the string that held it was too long. When the child, perched high in a spruce tree, would hang by her knees from a branch, the necklace would often slip off and nearly fall to the ground. Other times it would catch in the underbrush as she pursued a hare or a fox. When Seppo rained down blows on her over a cup of spilled tea or a broken saucer, the necklace would fall from her throat when she went flying through the air and crashed to the floor. But she always managed to grab it before any of the inn's customers could.

Zora loved to play with forest creatures. She was still small, but she had developed ways that let her approach the more docile of the wild animals and even touch them and feed them.

So it was, one fine day, she managed to approach a brown hare and play a game of patty cake with it. It was wintertime, a mild, grey morning. She had awakened at dawn from her bed of straw at the back of the kitchen, snuck a bowl of kasha and a half-gnawed piece of chicken leg from the counter, and crept into the dining room. Surprise! The hall was crowded to overflowing with indigents more dead than alive, lying this way and that, slouched over chairs, the counter, even on the floor! As she picked her way through the human wreckage, Zora recognized the revellers who had been making merry the night before. It was curious to find them there the next morning; as a rule Seppo never let anyone linger after he'd pocketed their last cent. For him, it was a question of principle. There were rooms to rent upstairs. If a customer was too drunk to go home after the last dance, all he had to do was rent a room. And that was that. What had happened for her father to allow a good three dozen drunks to sleep off their binge in the main dining room? Zora took fright at their moans of pain and strange postures. Behind the counter she found her father lying on the floor, legs bent under his heavy frame.

Here is what happened the night before. In late afternoon, an ambulant apothecary – a regular visitor to the cities, towns, and forests of the Grand Duchy at this time of year – dropped in to call on Seppo. For a mere seventy pennies ("A special price for you, so enchanted am I by that extraordinary moustache of yours!" the apothecary told Seppo), the innkeeper purchased from the smooth-talking visitor a full bottle of Amanien, an elixir reputed to cure cirrhosis and liver deficiency and, in regular doses, reinvigorate that precious organ so that even the inveterate drunkard would have a liver as healthy as a baby's, and could look forward to years of drinking without the slightest risk to his health. The white label on the bottle read, "Amanien. Prized by the Chinese, celebrated by the Ukrainians. Amanien. Revitalizes the liver, reinvigorates the kidneys."

Cash in pocket, the crooked apothecary bade goodbye and departed with a smile. That very evening, the credulous Seppo served a small glass of Amanien to each of the customers to test the product. A blend of absinthe, fly agaric, and charcoal dust, the potion quickly knocked everyone out.

In the end, there was only one fatality: Helena Hiksu, the woman who had suckled Zora. After daybreak, long after Zora had fled that sinister drunk tank to run off and play in the forest, the other customers finally awakened, vomiting and bleeding from their noses.

The innocent child knew none of this. She could not have cared less about the health of the sickly sleepers. Rapidly she gulped down her gruel, ate her chicken leg, and hurried out of the inn.

A fine layer of snow covered the ground. The frozen spruce needles crackled under the feet, and to the little girl's ears it was the sweetest of music. She had been padding through the woods for more than two hours when she spied the brown hare perched on a fallen tree, gnawing at shreds of bark. Zora approached slowly. The innocent creature observed her without moving. Patiently, slowly, softly, Zora moved forward with the tiny steps of a she-wolf on the hunt. When she'd crept quite close, the hare bounded away. Its tiny paws did not allow it to move very fast, and Zora could have easily overtaken it, but she enjoyed chasing it through the trees. Finally, growing bored and tired, she jumped on the tiny brown bundle and picked it up in both hands, smothered it with kisses, and hugged it to her chest as she stroked its head. How good it was to feel the warm, quivering body of a living creature against her neck! How she would have liked to spend the rest of her life just so, her forehead and hands thrust into the bristly fur of a consenting mammal.

For the fun of it, she removed her necklace and fastened it around the hare's throat, winding it several times to adjust it properly, then deposited the little creature on the ground. Irritated by the unwanted adornment, the hare turned and twisted its head before bounding off into the bush. Zora leaped to her feet and gave chase.

Young and sprightly as she was, Zora was still very small, and pursuing the zigzagging animal strained her calves and heels. Her little heart was pounding. What a disappointment! After running this way and that for more than an hour, caught up in the excitement of the hunt, she was lost. She came to a sudden halt, struck by that knowledge. She was surrounded by black spruce, their branches hanging low, knitting together. The distance between the lowest branches and the ground was no more than thirty centimtres, and the hare had lost its pursuer in the dense vegetation.

Panic rapidly replaced the pleasure of the game. Zora began to run between the spruce trees, seeking the slightest opening. Now she felt the full force of the pain from the needles that lashed her face and lacerated her skin through her torn clothing. As she ran, she desperately sought a landmark that might remind her of some previous time in the woods. For naught.

The deeper she ventured into the woods, the more threatening the trees became. Their dark crests leaned heavily toward the ground, joining above the little girl's head to create a black ceiling of branches that masked the grey sky. On and on Zora ran, on and on. Her tears mingled with her sweat, and her heart was in her mouth.

Never in her life had she been so terrified! She thought of dropping to the ground, giving herself up to fear, anything to disperse that uncontrollable convulsion of her mind and body. Already, she was having trouble commanding her legs. Like tiny metronomes run amok, they carried her ever deeper into the dark woods.

At last, the darkness began to give way. Something like a spear of light pierced the dense wall of vegetation around her. She followed that light, and soon emerged into a curious clearing.

In a small space, all the trees had been felled and hauled away, leaving their evenly cut stumps. Atop each one rested a large block of hard-packed snow. Zora lifted her head. Lazy, skittering snow-flakes were pouring through an aperture in the sky between the treetops, floating downward as they whirled and spun among the monoliths. How many of those mysterious snow blocks could there have been? Far more than Zora could possibly count! Intrigued, she went up to a block to her right. From close up, she saw that the fine layer of snow concealed ice beneath it. With her sleeve, she wiped clean a surface the size of the skylight in the barn at the inn, and as a game, she drew her face close to the ice as though looking through a window.

There was something inside the ice.

Zora leaped back, tripped over a root, and fell to the ground. She got up, rubbing her behind, but kept her eyes on the block of ice.

It was a fox. A fox frozen in a bizarre position, mouth gaping wide as if threatening an attacker. Though she wasn't entirely certain the fox was dead, Zora instinctively realized this particular creature could no longer scare anyone.

Once her initial fright had passed, she went to another block and carefully brushed away the snow with her sleeve. This time she had to look long and hard into the ice before discovering anything, but she eventually could discern a frozen creature, a small snake that seemed to have been caught as it was forming the letter *S*, much like the fox.

That clearing … it was no playground, Zora understood. Yet she could not keep herself from looking at what was inside the other blocks of ice. In her movements and expressions she concentrated all the attention she could muster for a girl of six, and set about examining each of the huge, rigid concretions that lay scattered across the clearing.

Within the blocks of ice could be found specimens of almost all the creatures that inhabited the Fredavian Forest: elks, ermines and badgers, lemmings, wolves, and even reindeer. Some of the animals seemed in vigilant postures, while the rump and back muscles of others were strangely contorted, as if the ice had caught them in an expression of surprise. Fascinated at first, Zora stuck her nose and fingers against the ice. The surfaces of the blocks were marked by irregularities, grooves and channels, and it was difficult to see what they held. She looked into the eyes of every beast, seeking in their black pupils an image that might help her unravel the mystery of their confinement. But the frozen orbs spoke nothing meaningful. All she could discern was a nameless terror. As she made her way among the blocks, Zora experienced the same sense of dread she felt before reaching the clearing. Her tiny bare legs began to shake like straws in the wind. This lugubrious garden exuded an air of great age and abandon, as though it had been designed as a museum, but had fallen into disrepair over the years. Zora found the place horribly frightening. The rancid stink of aged flesh reminded her of the smell of her father's inn … All around the clearing, striking ice formations hung from the branches and the leaves of the tall, ice-encrusted trees, large congealed drops of water, sorrowful laminated tears that illuminated the area with soft bluish light. Zora thought she heard a carillon tinkling from far away. She stopped to listen and, as she did, the sound ceased. Perhaps it was the wind combined with the crunch of her footsteps in the snow that made her believe she was hearing things.

She forced herself to brush the snow from each of the enormous diamond-like coffins, and took a close and careful look at the animals entrapped within. When she had completed her round, she angled back to the middle of the clearing. There, she was sure she was seeing things: on top of the biggest puffball mushroom she had ever laid eyes on was a strange creature that gave every indication of being alive.

It had a gigantic head, as tall and wide as Zora herself, but its body was diminutive, its arms stubby, its legs spindly and straight like sheaves of oats. It wore a blue jacket over a red vest, and short pants with black and yellow stripes. Atop its head perched a red cap of the same colour as its well-worn vest. It was a middle-aged Fredavian. And it was sweating profusely, as if suffering from a bad cold. In all her young years, Zora had never seen anyone outside of the grotesque faces of the quarrelsome and violent adults who came to eat and drink at the Farting Bear, and her own father who poured their drinks and served them victuals, and those raggedy travellers who stopped to beg for food and often set up camp in the environs of the inn. No one missed the opportunity to heap slights and insults on her when they saw her, and though she had no idea why they treated her this way, Zora imagined they must have a good reason. She was different, certainly. But different how?

And now, in this mysterious opening choked off by the dark woods of the Fredavian Forest, she had come upon a singular and strangely different creature. Who knows? Maybe it too dwelled in a remote public house somewhere in the forest? Maybe its father also beat it, and it had come to this mysterious clearing to protect itself from harm? What if this was Zora's long-awaited chance to make a friend? Following a very human inclination, she approached the gnome to learn more about its nature.

The Fredavian's eyes, the size of duck eggs, bloodshot and infested with tiny yellow worms, darted this way and that in confusion. Much time passed before it even noticed Zora standing there. It said something that the little girl could not understand; its language was not spoken in this land. The creature's voice was high-pitched, coarse, and nasal. Its mysterious croaking made Zora ill at ease. The Fredavian spoke again, this time in impeccable Finnish.

"We are seeking someone to bring us relief."

The Fredavian's eyes went back to wandering again. Quite strangely, it did not seem surprised by Zora's presence. Its gaze was indifferent, empty, mindless; Zora did not know whether to be happy about that, or concerned. Just then, she spotted, on the left, a huge axe leaning against the puffball mushroom. Its handle was even longer than the one her father used to chop wood, larger than the Fredavian itself, and she wondered how such a creature with such tiny arms could possibly lift it.

Zora asked the Fredavian, "Relief from what?"

"We're in deep trouble under our hats! And it's been going on for – what? – six or seven winters."

"You mean your head hurts?"

"Real bad! And why? I ask you. Why?"

"Well, why?" the child breathed.

Pensively, the Fredavian inserted its index finger into one of its huge nostrils and extracted an enormous gob of snot, then flicked it away. Its voice, nasal because of its stuffy nose, became clearer.

"Do you know how to carve a throne into a puffball mushroom?"

"No ..." Zora answered quietly.

From a sheath attached to its belt, the Fredavian pulled out a knife with a pitted blade. It stared at the blade as it spoke.

"Ah! It's really tough. With the first cut, pfft! The puffball shrivels up and deflates. And you get black dust blown all over your face! It's really no fun, because *he* commanded me to carve a throne in a puffball mushroom and now look ... OYYOOOYYY!"

Zora jumped. The Fredavian cried out in pain, lifting its hand to its cap.

"Oy oy oy oy oy! It really hurts."

The creature brought its hands to its face to cry, but seeing as they were so tiny and its head was so large, the best it could do was clap its hands on either side of its fat round nose. Tears rolled down its purple, feverish cheeks. Zora wavered between fear and pity.

"Who will bring us relief? Who? How many moons have we been here? Suffering. We tried to get a hold of him, the old man, before he could take off, but what could we do? We got there too late!"

Forced to prompt the creature, Zora repeated in a tremulous voice, "Too late …"

"Yes, too late. The whole way, in the diligence, *he* put us on notice, me and the others. 'Overtake his carriage, grab him before he can flee, and hand him over to me.' But when we overtook the britzka, sorcery! Sorcery!"

In a sudden, violent gesture, the Fredavian clapped its hands together. The puffball on which it was sitting spat out a plume of blue smoke with a mind-numbing stench. Pushed by fear to the limits of her childish rationality, Zora felt like she was about to crack. She mustered her last shreds of courage.

"My hare! I'm looking for my hare," she murmured.

Did the Fredavian even hear her?

"The alchemist flew away! Flew away! Like a soap bubble! 'Hurry up! He's taking off!' Palamede called. He could see everything. He was driving the diligence. So we piled out as fast as we could to try to spear the old man before he got too high up. But *he, he* stayed right there, in the diligence. And the old guy, the alchemist, was already high up, too high. He was carrying something like a maggot, would you believe it?"

So saying, the Fredavian raised a finger sententiously, as if to admonish the little girl. The gesture was completely at odds with its words. The outsized gnome's cheeks had turned crimson. It was sweating so profusely that fat drops rolled down its forehead and blurred its vision.

"So furious was *he* at having let the alchemist get away, *he* ordered us to return to the forest. The others, I don't know exactly what happened to them … Whatever the case, *he* brought us here. And then, with his pocket knife – nothing but a pocket knife no longer than your little finger – *he* hurt us … Oyoyoyoy!"

The Fredavian closed its eyes, seemingly overcome by more pain than it could bear. As though contemplation of its own knife only increased its hurt, it thrust the weapon back into its sheath. Then it did something that horrified Zora: with its atrophied hand it picked up the giant axe standing right beside her and lifted it to its shoulder as easily as if it had been a willow bough.

But then it said, "Oh ... our axe ... how heavy it is ... When *he* abandoned us here, when was it, I can barely remember, seven or eight winters ago, *he* insisted we carve out a throne for him from a puffball mushroom with our sheath knives for when he would return ... The whole thing made him laugh ... *He* laughed and laughed ... All that was long ago ... Lucky *he* hasn't come back, seeing as how we haven't been able to make the throne ... With our knives we punctured every single puffball mushroom in the forest! They are harder and harder to find! What can you do? We'd have done it long ago if our noggins didn't hurt so much. What were you saying, missy?"

"My hare ..."

"Ah, yes, a hare ... there he is, over there ..."

And the creature pointed to the exact spot where Zora had entered the clearing.

"He looks at us long and hard," it went on, "and we turn cold inside, icy cold ... so cold we can't even budge our little toes, paralyzed, we were! And then he pulls out his sharp knife, but he only scratched the top of our heads, here, right under our hats. Ever since, oh, how it itches!"

Then, for the first time, the Fredavian seemed to take an interest in Zora.

"But you, you could bring us some relief, couldn't you? With your little paws. Scratch, scratch, scratch with your little paws! Scratch, scratch, scratch!"

With its tiny hands, the Fredavian scratched at the air like the hind paws of a dog burying its shit.

"I just came looking for my little hare," whispered Zora, "I just came for ..."

Then the Fredavian whipped off his cap.

Zora recoiled. The top of the Fredavian's skull had been neatly sliced off and removed. The creature's enormous greenish brain protruded above its face, giving it the appearance of a half-peeled fruit. The trepanned gnome stared at Zora with its round, credulous eyes.

The girl, cast into the depths of horror, lost all control of her limbs. Despite herself, she took a step backwards. A great mistake! Her movement revealed her fear, and the Fredavian quickly reacted. In a fever of sudden amok, it rolled its wild eyes.

Then lifted high the great axe.

Zora flew off at top speed. She heard a roar of anger: the Fredavian had climbed down from its puffball mushroom and was pursuing her. The child took the same path by which she'd come, running as fast as her little legs would carry her. There, a hundred metres in front of her, where she'd entered the clearing, she could make out only a wall of impassable branches. No more path! All the same, she dove straight into the wall, hoping to mingle with it and disappear. After a good twenty paces she turned to look back. Because of its short legs and monstrous head, the troll could not catch her, which did not keep her from shivering in fright: the Fredavian was still brandishing its outsized axe.

She was almost safe ... almost. Ahead of her, the compact mass of spruce boughs drew closer. A few more strides – twenty at most! – and she could shelter in the underbrush thicket. The Fredavian with its elephantine cranium could never follow her into the impenetrable thicket.

Then, all of a sudden, Zora stopped in her tracks.

The little brown hare she'd toyed with that morning was right there, perched on a stump. Motionless. That was the one, no doubt about it. It still had the necklace around its neck.

The little hare was sitting on its haunches, eyes alert. For a moment Zora thought it was looking at her without moving, as animals often do when they sense danger. To urge it to escape with her, Zora stretched out her hand and tapped it on the muzzle.

Cling!

It was hard. The hare was completely frozen.

Cling!

For a brief instant, Zora thought she was having a nightmare. How could a healthy hare suddenly be frozen solid?

She glanced quickly to her right. The Fredavian was rushing toward her as fast as its legs would carry it. No time to mourn the little hare. With two half-frozen fingertips, she grasped the necklace. The leather was stuck in the ice but, with energy born of desperation, Zora mustered all her strength and pulled it free. This was not, in itself, a difficult thing to do, but she had to unbraid the knotted cord from around the animal's neck, and that took precious time. Feeling her life in danger, she gripped the necklace in two places, pushed her muscles to the limit, and pulled upward. The ornament came loose with the curls intact. Zora pulled it over her head. She was so hot, and so frightened, that she did not feel the icy leather necklace scorch her skin.

Zora grasped the hare in an attempt to extract it from its icy plinth. She knew nothing of death. The frozen creature she hugged to her chest, its globular eyes bulging from their sockets and focused on faraway nothingness, might have been cold and unmoving, but only temporarily; perhaps soon it would recover its life breath. But no such luck! The hare's paws were trapped in a thick layer of ice. This time, pull as she might, the animal did not budge a whit.

Zora turned toward her pursuer. The monstrous elf was bearing down on her, and it was only a matter of seconds before it would decapitate her with its axe. She could make out the taut, reddish skin of its cheeks, its hateful glare. She closed her eyes, pulled one last time with all her strength. *Hmmmfff!* No use – the hare was imprisoned in ice.

When she opened her eyes, the Fredavian was upon her. He raised the huge, rusty axe high above its head.

Ffffttt!

Downward swept the axe! The little blond jumped aside to dodge the blade and dashed off. A strange sensation of warmth on the right side of her face, as though a trickle of warm water was flowing from her ear and running down her neck and shoulder …

Driven by panic, Zora ran with all the speed of a hunting hound.

With long strides she reached the edge of the clearing in no time. Before dashing into the thicket, she glanced behind her one more time.

To her great surprise, the Fredavian had stopped beside the hare. It glared at Zora and threatened her with its tiny fist, scarlet with rage. Then it picked up the axe and with violence altogether extraordinary given its tiny stature, it smashed the hare's head with the flat side of the blade. The little cranium exploded in a geyser of scarlet ice and bloody fluids. Zora resumed her headlong flight and rapidly vanished among the trees.

It took her a good two hours to rediscover the path to the inn. The blood that had spurted from the nasty cut she'd sustained on her ear had coagulated and now formed a thick crust on the side of her head. She was crying lustily when she stepped into the dining room, and disturbed some of the customers, who were quick to complain to Seppo. The innkeeper strode over to his daughter, grabbed her by the hair, and threw her out with a kick and a volley of insults.

CHAPTER 5

Captain Gut and His Flourishing Trade

Every year, in the spring, a man known throughout the region as Captain Gut came calling at the inn. Put bluntly, the Captain trafficked in women. His headquarters were in the south of the country where, during the winter, he and a bunch of hired thugs kidnapped women from the wealthy cities of the coast. Come spring, Captain Gut clapped heavy iron collars around his captives' necks and chained them together. In March, he and his captives travelled as far as Karelia in a livestock wagon (the Captain had accomplices among the Helsinki railway workers). Once he reached Grigol, this cruel and shady character, his face laminated by dust and deep cold, traversed Karelia from north to south, selling off his merchandise. More often than not, the poor women were sold off to whorehouses or pimps in village dives and lumber camps. In good years, the lineup might include as many as thirty women. Some peasants would pay up to five hundred marks for a wife; in a nice whorehouse, you could buy a good-looking girl for the same price. To keep the women quiet during the trip, the Captain relied on a dozen grim and ill-tempered mastiffs he fed on jerky and dirty water. They would bite the prisoners for sport and devour anyone who attempted to escape. But their lives were not much easier than those of the women they were assigned to keep watch over. They were no better kept than slaves and beaten regularly. Their coats were sparse and spotted with bloody scabs.

The Captain's business was not looked upon with favour, and that is easy to understand. As a result the merchant, in his peregrinations, avoided the larger towns and made it a point to follow less well-trodden paths. Haunted forests, vast deserted plains, mountain escarpments; the Captain travelled where others would not venture. The women, beaten, starved, and raped, were herded across hundreds of kilometres, most often at night, only to end up whores or peasants in the most hostile regions of the Grand Duchy.

During his swing through Karelia, Captain Gut passed through the Fredavian Forest. The place suited him to perfection. The inhabitants of the forest were degenerate scum. There was no risk of encountering representatives of the law. The woods were so dense they could keep any secret. And, above all, in the western quadrant of the forest lay the Inn at the Sign of the Farting Bear. A lover of innards (to which fact he owed his nickname), the Captain knew none better than those prepared by Seppo Petteri Lavanko.

The Captain was a massive specimen. His paws, bulky as loaves of bread, were brown and coarse; they were hands that had forced, twisted, strangled, and crushed. His fingers, fat as sausages, were covered by enormous exanthemata. But what stood out most were the Captain's teeth. They were monstrous, forty-two in all, forty-two bulging stumps that overlapped one another in frightening disorder like so many horse's teeth in a human mouth! He had several rows, like a shark. Some claimed that the Captain had a set of teeth at the bottom of his feeding tube, and that he could easily continue to masticate in his throat or his stomach. In any event, that toothsome battery stuck in a large and muscular jaw terrorized any and all who encountered Captain Gut. It was said in the region that he marked his women by biting their thighs, as though branding livestock with a red-hot iron.

It was hardly surprising that whenever the Captain came calling, Seppo bent over backwards to please his intimidating guest, and hastened to agree with whatever he might say. If perchance the Captain spat upon him – it happened all the time, for the Captain, like his other customers, liked nothing better than to torment him, that greasy half-wit – he would wipe off the sputum without a word. Seppo was one of those lower creatures that entered near-mystical ecstasy at the spectacle of the strength and self-assurance of someone else. Coming from the Captain, he was prepared to suffer any humiliation.

Of a cold April day in Zora's ninth year, the Captain and his procession of women arrived at the inn. The chain gang numbered twelve captives. After long weeks of walking, the women were haggard and silent. Violence, privation, and humiliation had reduced them to empty minds trapped in half-dead bodies.

In front of the inn they were given permission to sit on the ground. The dogs also rested, while the Captain strode into the inn.

"Seppo! Seppo, you old tub of lard!" he cried out.

Seppo was in the kitchen among his pots and pans. When he heard the Captain's voice he jumped, shivering the way virgins do when they hear the spiked boots of their husbands rattling on the floorboards after the wedding. The innkeeper rushed out to welcome his guest.

"Seppo, you fat, filthy bloodsucker! How are you?"

"Ah, fine, just fine! So, back in our area, eh? How's business? I won't shake your hand, milord! I just gutted two pike this morning and I've got the stink of fish all over my hands."

"Rustle me up a roast of reindeer."

"Yes, sir! Whatever you say, admiral! But I have to warn you: my cuts of reindeer have been smelling funny of late."

"Bah! Just give me whatever you have, do I give a damn? And find me some bones and dump them outside for my bitches to chew on, with some water. And scare up something for the dogs while you're at it."

So saying, the Captain burst into guffaws that made the walls tremble.

Seppo bowed obsequiously and exited the inn. Outside, he cast an eye at the chained women who were sleeping or scratching at the earth with their toenails. Then he walked to the knacker's shed and gathered up everything he found lying about in the way of bones and rotten innards, returned, and threw the whole lot to the women and the dogs. He filled a large bucket with cold water so the prisoners could drink and wash off some of their accumulated filth. Coming back inside, in a high-spirited mood, he hailed the Captain.

"You will forgive me, milord, for chatting with you as I stuff these plump bald eagles for tonight's customers! When I'm done, we'll eat one together, if that's to your liking."

"Go to it, fatso, and stuff 'em proper. But first, bring me a bottle of vodka."

"Wouldn't you rather have a drink of our polecat juice?"

"No way! No human would drink your poison, Seppo. Makes me puke."

"Whatever you say … Ever since I started collecting the customers' piss in a big barrel out behind the inn I've quadrupled production, but it's true, the stuff doesn't taste the same."

The Captain frowned. Exhausted, he laid his arms on the table and his head atop them.

"Go to it, you compacted stool! And quick with the vodka! Serve my bird with blood gravy when it's ready."

"Consider it done, commander!"

Seppo plopped a glass down on the table and poured a shot of vodka. Slowly the Captain straightened, shook his head, and swallowed it in one gulp. Then he took the bottle from Seppo's hands and refilled his glass.

"And how is the flesh trade going, as good as usual?" asked Seppo.

"Not as good as yesterday, better than tomorrow, Seppo. If you only knew …"

The Captain pulled a large wooden pipe from his pocket and filled it with black tobacco. He smoked slowly. The grey fumes that billowed up from his pipe imparted his craggy face with a dark and threatening aura. Seppo hurried back to the kitchen. On the wooden cutting board that lay before him on the counter, he laid out the eagle's gizzard and liver. Then he set about chopping them and the silence of the afternoon was filled with the click of the knife against the wood.

In the dining room, the Captain knocked back two more shots of vodka. He spoke loudly enough for Seppo to hear him.

"Trouble, trouble, nothing but trouble. One bother after another with those damned sluts. Nothing but whimpering and crying … 'The more you cry the less you'll piss,' I tell them. But no. Not only do they squeak like lambs, they stop every five minutes to water the weeds. Let me tell you, if I was to stitch up their lips to stop 'em from pissing, I'd get where I was going in half the time."

In the kitchen, Seppo threw the eagle innards into a pan and browned them in bear grease with onions, garlic, some topsoil, and one large dry reindeer turd.

"When I think how much I have to invest just to get my hands on 'em!" the Captain went on. "Times are tough everywhere, even in the southern countryside, and fathers are ready to drop their daughters, especially when they're pickpockets. But I can't get by on that. To make money, I've got to kidnap one or two dozen. And then, my big fat Seppo, I can't tell you how tough it is! I never get off without scratches and bruises … Sometimes I get so steamed up I have to treat 'em really rough. Why, just this year one little harpy punched me so hard in the nose that she almost broke it. The little slut!" With those words, the Captain slammed his fist on the table. "I was so furious I peeled the skin off her back with my penknife before I disembowelled her. Too bad … She would have been a good milch cow …"

Back in the kitchen, Seppo tossed some smoked bullfrog carcasses into the frying pan along with the *Amanita phalloides,* a mushroom highly esteemed by the inn's regulars for its calming effect and delicate flavour. The Captain went on with his soliloquy.

"And to tell you the whole truth, Seppo, I've had it with travelling from one end of the country to the other with my livestock. It's the same thing everywhere in this rotten Duchy. Nothing but drunks, beggars, and poltroons. Which group do you belong to, you big imbecile?"

In another frying pan, Seppo mixed dry bread with sow's milk. When he heard the Captain's evil words, he smiled stupidly and, to impress himself, stuffed a handful of milk-soaked bread into his mouth.

"You're nothing but a poltroon, Seppo Petteri Lavanko, a thick-headed turnip like all the rest of them. You like to eat pig shit, you tell your customers the same old stories and they try to be as stupid as you, you jack off like a leaping toad and then go and fuck a sow ... and you're happy, right?"

"Jusht as you shay, milord!" Seppo's mouth was still stuffed with sodden bread.

He tried not to show it, but he found the Captain's insolence hurtful. How he would have liked to attract that mammoth's admiration and true friendship! After that Tuomas Juhani Korteniemi of many years past, Seppo had never found a single friend, not a soul who cared a whit about him. Tears welled up in his eyes. He salted and peppered the mashed bread, removed the pot of innards from the burner, and poured its contents into the bowl. Then, with his stubby fingers he mournfully mixed the eagle giblets and the bread.

"Ah, Seppo! Seppo, you fat-assed shit eater!" the Captain went on. "You call this a life? Why didn't I become an innkeeper like you or just open a whorehouse? Or herd reindeer! I'd send my animals to pasture on the tundra and while away the happy hours with my dogs and some big-breasted herdswoman."

Deep in the cramped kitchen, eagle carcasses were aging at the end of strings hung from the ceiling. Seppo pulled down a half dozen. The Captain was silent, puffing on his pipe. Seppo stuffed each bird with the forcemeat he'd prepared. Then, with a rusty needle and thread, he stitched shut the wings and legs of the eagles and put them in the oven to roast.

Then he returned to the dining room to join the Captain. The two men drank shots of vodka as they waited. After two hours had gone by, Seppo removed the roasted eagles from the oven. He and the Captain ate one bird each; the remaining ones he would serve to customers that evening.

After they'd polished off the eagles, Seppo brought two bowls into which he'd placed pigeon jabots macerated in fermented sow's milk. Seppo and his guest were belching with contentment! When he'd eaten his fill and drunk to his heart's content, as he was accustomed to whenever he called on Seppo, rather than pay for the meal and the drink, Captain Gut offered the innkeeper the prisoner of his choice to furrow.

Out of the inn they wobbled. The captive women had long since finished gleaning what they could from the old reindeer bones and scraps of dried tripe. Some of them were sound asleep on the ground. Others were gathered in silence around the pail of water, splashing their fingers, and now and then dipping their hands and rubbing their faces, arms, and shoulders.

Seppo selected a hairy brunette leaning against a tree. She had her principles. When Seppo wanted to touch the merchandise, she spat on him and hissed like a lynx. He administered a ringing slap, lifted her by the hair and struck his face against hers.

"I like the looks of you, my little strawberry, even if your manners are a bit barbarous. But I'll soften you up, I will. Just you wait and see. And don't go pissing when I stick it in you, you'll stain my clean apron."

Turning to the Captain, he explained, "It wouldn't be the first time, so I'm extra careful."

He couldn't wait to haul the brunette up to his bed. He dragged her into the underbrush and raped her right there, with pine needles stuck in her behind.

After he'd had his way with her, he beat the poor woman so badly that when she emerged from the woods, she was covered in bruises. The Captain was sitting on a stump, smoking. When he saw his prisoner's welts, he frowned.

"Was it good?" he asked Seppo in a flat voice.

"No big deal. When you've stuck it to one you've stuck it to 'em all. Plus her twat was a little sticky."

"You can say that again! You'll never forget this one! She just gave you a healthy dose of the clap!"

The Captain burst out laughing. He laughed so hard he toppled off the stump he was sitting on, and it took him two long minutes to catch his breath.

"Oh no," groaned Seppo. "That's the third time! I've had it up to here! The remedies, the mustard cures … they put my prick to sleep for weeks!"

By now the Captain was laughing so hard he choked on his spittle. He turned red, thumped his thighs, and spat profusely until he finally brought up the phlegm from his breathing tube with a gulp of water from the same bucket Seppo had left for the women. As for Seppo, he was still seething. He strode through the group of captives as he buckled his belt. A lad of thirteen or fourteen caught his eye, attached to the end of the chain.

"Who's the youngster?"

"Oh, him?" said the Captain. "He ended up in my flock by accident. It was his mother I had my eye on. A pretty blond she was, who rented out her charms on the sidewalks of Porvoo. Seeing as how her son was with her, I picked 'em both up. Sold off the mother in Grigol, but the buyer didn't want the youngster. When we got to the forest, to Wolf Creek, I was going to drown him, but when I thought it over a bit, I said to myself that maybe I could sell him off up north. At the Sailio family hamlet, for instance. There are more buggers per square metre in that godforsaken hole than in the rest of the Duchy."

Seppo went up to the boy. "The face of an idiot!" he thought. True enough, the youngster had a ridiculous mug. His head was shaped like a coconut, topped with a cap of yellow hair that fell in his eyes. To top it all off, one short lock stood straight up, which gave the little bugger a simian appearance. He had the glassy look of a stuffed reindeer head, the kind you mount on the wall. Was it the long journey he'd endured, or had nature made him that way? One way or the other, he looked puny and feeble. Seppo brought his face close to the boy's and examined the odd-looking yellow stains around his mouth.

"What's his name?" Seppo asked the Captain.

"No idea … I call him Mustard."

"On account of these spots?"

"You got it."

Seppo grabbed the youngster's chin between his fingers and with the pad of his thumb rubbed the stains for a moment. No. They were stuck on.

"Let me suggest, my fine fellow," he called out to the Captain. "I need someone to knack my reindeer carcasses. Plus there are all the little jobs around the inn, not to mention the repairs that need doing ... I'm always in the kitchen or looking after the customers. Where am I going to find the time to refinish the entrance or cut the wood? What's more, in the best inns, it's all the fashion to have a dishwasher. If you agree to let me have the youngster, I'll give you my daughter!"

In pronouncing those words – "my daughter" – Seppo grimaced, as if mentioning his relation to Zora would reveal some horrible reality he did his best to conceal.

"Your daughter? What daughter? What are you talking about, lard-ass?"

"Uh, well, my daughter. Wait a second."

Seppo stepped behind the knacker's shed and the Captain heard him shout, "Zora! Come here now, or I'll whip you within an inch of your life!"

Several minutes went by. Seppo continued shouting in the direction of the woods. When he reappeared, he was dragging a little girl with wispy hair by the collar of her dress.

Zora turned nine that summer. She had always been large for her age, and boasted the well-padded shoulders of a peasant girl. She wore an ill-fitting, splotchy grey dress. Scratches cross-hatched her legs. As she always did, she'd gotten up early that morning to roam the woods. Once she'd had her fill of the forest, she returned to the inn in hopes of resting on her straw mat. But as she drew near the establishment, she heard her father and a man whose voice she did not recognize laughing and conversing as they ate. Leaving them to their delectations, she went off to stretch out under a tree at some distance from the inn, piling up some fallen branches to make a pillow. The sound of her father calling awakened her. Which was why, standing there, hair dishevelled, she stared at the two men with a nasty look. Seppo and the Captain stared back.

"Well," said Seppo. "What're you up to, you little wench? Didn't I teach you it's rude to gape at people like that?"

The Captain looked the child over.

"Who is this little fleabag?"

"My daughter."

"Your daughter? Well, onto the next, you jerk-off! You must have nicked her in town, poor child!"

Seppo said nothing and scratched the earth with the tip of his boot, a pained look on his face.

"By the tsar's beard! It's really your child, then! How come I never saw her before?"

"She's a lost cause ... spends all her time in the forest with the animals. A real minx. I don't want her hanging around here all day bothering the customers."

The Captain pinched her chin between two fingers and slowly turned her head from left to right.

"No beauty, that's for sure ... She's got eyes ... a couple of caves. Pirate eyes! But nice skin ..."

He placed his index finger on the little girl's face, close to her eye. Then, slowly, he slid his finger down her cheek, and stopped when he reached the corner of her mouth. Zora didn't move, but her eyes rolled crazily left to right to avoid the Captain's gaze.

"I got no use for her," Seppo declared, "and I'd be happy to let you have her, because in exchange, I could use the strong arms of that lad over there to haul sacks of flour and salt herring. What say you, colonel?"

"She's nothing to look at," replied the Captain, "but she's already well built. She'll make a perfect farm girl."

And suddenly, with his two massive paws, he struck Zora three times on the shoulders. Her knees collapsed.

"Ha ha ha! What about that? My little milk cow! How'd you like to travel with Uncle Gut?"

It was then that Zora put on an astonishing display of defiance. She burrowed her two black eyes into the Captain's and stared right at him. The big hulk was shocked, and his grin suddenly turned sour. He pinched the plump part of the girl's cheek, and she let out a screech of pain.

"Don't you try to look me in the eye, got it?" he hissed.

With his two fat fingers he kept up the pressure on her cheek until tears welled up in the poor girl's eyes. Only then did he turn and look at Seppo.

"She's too young. I don't need another mouth to feed. The hussies I've got eat like sows ... But in a few years, when she turns fourteen or fifteen – how old is she, anyway?"

"Nine."

"When she turns fourteen or fifteen."

He looked at the girl for a moment or two, as if deep in thought. Then he spoke in a tone that sounded more like an order than a proposition.

"Here's what we're going to do, Seppo, you fat ass. I'll give you Mustard, and you can turn him into your butcher boy. In exchange, you promise me not to sell your daughter to anybody till she's fourteen, and not damage her before then. Get what I'm saying? I don't mind if you groom her a little now and then – little vixens like her can't tell their head from their ass, and even the most upstanding man finally runs out of patience – but nothing to cripple her. When she reaches the agreed-upon age, if I've got a bit of luck, she'll be better looking and you'll hand her over with pleasure, keeping in mind Mustard here, who in five years will be stronger and worth more than he is today."

Seppo had no reply. Sure, he was irritated at the thought of putting up with the girl's comings and goings for another five years, and he pretended to urge the Captain to take her immediately. The latter would have none of it. In her present state, the girl was too ugly. You could always find a taker for a boy. For little girls who were attractive, you might be lucky. But with a louse like Zora, you were stuck. For the sake of the Captain's commerce, it was better for Seppo to keep on wiping the little fart's ass for a few years more.

"But don't sell her off to anyone in the meantime! And I'll tell you something else, you big boar: I'm not about to bet on your honesty. Just to make sure you don't try to palm off some other girl on me five years down the road, I'm going to brand the youngster."

The Captain began by going over to Mustard. He pulled a key from his pack and unlocked the iron collar around the boy's neck that kept him linked him to the chain.

"You're lucky, little man. You're going to be the manservant of Seppo the imbecile!"

He led Mustard to Seppo and shoved him violently into his arms. The little boy staggered, but kept his footing. His features betrayed no emotion to speak of.

Meanwhile, Zora stood off to the side, observing the trade with indifference. Was she aware that her father had just promised her to this immense hulk with the grease-stained hands? There was no way of knowing. She was nine years old, but she looked so simple-minded, and spoke so little, you would have thought an adult conversation reached her only in the form of a distant murmur.

Then the Captain seized Zora's leather necklace with the little pouch containing a lock of her hair, and dragged the girl toward the inn. The leather cut into her skin. Zora resisted and began to shriek and wriggle like a she-devil. The Captain picked her up and threw her over his shoulder. Once inside, he dumped her on one of the dining tables.

The tiny ball of fury! Her arms and legs pumped furiously, right and left, to escape his clutches. The Captain stretched her out on her back. With one hand he pinned her neck to the table, and with the other he restrained her legs, though she was wriggling like someone possessed, the little piglet! The girl was caterwauling now, terrified of what was coming. She howled, she writhed, she begged! Then, in one last attempt, she lifted her head, her eyes wild, and at the top of her lungs she shouted a word that everyone, including the women sitting outside, could hear.

"Papa!"

Silence fell over the inn.

Standing in the doorway, Seppo turned his eyes to his daughter and blushed visibly.

On the windowsill close to where he stood lay a heavy razor strop, which the itinerant barber Kimmo Makkonen had forgotten the day before when passed by to cut his customers' hair. Seppo grabbed it, strode over to the table, and with all the strength his fat arm could muster, he raised it high above his head and brought it down on the little girl's bare thighs. *Thwack!*

Zora let out a final scream of pure pain. Eyes brimming with tears but without a sound, she lifted her head again and stared her father in the eyes. Seppo took a step backwards, turned to the Captain, and nodded his bulbous, porcine head, as if to say, "You may proceed."

The Captain rolled her over on her stomach, then lifted up her dress to where her buttocks began. He kept a hold on her, but it was no longer necessary. Zora had stopped squirming and screaming. The Captain bent over, lowered his head to her right leg just below the buttocks, and bit her violently on the fleshiest part of her thigh. Through the ten seconds of that ordeal, Zora let out not so much as a whimper. And when the Captain stood up, blood was spreading across the little girl's skin like spilled wine on a white tablecloth.

The Captain went to Seppo and imparted to him some pedagogical advice.

"Make sure you get the little hussy's temper under control before she's thirteen. Slap her around, whip her, beat her with a stick, don't spare the rod, really give it to her. If you're too soft, they turn out like unbroken mares, and then it's too late to get the bit between their teeth. I'll be taking over your daughter, and I don't want an unbroken mare."

The Captain and Seppo sealed the deal with a glass of vodka. Then the Captain ambled outside for a nap under a tree with one of his women. Later, as he was preparing to hit the road with his captives, Seppo bade him farewell and slid some wild boar's ears into his hand. "Something to gnaw on as you go." Captain Gut whistled for his dogs, whipped his women, and went off with his chain of prisoners. When she heard the rattling of the metal, Zora, who had been lying face down on the table, raised herself. She looked at her thigh; the vicious, deep wound was still bleeding. She felt her neck. Her delicate skin had been nastily scratched when the Captain yanked her by the necklace. A long bleeding scar stretched like a thread, from her left ear to the back of her head. But the necklace was still there. Fortunately.

She tried to shift her wounded leg and climb down from the table. The contraction of her thigh muscle touched off a pain so sharp she felt she'd been struck by lightning. About to faint, she lay down again on the table with piercing cries.

CHAPTER
6

Mustard and the Little Woodland Fairy

On the day the Captain visited the inn, Mustard felt quite pleased with himself when he realized he would be staying with the fat bald man instead of continuing on that exhausting journey. He had not the remotest idea of what lay in store for him in this immense, rotten edifice buried deep in the terrifying forest. But for the time being, none of that mattered in the slightest. When the silent, unkempt little blond girl appeared, summoned by her father from the woods, Mustard felt a curious kind of wonderment. He could not have expressed it in words – in truth, he was as dull-witted as the Captain claimed – but the sight of the girl had a calming effect on his small heart. He found himself dreaming of what it might be like to play, to run with her in fields where the wheat would dance in the wind like her short, dishevelled hair, ill-defined promises of unutterable happiness.

Soon enough, these pastoral reveries would collide with the pitfalls of dire reality. A first disappointment, and such a painful one at that! After being dazzled by the little girl's apparition while Seppo and the Captain carried on their outrageous haggling, Mustard looked more closely at Zora in hopes she would notice him. When she finally turned her head his way, she drilled him with a scornful glance, then quickly looked away, as if to say, "Who do you think you are, you tadpole in rags?" Then shortly afterwards, the Captain began to abuse her. Mustard listened to her howls that seemed to go on forever. Finally the Captain went off with the women and left him there with the innkeeper. He had no way of knowing that a thirteen-year ordeal was about to begin.

The day after Mustard's arrival, Seppo went off to Grigol, returning late in the day with a huge roller whose handle was longer than his new charge was tall. For months, several dozen huge sacks of crushed rock had been stacked beside the inn.

"Before you hit the sack, pave the path that leads to the clearing."

So began young Mustard's life of servitude, from which he would find no rest until the day of his death. Seppo forced him to haul bricks, logs, and beams from dawn to dusk. The lad ate two bowls of poor gruel a day, with a slice or two of spoiled bread if he was lucky. There were times when his forced labour was too much to bear, and he collapsed, exhausted, axe in hand or wood on his back. Seppo would fly into a rage, rush over, and kick him in the ribs, cursing him all the while. One day when he'd dented a rainwater catchment tank by accidentally hitting it with the manure hamper, Seppo beat him so hard he passed out. He came to thanks only to the mirthful customers who rubbed his back with polecat juice. He got to his feet, vomited, and took a few wavering steps before collapsing once more. For the rest of the day, Seppo had no choice but to cut his apprentice some slack; he had him shine some trout that had begun to go off with powdered cinnabar. "And make it snappy, it's for tonight's customers."

One evening Mustard was sanding the frame of the tool-shed door when Seppo came looking for him.

"Grab the shovel and follow me."

They walked for a good half-hour through the woods. Then, at the foot of a tall, lonely pine on a bare hillside, Seppo ordered him to dig. Two metres down, the shovel struck something hard.

"That's where I keep my money," Seppo told the lad as he opened the ash-wood chest that he had helped him pull from the hole.

Inside the chest, bundles of dirty marks and coins thrown pell-mell filled about a third of the space.

"Once a month I deposit the take here. I keep almost nothing for myself. Just a few pennies to pay the tobacconist when he comes by, or the odd time for the wenches in Grigol when I get an itchy dick. From now on, you'll be making the deposits. At night, when nobody can see. The beggars in the forest are like hogs, they've got nothing better to do than wander the woods like animals. The way Zora does. You'd think she'd be kind enough to help me at the inn, with the customers and all the rest? Forget it! The little hussy would rather run hither and thither through the woods, playing little games with the leprechauns and wild pigs, and turn up when she really gets hungry. You try to figure out what she's up to, morning to night … She's just like all of 'em, she is. A peasant. A mudpout. A do-nothing."

Seppo pulled out a few banknotes and a handful of coins from the tightly drawn purse he kept in the flap of his apron.

"There's a little more than twenty marks this month. There would have been more, but I had to shell out a pile to buy me a new pair of shoes last week. That shoemaker, what a jerk! Three whole marks, that's what he charged me."

He deposited the money alongside his savings. Mustard buried the chest while Seppo puffed on his pipe. As the sun slipped slowly below the horizon, its light touched the clouds with purple. When Mustard had finished trampling the earth to remove their footprints, Seppo grabbed him by the hair and stared him straight in the eye.

"I'll be counting the money and nothing better be missing. Make no mistake, young man. I may not be able to read but I know my figures. And if I find out that so much as a penny isn't accounted for, watch yourself. I'll make you shit vinegar, by my word! I'll pry your eyes out of their sockets and slice open your stomach with my fish knife, and your guts will be hanging out down to the ground and your face will be covered in blood. Do you understand what I'm saying?"

Mustard never spoke. Could he hear? Seppo didn't know. The obese innkeeper took the boy's brief blink as acceptance.

For his first months at the inn, he almost never encountered Zora. He toiled like a mule the livelong day. At night when Seppo was busy serving his customers, he went up to the second floor and slept in one of the empty rooms, the one at the end of the L-shaped corridor. He'd adopted that room from his first night, without Seppo's permission. The innkeeper noticed it at the end of the first week, but said not a word; the child had to sleep somewhere at the Farting Bear, after all. Rarely did the customers stay the night.

Come morning, Mustard was always the first one in the house to rise. He rummaged through the cold innards the previous night's customers had left on the tables, then went off to Devil's Creek to haul the day's water. If, the night before, Seppo had instructed him, "Wash my underwear and my clothes before I get up," he took the laundry with him as well. At the creek he wrung out the soiled clothing and filled two large buckets with cold water. On the return trip he checked the traps he'd set out the day before and set new ones. If he caught a hare or two, he brought the game back to the inn with the innkeeper's damp laundry and the icy water. The odd time, if he returned early enough, he would see Zora wake up. How happy he was! He hid in a corner of the dining room and observed the half-asleep girl padding through the inn. She pecked at the leavings on the tables, just as he had done earlier, stretched herself with a yawn and looked out the window to check on the weather. Some days, she would come upon Mustard hiding behind a keg or under a table. When she did, she would throw him a withering glance and hasten out of the inn. At times when he had nothing else to do, he would follow after her, pursuing her into the forest, always keeping his distance. What he liked best was when Zora thought she was alone and lowered her guard. Only when the little girl believed no one was watching did her roam through the woods take on the rhythm of a dance, an enchanted waltz, and her tiny steps, the way she paused in ecstasy in front of flowers, mushrooms, and insects, combined in his simple mind to produce the most marvellous of spectacles. But whenever he found himself deep in contemplation of the little woodland fairy, time would speed up, and all too soon he had to return to the inn to make sure he was on duty when Seppo awoke.

CHAPTER
7

Leon the Apothecary and
His Most Excellent Pomades

"Ah, what a charming lad! And what an ass, like two loaves of white bread, I wager!"

Sighing as he spoke, Sagadat Leino stuck out his lower lip and breathed out a long wisp of black smoke toward the ceiling. He was lounging on a bench, one arm thrown over Little Lulu's shoulders. The other customers found the scene amusing, and were splitting their sides with laughter. Zora, sitting a metre's distance from Sagadat, was rubbing her gums with a finger. She seemed not to have heard his insolent remark. Sagadat stuck out his left arm and prodded her buttocks.

"Ugghh! What disgusting little joints! Nothing but bone, not a shred of meat on them! From behind you look like a boy and I like that just fine, but as soon as you turn around, ugh! What an ugly little bird, really! Off with you, pug face! You're making us ill!"

The customers laughed all the more heartily and heaped more insults over the innkeeper's daughter. Turo Loikas attempted to splash the poor girl with the beer left in his tankard, but he was too far away and the brew soaked the two customers seated between him and Zora. One of them, a hefty bearded man, lost his temper and smacked Turo. The blow touched off a brawl and, before you could count to three, the forty-two revellers crowded into the dining room were at one another's throats. Taking advantage of the uproar, Zora fled the scene.

At fifteen, Zora was all bones and sharp angles. She was extremely tall, towering over her father by a good twenty centimetres. Beneath her patched dress, she held out a promise of handsomely solid shoulders, a natural robustness undermined by a deficient diet, the result being that the young woman displayed little more than two protruding shoulder blades and long, stringy arms, whereas nature intended her to have strong shoulders and fine, full, and well-proportioned white arms. The terrible abandon that was Zora Lavanko's lot was most clearly visible on her head. Her blond hair lay on her forehead and neck like a golden lawn that no one attended to.

Zora's skin was fine and white, with just the right amount of blush when she was active. All her physical strength, all the rough-hewn good looks for which she could thank the days spent playing in the woods, was concentrated in her milky skin, for which the great queens of history would have gladly sold their souls. The girl's cheeks had the fineness of precious stones.

Every day she ranged through the forest, and bathed in the Serpeille River at the foot of Pöysti Falls, exactly where – how could she possibly have known? – her mother had taken her life sixteen years before. She observed the creatures of the forest, gathered and ate its mushrooms, wandered between its great trees. On the steep slopes of rocky hillsides, she sought out crevices large enough to wiggle into. When she located one, she would slip into it and remain there for a moment, shivering. Rapidly enough she would tire of the darkness and the damp, and when she emerged she appreciated the light of day all the more, the clear sky, the gentle autumn breezes that caressed her skin, the chirping sparrows. At dusk she would climb the tallest trees and watch the sun set slowly beyond the Plains of Archelle. The great pink halo of the shiny disc would drop behind the rounded shape of the Drunkard Hills, far to the northwest; there were times when, if the tree was tall enough, Zora could make them out on the far horizon. In the penumbra that followed the dying of the light, before clambering down from her perch, Zora would turn her eyes to the south. There, at the far reaches of the forest, the lowering bulk of Mount Bolochel reached up into the sky like a dagger's tip, a steep, sharp point against which the daylight of this world came to die. Each time she witnessed the spectacle, an icy shiver ran down the young woman's spine. The silhouette of the mountain was blacker than night itself. Zora knew that, come morning, when the entire forest would be bathed in the triumphant brightness of the rising sun, the mountain would cast a shadow over the many kilometres of the region that stretched out at its feet, and huge flocks of ravens would depart the sunlit woods to seek refuge beneath its dark cloak. In all her young life, Zora never dared venture as far as the mountain. Gladd the Argus lived atop its summit, that was what the customers at the inn claimed, and she often heard their horrifying tales of the Black Bard.

Come summer's end, thanks to lower waters in the Serpeille, she would cross the river at the ford. She cautiously explored that part of the forest to the west of the water in hopes of spotting wolves. They were rarely seen in these parts, live wolves least of all. The trappers who would stop off at the inn often carried wolf carcasses slung over their shoulders, and they would fling them to the dining-room floor before sitting down at a table. The sight of dead animals never moved Zora, a tripe butcher and cutthroat's daughter. The sight of blood-drenched wolves bothered her no more than the partridges aging in the kitchen or the skinned wolverines hanging from hooks in the knacker's shed. But in her eyes wolves were handsome, even in death; in their features she detected a dignity that would have been magnified had the beasts still lived. Still, wolves were wary creatures, and could easily sense the presence of humans. How to approach them? Zora had spent her entire life in the woods and could, with a bit of effort, observe flying squirrels, lemmings and hares, reindeer, and even wolverines at close range! Lynx avoided her, but she didn't care, for she did not like them one whit. She also steered clear of bears, whose behaviour could be unpredictable. But wolves … how she dreamed of seeing one up close!

The sickening odour of a traditional Finnish dish made her dream come true.

One winter afternoon, while Seppo was snoozing, Zora crept into the kitchen to find something to eat. There, next to the oven, she found seven large *kalakukot*, still warm and steaming, that Seppo had stuffed with pike filets and pork fat. The *kalakukot* had spent the morning in the oven, and Seppo left them to cool on the table before going off for his nap. Zora wrapped one in an old apron, and with her free hand poured herself a full goblet of buttermilk. She knew Seppo would get angry and beat her. "No matter," she said to herself. "I'm too hungry."

She left the inn with her lunch and moved quickly northward for a quarter-hour, sat down beneath a spruce tree, and started to eat.

She heard the wolves before she saw them. The crackling of pine needles and dry sticks being trodden underfoot alerted her. Her mouth full, she stopped chewing and did not swallow. As she was expecting a hare or a fox to appear, she almost choked when she beheld two extraordinary wolves. How could they have come so close without making any more noise than a mink? A surge of terror paralyzed her. The two beasts slowly made their way toward Zora, neither growling nor showing their fangs.

It could only have been the smell of cooked fish that drew them. The wolves – a male and a female – came over and poked their muzzles into the *kalakukot*. The male licked the fish and the crust but did not open his mouth. The female moved off after two sniffs. Zora could not take her eyes off her. How beautiful she was! Her eyes the colour of jade, her breast and head dark grey except for her muzzle, which was pure white. And the lighter colour formed a strange motif against the grey fur of her forehead, like a cheese bell or a covered rowboat.

Not for an instant did the wolves show the slightest interest in Zora. They sniffed the *kalakukot* without eating; the male was satisfied with a slurp of the buttermilk that filled Zora's goblet.

After a few moments of slow-motion ballet around the child, nosing this way and that and glancing in every direction, the two magnificent beasts turned slowly back in the direction they had come from, giving the young woman not so much as a glance. By then the *kalakukot* were cold. Famished, Zora ate it anyway.

In the following days, she would take refuge in the enchanting recollection of those two beings that lived together in the woods. In the sad and serious tranquility of the wolves, in the apparent indifference of their behaviour, in the distrust they showed toward all that did not belong to their world, Zora saw the reflection of what she herself was. The wolves possessed something she did not, and which she cruelly craved: siblings, companions, a brotherhood. Never did you see a lone wolf. They always travelled in groups, or at least in couples, like the two celestial specimens that she encountered that day.

And so it was that Zora created an imaginary lupine brotherhood. In her imagination she conjured up five wolves; to each she gave a personality and distinctive features. She spoke to them in the language of humans and the wolves responded. And when the cruel moment came when the pretty dream that enveloped her burst like a soap bubble – the burbling stream of her imagination would run dry by day's end – she would come to an abrupt stop. She looked around her. Night was falling. Not a living creature, with the possible exception of a dull-witted partridge perched atop a stump or a couple of ravens in the branches. These moments of awakening were more painful than all the blows her father inflicted. She understood then that she was alone in this world, alone forever.

Of course there was Mustard, who by virtue of the indignities he suffered at her father's hands shared the same cruel destiny. But she did not like him, did not like him in the slightest!

If Zora was a she-wolf, Mustard, from the moment he arrived at the inn six years earlier, was an ass, a vacant soul, an empty mind whose vacuity was confirmed by his eyes, with their look of perpetual astonishment. Obedience was his destiny. Seppo had started him off with the heaviest tasks around the inn. He trained him to carry water, haul wood, patch the holes in the roof – jobs of that magnitude. Then, gradually, the innkeeper initiated him into the butcher's trade. Cooking and serving his customers kept Seppo's hands full. He needed someone to work in the knacker's shed, hang the game to age, butcher the animals, draw out their innards, and occasionally tan their hides to sell later in Grigol. In a word, Seppo taught him the tripe-butcher's trade. The child would become a tripe-butcher's boy and know nothing else.

Mustard may have been tall and skinny, but he was tough as a Russian! And since he was dim-witted and docile too, after he'd spent two years at the inn, Seppo figured he could make more of the lad than a simple slave; he could turn him into his right-hand man. He initiated the boy into the arcana of a technique far more sinister than simple butchery. No longer the ass, Mustard became a tiger. On occasion Zora would cross his path by the knacker's shed. The lad would be carrying quarters of some strange meat whose origin she could not determine. And then, perhaps because he slaughtered the animals clumsily or used poorly sharpened knives, since he had taken charge of those tasks, Zora found the shrieks and cries that echoed from the knacker's shed far more disturbing than when Seppo handled the task. Zora would go well out of her way to avoid passing within proximity of that place. The screams that issued from it were too horrible.

Zora knew that Mustard would sometimes follow her into the forest. He kept his distance and tried to stay out of sight, but Zora knew the woods as well as she knew her own body. In that dark place there was not a hideaway, not an excrescence, not a bulge with which she was not intimately familiar. All she had to do was cast her eyes over a forest scene – any scene – to immediately detect any foreign presence. A glimpse of a head, a flash of human skin in the underbrush, a shred of clothing that stuck out from behind a tree, even an unaccustomed sound had the same effect on her consciousness as a nick makes on fingers drawn along a knife blade. She was angry when she realized this low-life was following her.

She took off through the trees and vanished into the underbrush, and he would never find her.

One evening at the inn, after Sagadat Leino made sport of her and a brawl broke out, she made quickly for the exit. Before she crossed the threshold, she reached out and plucked Footpad's pipe and tobacco pouch from his table. He saw nothing, too intent on trading blows and scratches with Erik Loppi. She had a toothache, one of her molars, at the back of her mouth, on the upper left. She'd heard the inhabitants of the forest say that tobacco smoke could sooth a sore tooth. Her catch in hand, Zora vanished into the night.

Beneath the inn's front porch was a cavity, not large enough to stand up in, but wide enough to lie down comfortably. Zora often sought refuge there during the cold of winter when Seppo expelled her. There, flat on the ground, she wriggled beneath the floor of the inn. Heat from the woodstove, which was not too far from the main entrance to the dining room, warmed the floorboards and Zora, hiding under the porch, enjoyed a bit of warmth. But it was still too cold there for sleeping, and she would often awake during the night and warm herself by vigorous exercise outside. Come morning, she was shivering so hard and her head was aching so badly that she felt she'd been trampled by a herd of reindeer. Thankfully, it was April now, and the weather was mild. Zora curled up in the tiny enclosure. The footfalls of the customers entering and exiting the inn bothered her a little at first, but she soon became accustomed to the noise. She lit the pipe, drew a couple of deep draughts, swirled the smoke around inside her mouth, and spat it out, coughing. The relief she felt was no better than the nausea; she extinguished the pipe by sticking its bowl into the cold earth, and fell asleep.

The next day, she opened her eyes and touched her left cheek. "Ouch!"

The discomfort, bearable the previous day, had turned into shooting pain. Zora noticed that her forehead was hot and moist. She slid out of her refuge and climbed the steps to the porch. It was a reflex: every morning, when she'd spent the night out of doors, she would sneak back inside to scavenge for food before Seppo woke up. But today, with that tooth of hers and the fever that was wracking her, she wasn't hungry. She turned around, went back down the stairs, crawled under the porch, and attempted to sleep some more. For naught! She felt as if someone were slicing her gums open with a butcher knife! She lay there for two hours, in the deepest despair. She smoked more of Footpad's tobacco, but this time it brought her no relief. At wit's end and in pain, she rose and tramped into the woods.

She followed her footsteps for some time, finally ending up on the banks of the Serpeille. Crouching at the edge, she rinsed out her mouth with cold water to numb her gums. At first it seemed to help, but when she spat out the water, the pain was still there, more intense than before.

Zora wandered in pain through the tall spruce of the forest the whole afternoon. At dusk she emerged from the deep woods and came out on the path that wound through the western section and led directly to the Farting Bear. She knew a kilometre and a half separated her from the inn, but she didn't want to go there and risk an encounter with her father. There could be no doubt he would beat her, and the pain of her toothache was enough! Where was she to go? She turned westward. Three kilometres farther on, the trail reached the Serpeille, then ran along its banks to Pöysti Falls, then the Asswiper Bridge before angling off to the west, toward those regions of the forest where Zora had never ventured, to the fabled Plains of Archelle and beyond … Beyond? What lay beyond? "For certain, nothing and nobody," she thought to herself, "to help ease my pain!"

Zora sat down on the ground in the middle of the trail, her long thin legs crossed in front of her. She began to sob, face red and streaked with tears.

At that very moment a man appeared and drew near her. He had come from the west, along the same path, but Zora, absorbed by her pain, had not seen him. The dirty tips of two hefty boots presented themselves in front of her puffy eyes. She raised her head.

The man standing in front of her was tall and powerfully built. He was loaded like a pack mule, as you will soon see.

Attached to his back by shoulder straps hung a hefty blue-and-white striped rucksack full of useful objects. From an aspen branch on his left shoulder, a red bundle was suspended like a fat, poached cherry! Around his waist he wore a broad belt and a snakeskin pouch (considered poor taste in Karelia but esteemed, so they say, among the Russians). Hanging by a strap across his right shoulder was an elongated, irregular-shaped valise that may have contained a musical instrument. But what instrument could it have been? The story you are reading will not tell you, for even the author of these lines knows nothing of its contents! To top it off, swinging from his belt were three fat purses full of marks and pennies, but also of banknotes and coins of distant lands, countries where people do not bathe more than once a week, where they eat with their hands and clean their teeth while gargling with tea!

The man was of porcine mien, beardless and running with sweat. His tiny eyes were buried deep in the folds of his splotchy skin.

"And what might you be doing here, my fine doe? And why the tears, like boiling water?"

Zora recognized the guttural and ill-spoken Finnish of the Russians. They would occasionally stop by at the inn, and she could not get enough of listening to them. Their talk was ugly, but God knows it was funny! But, in the shadow of this giant piglet, she felt only one urge: to get to her feet and flee as fast as her legs would carry her! A shame, because her fever had grown worse and the ground was her bed, and now the man was upon her, leaning over and putting his hand on her forehead.

"Oyoyoyoyoy!" he whistled. "Look at face of hers, red as beet! And she look like she's hurting, the big stork! She's burning hot and sweaty, the ugly little pussycat!"

(For to tell the truth, Zora was no princess.)

Then the man slowly slid his hand across her face and parted her lips with the fat tip of his thumb. Zora froze as the man licked his chops.

"You must be hurting, my little ugly duckling, yes? You have toothache, my long drink of water? So bad, like woodpecker pecking away at inside of mouth, peck peck peck in your little mouth, yes?"

The man reached down to his belt buckle.

"Well, weep no longer! I fix your problem in two shakes! You want me to make you feel better? Because you know – or maybe you don't know – but I tell you, Leon the Large, that's me, all right, Leon the Large knows how to make mouths and plenty of other places feel better."

So saying, he opened his belt pack, then brought his hand to Zora's mouth.

"Open wide."

Zora attempted a cry, but no sound issued from her mouth.

"Open up, I said!"

The Russian spread her lips with his thumb and index finger. Within an inch of fainting, Zora had no choice.

Using his index finger as a tongue depressor, he looked closely at the infected area, next to the molar. He let out a long, pensive sigh. He saw what he'd expected to see.

"All nasty and inflamed! And swollen too! The root of your tooth full of sewage, my big dishrag! But look at your good luck! To happen upon Uncle Leon on fine evening."

Leon the Russian slipped the large striped rucksack off his shoulders and set it on the ground. He undid the cord that held it closed and withdrew various vials and small jars. With delicate but sure-handed movements, he unwrapped his wares, and on his face he wore the expression of a fisherman picking through his flies, wondering with which one he should bait his line.

"Thank your lucky stars, my ugly little wench, for Leon is apothecary, and by no means the worst of apothecaries, let me assure you! I say, in fact, there is no apothecary as fine as me anywhere in Grand Duchy, my little one! Often I pass through Fredavian Forest! I'm on way to sell my new ointments in Grigol! But now, who's going to get benefit of my new ointments? For free, at that!"

Zora shrugged her shoulders.

"Well, you, of course!" the apothecary chortled. "It will be game, you'll see. You're the one, peasant lass, whose toothache Leon will soon cure!"

The wandering eccentric was getting more excited by the minute, like a child in a candy shop! From one of the pockets of the rucksack, he swiftly removed a small jar that resembled a lady's compact. It contained a beige gel that gave off the pungent aroma of overripe fruit. He sprinkled the gel with three powders taken from as many coloured vials.

Her fear dissipated, Zora watched him with some interest. Already the raving pain in her tooth seemed less intense. The man unhooked a shallow tin bowl from his belt. Into it he poured the gel he'd sprinkled with the powders, and using his sausage-like fingers, he added a dash of red liquid with a strong odour. Using his finger again, he stirred the decoction until it seemed unctuous enough. He tasted it and pronounced it satisfactory.

"Now, my little not-too-pretty one, open your mouth wide and point to where hurts most."

The man was harmless and had nicely gained our little Zora's confidence. With nary a second thought, the little blond opened her mouth and pointed to the spot that the apothecary had earlier identified.

"Ahhhh! And now, down to work! Leon rub your little pink gums, like this ... Mouth wide open, my ugly little toad! That's it!"

With the tip of his finger the man applied the ointment to the infected area. A thick glob slid down Zora's throat. It was intensely sweet, and she winced.

"Ha ha ha! Sweet remedy ... but fast effect."

That was an understatement! At first, Zora felt her gums go numb. It was a curious sensation, and not the most pleasant one, to tell the truth, but the pain had stopped pursuing her, and that was wonderment enough for Zora. She cracked a crooked smile that seemed to enchant the hulking Russian.

"Feels better, eh, my little hayseed? Listen carefully, little lady! It's magical jelly, but tomorrow or day after, when you wake up in morning, your tooth ... *Plop!* Spat out on pillow or caught in your greasy hair! That's life, my little cucumber: no pain, no cure, you have to lose something for good ... If I had some gold, needle, and right medicaments, I'd make little hole in your tooth and fill it with gold, but what can I do? You're just little poor girl anyway, no? Where will you find money for gold? Plus the tooth is at back of your mouth, nobody will notice when it's gone. Don't cry tomorrow morning if you find your tooth on pillow. Understand?"

Zora nodded yes.

"You live here close by, my little frog?"

Zora nodded again and pointed east.

"Ah, you live at the inn that makes tripe, right? The Happy Innards, something like that?"

"The Farting Bear."

For the first time the apothecary heard Zora's voice. He was hardly impressed and scratched his head dubitably.

"That's it, the Farting Bear. Your daddy's the innkeeper?"

"Yes."

"Yes, yes again. Leon hear of the inn. But Leon ... eat intestines, eat spleens ... Brrr!" He pinched his nose to signify disgust, which brought a smile to Zora's lips. "Leon rather keep walking to Grigol and take room in normal inn. You know way to Grigol, my little weasel?"

"That way." Zora pointed east, in the direction of the inn. "You have to pass by the inn," she added, "then follow the trail to the east. After the forest comes the Ritva Swamp. It's muddy but you'll find a paved road with a lot of traffic, and signs that tell you the way to go. On foot ... on foot from here, you'll need seven or eight hours, moving at a good pace."

By now it was dark. The man looked around at the darkness as if to estimate its depth. Then, in a decisive tone, he proclaimed, "Off we go! With us God! I'll go through woods to miss inn. After, find east trail and way to Grigol. To travel by night, Leon likes!"

Zora said nothing. She approved of the husky Russian's plan. If she could only avoid the inn herself…

"Stroll in forest with owls and wolves before town! And you, my little garter snake, you go back home now? Because night has come."

The Russian then bowed low, and so surprised was Zora by his curious behaviour that she leaped backwards! Husky Leon burst out laughing, waved his hand, veered off the trail, and headed into the woods. Before vanishing completely, he turned back one last time.

"If you have toothache again, go see apothecary who uses sandpiper grease and spruce balm. If he use sandpiper grease, he true apothecary, do good job."

And after a final wave, the man disappeared into the woods. Zora made her way back to the inn along the trail.

It was a festive night at the Inn of the Sign of the Farting Bear; the forest dwellers were celebrating the feast of Saint Xanthine. From outside the huge slouching structure, Zora could hear the sounds of carousing. Now that her tooth was no longer aching, she was hungry, but she didn't dare go inside for fear someone would see her and try to fondle her or make fun of her. With muffled steps, she crept around the inn and came to the kitchen window. The shutters were ajar, but there was no one inside. Seppo would be in the main room, serving alcohol to his customers. A grey partridge hung there from a cord. The window was not too high above the ground. Zora reached up and grabbed the sill with both hands, then hoisted herself up until her torso was inside. Then she freed her hands by balancing on her tummy on the sill. An outstretched arm and … *Fluppp!* She clutched the dead fowl's warm body. Instead of dropping back to the earth, she tossed the partridge over her shoulder to free her left arm, since Seppo had left some mint cakes on the little table beneath the window. Arm outstretched once more, Zora grabbed three of them! "With the berries I can pick in the bushes by the latrines ... Mmm! I'll eat to my heart's content!" she said to herself, licking her lips.

Then she tipped herself backwards and landed on her feet. She picked up the partridge and circled the inn to take a drink of water from the rain barrel near the knacker's shed. She took a deep gulp. Along with the frigid liquid, she felt tiny spines, like wood shavings or cement chips, sliding down her throat. She stuck her finger in her mouth to touch the diseased tooth. Rubbing it, she felt scales sloughing off: the tooth was disintegrating. "What of it," she thought, "as long as it stops hurting."

Baddabing!

A cascade of deafening noises resounded from the knacker's shed in front of her. It was Mustard ... He was looking for a particular knife and had scattered all the others across the floor. Zora froze. She heard the sound of a knife against the grindstone. When he finally emerged from the knacker's shed, it was no knife he held in his hand, but a short cudgel, no longer than a man's forearm. Zora recognized it as the tool he used to stun the beasts before plunging them into the scalding vat.

His unexpected appearance startled Zora, who kept as far away from the dim-witted lad as she could. She was right next to the water barrel, close to the knacker's shed door that had just flown open violently – impossible to escape without attracting his attention. But to her astonishment, the boy passed by no more than a metre away and took no notice of her. As he strode toward the forest, Mustard was breathing heavily. The night quickly swallowed him up and Zora, struck by the curious haste of the usually sluggish lad, made up her mind to follow him. Tracking was an art she knew well.

In the darkness, she followed the sound of his footfalls. Occasionally, in the moonlight, she could catch the gleam of the cudgel. He bulled deep into the woods, following no trail. He moved rapidly, with assurance. When he halted, Zora stopped too. The boy pricked up his ears, listening for something, but she was sure he didn't know he was being followed. No, Mustard was *after something*; he was tracking an animal.

Was he tracking a reindeer, a bear, a wolf? Halfway down a gentle slope he came to a full stop, slightly below where Zora stood, well hidden. She could make out only the top half of his coconut-shaped head, and even that was little more than shadow.

Time went by. He stood motionless. When finally her legs began to tingle and she could not stand to wait anymore, she climbed silently up the trunk of a tall spruce. There, halfway between the ground and the crest, she could see his silhouette, from head to toe.

The boy was as taut as a bowstring, like a wild animal about to leap. A soft breeze rustled the leaves of the birch trees. An owl hooted.

Five long minutes passed. Then a new noise could be heard, footfalls mingling with the gentle harmony of the wind, growing ever more audible. The person approaching had no idea he was being spied upon. He whistled gaily, ornamenting his refrain with short bursts of song. A man's voice. The distance kept Zora from hearing the words to his song.

From high on her perch, she watched as Mustard slipped between the trees, taking advantage of his insouciant victim. He drew closer to his prey and when he'd come within two steps of the walker ... *Whack!* He pounced like a lynx.

Sitting on her branch, Zora did not budge. Mustard brought down the cudgel on his victim's head. Did the man even understand he was being attacked? He fell to the ground without a cry, like a sack of dead rats.

Mustard stripped him of his belongings: rucksack, sash, pouches, and pack. He strapped all the gear to his body and set off for the inn, leaving his unconscious victim on the ground.

When he had left, Zora scrambled down from the tree and went over to the body. She was only half-surprised to recognize Leon the apothecary, the man who had healed her toothache. He had a nasty wound on his head and a rivulet of blood was trickling down his round face. But he was still breathing.

Zora wondered if there might still be something of interest on Leon's body. Something to eat, perhaps? Zora always needed more food. But she couldn't remember seeing him pull anything but vials, packets, compacts, and a bowl for preparing pomades from his various sacks and pouches. Mustard had made off with the whole kit and caboodle. She rummaged through the husky apothecary's pockets and came upon a handful of pretty, multi-coloured vials, but what could she possibly do with ointments and philtres? Nothing there could relieve her hunger. And worse, if Seppo were to find those little bottles on her, he would make a big deal of it and give her a whipping. Worse yet, none of Leon's clothing suited her. What a waste of time! And now, someone was coming! It had to be Mustard with her father. They were coming for his clothing. Zora climbed back in her tree.

When they reached the dying man's body, Seppo asked, "That's all he had for the taking?"

Mustard nodded.

"All right, let's haul him in."

Seppo dropped a coil of rope. Mustard tied the Russian's legs together, and with the rope he and Seppo dragged their expiring victim off toward the inn. At the speed they were travelling, they would need at least an hour to get there, Zora calculated. She decided to stay right where she was, in her tree, for a little longer.

Once she could no longer hear Seppo and his protégé, she clambered to the very top of the great spruce. As every time she perched on a lofty treetop in the dead of night, the beauty of the canvas beneath her took her breath away. Seated on a tall branch, her back against the trunk, she swayed back and forth, whistling.

For Zora the contemplative, the whippings, insults, and dis-honour inflicted on her at the inn, and the hunger that made her stomach writhe during her long wanderings through the woods, were not too high a price to pay for the moments of occasional bliss as the Fredavian Forest unfolded its beauties and wonders before her. All around, the forest stretched out seemingly to infinity. Only Mount Bolochel to the southwest and the Drunkard Hills to the north broke the smoothness of the prospect. An immense moon shed its smoky light on the forest. Zora felt so contented, so at peace that she would have surely fallen asleep on her branch if something utterly stupefying had not happened.

Her eyes were slowly closing when she spotted something that gave every indication of being a flying man, passing before her between earth and sky.

"What?"

She opened her eyes wide and rubbed them vigorously. The man was at some distance away, two or three hundred metres. Yet she could perfectly make out his dark form against the deep blue backdrop of the night sky. He was far higher than Zora, and moving slowly through space along a nearly perfect horizontal axis. He was seated, but on what? Upon nothing at all! Look, he was passing in front of the great disc of the moon! No doubt about it. It was a man and nothing else. He wore a top hat and a frock coat whose flaps fell on both sides of his thighs. He was floating inside a great sphere of smoke ... Good Lord! He was exhaling the smoke from the pipe in his mouth!

Dazzled, Zora observed the flying man's deliberate and graceful transit. He crossed her field of vision from west to east, and then began a slow descent as his flight path curved broadly toward the earth. When he reached a point opposite her, the girl despaired of seeing him sink beneath the hilltop. To watch him for as long as possible, she stood up on her branch.

A moment later, he was gone. But she could have sworn the man waved at her before sinking out of sight. Actually waved at her! That must mean he'd seen her.

Zora clung fast to the mad hope that the man would reappear. But after two hours, overcome with fatigue, she climbed down from her tree and, in resignation, headed back to the inn, promising herself to return the following night.

Her heart still upside down from her misadventure, she followed her footsteps back to the inn. Before sneaking inside to lie down on her straw pallet, she went to the water barrel next to the knacker's shed. Her head was in the barrel and she was drinking like a horse when she heard strange sounds from within the shed. Curious, she wiped her mouth on her sleeve and snuck over to peek inside.

The double doors of the building yawned open. From inside came the sound of moaning. Everything was dark. Zora could barely see a step in front of her.

She went in, following the wall on her right. When she was all but certain there was no one there but the poor soul making that sound, she felt her way through the quarters of meat hanging from the ceiling and bumped into the scalding vat. A cloud of fatty steam, hot and stinking, rose up from the tank, and when it condensed, it fell to the ground in heavy droplets. Quite clearly, something had just been scalded. Standing on tiptoe, Zora clutched the rough edge of the tank. In the steamy darkness it was impossible to tell if there was anything in it. She turned away and headed for the main room. That was where the lamentations were coming from.

The closer she came, the more the moaning wrenched her heart. In the knacker's shed, she could see no more than two steps in front of her. She happened upon a candle stub and some matches on a stool close to the tank, and lighted the taper.

Once the flame had sputtered into life, she saw that the floorboards beneath her feet were covered with a kind of spongy red crust. In disgust, she covered her mouth with her sleeve, and forced herself to look straight ahead.

A few steps from the back wall, in the feeble light of the candle, she found where the moaning was coming from. Three indistinct forms hung from butcher's hooks. The one in the middle was motionless; the other two, suspended in midair, twisted and turned slowly, the creaking of the pulleys mingling with the whimpering that came from one of the forms.

Terrified, Zora leaped backwards and hid behind a huge reindeer quarter.

From the right and middle hooks hung wolf carcasses. The blood-drenched creatures had been hacked to pieces. Zora recognized the two wolves she had encountered in the forest a few weeks before.

The male, in the middle, was already stiff. To his left, the female, two hooks dug deeply into her flanks, was pedalling her two hind legs in thin air, a look of resignation on her face.

To the left of the wolves hung Leon the apothecary. Zora recognized him by his tiny porcine eyes. The rest of his head and his body were nothing but steaming magma of melted flesh and muscle. Mustard and Seppo had stripped him and plunged him into the boiling water of the scalding vat, then hung him from a butcher's hook. The pot-bellied Russian was now nothing more than a half-liquefied mass of human fat and broken bones. All that remained of his arms were two stumps that waved this way and that. Even his head had melted. Only a large fat bulb was left, along with a few shreds of skin that hung from the sides and back of his skull. But his eyes remained, looking in Zora's direction. His mouth had been replaced with a small, gaping, lipless round hole revealing yellowed teeth.

The hooks thrust between his ribs, and he dangled there, a metre off the ground, in an upright position. Zora thought he was dead, and stepped away. She turned her attention to the wolves; suddenly, the apothecary raised his head. It was as though a smouldering spectre had emerged from the earth to confront her.

Leon stared down at Zora. He gurgled incomprehensibly three times, then succeeded in articulating these words: "Come, little girl ... come help me ..."

His murmuring voice cut through the dense silence of the knacker's shed.

For a few seconds, Zora, candle in hand, considered the man with a blank, neutral gaze. Then she turned to the she-wolf to her right, which was still quivering, frightened by the movement and the voices around her.

Zora examined the animal. Yes, it was indeed the she-wolf that had approached her to sniff her *kalakukot* three weeks before. She recognized the bell-shaped spot on her forehead. The hooks had penetrated deeply into the fleshiest part of her flanks. The beast hung there, and the skin was distended where the steel claws had entered her flesh. How horribly painful it must be! Zora returned to the scalding vat. Beside the tank stood a small table where Mustard would bone the game. She threw the knives to the floor and pushed the table underneath the wolf. It was just the right height. She looked to the right and saw the apothecary staring at her in his delirium. She threw him a hard glance. The apothecary lowered his head. He was half-dead, slipping in and out of consciousness.

The table was shaky, but high enough so the she-wolf, hung in the vertical position, could put her four paws on it.

Zora knew that the most delicate part of the operation had come: remove the hooks from the animal's flesh. But at this point, it was too late to stop. Mustard or Seppo could walk into the knacker's shed at any moment. Paws on the table now, the she-wolf wobbled, but did not fall.

Zora placed one hand on the creature's right flank, near the entry point of the hook. Pressing gently against the skin around the wound, with the other hand she slowly slid the metal from the flesh. A good fifteen centimetres withdrew from the wound. Throughout the operation, the she-wolf breathed a long whine of muted pain, as if she knew she must remain as quiet as possible to keep from tipping off her tormentors.

With the first hook removed, Zora began the same procedure on the left side. This time the she-wolf let out a howl, and her limbs shook. But she stood fast.

In the end, freed from her steel bounds, the animal attempted a few steps on the table. After, she turned to her dead companion and licked his fur, whimpering. Then she jumped from the table and with laborious, short steps, hurried out the door.

Zora replaced the boning table where she had found it, next to the scalding vat. She couldn't be bothered to replace the knives, not when the place was always a mess! She threw a quick glance at the apothecary. The bulky man now wore a beatific look. Blood had begun to gush from the holes where his nose had been.

Far away, she heard a door slam. It was the front door of the inn. The sound of steps … Horror! They were coming!

Zora blew out the candle. Impossible to sneak out without

being seen. The back door of the inn lay just opposite the entrance to the knacker's shed, only fifteen metres away. She had no choice but to crouch in a dark corner and pray that they not notice her.

Hunched over, she tiptoed past several quarters of meat hanging from the ceiling. She stumbled over a piece of wood. *Bangadabang!* She froze for an instant. The footsteps drew nearer. In four quick strides, Zora reached the wall on the left, found a corner, and crouched down, arms around her knees.

The knacker's shed was not square; it was shaped like a flask. The entrance was at the bottom of the flask, while the wolves and the apothecary had been hung at the back, at the flask's neck. Zora had hidden in the corner that formed the right shoulder. From where she crouched, she could see neither the wolf nor the apothecary. When Mustard came in and closed the two large swinging doors, the darkness was complete. It lasted a few seconds, then a halo of light, with Mustard at the centre, appeared near the entrance.

Zora watched as the half-wit made his way across the shed in the light of an oil lamp. He passed close by without spotting her. When he reached the hooks, she lost sight of him.

Mustard's low muttering and the sound of metal on metal broke the silence. Slowly, Zora crept along the wall to the point where it curved inward to the right to form the neck of the flask. Only her head stuck out, turned in the direction of the hooks. Hugging the floor, in the darkness, she could see without being seen.

Mustard stood there in front of the hooks with a huge butcher knife in his hand. Zora recognized her father's heavy hatchet, the same one he used to cut up skua carcasses. That butcher knife had been part of the Farting Bear since the day she was born.

The boy stared at the empty hooks and the chains where the she-wolf should have been. Zora felt her muscles seize up. What if the simpleton decided to search the knacker's shed in search of his prey? Then what? What if he came upon her? With his sick, feverish mind, who knows what he would have done to her, who knows if he might inflict some abominable chastisement on her as punishment for her misdeed?

Then suddenly, Mustard began to shift from one foot to another, whining and growling! Bleating, he waved the slaughtering knife above his head, and in the glitter of the long blade Zora caught a glimpse of herself, like in a mirror. She was terrified at the idea that he had seen her reflection, but Mustard had slipped into madness, and nothing around him seemed able to save him from it.

Zora could see nothing of the apothecary, but she understood that the man was feeling true terror; his pleas were growing clearer. Mustard's hopping and jumping must have shaken him from his pre-death coma. He began weeping like a baby.

"Oh no! Oh no! Not that ... not ..."

He was begging as loud as his scalded vocal cords would let him. Using her arms, Zora crept forward to look. She saw Mustard grab the stub of the apothecary's right arm, lift the fleshless member, and with feline rapidity bring the knife down on the victim's shoulder. This time, the Russian found the strength to shriek with pain. Zora jumped and covered her ears. But she could not keep from watching the scene.

Was the knife poorly sharpened? Whatever the case, the blow chewed up the flesh and only half-detached the arm from the shoulder. It was as though he had sliced open a pie overflowing with soft, juicy red cherries. The gaping cut exposed fat globules of bloody pulp.

Mustard began delivering blows in rapid succession, his arm waving like a windmill. *Thwack, thwack, thwack, thwack!*

The apothecary was screaming. With his cries came strange exhortations uttered in a language that neither Mustard nor Zora understood, imprecations whose demented melody mingled with the distant sound of shouting and vulgar drinking songs issuing from the inn, in the distance. The knife blade whistled as it cut through the air.

In the endless clamour, Zora lowered her head and vomited at the base of the wall. She crouched motionless for a few seconds above the small pool of bile, gasping. The din was deafening: Mustard's grunting, the swish of the blade as it rose and fell, biting into living flesh, cartilage, and bone, again and again in the same spot, directly on the clavicle. Zora covered her ears again. She watched as Mustard delivered the final blow, the one that cut the stub of the arm loose from the body. She saw Mustard hold it for a moment, throw it to the floor, then begin to hack away at the apothecary, striking everywhere on his body. Leon's cries grew fainter and fainter. Before he fell silent entirely, Zora got to her feet, gasping. With muffled steps she snuck out of the knacker's shed, hardly caring whether Mustard saw her. Outside, she walked slowly to the door to the inn. The customers were eating and drinking, and no one paid her the slightest heed. She wanted to reach her pallet in the kitchen, but Seppo was busy coating bear tongues with sow butter. She hid under the porch and prepared to spend the night there. It took her many hours to fall asleep. The din of the carousers mingled with the screams of the apothecary that still echoed in her head.

The next day, when he discovered the she-wolf was gone, Seppo grabbed Mustard and gave him a beating that sent him reeling into a heap of rotten barrel staves. "Next time that happens, I'll hang *you* from a meat hook. Got that? Yes or no?" Had Mustard agreed? There was a long cut above his left eye and his face was splotched with blood. "I want all those staves chimed before dark. And seal the casks of reindeer kidneys that came from Lapland two weeks ago, the ones that are still sitting there near the storeroom. The customers have been complaining about the smell. And hoe the vegetable patch. And I don't want your eye wandering over my daughter while you work. Next time I catch you fooling around, I'll lose my temper and slice off your dick with one blow of my axe." Seppo picked up the cooper's plane that was lying on a barrel and threw it full force in Mustard's face, then headed back to the inn to prepare an order of rolls stuffed with white meat, wild herbs, and coarse salt.

In the days that followed, the rolls stuffed with meat caused a sensation among the inhabitants of the forest. Seppo sold out the entire batch for a pretty penny in less than a week. He served them to customers with glasses of black bile. When he was asked, "Chef Seppo, when will you be cooking up another batch of those succulent little meat rolls?" the master butcher answered, "I'm fresh out of meat, but I promise you I'll find more."

As for our brave Zora, the morning after her encounter with Leon the apothecary, when she awakened beneath the front porch, she found the stub of her rotten tooth next to her on the tamped earth. The tooth had fallen out by itself, painlessly, during the night. She picked it up and examined it closely for a moment. "So," she mused, "how fortunate I was to happen upon Leon the apothecary last night."

CHAPTER
8

Finland the Lower,
Finland the Upper

I n the summer of her sixteenth year, Zora witnessed her father achieve a gastronomic exploit of unprecedented proportions. In August of that year, Seppo invented a new recipe: rib-breaker tripe. The discovery was purely accidental. Here, for the sake of brevity, was how it came to pass.

In late July, numerous customers had begun to complain that Seppo's wolverine bladders with molasses were giving them intestinal worms. Reluctantly the tripe butcher was obliged to remove them from the menu, but he had to replace them with something else. So, one fine afternoon, Seppo locked himself in the kitchen to figure out what he could possibly concoct from the lungs, hog's caul, and rancid kidney fat that accumulated in various pots while he was preparing other meals.

When he emerged from his kitchen at nightfall, he had created a brand-new recipe: tripe à la mode de Seppo. That very evening he asked one of his customers to add the dish to the blackboard that hung outside the front entrance.

The next day at noon, Anssi Kovanen and his friends arrived at the inn after a morning of foraging for wild herbs and mushrooms in the forest. It was the busiest time of the day, so much so that Anssi and his band were almost turned away for lack of a free table. Poor, poor Anssi! Never could he have imagined how much better it would have been for him to eat somewhere else, or to not eat at all!

For, you see, Anssi had ordered a serving of Seppo's new tripe concoction. He was in an adventurous mood and eager to sample something completely different. "You'll be the first to taste my tripe, my fine fellow," Seppo assured him as he took the order. Anssi's friends ordered various other dishes, and a big platter of fried minnows and rhubarb dusted with sugar. Then our rascally publican tripped off to the kitchen to prepare the order.

A half-hour later he re-emerged to serve the guests. While waiting, Anssi and his pals, who lived the life of free spirits, had knocked back several shots of polecat juice and were already halfway under the table. No sooner had Seppo set the plates on the table than the famished scavengers dove in, some with forks, others with their fingers.

It quickly became apparent that there was a problem with the tripe preparation, for after a single bite, Anssi jumped to his feet, his face crimson. He clutched at his thorax and –

Crack!

The sound echoed so powerfully through the inn that it silenced the customers. It was as if a giant had seized a thick aspen branch and bent it until it snapped. But it was no branch that had snapped; it was (you could see as much from the way he was holding his sides) one of Anssi's ribs.

"Well, what do you know!" exclaimed Seppo. "It's that bad, my tripe? Maybe I added too much trotter broth, or maybe that scoundrel of a vinegar merchant –"

Crack!

Anssi Kovanen had just sacrificed another of his twenty-four ribs on the altar of Finnish regional gastronomy. This time, the customers, all together, shouted in horror.

Crack!

Before the horrified eyes of Seppo and his customers, Anssi lost his ribs, one after the other, in transports of indescribable agony. By the end, he was writhing on the floor like a fish about to be thrust into the cooking pot. The flesh of his chest collapsed to the point that it almost touched his back, and you would have sworn that an irresistible vortex was sucking up Anssi from within. Within five minutes he was dead. His friends (and later his family members) blamed Seppo and his "rib-breaker tripe," but it went no further than that, given that the plaintiffs were unable to demonstrate the existence of a cause-and-effect relationship between the dish and Anssi's curious death. In any case, people died nearly every month at the Farting Bear, sometimes in fights that ended badly, but often due to the food. In this miniature society totally bereft of laws or morals, the time was long passed when anyone would have held the innkeeper responsible for anything untoward that occurred within the four walls of his establishment. You entered the Farting Bear at your peril, and everyone knew it. And should complications arise, you had no one but yourself to blame.

Seppo duly removed his rib-breaker tripe from the menu, but the incident with Anssi so fascinated him that he prepared several new portions and fed them to a sow, a reindeer, and a fair-sized dwarf he'd bought from a passing livestock merchant. He wanted to ascertain whether his rib-breaker tripe, as the dish was now known throughout the forest, really did break bones. When he'd finished burying the remains of the dwarf in the empty sow's pen behind the inn, he stuck his shovel in the ground, scratched his head with one hand, and hitched up his britches with the other. Yes, his tripe truly did break bones. Seppo had outdone himself. Already, the year before, some customers had complained that his ragout of fatted chicken with night soil had ulcerative properties. But to invent a recipe that actually caused bones to snap, that was a prodigy never before witnessed in the annals of gastronomy!

Zora had not been at the inn the day Anssi died, but she quickly got wind of the incident. That her father had succeeded in killing a man by the power of his cooking alone fascinated her. So when Seppo prepared the second batch of his tripe à la mode, with his intent to experiment on a sow, a reindeer, and a dwarf, she made certain she was in the kitchen that day, in the background, to observe how he prepared the delicacy. Seppo paid her no heed; over the years, he'd become accustomed to the silent presence of this gangly ostrich. As long as she did not interfere with his comings and goings, he let her hang around. Not only that, he was getting old, and had grown tired of beating the youngster twenty times a day. He made no fuss when Zora looked over his shoulder, so to speak, as he prepared his tripe specialty. Little could he have imagined that Zora, as she looked on, was actually making mental notes. To memory she committed the list of ingredients and different phases of the preparation. You never knew when they might come in handy.

During that particular summer – as we will now see – exceptional moments of calm carved out a place in the girl's daily routine. Seppo and Mustard had taken to installing large grills outside the inn, in which they prepared beds of glowing coals. This they always did early in the evening, when the sun began its long, slow descent toward the horizon. On the grills they roasted pigs' heads and ears, reindeer tongues, bear paws, and the livers and stomachs of any and all species. Lengths of intestine sputtered over the fire as Mustard seasoned them with spices and sow butter. The offal produced a blue smoke that rose into the sky. The customers wandered out of the inn with their goblets of alcohol, gathered into groups of six or eight around the grills, and gossiped placidly. Just outside the ring of onlookers, scrawny chickens pecked at the ground, scattering only when someone lashed out at them with a kick. As it was sundown, no one was really intoxicated yet (except for one or two drunkards, but even they could not perturb the peace and quiet that prevailed). Only at those moments, come sundown, when the lower cuts were roasting over the coals, did Zora dare mingle with the customers of the inn. She joined them as they stood around the grills and watched the pieces of offal brown, then blacken, letting herself be carried along by the rustle of conversation as though by music. These were the only moments of her life when human voices did not take the form of infuriated shouts, cries of madness, or hatred. It even happened that someone would engage her in small talk, not for a long time, mind you, "just long enough for Seppo to grill my skewer of robins." These were never more than prosaic exchanges: "The she-dog pudding looks nice today," or "You know Jari Järvinen's son? He got work at a gravel pit near Lake Ladoga." "You can't deny that the afternoons have been lovely of late." But Zora asked for nothing more. She was delighted, above all, that no one importuned her.

When the meat was cooked to perfection, Seppo removed it from the grill with a hook and served it to the customers. They ate standing up and washed down the food with mouthfuls of polecat juice or patantine. Everyone seemed soothed by the odour of roasting tripe and joints, entranced by the smoke billowing upward, moved by the beauty of the sunset that made the leaves seem aflame. Zora, on occasion, would help herself to a skewer of grilled cuckoos or a plate of pig's ears, and her father, who would normally smack her if she got underfoot, lifted not so much as a finger.

Then, at the beginning of August, something extraordinary took place.

One afternoon, Seppo was busy preparing a facial with strips of lard – it would rejuvenate his skin, he believed – when he heard the handle of the inn's front entrance click.

There, in the doorway, stood Tuomas Juhani Korteniemi.

Seppo's reaction would not have been more violent had a phantom appeared before him! And indeed, Tuomas strangely resembled one as he stood there in the doorway. Around his dark silhouette, sunbeams poured into the inn, and the light shone around the alchemist like a glorious halo. Seppo beheld the scene, speechless, astounded, and terrified at the same time. A slice of lard slid from his forehead to the tip of his nose and then into his open mouth. Involuntarily he swallowed, almost choking in the process.

Tuomas took a step forward. In the dimness, Seppo could at last make out his features. Yes, it was well and truly Tuomas Juhani Korteniemi, the benefactor of the little people, the sorcerer, the kidnapper! Damnation! He hadn't changed one bit. After how many years, fifteen or sixteen? His face showed not so much as a wrinkle, and his fine white hair had lost none of its lustre. Standing as erect as a stepladder, he was as short and thin as ever, with that fine burgundy frock coat of his and his perfectly pressed black corduroy trousers.

Seppo's mind was racing. What could that schemer of a Tuomas be looking for after all these years? Was it vengeance he sought? On that day sixteen years ago, on the Plains of Archelle, when he rose up into the air, had Tuomas seen Seppo below on the ground? Did he know that it was he, Seppo, who had put the Fredavians on his trail? Did Tuomas want to square accounts with him for taking back his daughter and raising her himself? But for dog's sake, by what right? She was his daughter, after all, Seppo Petteri Lavanko's! She issued from his seed! And what of that old sorcerer who lulled him to sleep with his magic tobacco on that day long ago? Ah, what a stratagem! How by falsehood he obtained consent to steal Seppo's own progeny! The innkeeper had no reason to be ashamed of what he had done. And as for whatever might have happened between Tuomas and the Fredavians, what did that have to do with him?

Emboldened by these thoughts, Seppo stood up to confront Tuomas. "Ah," he thought, "why should I be afraid of that pantywaist? Just look at him, thin as a rail and frail as a sandpiper!" To lift his courage, he clenched his fists and belched.

But strive as he might to intimidate, it did not work. There was something in Tuomas's majestic bearing that diminished him. A long interval passed during which the two men said nothing at all, staring at each other, expressionless. Tuomas appeared to be enjoying the silence that slowly swelled to fill the room, the sense of discomfort that was becoming palpable. He smiled.

Seppo looked away. Red faced with shame, he strode behind the bar and poured himself a goblet of rotgut, turning his back on Tuomas. He heard the soft footfalls of the alchemist.

"I've come to see your daughter. Zora."

Seppo grew nervous. How, he wondered, did Tuomas know the name of his daughter, when the little wench hadn't even been baptized at the time she and the old man were separated?

He stammered, "Zora? So, it's still her you want? Well, damn me! If you had only … If I had only known before … Damnation! I would have sold her to you!"

"Sold her?" exclaimed Tuomas.

Seppo raised his index finger to silence the old man, then went into the kitchen on tiptoe. He soon emerged, pulling a gangly teenaged girl by the ear. The girl had clearly been awakened from a deep sleep.

It was late in the afternoon, and Zora had been whiling away her idle hours on the banks of the Serpeille River. Her faculties dimmed by the long hours spent alone, exhausted from lack of sleep due to the din of the inn, she would often sleep in the afternoon on her pallet whenever her father had work to do out of doors.

But that particular afternoon, a nasty migraine accompanied her usual fatigue. She had been sleeping barely an hour when Seppo roused her from her nap. She felt numb, and that wretch of a father was hurting her as he twisted her ear. She did not even look up at Tuomas, which seemed to enrage Seppo all the more. With a flick of his wrist he sent his daughter spiralling into the air. There was an instant – a microsecond perhaps – during which Zora found herself between heaven and table, in a ridiculous fetal position. *Whup!* Her father brought her down with a crash on the table and held her there by the throat.

"Your head's stuck so far up your ass that you don't even see who's come calling, you sluttish lass?" shouted Seppo. "Is that the way I raised you? Too stupid to talk, but never short of ways to make me look bad when I receive important guests, is that it, my fine, feathered friend?"

Zora was wriggling like a hooked salmon.

"The snooty little slut! Too fatheaded to show any respect!"

Tuomas the old alchemist leaped forward and caught hold of Seppo's arm, which had begun to descend in an arc, aiming at Zora's face. Tuomas's cry was louder than Seppo's.

"Enough, you gross gallows bird! You can't go hitting your own children, especially a girl."

Her father having loosened his grip, Zora wriggled free and scurried away. Tuomas continued to admonish Seppo, though he reserved the worst reproach, gentlemanly in his very contempt.

"How can you possibly strike your own child? Have you not in your heart the merest drop of that water of love that bubbles up when a man becomes a father?"

Seppo, to say the least, was not given to abstract thinking. He stared uncomprehendingly at his interlocutor. Tuomas pointed to a stool and said, "Sit!" as though addressing a dog. Seppo did what he was told.

"While you were mistreating your daughter on this very table, the edge of her dress came up and I saw a scar on her thigh. A scar shaped like a bite. How did it get there?"

Seppo opened his mouth to speak, but Tuomas cut him off.

"I remember when I still lived in the area, every year a character named Captain Gut would come visiting the forest. He stole girls, chained them, and led them away ... I doubt he was kidnapping them to turn them into nuns. He would have passed this way, isn't that so? And I don't believe for a minute that you would have pleaded paternal guardianship when he offered to purchase your daughter. I am aware of his methods, you know. I know that sometimes he brands girls by biting them on the fleshy part of their thighs."

"She's my daughter, my spawn. Seppo Petteri Lavanko does whatever he wants with whatever is his."

It was the first time Tuomas had heard Seppo pronounce his full name: "Seppo Petteri Lavanko." He had not anticipated that the innkeeper would correctly labialize the three *P*'s of his name. Seppo had a speech defect and pronounced labials indistinctly.

"Seppo," said Tuomas, clearly enunciating the *P*'s, do you know what happens to girls the Captain kidnaps or steals? In the best of cases, the poor things end up in wealthy families where the master of the house repeatedly rapes them. They work as domestics and are the unwilling instruments of his ancillary phantasms. But most of the time, the Captain sells his catch to bordellos. There, they are assaulted for the most precious years of their lives, and then, when they begin to fade, they are thrown onto the street where they spend the rest of their lives working the sidewalks, begging and being insulted by every passing Tom, Dick, and Harry. Have you ever been to the capital, Seppo? Have you ever been to Helsinki?"

Seppo had no idea what Tuomas was getting at. What did these tales of raped domestics and Helsinki whores have to do with him? And what was this immoderate interest that the old man, after all these years, still had in that ugly duckling Zora? For Seppo, there could be only one explanation: Tuomas Juhani Korteniemi had bats in his belfry. Meanwhile, the old man continued to pontificate.

"I," continued Tuomas, "have resided for several years in Helsinki. There you will find breathtaking streets lined with great buildings of brick and marble, filled during the daylight hours with the hustle and bustle of passersby, their laughter and their cries. You encounter the gleaming coaches of princes, kings, and ambassadors … Carriages so beautiful, so finely gilded, that you would have sworn they were huge pastries on wheels. You want to take a bite out of them. There are lively markets, children playing, running, laughing … But far from the prosperous heart of the capital, far from the macadam and the marble, there are the dustbin districts, where everything stinks, everything is disgusting, everything cries out in despair. The people there are poor, they live eight or twelve in tiny apartments, their front doors give right onto the sidewalks covered with bird shit, they spend their days walking the streets or drinking in miserable dives while their children play outside with dog carcasses and their wives rummage through garbage heaps. And, among the throngs of the banished, the lost, and the needy, those who awaken most violently the pity of men and women of heart are the whores. Behind their forced smiles lay hidden entire lives of pain. That is the ordeal that Captain Gut is waiting to subject your child to, the flesh of your flesh. You are damning your own child to hell, you wretch!"

"Maybe so, but he gave me my apprentice, the Captain did!"

And Seppo explained to Tuomas that the Captain had given him little Mustard in exchange for Seppo's promise to hand Zora over to him when she began her monthlies.

"You don't know what she's like, the youngster!" he explained to Tuomas. "Stubborn as a wolverine. I'm just looking out for her welfare. So I say to myself, I say, 'She won't listen to her father, who's so kind and gentle. Maybe what she needs is discipline … Perhaps she'll heed someone who won't put up with her whims …' That's how come I sold her to the Captain – people do what he says!"

What Seppo did not say is that three or four years had gone by, and there had been no sign of the Captain in the Fredavian Forest. The previous year, when Zora was fifteen, Seppo had hoped the Captain would come calling and was looking forward to finally getting rid of his daughter, exactly as he'd agreed to several years before. At last he'd be free of this bothersome little good-for-nothing! But the Captain had not come, nor had he given the slightest sign of life. For the past several months, Seppo had begun to wonder if perhaps he were dead, something that definitely belonged to the realm of the conceivable, bearing in mind his carefree existence and the company he kept. But if the Captain were dead, what was he to do with Zora? He would have to sell her to someone else. But Zora was as ugly as sin, a gangly, skinny girl with evil eyes and broad shoulders. Devil take her, she towered by a good half-head over most of the men in the forest! And she was only sixteen! Who would want to be stuck with that kind of a woman?"

And now, this fathead Tuomas Juhani Korteniemi descended from his fifteen-year-old cloud and made the oddest declaration.

"I want to purchase your daughter. Then I shall marry her. And you will give your consent."

Seppo was overcome with such powerful enchantment he felt he would burst into tears! Ah no, he must not do that! Above all, he must conceal his joy from the old mule and drive up the price. But it was too much for him … "What luck! What luck! What have I ever done that fortune should smile upon me so?" the innkeeper thought. And, in spite of himself, his eyes misted over. Tuomas frowned with disgust, but Seppo kept up the charade and put on an afflicted air.

"Purchase my daughter, my only daughter … Easier said than done! She's already promised to the Captain, the little ne'er-do-well.

If I sell her to you, I'll have nothing to give the Captain, while he gave me little Mustard, who's feeble-minded – that's understood – but has a strong pair of arms to help me out with the difficult chores. And the Captain is not someone to wipe the slate clean if somebody plays a trick like that on him."

By way of answer, Tuomas Juhani Korteniemi placed on the table a wad of banknotes neatly rolled up and tied.

"Five hundred marks."

Losing all self-control, Seppo Petteri Lavanko fell to the floor and wept tears of joy. He grasped Tuomas Juhani Korteniemi's polished boots and covered them with tender kisses, for it was indeed a blessed day. Five hundred marks. Five hundred marks! One year's wages for a farm boy or a butcher's assistant. Sufficient to live in a hotel in the capital for three months and be served lobster by waiters in tails. Enough to purchase a château, perhaps, and several parcels of land, to become king of a tiny country all his own!

When he'd recovered from the shock, he got to his feet. After having warranted his own daughter, Seppo Petteri Lavanko offered Tuomas a glass of polecat juice to celebrate the transaction, but the old man, looking downcast, declined with a shrug of his shoulders. He picked up the roll of banknotes from the table, peeled from it five ten-mark bills, and cast them on the table.

"You will get the rest after the wedding."

And so saying, he put on his hat and strode briskly out of the inn.

*
* *

The wedding took place two weeks later, in Grigol. Tuomas arrived bright and early at the inn on horseback. In addition to his own mount, a massive gelding with bulging muscles, he was leading a clean and docile white mare at the end of a long line.

"This one is for Zora," he told Seppo. "You will have to make it to Grigol on foot. Only two horses, three people … No matter how you look at it, someone will have to walk, and that person will be you."

Seppo protested, appealing to his status as father and innkeeper.

"You'll walk, and that's that," Tuomas replied. "If it were up to me, you would stay here and pull the lint out of your navel while your daughter and I are married in Grigol, but we need you to sign the registers. So you'll come. On foot. Either that or you'll not get a single mark."

Seppo swallowed his anger. To buck up his courage, he thought of all the splendid money that would pour into his purses at the day's end.

Zora had never ridden a horse and was fearful at first. Tuomas showed her how to stroke the mare's mane, then its muzzle. With the greatest deliberation, he instructed her how to mount the horse. Once she was firmly in the saddle, he took the reins and guided the mare through several turns around the inn. Zora was soon enjoying it; her cheeks turned cherry red and she began to flash awkward smiles at the trees, birds, and even the sun rising in the east. At the sight of the girl's happiness, Tuomas felt true transports of joy, and in his joy he began to whistle the old melodies of the country.

The journey to Grigol took them six hours. Zora's mare was slow moving, and they often had to wait for Seppo, that tub of lard, who trotted along behind them, huffing and puffing.

They reached the outskirts of Grigol in mid-afternoon. Rather than enter the town, they left the high road and turned off onto a well-maintained lane that brought them, fifteen minutes later, to a lively, tidy quarter. The streets were narrow and lined with long outdoor markets where the customers jostled one another as they prodded the vegetables, examined the pigs and cows, and bargained over the price of meat. Here and there, street musicians played the violin or the accordion. It was a modest district, which appeared to be experiencing its most prosperous season of the year. In the market stalls, long rows of glistening, colourful vegetables made their mouths water. Succulent-looking cuts of pink pork and recently plucked chickens hung from butcher's hooks. A single grand residence graced this district, and that was where they stopped, in front of it. The gracious manor was surrounded by flowering cherry trees. Tuomas dismounted and spoke to Seppo.

"This house belongs to a lady of excellent qualities whom I am fortunate enough to count as a friend. Zora will be clothed and coiffed as befits a marriage, no matter how discreet, and it is here that the ceremony will take place. The servants will assist her in her preparations while I take a cup of tea with my old friend. You are hungry, of course?"

"Oh yes!" exclaimed Seppo.

"You see this alleyway? Halfway down on the left, you will find a tavern called the Chimneysweep's Wife. The pheasant is delicious, and the beer is good as well. Go and eat."

"I'm going, I'm going. But, tell me, while we're at it, don't you think the time has come to fork over the money for my daughter? What I mean is, it's like the ring was already on her finger –"

"No. First you must exercise your prerogative as a father. You must sign the legal documents. I will present them to you when you return from the tavern. Once that has been done, I will hand over the money and you will make yourself scarce before the ceremony begins. For the moment," he continued, pulling a one-mark bill from his pocket, "you can make do with this. It should be enough for a bowl of stew and a pint."

Seppo stuffed the bill in his pocket.

"Umm, uh … the lady who lives there, do you think she'd let me use the commodities to shit? I hear that in town the latrines are in the houses. Makes you curious, that's for sure! And –"

"Yes. No … I mean, no, you won't be doing that here. Off with you now! I've seen more than enough of you! After you've eaten, you can shuffle off somewhere should you feel the urge. But be back before five o'clock."

Tuomas paused, as if he had swallowed a sharp word that had been stuck in his throat. Then he took Zora by the arm, helped her down from the mare, and guided her slowly to the stone path that led to the massive doors of the manor.

Seppo went down the alley the way Tuomas had directed him, but he did not find the tavern. Soon, the alley opened onto the main street of the quarter. Seppo looked around him at the grand buildings, the people hurrying about their business, the carriages, and all of that made a powerful impression on him, since he rarely came to town. As he wandered, a street urchin came up to him, hands in his pockets, a friendly smile on his face.

"You're not from town, my fine fellow, if I am not mistaken?"

"It's that easy to tell?" asked Seppo, surprised.

"Why of course! People from around here don't have ... let's say, your panache."

Seppo gloated over the compliment.

"Do you like little girls?" the lad enquired.

"Just as much as anybody else, except that I'm not really flush at the moment. I've got one lousy mark to my name."

And Seppo, the numbskull, pulled out Tuomas's banknote from his apron pocket and waved it under the youngster's nose.

"No problem," said the boy, "I know a place where, for a mark, they'll fix you up with a little cutie who's just your style."

"Really?" exclaimed Seppo.

"For sure! Here in Grigol, we know how to treat our countrymen who've come from afar. Follow me."

"What luck!" Seppo thought. "I've been blessed by Ukko himself!"

The boy led Seppo down an alley, through twists and turns that made the innkeeper's head spin, unaccustomed as he was to the narrow passages that ran between the apartment houses as crowded as chicken coops.

"Tell me, kind sir, have you eaten?" the boy asked.

"Oh, I've got a bit of an appetite. But it can wait till I've had me a quickie."

"Have you tried our local specialty?"

"There's a local specialty here in Grigol? What is it?"

"Prune pie, of course!"

An accomplice of the urchin, waiting at the window of one of the apartments overlooking the alley, emptied the contents of a chamber pot on the innkeeper's head.

Taking advantage of Seppo's momentary blindness, the scamp snatched the mark from his apron pocket and fled. By the time Seppo could wipe the shit from his eyes, the little nipper had vanished. Shaking his fist, Seppo cursed him long and loud, but didn't dare pursue him. As his voice echoed between the dark facades of the buildings, he heard a woman's voice yelling at him to shut up. Fifteen seconds later, the contents of another chamber pot came cascading onto his head. Two shit baths in one day, our doughty Seppo!

But who would shed a tear for the ill fortune of a tripe butcher from the Fredavian Forest? Let us leave him to unplug his seven orifices, and turn our attention to Tuomas and Zora.

At the threshold of the grand house, the gentleman came to a halt and cast a sidelong glance at Zora. The girl knew nothing more of proper etiquette than did the creatures of the forest, from which there was very little to distinguish her. Never had she been taught to mind her manners in the presence of certain people. There she stood at the entrance to this sumptuous residence with a confused look on her face, a face powerfully ignorant of the niceties.

Tuomas knocked softly on the door. Quite rapidly a lady of some fifty years opened. Zora was so struck by the lady's beauty that she could not suppress a cry of admiration.

"Oh!"

"Good afternoon, Zora. Welcome to my home. My name is Inari Makinen."

Madame Makinen … what a lovely voice she had! Low-pitched and cultured, a thousand leagues from the squawking whoredoms who hung out at the Farting Bear. The young girl essayed an awkward curtsy, since Seppo had ordered her to be deferential toward the townspeople, failing which he would whip her within an inch of her life, irrespective of the circumstances. He was no longer there to oversee his daughter, but in the almost celestial presence of Madame Makinen, Zora felt it entirely natural to bow. Inari Makinen responded with a slight nod, bestowing upon her a smile so pure and lovely that Zora was suffused by a surge of warmth.

The beautiful lady turned to Tuomas. She took the elderly gentleman's arm and conveyed such love in her movements and in these few words – "Tuomas, my dear Tuomas!" – that the affection Zora felt for Tuomas knew no bounds. A man who enjoyed the favours of such an elegant and beautiful lady could only be worthy of the loftiest recognition.

Madame Makinen invited them in.

The interior of the manor house was finished in dark wood. The vestibule opened onto a spacious sitting room filled with books and sumptuous tapestries and paintings of pastoral scenes. Zora found it difficult to forsake the blue sky and sun and be swallowed up by this immense, poorly lighted interior with its oppressive atmosphere. All the same, she followed Madame Makinen and trusted her.

In the capacious drawing room to the right of the vestibule, the servants showed them to seats around a table, and served them tea. It was strong, sweet tea, and Madame Makinen urged them to accompany it with small biscuits of a kind that Zora had never seen. Madame Makinen and Tuomas chatted blithely about this and that. Zora sensed they were avoiding certain subjects because of her.

The tea having been drunk, Madame Makinen said, "Now, my pretty Zora, be off with my servant Katariina. She will take you upstairs, and dress you in your bridal gown and coif your wild, lovely hair. I shall be joining you shortly."

A plump, pretty-faced servant, not too old – perhaps in her early thirties – took Zora by the hand. "Follow me!" Zora rose and then, unexpectedly, drew from the pocket of her dress a wildflower she'd plucked along the way. It was a large, round daisy, with all its petals intact. She handed the flower to Tuomas with a smile so guileless, so totally devoid of the slightest hint of coquetry or ingratiation that a domestic who happened to be passing through the drawing room with an armful of clean sheets burst out laughing. Tuomas took the daisy with a smile – "Thank you so much, Zora! What touching attention, truly!" – and pinned it to his lapel.

As Zora disappeared up the broad oak staircase that led to the first floor, Tuomas removed the daisy from his lapel and turned it gently between his thumb and his index finger. Pensively, he stared at the flower. Madame Makinen stretched out her arm and stroked the daisy petals lightly with her fingertip.

"What a strange young girl ... I've never seen anything quite like her!" she said. "Her face is an entire country whose geography conceals surprises and enchantments at every turn. You never tire of her milky cheeks, or dimpled little chin, like an eggshell ... But it is only when you step back and take in her features as a whole that you say, 'How beautiful she is!'"

"Yes, and her eyes are deep, dark abysses ..."

"Let us repair to the boudoir, Tuomas. Together we will drink this jasmine tea that my husband sends me from Nanking. Here, we won't have a moment's peace. People are forever going every which way."

Indeed, the manor house was humming like a beehive. When a gardener or a delivery man was not traversing the drawing room, galoshes depositing mud on the carpet, it was the dressmaker delivering Zora's wedding gown, or the local florist who had dropped off the bouquets and the two wedding wreaths at the front door, and was shouting instructions to the domestics. Tuomas followed Madame Makinen into the small boudoir to the right of the entrance. She closed the door behind them.

They sat down in two well-padded, purple armchairs, separated by a small coffee table. Tuomas lighted his pipe.

"What a curious chapter in your life you are about to write today, with this marriage, my dear Tuomas! What does your heart tell you?"

The alchemist slowly exhaled a long stream of smoke.

"I can barely believe it myself ... Getting married. At my age! And in such bizarre circumstances ..."

He smiled sadly, then took Madame Makinen's hand in his, and brought it to his cheek.

"Please forgive me. This unexpected marriage ... and the life I've been living for these past several years, you know so well ... They have been enough to cause an old man to lose his bearings. My head is spinning. It is all I can do to try to make some sense of it."

He still held between his fingers the flower Zora had given him.

"Zora is only half-human," he said. "By throwing that child out to fend for herself, by abandoning her to the Fredavian Forest and its horrors, her father transformed her into a wild animal. Why, just this morning I saw her spit on the ground three times and blow her nose by blocking one nostril and snorting. She can barely speak, and when she does, her voice is hoarse, as if stifled. Her body and her soul are marked with scars that will never heal. I cannot even dare ... cannot dare imagine what ..."

Tuomas's face had turned livid.

"I have been tormented by the thought that one day, sixteen years ago, I held that infant in my arms. She was only a baby then, nestled against me; close against my breast I held her future and her happiness as I lifted myself skyward to escape the Fredavians and Gladd the Argus. I wanted a better life for her. We would have wandered at length, no doubt, for I was being pursued, but once we reached security in the south of the Duchy, I would have taken the time to find her a good family. Today, she would not be this semi-wild girl who eats raw meat and spits out the bones, belching. She would be a normal young girl, with all a young girl's dreams, dreams of love and ascending in society, she would have that contagious freshness of beautiful young girls, she would walk down the street with a parasol and turn up her nose at an old man like me who would look her over from top to toe as he passed, and certainly forgive her indifference, since he had at once experienced the delight of receiving the light of the beauty of youth for a fleeting instant, and the satisfaction of crossing paths with someone full of contentment in this life. For truly happy people are so rare ..."

Tuomas placed the daisy on the coffee table and rubbed his face vigorously.

"But things did not work out quite that way, did they? Because I was clumsy, and perhaps even negligent, because throughout my life I have knocked over and broken my wine glasses as I ate, tipped over the salt shakers at formal dinners, broken not only my own precious objects, but also those in the houses that have honoured me by receiving me. For I am the clumsiest person in the Duchy, it was inevitable that I drop the most precious gift that life had bestowed upon me ..."

Tuomas held his head between his hands and broke into sobbing. Inari Makinen leaned toward him, laid her hands upon his, and gently chided him.

"That will be enough, Tuomas! Think carefully before you put yourself into such a state on your wedding day. For what possible purpose? A baby that falls from your arms as you attempted to save her – one of life's insults! Every day worse things, sometimes even fatal things, befall thousands of people."

"But I cannot come to terms with the idea that, in the great mechanism of cause and effect, I was the weak link, the reason why little Zora was beaten, humiliated, deprived of love, and suffered God only knows what other ignoble mistreatment ..."

Tuomas's voice was choked. Madame Makinen pulled her chair closer to his and took his face in her hands.

"And today, through marriage, you want to redeem yourself for a fault you never committed. Old fool!" she said, wiping a tear from his cheek with her thumb.

With a sniffle, Tuomas attempted a smile.

"I don't believe this marriage will change anything. Of course, much better for her to be married to an old man than to continue to live among those half-men, half-beasts. But what can I do for her? She is marked forever. And as for me, I will be forced to live out the last years of my life with the dark spectacle of the human void she carries inside. But, do I dare admit to you, my dear, good Inari? I dreamed of other things for my old age."

With those words, Tuomas burst into sobs again. Madame Makinen put her arms around the old alchemist, stroking his hair.

"Dear Tuomas, my dear compassionate Tuomas! Do not torment yourself so! You must understand you were only the powerless accessory to a quirk of destiny of which Zora was the intended victim. Be kind to her, as you have been your whole life through to the people around you. Be good to her and even if you cannot remove the dark veil that covers her face, with your kindness and loving care, you will take your revenge on fate."

Tuomas lifted his head, drew his kerchief from his pocket, and wiped his face.

"Undertake the task that awaits you with a brave heart," Madame Makinen continued. "That young lady has so much to discover ... Help her see beautiful things, and discover music, sing for her! Salt her meat and prepare her vegetables with cream, so that slowly, gradually, she can uncover all the beauty and sweetness life offers. She is still young ... Her soul is not a marble column. She surely must have been mistreated in her family, there can be little doubt, but you can modify the curve that circumstances have imprinted upon her life. Look upon it as a vocation. You will be a good husband, and you will awaken in her noble, peaceful, and altruistic feelings. There is, in the vocation that is now yours, something grand, Tuomas Juhani Korteniemi, and I wager that you will soon come to realize it. I believe that, rather than interfering with your excellent alchemist's magisterium, the presence of this young woman at your side will prove an inspiration to your research. And we will all be the beneficiaries. Is that not true, Tuomas, my friend?"

Madame Makinen got to her feet and deposited a kiss of consolation on her friend's cheek. She then went up to the first floor to see how the dressing of the bride was progressing.

Tuomas remained behind in the sitting room. His despair had given way to nervousness. "What ..." he said to himself, "what an idea, to get married at my age! And with a young girl, what's more? A fine plan for a heart attack before the year is out." He smoked pipe after pipe, drank cup after cup of tea, and often visited the facilities. Why had the women not come downstairs? Tuomas glanced at his watch … 4:37 … 4:46 … now 4:52! Unable to sit still, he went into the drawing room, picked up a large envelope that had been lying on the mantel above the fireplace, and exited the house. Seppo had returned from his wanderings and was pacing impatiently outside.

"Did you eat your fill?" Tuomas asked.

"Well, that's just the trouble. Not far from here, some street urchin robbed me! Grabbed my money and ran! Ah, what a fine place is Finland the Lower! What I mean to say is, my belly is empty, and I was on my way to see you to –"

"Is that so? I'm terribly sorry. Too bad, but I am not interested in hearing about your afternoon. You listen to me instead."

Tuomas took a step toward Seppo. His eyes were pure ice. Had a tiger looked Seppo in the eye, he would not have been more terrified.

"It may be that, one day, you come calling to see to some matter regarding your daughter, perhaps on that day you will feel the need to strike someone frail and innocent, or because you've invented some vile stratagem to extract more money from me. Perhaps, as well, dark thoughts of vengeance will have entered your mind after you have realized that in selling off your daughter, you have lost the only human being that could have brought you some consolation in this life. But that will all come to naught, for you will have long before abandoned all parental claim to Zora. This document so testifies."

Tuomas drew from the envelope the legal affidavit by which the innkeeper gave his consent to the marriage of his daughter with Tuomas. Once Seppo marked his *X*, Tuomas replaced the document in the envelope and removed a pack of banknotes from it.

"Four hundred and fifty marks. Count them."

Seppo counted. When he had finished he nodded. Tuomas stared at him for an instant in silence, fascinated.

"Are you not ashamed," he asked, "to sell off your daughter as if she were a cow or a sow?"

"Not at all. And I'm going to tell you something, you old fart." Now that he had his money in hand, Seppo no longer saw the need to bow and scrape before Tuomas. "If I'd known earlier that gawky sixteen-year-old girls could be sold for that kind of money, I'd have turned out a whole litter."

"Gone with you, wretch! I've come to hate you as I have rarely hated any man, Seppo the tripe butcher. Now clear out, and may Ukko grant that I never see your cabbage head and bovine eyes again."

Seppo shrugged his shoulders. What did he care about the remonstrances of that sly old fox? Already he had stopped caring about what might happen to his daughter and Tuomas, and begun to wonder how he would make his way back to the inn. Then he had a sudden inspiration, which he hastened to share with Tuomas.

"You know something? With the money you paid me for my daughter, I'm going to buy a cart and a reindeer. I can use 'em to haul heavy loads. And this very evening I can head back to the forest on a reindeer's back! But first things first! I'm going to have a drink and pay a visit to the girls to celebrate!"

And so saying, he waved his fistful of marks with a smile. Then he turned his back on Tuomas and went down the street in a westerly direction. In disgust, the alchemist watched him. When he had gone far enough, Tuomas followed him with deliberate steps.

Two streets from the corner where the manor stood, Seppo halted at the door of a tavern through which groups of dubious-looking individuals and shady women were entering and exiting. From within, you could hear someone bellowing a drinking song, and the customers joining in for the refrain. Even from a distance, Tuomas recognized the tune: it was "Flibustine," a nasty ditty that woodcutters would sing at the top of their lungs as they marched through the forest or made their way through Grigol. Tuomas watched as Seppo stopped in front of the greasy dive, sized up the place, then stepped inside. The old man kept his distance for a couple of minutes. Then, close to the entrance, he spotted a wiry youth with a suspicious look about him, sitting on a barrel. He walked up to him.

The lad boasted several days' growth of whiskers. A long scar crossed his cheek on a slant, from his left eye to the right side of his jaw. His brown cap hid half his face. When he saw Tuomas draw near, he threw him a threatening glance, as if to say, "Well, now, you old fossil, looking for trouble, or what?" Tuomas pulled three one-mark bills from his pocket and held them out.

"What's with the cash?" whistled the pimp.

"The fat man that just went in, the one smelling of shit, did you notice him?"

"Yeah, I seen him. Real stupid looking."

"Looks stupid and is stupid. Work him over. Do it with a pal of yours if you can. Or ten, if you can manage it. All I want is for you to bust his chops. If you do the job right, I'll come by later and give you two marks more."

"Two marks! Tut-tut … For five marks we can work your man over real nice, but not for less. But for a little extra … for a lot extra, we can really stomp him."

"I'm not asking you to kill him. I only want you to knock him out of action for a week or two. In fact, if you rough him up too much, say goodbye to your two marks. Take it or leave it."

"All right, all right, I get the picture. It's just not goddamn possible how picky and choosy customers are getting these days … 'Just hit him a little bit but not too much, don't get carried away, beat him gently …' Sissies, the lot of them."

*

* *

Later that afternoon, Tuomas Juhani Korteniemi became, for the first time in his life, a *husband*. He was eighty-four years old. It would be hard to imagine a more humble wedding. The only witnesses to that singular union were an elderly lady, friend of the groom, and a handful of domestics torn between surprise and derision ("You can't accuse the bride of being beautiful … She's got the face of a peasant girl who got kicked in the face by a cow! She looks so awkward in her bridal clothes. You'd think she's never worn anything

165

better than rags"), a dressmaker who was allowed to observe the scene as a way of thanking her for her work on the gown, and the cook who prepared the food for the reception.

But, had you ventured in front of that meagre gathering something on the order of, "Do you know old the groom is? Eighty-four years old!" and even sworn to it by all the gods, no one would have believed you. "Impossible!" the attendees would have answered. "In his early fifties, perhaps, fifty-five at most, but certainly no more! His hair is white, of course, but look how straight he stands! Look at his skin, still firm around the eyes, and those fine cheeks that look like fresh-baked bread! Those are the kinds of cheeks, my dear lady, you find on a young man! Eighty-four years old? You can't be serious! Unless the old trickster has discovered the fountain of youth."

Indeed, there was more than a touch of sorcery behind that apparent youthfulness of his. One is not an alchemist for nothing, after all. We will certainly have occasion, later, to speak again of the spells whose secrets Tuomas had mastered, and that could slow the deterioration of the body but, for the moment, let us simply say he was quite handsome indeed, quite elegant in the new dress suit he had made especially for the occasion. As for Zora, the wild girl, the lanky and bewildered bride, no, she did not look at all like a cowherd on whose face a ruminant had trodden. It is far too easy to make fun of others when one is a domestic and has spent one's life rolling among the trimmings of luxury that sir, madame, and their little cherubs might deign to let float down from their lofty perch atop the cirrus clouds of society. One night in the Fredavian Forest would have sufficed to drive those backbiters to distraction. Zora, who stood today beside Tuomas in her black bridal gown, had never, in her entire life, known anything but the forest.

The ceremony was brief. It took place in the salon of Inari Makinen's manor house. At the end of the afternoon, the beautiful lady spent two hours with Zora, in the same sitting room where she had consoled Tuomas. She explained what marriage was to her, and how it would change her life. To her questions, Zora answered with yes or no, and it was impossible to determine her sincerity. Zora stared at her with her cold eyes that seemed to say, "I have no idea in the world what you're talking about, but that doesn't matter. I'll do what you say, and whatever will be will be. I'm easy to please." Inari Makinen made every effort to keep her explanations as simple and neutral as possible. But when the time came for them to move to the salon for the ceremony, it was by no means clear whether Zora had understood that this event would bring changes to her life.

Curiously, it was only after the ceremony had ended, and the marriage pronounced valid by a representative of the mayoralty, that a handful of guests arrived. They were only slightly older than Zora. Their parents numbered among Inari Makinen's friends; she had invited only those whom she appreciated for their moral qualities, their gentle spirits, and open-mindedness. She wanted Zora, no doubt for the first time in her life, to enjoy the company of young people who were not rapists, alcoholics, or abortionists. The guests presented their warmest congratulations to the newlyweds. There was food and there was dancing. Zora paid scant attention to the festivities, but she did devour the red partridge pâté and country bread, the *gelée* of woodcock, the beluga caviar spread thick on hot, fresh blini, the citrus salad, and hermit crabs served with Manchu ravioli. She consumed slices of sugar pie, drank cups of coffee, and when the meal had all but ended, tossed back two full glasses of red wine that made her feel funny all over. At nine o'clock, she vomited into the cushions of the large divan and fell asleep, head on the armrest, while everyone around her was making merry.

Late that night, without waking her, they carried her to a horse cart, a gift to the newlyweds from Madame Makinen. The joyous guests decorated the vehicle with lanterns, bells, and multicoloured crepe-paper streamers, and wrapped its lights with garlands of white flowers. Tuomas's mare had been fitted out with a broad-brimmed straw hat, and paper cut-outs in the shape of stars and distaffs were stuck to its coat. After having bade adieu to Madame

Makinen and her friends, Tuomas climbed onto the driver's bench. Zora was sound asleep behind him, among the boxes of wedding gifts. "Away!" called Tuomas, and he and his new wife set out on the long trek that would bring them back home.

When they reached the edges of the Fredavian Forest, the disc of the sun was climbing above the eastern horizon, sending out giant golden cones that striped the royal blue of the heavens. Zora awakened. Tuomas turned the carriage into the woods, and the forest, normally so dark and threatening, seemed to celebrate the day of the union of spring and winter, revealing all that spoke gaiety and bright colour. Puffy, plump clouds sailed indolently across the azure sky.

It took them a good five hours to cross the forest. Three hours would have done the trick had they followed the trail that passed through the heart of the woods, but that would have obliged them to come too close to the Farting Bear. Tuomas chose instead to make a detour through the Drunkard Hills, farther north. At the end of their long journey, they emerged onto the broad Plains of Archelle. That was where Tuomas lived, in a small house some twenty kilometres from the edge of the Fredavian Forest, and not far from the border of another forest, the Misty Woods. It was almost noon when they arrived. The elderly gentleman brought the carriage to a stop in front of the house, hopped to the ground, and, for Zora, gallantly opened the narrow gate of the wooden fence surrounding the house and small garden. Zora stepped to the ground. She took several awkward steps to shake the stiffness from her legs and considered her new home.

It was a two-storey, whitewashed building topped by a steep red-tile roof. Freshly painted green shutters framed the windows. Pots of variegated flowers had been placed on the windowsills, inside and out. In front of the house, a small garden enclosed by a low wooden fence painted green to match the shutters held out the promise of leisurely afternoons in the shade of the sunflowers growing there. When he built the house a few years before, in laying down the paving stones that led to the front door, Tuomas had employed a mortar of a rosy shade thanks to a product of his own invention. The effect was simply charming.

The little house rose from the flatness of the surrounding plains like a thick, spotted mushroom. For kilometres around, not the slightest sign of human presence. Tuomas stood before his house, back to the door. He was still dressed in the simple, elegant frock coat he had worn the day before, at the wedding. He looked at Zora and smiled.

Tuomas, with his fine white hair, his smiling, gentle expression, his erect stature, still attired in the suit ever so slightly wrinkled from the voyage, but well tailored, in front of that pretty house: it was an image that Zora, as long as she lived, would never forget.

At the end of the day, the young woman was sleeping in a room of her own, a large, airy chamber that smelled of fresh bread and vanilla. Tuomas had ordered for her a headboard similar to the one he had as a child, and on which were depicted scenes inspired by the fables of La Fontaine. Before dropping off to sleep, Zora admired the images for a brief moment, then, exhausted, surrendered to the wide, embracing bed, and fell into a sleep so tender and deep she wished for a moment that she would never awaken. That night, and all those that were to come, Tuomas spent in his own room, at the end of the hallway. Much time passed before he could sleep. Four times during the night he rose and put his ear against the door to Zora's room, to match the wild beating of his heart with the peaceful breathing of the young life that slumbered just beyond.

PART TWO

Six Years Later...

CHAPTER
9

Death Within Us

Of a stormy evening one month of August, the man known as Footpad turned up at the Farting Bear with a mongoloid dog, which provided the assembled regulars with a source of raucous laughter and much delight. The dog was malformed, couldn't walk straight, and slobbered over everything and everyone.

"My brother Jani's the poor pup's father," explained Footpad. "Back home, Jani was always hanging around the bitch. Why, my dad came across him once in the cold room, sticking it to her. He was so furious he stuck the youngster's head into the beer barrel."

Everyone at the inn made sport of the dog. They danced around it, singing. They turned it upside down on the table to see if its underbelly was like that of normal dogs. They poked into its orifices to the sound of many jokes. They poured alcohol down its gullet. The dog staggered this way and that, threw up, and flopped down in a corner to the guffaws and applause of the assembled multitude. A good time was had by all. But was there ever an evening when people did not enjoy themselves at the Farting Bear? Was not each evening a splendid adventure, filled with surprises, keenly developed fellow feeling, with comic scenes of pissing contests and hilarious attempts at gang rape?

After having regaled his pals with his mongoloid dog, Footpad leaped atop a table and danced bare chested, as he was so often wont to do. The other customers brought down the pots and pans from the walls and clanged the implements to make music.

Suddenly, just before midnight, the door to the inn swung open and a curious personage stepped inside.

The visitor was a young man – perhaps all of twenty years old. He was as handsome as Jesus. The women in the room stopped their banging and shouting and cried out in admiration as they watched him walk up to the bar. His black locks cascaded upon his shoulders in generous curls seemingly undisturbed by the torrential downpour drumming down on the forest outside. He was tall, and almost feminine in his slender build. The only discordant touch in an otherwise near-perfect portrait: dark circles ringed his eyes, as though he had not had a proper sleep for months. And as he was clad entirely in black, from head to toe, he had a spectral appearance that caused the men to shiver.

Unsurprisingly, all heads turned toward him. Seppo paid particular heed to the young man's boots, which were so highly polished that the innkeeper could make out his reflection at two metres' distance. He himself had worn the same stinking, perforated socks for more than a decade. He immediately took an intense dislike to the visitor.

The latter could not help but notice the effect of his arrival upon the throng, and he seemed discountenanced.

"Good evening, and a thousand pardons for the disturbance. I would like a room for the night. I have been travelling for some time through the forest. It is all I can do to stand upright."

He could hardly have put it better: he was wobbling in his weakness. But his voice remained firm, low-pitched, and suave, and it made the ladies in attendance hot and bothered. His elegant speech was that of a townsman.

"That will be one mark, payable immediately," Seppo answered.

A price that, it goes without saying, was well above what one would generally pay elsewhere in the region for a room in such a miserable inn. The visitor did not so much as blink. He reached into the pocket of his trousers and pulled out two worn bills, which he handed to Seppo.

"Here you are, two marks. And now, please allow me to sleep, if you would be so kind. I am so tired ... I will cause you no problems, I assure you."

"It's the upstairs room, on the right."

"The key?"

"There is no key. There's no door."

The young man was about to make his way upstairs when the Stroller, who adored striplings, hailed him.

"You there, fine fellow! You're not going to turn in before drinking a pint, are you?"

The other customers roared their approval. After the mongoloid dog, they were in the mood for a laugh at someone else's expense. They pulled up a chair and forced the handsome lad to put down his heavy rucksack and take a seat. Seppo served him a bowl of potted martin kidneys and a boiled sweet potato. The Stroller poured him a shot of polecat juice in a filthy goblet and pushed the beverage in front of him. The customers gathered around, scrutinizing him with a mixture of curiosity and derision. The Stroller sat down on his lap.

"What's your name, my fine young tyro?"

Ill at ease, the traveller wrung his hands and touched neither food nor drink. He finally ventured a few gentle shoves to show the whore that her presence on his lap was unwanted.

"If you would be so kind as to get up, I –"

"So you'd like to dance, you and me? That'll loosen you up. And while you're at it, tell us what you're doing in our neck of the woods."

The young man froze, clearly in no mood for pleasantries. He raised his head and with his fine black eyes looked directly into the Stroller's. The whore straightened up, as though chastised, her eyes downcast. The young man, who had stopped wringing his hands, turned toward Seppo the innkeeper and spoke in a calm voice.

"I would like a pint of cold beer."

"Coming right up."

Behind the bar, Seppo filled a goblet with beer and set it down in front of the young man. He stared at the bottom of the glass.

"There's an eyeball," he complained. "A bull's eyeball in my beer."

"That's how we serve our brew here," Seppo replied.

"Yeah!" shouted Footpad. "A bull's eye in the beer and as for the bull's fat, the Stroller smears it over her smallpox scars."

The customers hooted with mirth, all except the Stroller, who attempted to scratch Footpad, but to no effect. Everybody wanted a beer just like the young man, and all of a sudden, Seppo had his hands full.

When everyone had their drinks, they gathered around the visitor. The most ill-mannered fondled his handsome black hair and uttered insolent and tasteless remarks. The women were tittering, each one trying to imagine what it would be like to have her twat tickled by the dark-faced beer drinker.

"So, pretty boy, are you going to tell us what you're up to here in the Fredavian Forest?" someone piped up.

Abruptly, the young man shoved the beer to one side. He had drunk not a drop.

"I have heard tell that in the Fredavian Forest there lives a famous storyteller who knows many ancient tales, tales unknown to the other storytellers of the region, and the Duchy. I am greatly interested in meeting him and listening to him. Is there anyone here who can tell me where I can find Elijah Saariaho?"

All at once the assembled scum let out a shout of collective disgust.

"Ha! Elijah Saariaho! Feh! Feh!"

An old woman came up and spat in the visitor's face. Others heaped insults on him and jabbed their fingers at him. But in the rolling thunder of curses, the young man was unable to understand what exactly they might have against him. What was it that made these people so hate Elijah Saariaho?

Marko Sahlstedt, a former mushroom smuggler who now worked as a travelling caterer, liked to believe he was superior to the other customers at the Farting Bear. True, he was seen as a bit of a leader. And it was he who waved his arms to quiet the crowd.

"Elijah Saariaho is an evil-tempered and dislikeable person, who takes no pleasure in laughter. In the days when he lived in the forest, he would kick the ass of anyone who tried to harvest rhubarb near his house. Back then, he lived at the far western reach, in the Pisan Hills. And one fine day, he upped and left. No one knows where he went, and that's a good thing, because no one cares. We don't want him anywhere around, for sure. If he was ever to show his mug in these parts, there'd be fifteen of us, me and the other men of the forest, who would slice off his nuts and make him eat 'em!"

All the men present at the inn raised their tankards. "Most certainly! For sure!" Bitterly disappointed, the young man announced he was retiring to his room to sleep. But the customers of the inn were in a teasing mood, and fully intended to enjoy themselves a while longer with their hoity-toity visitor. They forced him back into his chair. The Stroller, who did not like to end her evenings on a note of failure, crept up, grabbed him from behind, and on his cheek planted a kiss that stank of wet feet and cold tobacco.

"You don't mind if I sit a little longer on your lap, my little pullet?"

"Really, that's enough …"

"Ah, you pantywaist! The chairs are hard here, and I've got a sensitive bottom."

From the back of the inn, a customer shouted, "That's because you spend all your time sitting on prongs!" Everyone roared with laughter. The visitor did not have time to protest. The Stroller settled on his lap and wrapped her scrawny arms around his neck. The whore was no longer young – going on fifty-five or thereabouts – and had coarse, granular skin striated with protruding purple veins.

"In exchange," she croaked, "I'll show you my assets! Now isn't that nice of me?"

So saying, the Stroller licked his ear and nuzzled his nose. To rid himself of the old harpy, the fine young man stiffened his back and shook his arms, but his abjurations only caused the motley throng at the inn to laugh louder, and they began to dance a rowdy jig around the couple. By now the whore was clutching the visitor's clothes, teasing him and whispering sweet nothings in his ear.

"Might as well get used to it, my pretty little virgin, I just love to lick! But why are you trying to get away from pretty Tiina that way? Calm your heart and rejoice! When we're married, you and me, I'll let you taste my piggy bank, even before, if you like. Why not tonight? You won't be able to get enough!"

The low-lifes gathered around them were laughing until they were about to burst. Suddenly, in a moment of panic, *smack!* The young man slapped the Stroller in the face.

The old harpy fell to the floor. Getting to her feet, she began to harangue the dandy.

"So that's it? You're the kind who likes boys, my fine, flouncy aristocrat! But what I won't stand for is being slapped! You're going to pay dearly for this! I'll give you an itch you can scratch!"

The old hag picked up a teapot and threw it at the young man's head. It hit him full in the face, and opened up a gash above his eyebrow; in the room, the laugher grew louder. Blushing with shame, his fine curly black hair viscous from kelp infusion, the young man picked up his sack, lowered his head, and made for the exit, scattering the mirthful revellers as he went.

Seppo watched the entire scene with a smile. When he saw that the young man had chosen to flee, he turned to Mustard, who was standing in the kitchen door. The tripe butcher nodded to his apprentice and pointed to his boots. Mustard understood. He picked up his jacket from a stool behind the bar and snuck out of the inn unnoticed.

Mustard was now twenty-eight, rangy and thin, with long, stringy muscles. He had grown taller and stronger than his master but as he was little more than a workhorse who had no one in the world but Seppo, the tripe butcher's domination over him, far from lessening with the passage of time, had only become stronger.

Outside, Mustard yanked an axe from a nearby stump. Hidden in the underbrush he watched as the visitor vanished into the night along the trail that led westward from the inn. He let him gain a lead of several strides, and then, moving carefully, set off along the trail after him. The two men walked for a full half-hour, one in pursuit of the other.

The lone traveller's only light was that shed by a pale moon. Not knowing the trail, and gripped by terror, his steps were hesitant. Frequently he came to a stop and looked around him. When he did, Mustard, a few steps behind, would halt as well.

A few moments later, terrified by the hooting of an owl, the young man picked up his pace and ran straight into the trunk of a dead tree that lay across the path, falling backwards. Mustard seized his opportunity!

In five long strides he covered the few metres that separated him from his prey. The young man lay there on the ground, rubbing his aching forehead, when suddenly, looming over him, he made out the black form of Mustard. Crying out in terror, he babbled a few words to calm the savage beast, but his assailant could not fathom them. The butcher boy raised high the axe, drawing a bead on the head of the unfortunate young townsman. The latter realized he was about to die, and his horror knew no bounds. His cries grew shriller. Mustard raised the axe over his head, raised high the axe … Oh, how the blood would spurt over the dark ferns! There would be enough for an entire family of wolverines! Now was the time, one good blow and …

Ouch!

"Whazzat?" thought Mustard. Just as he was about to bring down the axe, a hard object moving at high speed struck him in the head! Mustard bent over … So, that was it! An acorn … It hadn't really hurt, but where could such a projectile have come from? Mustard looked around, but nothing could be seen in the inky darkness.

The traveller, moved by the survival instinct, took advantage of the diversion to roll into the undergrowth. After three rotations he attempted to get to his feet. But the noise alerted Mustard, who surged toward him, tripped him, and knocked him down.

Yet again our townsman found himself stretched out on the ground, and the blood drained from his face. His expression, as he looked up at Mustard, was no longer imploring; it was wild with terror and nothing less. The butcher boy, who had by then forgotten the acorn and was about to begin his work, raised once more the heavy axe and...

What on earth? A deafening roar!

A blood curdling noise – you would have said the neighing of some otherworldly gelding – rang out behind Mustard, paralyzing him. The wretch did not have time to turn his head. The fore hooves of a gigantic black steed sent him violently flying against the trunk of a towering birch. The shock was brutal, and Mustard slumped heavily onto the ground cover, unconscious.

The young townsman had seen the outline of an enormous horse rear up behind his tormentor, an infernal steed one and a half fathoms tall. Astride the beast he had clearly distinguished the hooded shape of a spectre, and the sight was enough to make him faint dead away.

*
* *

When he opened his eyes, his ears filled with fluid and the morning cooing of the cuckoo, Mustard lay with his head across a bed of ferns pearled with frigid dew. His cranium throbbed in dull pain. Propping himself up on one arm, he managed to assume a sitting position. First he spat out a gob of sputum, then a mouthful of dirty grass that had turned his saliva bitter. Back against a tree, he rubbed his forehead, eyes closed, for a few minutes.

It took him several attempts to get to his feet. His head ached so painfully that waves of nausea swept over him. Every contraction of the muscles of his body made him want to vomit.

When at last he'd gotten to his feet, he took a few steps to stretch his legs. He snacked on nuts and juniper berries, but hardly appreciated his repast, for dark thoughts were passing through his mind. He knew that Seppo would heap insults on him and deprive him of food to punish him for not bringing back the boots and the corpse of the previous night's visitor to the inn. Undoubtedly he would beat him. Bringing his hand to the back of his head, Mustard noticed that his hair was matted with blood from a wound a good three centimetres wide, just above the neck. Once more he thought about what had happened that night. He saw his victim, yesterday's easy prey, lying there at his mercy, on the ground, arms covering his face. Then came the impact on his forehead, the acorn that had disturbed his work … He'd thought nothing of it at the time and had lunged once more at his victim … and then … and then … then it wasn't an acorn that hit him, but a veritable cannonball!

At his feet he saw crushed brambles, trampled most likely by a horse's hooves. But there remained not a trace of the young man from the night before, nor of his fine boots. Mustard squatted down and ate the rest of his berries. When he stood up, dizziness overcame him once more. So weary and so unhappy did he feel that he could not muster the courage to return to the inn. He lay down again in the ferns and tried to sleep.

Day was dying when he awoke. Perched on a tree stump, a plump partridge was looking him over. Mustard crept forward, snatched the bird, wrung its neck, and plucked it. He attempted to light a fire, but saturated as it was with rainwater, the undergrowth would not light. The lad ate the bird raw.

*
* *

The young townsman awakened in an environment that could not have been more inviting. He opened his eyes with first light to find himself in a cozy little room that exhaled the sweet smell of sugar pie. He closed them a few seconds to make sure that he was not dreaming. Where the devil could he possibly be? All around him was silence.

Then the memory of the previous day's events struck him like a ton of bricks, and he shivered beneath the thick quilt. But the sky was blue; he could see it through the gap in the flowery curtains that veiled the window. Outside, birds were chirping. Slowly he got up. His head ached – it had been aching for weeks now, nothing new there, that's how you feel when you get no more than two or three hours of sleep a night – but the pain was less piercing than it had been of late.

On a small table next to the bed he found his clothing, covered with earth, stained with filaments of grass and small leaves, and torn in several places. But he put it on nonetheless, considering that he had nothing else to wear.

The room opened onto a short, narrow hallway, and a circular staircase led to the floor below. The silence that reigned in the house inspired near-mystical respect.

Down the stairs on silent feet the young man crept, and he stepped into a spacious salon. Immediately he was charmed by the extraordinary smell of pie that filled the room.

He found himself in a drawing room typical of the country houses in this region of the Duchy. Out the broad windows through which daylight flooded, the traveller could see broad green meadows that stretched as far as the edge of the forest, far away. Not a sign of human activity for kilometres around.

He looked around him. The house – there could be no doubt – was the dwelling place of educated people, notables perhaps, for everything was sparkling clean, and the room was full of fine objects. The furniture was simple and elegant, like the round table close to the counterpane, covered with a Vichy tablecloth with a rustic motif atop which stood a pretty vase of fresh-cut flowers. The back wall was broken by a fireplace above which were bookshelves fashioned from pine. The young man walked across the room to examine the meticulously classified books. There he found the great novels of the century in fine collector's editions, the works of the ancients in Greek and Latin, as well as others in French, Russian, and other languages he did not recognize.

On a well-stuffed divan to one side of the fireplace lay an article entitled "Chinese Hyper-Alchemists, Spit Gobs of the Son of Heaven" that appeared to have been torn from the pages of a magazine. Atop them rested a pince-nez.

To the other side of the fireplace, a door yawned open. From beyond it came a chorus of gurgles and hisses, along with a persistent odour of humus. Intrigued, our traveller stepped cautiously over the threshold. And thus stepped into the most incredible room he had ever encountered in his life.

Clearly enough, it was a scientist's laboratory, but what manner of occult and impenetrable research could be taking place here, our traveller could not venture to presume. Large work tables in yellow birch lined the walls, and atop them plants of every size and shape competed for space with books of spells and scientific instruments. An almost artistic disorder prevailed: great piles of chapbooks, measuring devices, yellowed parchment covered with formulae, quadrangles, and pentacles ... You would have sworn you had happened upon the workshop of Merlin the Magician.

The young man slowly let his fingers glide over the leather cover of a thick chapbook entitled *The ABCs of Alchemy: The ZYGs of Zygomancy*, tilted at an angle among the cabalistic texts and other titles of like obscurity. On every parcel of available space stood graduated beakers, Bunsen burners, vials, test tubes, and newspaper articles atop which had been placed blocks of kainite to prevent them from flying away when the windows were opened. Alembics of various sizes emitted pungent fumes that caused the young man to reel back. Hermetically sealed vials contained what appeared to be organic matter, some of it in an advanced stage of putrefaction, while others held multicoloured vapours that seemed to dance in a fine shower of crystal. There appeared to exist in that room as many odours as there were objects, and whiffs of sulphur, of germination, of rotting fruit, of human excrement, and of ash began to make the young man feel queasy. Standing beside a lighted candle, a sealed alembic contained a shredded substance. He stepped forward for a closer look, and was about to retreat when a voice close by startled him.

"It is sperm liquor from a hare. Putrefied."

An extremely handsome elderly gentleman, with luxuriant hair and an amenable look on his face, was seated at a desk at the far end of the room.

He stood up and stepped forward to meet the visitor with an expression of mild embarrassment, as though he were the one surprised while strolling through a stranger's house. To regain his composure, he leaned over the alembic that contained the spermatozoid fluid and examined it, pretending to be absorbed.

"My young wife, believe it or not, has gotten it into her head to create a homunculus. A tiny human being, if you prefer, no larger than a flower petal. That which nature creates, she feels capable of creating as well. She has come upon that nonsensical formula of Paracelsus" – the gentleman pointed to a parchment affixed to the wall, directly above the alembic – "and desires first to create a hare to put the formula to the test."

He straightened up, still looking at the alembic. Then he smiled.

"The sperm has been rotting in that container for thirty days now. My wife is preparing a series of decoctions in preparation for the fortieth day. Just between you and me, I might add, she is most likely to be disappointed. Very disappointed. But I cannot bring myself to dissuade her from carrying on with her experiment. Her obstinacy and her curiosity are most touching."

He turned to the young man and for the first time looked him in the eye.

"Please do not misunderstand me! I believe in homunculi, and I have even encountered some, here and elsewhere. And one can indeed create such a being, providing you have the necessary ingredients and the proper formula, that of the French alchemist Eugène Maniguette, for instance, or the Chinese sage Gao Dongdong."

Then, abruptly turning away from the spermatozoidal fluid, the elderly gentleman pointed to a watercolour hanging on the wall, next to the Paracelsian formula. It depicted a wading bird with white plumage and black wings; the posterior segment of its interminable beak was orange in colour. It was not, in truth, a particularly successful painting.

"An African jabiru," said the gentleman. "My wife dreams of seeing one with her own eyes, and she imagines that after the tiny hare and the homunculus, she will be able to create an entire colony. She can picture them lapping water from the little pond behind the house. An acquaintance of ours lives in Africa and has promised to send us a jabiru egg at an opportune moment. But before that happens, I hope to be able to persuade her to listen to reason. Can you imagine? Birds of Africa in our Nordic lands … they would never survive the first frost of autumn."

Reassured as to the intentions of his host, and more at ease in this baroque laboratory, which he now knew to be maintained by an honest man, the traveller grew less wary.

"Pardon me," he said, "for entering without being asked. Please do not think I was attempting to make off with anything."

"Think nothing of it. It is I who must apologize for receiving you in all this disorder. Not to mention the odour. Let us retire to the salon, where there is bread and coffee. Ah! And blueberry jam that my wife has prepared with an intelligence that quickly makes one forget her eccentricities. I will toast some bread for you and serve you a wedge of pie. You must be hungry, young man. After you have eaten, we will talk. But only after you have eaten. If you are like me, you must loathe being obliged to speak and eat at the same time."

Our traveller felt keenly embarrassed to be given breakfast after all that had already been done for him, but the master of the house insisted on serving him toast, jam, and coffee. He then withdrew to his laboratory to allow the visitor to eat unhurriedly, a gesture of politeness that enchanted the young man, for there was nothing he found quite so displeasing as to eat while being observed. It was only when he returned to the drawing room that his host at last introduced himself, not failing to beg pardon for not having done so earlier.

"My name is Tuomas Juhani Korteniemi. You are in my home, on the Plains of Archelle, on the edge of the Misty Woods."

The young man swallowed a last morsel of toast and raised his head.

"My name is Tero Sihvonen, sir."

The two men shook hands.

"I am a bit confused," Sihvonen went on. "Last night – was it really yesterday? – I ventured into a terrifying woods ... the Fredavian Forest ... there I found an inn ..."

"The Inn at the Sign of the Farting Bear."

"Is that what they call it? It was pitch dark and I could not read the sign. But it was brightly lighted, and people were laughing and dancing. I went in. To tell the truth, I was very poorly received. I left as rapidly as I could. As I was making my way toward the exit, the customers poured beer over my head, pointed their fingers at me, laughed at me, and insulted me. It must have been half past one in the morning ... Outside, I headed west hoping to find a lumber camp or a peasant hut where I could spend the night. Then along came this ... this individual ..."

Tero rubbed his forehead, as though the very recollection had given him a headache.

"I'd noticed him there, among the carousers. He must have followed me when I left. I'd been walking through the woods for ... for a good twenty minutes, I estimate. And then –"

Perceiving his young guest's disarray, Tuomas broke in.

"His name is Mustard. At any rate, that's what he's known as in the forest. A ne'er-do-well who takes care of the dirty work for Seppo Petteri Lavanko, the owner – you must have seen him last night. Believe me, my friend, Mustard's prey rarely gets away. Of the bandits who work by the light of the moon, he's one of the most ferocious and pitiless. You are indeed fortunate to be alive this morning."

"I could hear nothing. I was on the ground ... I saw him raise his axe, a huge axe it was! Just as he was about to bring it down, there was a sudden movement behind him, as though some giant had suddenly emerged from the trees, and then came a terrible roar … And then, nothing … I must have blacked out. I have no idea what happened to my attacker."

Tuomas got to his feet and refilled Tero's coffee cup. He was smiling.

"A giant … a giant indeed! Astride a steed worthy of the queen of the giants! It was my spouse, Zora, who rescued you. Caution her though I may not to enter the Fredavian Forest … she's a stubborn woman, my wife. Yesterday, when I saw her return home in the middle of the night with you, in a state of unconsciousness, slung over her horse, my first reaction was to admonish her! And, please forgive me, my fine lad, it was only later, when I appraised myself of your condition, that I undertook to look after you."

Tuomas sat down beside the youth and lit his pipe. From the bowl, clouds of indolent blue smoke began to rise, whose odour immediately enchanted the young guest.

"I would wager," continued Tuomas, "that even as we speak Zora is hatching a plan of reprisal against your assailant. She is normally sweet and conciliatory, but she cannot be dissuaded from carrying out special missions against the fine folk of the Farting Bear for her personal diversion."

"But, sir, if we are not in the forest, where then are we?"

"As I have told you, my dwelling lies on the Plains of Archelle, at the edge of the Misty Woods. We are some twenty kilometres to the west of the forest. Here you are safe. All the miscreants of the region congregate in the Fredavian Forest, so there's no one to trouble you here."

No sooner had he spoken those words than the muffled sound of horseshoes striking macadam resounded from outside. The young man lifted his eyes. Through the open window he saw a gigantic horse pass in front of the house, immaculate of coat and black as night! Tero was a peasant's son and in the countryside of his birth, there was not a single family that did not possess a draught horse. Which is another way of saying he had certainly seen horses in his life. But he could never have imagined that such a huge specimen existed in this world!

His eyes widened; he got to his feet and stepped over to the window to observe the beast. Not a single part of the animal was not jet black, from its large round eyes down to its withers and the inside of its nostrils. Even the war saddle upon its back was an inky black. Tero was so struck by the horse that he barely noticed the horsewoman dismounting from it.

Tuomas found his guest's astonishment amusing.

"A Victurnian. A breed, the kind of which you are unlikely to see many examples in your lifetime, let me assure you. Your astonishment flatters the conceit of an old man, whose only remaining distraction is to surprise his entourage with the inconsequential. I gave it to my wife last year. Consent to flatter me further by granting me the honour of stepping outside to examine it more closely. What say you? It's a fine day. We could chat as we walk a bit with Yatagan – that is the horse's name – and also, quite obviously, with my wife …"

"What an extraordinary horse!" thought the young man, very moved, as he approached the animal. Next to the enormous mount stood a tall young woman, long legs sheathed in riding pants. Her blond hair was drawn behind her head in a heavy braid that gave her the appearance of an Amazon on a spree. A fine grace of movement and the gentle roll of her shoulders and hips offset her imposing height and lent her a femininity that would easily have attracted the eye of any rakish dandy in the capital. Her tall slender physique combined the healthy complexion of a country girl with the distinguished appearance of the cultivated ladies of the European aristocracy. It was a warm day, and the horsewoman's forehead was beaded with perspiration.

Tero bowed politely. Earlier, when the elderly gentleman had spoken of his "young wife," Tero was expecting to encounter a slightly older individual. As a man of the world, he concealed his surprise. That was not so difficult: the shock caused by the sight of the extraordinary horse eclipsed all the other singular aspects of this curious household.

The young lady returned his bow.

"Sir, you are looking much better! My husband and I were concerned for your well-being last night as we kept watch at your bedside."

Tuomas nodded in agreement.

"True indeed, and our happiness at seeing you in good health and spirits this morning is all the greater. Sir, allow me to present my spouse, Zora Korteniemi."

Tero bowed once more.

"Madame ... my name is Tero Sihvonen. I doubt that whatever I might possess in this earthly life would suffice to thank you for what you did for me last night in the forest."

"Oh, that was only a half-hearted effort hindered as I was by the trees. And Yatagan was the one who did most of the work!"

They exchanged pleasantries for a few more minutes. As he stroked the flanks of the majestic steed, Tero Sihvonen explained to his hosts that he had also had a horse, but that the beast had died the previous day, drowned in the Ritva Swamp. Which was why he had undertaken to cross the Fredavian Forest on foot.

"Oh! A tragic error!" exclaimed Tuomas. "To make your way through the Fredavian Forest on foot, imagine! And while you're at it, why not swim the Atlantic? My boy, it is clear you are not from these parts."

Tuomas explained to his guest the nest of cutthroats he had ventured into the previous evening. He would certainly have not come out alive had Zora not been in the immediate vicinity. After more effusions of gratitude, the young man, who feared to have lacked proper manners by not introducing himself earlier, wished at last to relate his own story. Tuomas stopped him.

"Tut-tut. First of all, you must have a nice hot bath. You are still muddied from last night's misadventure."

In a log cabin behind the house, there was a bathtub. Earlier that morning, the Korteniemis had filled it with boiling water.

After he had scrubbed himself from head to toe, Tero lingered in the warm water, tasting the happiness of still being alive. The old man was right: he had escaped the Grim Reaper's clutches by a hair. He forced himself to gulp soapy bathwater to rid his mouth of the taste of that monkey-woman who had pressed her lips against his at the inn. But did there exist water that would wash from his memory the sinister eyes of Mustard the hatchet man? More than the spitting, more than the insults, more than the stench of dead dog that filled the dining room of the Farting Bear, more even than the flash of the axe in the night, the mindless, bilious gaze of the would-be killer caused nausea to rise in his throat and gave him cold sweat.

Yesterday, a nightmare. This morning, sunlight, fruit preserves, and the company of excellent people. The counterpoint was brutal.

But who, he wondered, were his two hosts? Tero, certainly, was deeply recognizant of their care and consideration, and above all, he well measured what he owed to that tall girl who was built like a weightlifter and who had saved him from certain death. But something didn't add up. What was it? It was not the difference in age. True enough, Tuomas Juhani Korteniemi was as old as Väinämöinen, and Zora could be no more than twenty-five. Yet the young woman appeared entirely satisfied with her life here on this vast and empty plain. No, it was something else. A strange flawlessness in their manners and their humours, an irritatingly impeccable harmony. Everything here was perfect, too perfect. In this bucolic theatre, where they lived alone, far from the world, the gentleman and his wife performed their lives like actors. That was it. There was something staged in their conversation, the decor of their house, the hospitality they lavished upon Tero.

He felt a profound sense of unease at the idea. To rid himself of the impression that the mysterious couple was forcing him to play a role in the strange fiction of his own life, he resolved to do something spontaneous, something repugnant. Standing in the bathtub, he made love to Rosy Palm and her five sisters while visualizing the lady of the house, then shook himself dry by dancing around stark naked. Once that was done, and done well, he exited the bathhouse.

As he approached the garden, and saw his hosts breakfasting

indolently on capon and orange juice beneath a pretty pink-and-white striped parasol – more artificial pastoral charm, as if you had entered a watercolour painting – Tero concluded it would be wiser to conceal his true intentions. Throughout breakfast, he limited himself to formalities.

Born and raised in a small village to the north of Hämeenlinna, Tero studied medicine in Helsinki, where he had graduated a little more than a year earlier. After a residency in the capital under the supervision of a long-time family physician, he had entered the employ of the Lake Ladoga Company, which held the logging rights for several forests in the Northern Lands. The company maintained camps at different locations in Karelia, Savonia, and Ostrobothnia. Each camp boasted its own dispensary, nurses, and medical orderlies. At the same time, the company employed a certain number of itinerant physicians who travelled by horseback from one camp to another, spending several weeks in each to look after the woodsmen's health. It was hard work, perfect for young men of an adventurous bent, able to endure the solitude of months on the road. Tero was cut from such stock.

"The truth is this: though I have made medicine my profession, my great passion in life has nothing to do with the science of Hippocrates. I scour the forests of our land out of love for the ancient legends of Karelia. When I was a lad in Parola, I loved nothing quite so much as the long evenings of storytelling where the bards of the canton would declaim their tales and poems, and on every occasion, the stories of Karelia were those that enchanted me the most. My fascination with Karelian folklore has never left me. At seventeen, I left my home village to study in Helsinki. At first, I found the nights in the big city long indeed, and my medical studies only half-interested me. What I missed most was just those long evenings of legend and song from my village. To escape the tedium of my lonely life, I began to write down my favourite songs in a thick notebook. At first, my output was hesitant. Our tales and legends have been passed down for thousands of years. When you consign them to writing, it is like attempting to put them in a cage. Yet I came to enjoy the task, and it soon occurred to me that the fact of transcribing them would save them from oblivion. Not just my oblivion, but everyone else's, the forgetfulness of our descendants. That's when I conceived of the idea of criss-crossing the country and collecting all the ancient songs that I heard from the mouths of all the bards I encountered, which I would eventually compile in written form. I would, I imagined, draw up an exhaustive and eternal inventory of the poems, songs, and lamentations of the ancient Finns."

Tero Sihvonen stopped speaking for a moment, as though hesitant to continue. For a short moment he observed Yatagan, the great steed, who was wandering between the rows of sunflowers.

"My parents are poor peasants. They worked hard to send me to school. I repaid them by applying myself to my studies. I was first in my class. The people of my village, particularly the notables and army officers, collected funds to allow me to continue my studies in the capital. It was an extremely generous gesture, but it placed a weighty moral obligation upon me. Not only must I study seriously and assiduously, I also must choose an area of expertise that would allow me to contribute to the betterment of my benefactors. Peasants are practical people. They are happy to help a boy from the village go off and get an education in the big city, but not a greenhorn who would fritter away five years of his time daydreaming in some literature department. They are not interested in a lay-about who spends all day reading and reciting sonnets while sipping French wine. Against my better judgment, I elected to study medicine at the Imperial Alexander University. But just as you cannot stop a heart from loving, throughout my long years at university, I never ceased to nurture my passion for the ancestral tales of our land."

"How sad," sighed Zora. "Considering the political subjection and the dearth of culture in which our Finland currently finds herself, we need men of literature no less than physicians."

"I entirely agree," said Tero Sihvonen. "In that spirit, the idea of going to work for the large forestry companies occurred to me after I completed my first year in medicine. I owed it to my family and my fellow citizens to become a doctor, I owed it to myself to be faithful to the calling of my heart. The job of itinerant physician for the Lake Ladoga Company would make it possible for me, in my prime at least, to travel across the country, meet its bards and aged storytellers, and gather ancient tales and poems from their very mouths, all the while placing my medical skills at the service of the woodcutters and peasants of the Duchy. I completed my studies with the grade 'prodigious.' The company hired me less than a week after I received my diploma. I would be a doctor and, as I travelled, I would compose a grand work bringing together the poems of the Finnish oral tradition. Now an arch linked the two principal pillars of my mature life, and would give it coherence. I was reassured to know I could now spend the rest of my days doing what I loved the most. I was as happy as it was possible for a young man to be. Before beginning my work in the far north of the Grand Duchy, I returned home to spend four months in the village of my birth, where there was no doctor, only two young nurses who ran a relatively well-equipped dispensary. Whenever they fell ill, the people of Parola were forced to travel to the city. I took care of the elderly, delivered four children, gave everyone advice about proper hygiene, and before leaving made it a point of honour to promise the villagers I would return as often as possible. That was more than one year ago – seventeen months, to be exact. Since then, I have been travelling the Northern Lands on behalf of the Lake Ladoga Company and, wherever I go, I make friends with the local bards, lend them an attentive ear, and transcribe their stories."

Tero paused for a sip of orange juice.

"What an extraordinary journey I have had over the past year and a half! It is astonishing what beautiful forests and vast, poetic plains this country of ours possesses! I have beheld much that is beautiful, and much that is amusing. Up until last night, I never encountered any danger. Not a single serious accident, not a single thief, no one sought to harm me … The peasants are kind and hospitable and provide me with a bed and a meal. Often they will guide me into the depths of faraway forests, where they introduce me to toothless, reclusive, and melancholy bards. It is almost always the same story: at first, they refuse to share their songs with me. They suspect me of being a Lutheran zealot come to persuade them to abandon their ancestral faith and force them to accept that of the Church. I show them the tales I have collected, and speak to them of the villages I have visited, the bards I have encountered. There always comes a moment when they finally overcome their mistrust, and then they open up like books."

Tero stopped speaking. His deep black eyes focused on a point on the far horizon. He seemed to be reconstituting the events of the past days. Though his face was wracked by fatigue, he was a handsome young man. At rest, his eyes absorbed in the distance, with his fine nose, his long, cultured face, and his long curly black hair, he bore comparison with a hero of legend.

His visitor fell silent, and Tuomas prodded him gently.

"And it was pure happenstance that you found yourself in the Fredavian Forest? Or did some loudmouths send you there under false pretexts?"

"Well, uh ... yes, I ... to tell the truth, I'm a bit lost," mumbled the lad.

He shook his head vigorously, as if to get his ideas in order.

"Since I have been travelling across Karelia and Ostrobothnia for more than a year now, the company authorized me to spend a few weeks with my family. The visit did me a world of good. My parents ... they're growing old, you understand. My father turned fifty-five in September. He has a heart murmur. My mother is not in the best of health either; hers has been a life of hard work. You can imagine how happy they were to see me again. And I too truly missed them. I spent some time with them, but had to be on my way all too soon. The company notified me by mail that I would be needed come autumn at a new sawmill near Plabet. Before leaving, I promised my parents I would not stay away another year without returning to see them. I took a train from Hämeenlinna as far as

Grigol. As I wasn't expected at Plabet until next month, I decided I would spend a few days in the village of Rat River."

"Rat River?" exclaimed Tuomas. "What could you possibly want to do in Rat River?"

"It's … it's because I am looking for a particular bard … a man someone told me about during my last visit to the region, seven or eight months ago. I travelled there, but could not find him. In my disappointment, I decided to return to Plabet. I purchased a horse, an old nag that unfortunately drowned in the marshes beyond Grigol, on the outskirts of the Fredavian Forest. That's when I had the outlandish idea to make my way through the forest on foot … You know the rest of the story."

He turned to face his hosts and noticed that both of them were examining him with devouring empathy. Something in the sibylline smile of the young woman was inviting him to reveal more, to enter into the fine details of his life, to tell of his tribulations and his literary avocation. The elderly gentleman sat upright in his chair and drank in his words, patting his stomach. Tero did not care for such close attention. He had spoken more about himself than was appropriate with strangers.

"I regret having ventured into the Fredavian Forest," he concluded. "I experienced events and saw faces I will never forget. I owe you my life, Madame Korteniemi" – and here he turned to Zora and nodded politely – "and, by the same token, I owe you my successful passage through the forest. How far are we from Plabet?"

"You can count on two days on horseback, half of that with Yatagan," said Zora.

"Tell me," Tuomas interrupted, "were you introduced to any bards at Grigol or Rat River?"

"No one introduced me to anyone, but I was given some names. In Grigol, the owner of a bakery at Untamed Butte told me of an aged uncle of his who lived in the Sailio family hamlet and who, he swore, knew thousands of verses by heart."

Tuomas's tone had turned inquisitorial. Zora looked at her husband with narrowed eyes.

"And here, in the Misty Woods? Did they mention any names?"

"No … no one. Why?"

"Ah! That is strange!" exclaimed Tuomas. "No one ever gave you the name of Elijah Saariaho?"

"Ah yes! Elijah!" Zora exclaimed, a look of enchantment on her face.

Tero's face displayed nothing but sincere ignorance.

"No," he replied. "I've never heard the name."

Tuomas turned his gaze toward the edge of the forest visible to the west.

"Elijah Saariaho … He operates a forge in the heart of the Misty Woods. When was the last time we visited him?" he asked Zora, turning to her.

"A little over a year? Have you forgotten? It was in early spring, last year."

"Yes, of course! Early spring last year … We cannot go there often, you will understand. It's a whole day's journey. Not so long ago, Elijah lived in the Fredavian Forest. Then, six or seven years back, a pastor from Grigol accused him of abjuring his Lutheran faith and began to harass him. The courts got involved. I'll spare you the rest of the story. Elijah decided to move farther away from Grigol. He left the Fredavian Forest to set up shop in the deepest part of the Misty Woods. There he built a forge. Two or three times a year he sells his products in the marketplaces of the towns and villages to the west. We hardly ever see him in these parts."

Tuomas shifted in his chair and waved his diminutive fists in the air, as though the memory of the blacksmith had breathed young life into him.

"He's an odd bird, this Elijah. An exceptional person, for sure. Heart as big as the earth. I am flattered to number among his friends. He comes from a tiny village located at the foot of Koskela Gap. His father was an onion merchant, and his mother, a clog maker. Even in his youth, he was a wonderful storyteller. He had a phenomenal memory. When I first met him he was around eighteen, and already knew thousands of verses. But I doubt he still recites his tales these days. He has long taken leave of human society, and even his old friends hardly ever see him. But Zora and I occasionally visit him at his smithy, and it is always a great pleasure. At first, when he began to work his forge in the Misty Woods, he could be seen crossing the Plains of Archelle, leading his mare carrying a large bronze canister full of pieces of metal, on his way to sell his wares in Grigol or the neighbouring villages. As he led the old mare, he would sing those ancient airs that you love so much in his fine bass voice. Then he stopped going to Grigol because of that half-wit pastor. By heading west from the woods, as he does now, Elijah can reach a string of good-sized villages, and even a couple of major towns."

Tuomas struck a contented pose, as though he had just concluded a favourable transaction. He stretched out his legs beneath the table and put his hands behind his head.

"Tell me, my friend, would you be interested in meeting him?"

"I would indeed!" exclaimed Tero. "Would you take me to him?"

"Indeed I would. Here is what I suggest: stay with us two more days, long enough to recover from your misadventures. In an hour's time I will send Elijah a pigeon to ascertain whether he is at home. If that is the case, we will depart the day after tomorrow. We will need between eight and ten hours to make the journey. Alone, on a horse as fast as Yatagan, you're there in less than a third that time – Zora can tell you; she makes the trip more frequently than I do – but as far as I'm concerned, I never go empty-handed. I fill the cart with gifts and proceed slowly to make the most of the natural beauty that surrounds us ... Ah! Before I forget, I must tell you that the Misty Woods is an extraordinary place. You will not regret having visited it once in your life, young man."

Zora nodded in agreement. "It's true! A more enchanting place could not be imagined."

"So then, you will rest here today and tomorrow. Make yourself at home. But I warn you: soon I won't be able to contain my almost obscene interest in your great task of collecting the songs and poems of our people. You would certainly be making a very human gesture should you agree to show this old soul a bit of the material you have collected up until now."

They postponed until the dinner hour a more detailed examination of Tero's work. The young man spent most of the afternoon putting his affairs in order. During the previous night's attack, dust and mud had found their way into the satchel in which he carried his notebooks. Luckily, no document had been irremediably damaged. He brushed the grit from the worst-stained pages and carefully separated those that were stuck together with mud and moisture.

Meanwhile, Tuomas and Zora spent the afternoon packaging the array of gifts they intended to offer Elijah the blacksmith.

At sunset they supped on grilled beluga steaks and Plabet wine, once again around the little table in the garden.

After they had eaten their fill, Tero and Tuomas felt the urge to smoke. While checking over his belongings, the young man noticed his pipe had been broken in the altercation with Mustard. He mentioned it to Tuomas. The older man smiled, patted him on the shoulder, got up, and went into the house.

"He's going to give you one of those hellish pipes of his, and have you smoke one of his homemade tobacco blends," Zora said to Tero.

"He grows tobacco?"

"Yes, in a small field a little farther off, on the plain. Some of the plants come from regions ... I could name them for you, but you would not even know what I was talking about. Each year we spend time in Helsinki at summer's end. In the cafés down by the docks, Tuomas negotiates with traders from all around the world. He purchases great quantities of things: instruments for his research, books, ingredients to be used in his experiments, trinkets ... and tobacco of every kind. He's maintained relations with some of those traders for several decades. Long before I was born, in fact!"

The memory of those journeys made Zora Korteniemi particularly gay. She smiled a toothy smile.

"He grows his own tobacco right here, then subjects the leaves to one bizarre experiment after another, using antimony, mustard, buffalo grass, and just about anything else you could think of … Sometimes the effects are surprising. He doesn't tell me much about his experiments; he knows that, the better part of the time, they bore me. The Helsinki doctors who study tobacco addiction are always pestering him to share his results with them. But you know Tuomas and his research … they don't exactly belong to the same type of science that those gentlemen in Helsinki teach in the universities."

She pronounced the word *gentlemen* with a disdainful frown.

"Are you saying he is an alchemist?"

"Yes … yes, I am, when you get right down to it … Yes. That's it."

"And yet earlier he told me he once taught physics in Helsinki."

"He was not deceiving you. He was a highly regarded professor. But his true passion … Ah! Look, what was I saying?"

Tuomas had returned. On the table he placed a small blue metal box with Chinese ideograms painted on it, and handed Tero a handsome carved meerschaum pipe.

"Please accept this as a gift," Tuomas said.

And to Tero, who declined, Zora added, "I implore you, keep it. I can't stand seeing all those pipes littering the house!"

Tuomas took the pipe from Tero's hands, the one he had just given him, and was hastily filling it. Zora picked up the tobacco box and handed it to Tero so he could smell it.

"Oh, what enchanting tobacco!" thought Tero, a beatific smile on his face.

"This kind of tobacco," Tuomas said proudly, "you will not find at the tobacconists in the capital!"

The two men smoked voraciously, the thick blue cloud that rose from their pipes dissipating in the moonlight. They discussed tobacco while Zora went to fetch a third bottle from the cellar. Tero showed his hosts the notebooks in which he recorded the folktales and poems he had heard in the course of his travels. With a graceful hand, he had transcribed no fewer than fifteen thousand verses in these past thirteen months. Each page was dated, and in the margins Tero had set down the bard's name, his age, his certified or approximate birthdate, and the name of the village or forest in which he resided. With Tuomas he shared some of his most fascinating discoveries. Zora leafed through one of the notebooks, and occasionally interrupted the conversation between the men to read aloud the songs, verses, plaints, riddles, or lamentations that caught her fancy. Tuomas was moved to discover in these very pages the old, long-forgotten folk tales of his childhood. When Zora closed the notebook, Tero asked her to tell him frankly what she thought of his work.

"I am very impressed," she answered. "I just adore the old folk tales. I know more than a few of them myself, which I heard where I grew up. Some I find pleasing, while others … well, others, I'd prefer not to think about, for they only bring back painful memories. But then, is it really necessary to remember everything indefinitely?"

"What do you mean?" asked Tero.

"For instance, those tiny paper cranes that the Japanese make are beautiful because they are so fragile. They are fragile because they are made of paper. By writing these things down, are you not fearful you will destroy everything that is so fragile – and so beautiful – about our national legends?"

"You cannot compare the two," said Tero. "The paper crane is beautiful because it derives from something eternal: the idea of the crane. If a paper crane disappears, you simply take a piece of paper and fashion another. The age-old tales of our ancestors are something entirely different. When one tumbles into the uncreated abyss of oblivion, it is never seen or heard again. When the last person on earth to remember the legend dies, what dies with him are the characters, the places, the events, and the relations among all those things. And their emotions as well. None of this can ever be recreated. That is a tragedy I cannot accept."

Tuomas nodded. "I agree with Tero," he declared. "And by transcribing them, we not only immortalize the old tales, we also make them known. The charm of our ancient legends will not wither because they have become more widely accessible – quite the contrary. It is not like emptying the king's tomb and delivering his treasure to grave robbers and dogs. The inestimable worth of these tales is of an essence that cannot be profaned, cannot be bought and sold, cannot be diluted."

Zora threw up her hands as if to surrender. "All I was saying," she replied, "is that there are in this world beautiful things that carry their death within them. By forcing permanence upon them, you risk dislodging all that is beautiful about them."

She fell silent and, at length, observed the silvery moon as it pierced the night sky to the west.

*
* *

In the feline realm, every night is Sabbath
In the ancient graveyard, O pussy, take my claws

In the middle of the night, Tero Sihvonen crept from his room with muffled steps. Before he made his way down to the ground floor, he paused in the corridor and noticed that, aside from the one in which his hosts had settled him, there were two other rooms on the first floor, and that gentle snoring reached his ears from behind both doors. So, old Tuomas and his young wife slept in separate rooms ... What could that possibly mean?

He went downstairs and stepped outside. It was an extraordinarily beautiful night. Barefoot, he strolled across the soft grass of the plain, his eyes focused on the distant silhouettes of the trees that marked the boundary of the Misty Woods. The Misty Woods. "Elijah Saariaho," said Tero in a loud voice.

Our one hundred and one friends slide from the grave
One hundred and one stars stab the dying day.

He came to a stop only when the Korteniemi house was no more than a tiny bright dot far behind him. He lay down on the dewy grass and placed his head on his hands as if preparing to sleep. He would not sleep, of course. For the past six months he had barely slept. The night before, in order to get forty winks, a bloodthirsty mental retard had to attack him in a haunted forest.

> *See the cats from below, spewed up by the catacombs*
> *Never singly do they come, march they only in pairs*

In his body, in his joints, in his bones, down to the depths of his viscera, and above all in his mind, he felt as though he were 120 years old.

> *Three dozen this night, thirty-six zombie cats!*
> *For the zombie cats, let us kill the gravedigger!*

"Elijah Saariaho," murmured Tero, head turned toward the Misty Woods.

CHAPTER
10

Tero Sihvonen in the Feline Realm

In the morning it took Tero Sihvonen quite a while before he could muster the energy to get out of bed. Breathing heavily, he splashed water on his face, dressed, and stepped out of the room. He paused a few seconds in the hallway: loud snoring could be heard from one of the other two bedrooms.

On the table downstairs, Tero found a basket of bread, a large pitcher of fresh milk, three jars of jam, butter, and a pot of coffee, but he was not hungry. He left the house without eating and walked to the stable where Yatagan was kept. It was a magnificent day, though a little warm.

Yatagan was not in the stable. As he had not encountered Zora Korteniemi, Tero deduced that the young woman had left for a ride on her fine horse. He returned to the house and took the liberty of pouring some of the coffee that was growing cold in the pot, but did not dare help himself to the bread and jam before being invited to do so by his hosts. Seated there, he sipped his coffee and examined the charming, comfortable house.

A few moments later, old Tuomas finally roused himself.

"Please eat!" he instructed Tero. "But wait, allow me to toast the bread and reheat the coffee. Have you seen my wife?"

"No. I strolled out to the stable but she was not there, nor was the horse."

A look of concern passed over Tuomas's face. He stepped to the window and looked silently out over the landscape. Tero coughed to shake him from his reverie. The elderly gentleman was startled, then hastened to toast the bread.

Zora returned home several hours later, in the afternoon. On the table, she deposited a box that contained a pair of trousers and a man's shirt, vest, and jacket.

"I would have happily mended your clothing," she said to Tero, "but with all those holes, they would not have looked very nice. Here, try these on. They are not of the finest quality, and you may find them a bit too large, but they are the best I could find in Grigol."

The clothes, in fact, fit him perfectly.

In the hours that followed Zora's return, Tero thought he detected a coolness between the two Korteniemis, but could not identify the cause.

In the evening a pigeon arrived with news from Elijah Saariaho the blacksmith. He was indeed at home, in the Misty Woods, and was impatiently expecting a visit from Tuomas and Zora, whom he missed. They made their final arrangements for the voyage. They dined on nettles, Chinese cabbage, and carrots in honey, washed down with a powerful arak that dispatched Tuomas and Zora to bed at nine o'clock. That night, Tero could not sleep.

The next morning, after a light breakfast, Tuomas and Zora loaded their personal effects and a number of gifts for Elijah onto the horse cart. Then they harnessed Yatagan and set off for the Misty Woods after having closed the shutters.

The edge of the Misty Woods was, as we have previously noted, only a few kilometres from Tuomas and Zora's house, so close in fact that from the windows of their living room one could see, far off across the fields, the long line of close-grown conifers running north to south. A lyrical imagination might have seen the tall spruce as the first ranks of a powerful army gathering on the plain. As they drew closer to that extraordinary wall of green needles, Tero, seated on top of a sack of flour, kept watch left and right; the line of trees seemed to stretch off endlessly in both directions. And as they entered the woods, he could not repress an icy shiver. He felt he was being swallowed up by a monster of the vegetable realm whose dimensions were not of this world.

Yet Tuomas and Zora seemed as relaxed in these great dark woods as if they were back on their overstuffed divan. That reassured the young man, who calmed himself and soon became accustomed to the majesty of the trees and the darkness. Quite soon, he began to appreciate the coolness of the woods and the sounds of the birds and the animals echoing in the trees. And what trees they were! How they towered above him! He took delight in watching the ascending curve of the maples that encircled them. So lofty were they that he could not even see their peaks, and his gaze remained a prisoner of that celestial foliage. After an hour of such contemplation, he had stretched his neck so far that he cried out: "Owwww!"

The cart rolled on for another good four hours. At one point, thick grey clouds covered the sky. "Had I known," said Zora to Tuomas, touching his arm, "I would have put some straw on the carriage floor." A few indolent drops spattered the travellers, but the clouds moved on before they could empty themselves on the woods. Tuomas finally stopped the cart and announced they would take their lunch at the base of a tree.

"Only two or three more hours and we should be entering the heart of the Misty Woods. You will soon see, Tero, it is an unforgettable spectacle."

Zora gave Yatagan his ration of oats. In the dampness of the woods, the three travellers sat and ate buttered bread, sausages, and green apples. Zora had also brought along some cakes. When the repast was over, Tero, enveloped by the dampness and silence of the forest, wanted to rest a while more. But Tuomas insisted they continue without delay. "We still have a long road to travel," he explained.

On they ventured, for the better part of the afternoon. To pass the time, Tero stretched out on the tarpaulin that covered the luggage and consulted certain of his notebooks. Then he read a few chapters of the short novel he'd been carrying in his rucksack, Leo Salmela's *Elämän Korkeakoulussa*.

Finally, at around three-thirty, he nodded off.

An unhoped-for blessing: he fell asleep. Not for long, but long enough to rest, and enough for the world around him to be completely transformed. Tuomas awakened him by shaking him gently and calling his name in a low voice. His head knocked against the side of the cart. He opened his eyes and rubbed them to get a better look at what seemed to him to be the most astonishing landscape. Never would he forget the spectacle that lay before him.

The leaves of the trees were of a green so pure that their gleaming tinted the air around them and bathed the forest in a thick purée of luminosity. The air itself was almost dense enough to grasp. Tero extended a hand to see whether he could seize a piece of the concentrate of ether that the cart appeared to be slicing through as it moved along the trail. The exquisite green of the tiny branches bore a patina of leafy silver that showered the blueberry bushes with its brilliance. Branches hung low over Tero's head. He wanted to tear off one of these extraordinary silvery leaves to look at it more closely, but at the last moment restrained himself, as though he were about to commit the most grievous of crimes.

The bronzed bases of tree trunks seemed to emerge from tiny nests of scarlet mist. Vapours danced around their length. Higher up, among the larger branches, openings in the foliage revealed patches of pink sky. On the forest floor huge white flowers unknown to him thrust up from the undergrowth at the ends of inordinately long stems. Some of them had broad lips upon which nature had inscribed, in black and yellow against a pink field, strange and indecipherable runes. Others, as weightless as the skins of trout, deployed then withdrew their corollas with the same graceful movements as Sabellidae whose fronds sway to and fro in the depths of the sea.

From all directions birdsong rang out, high-pitched and plangent. Tero watched foxes scurry for cover as the wagon came into view. On high branches he spotted several partridges. At one point the group skirted a broad pond whose viscous water gleamed bright with flashes of silver, as mysterious red flowers floated across the surface. As he beheld the scene – the pussy willows, their jade-oil-saturated leaves coating the dark waters of the pond with their honey-like swaths, the lambent animal life that seemed to punctuate the static nature with its slow and colourful movements, this curious landscape so striking that not even the finest painter could have imagined its equal – Tero, spellbound by the beauties of creation, felt a knot form in his throat. He would not have been more startled, or more amazed, if he had been told that between the moment he had dozed off and the one when he had awakened, the cart had leaped from star to star to finally come to rest on another planet.

Lost in contemplation of these supra-terrestrial woods, he had all but forgotten Tuomas and Zora. He turned toward them. Tuomas was holding the reins, and his wife was seated beside him, her head resting on his shoulder. She was asleep.

With his eyes on the trail ahead, Tuomas said to Tero, "There is something in these woods so removed from earthly life ... Each time I come here, I feel as though I have forgotten who I am. As though I am being dissolved in the landscape, in all this beauty."

And he drew the fingers of his right hand through his wife's hair.

"Do not think that Zora is insensitive to the beauty of the Misty Woods. She comes here often ... Since the first time I brought her here, she was so taken with this place that hardly a week goes by that she does not return astride Yatagan."

Wherever Tero looked, the lines and shapes were in perfect harmony. These woods could have only been the creation of a great artist-demiurge!

The three travellers penetrated ever deeper into the enchanted forest. They skirted a second pond, even more extraordinary than the first. Astonishing spheres of light danced atop the waters. The light seemed to have been deposited there by the bushy foliage of the weeping willows lining its banks. These small luminous bulbs emerged languidly from between their branches, quivered for a moment in the air as if fitted with invisible aigrettes, before dropping to the surface where they continued their pirouettes without sinking. From the point where it encountered the pond, the trail followed the shore for a good half of its circumference, in the shape of a slightly irregular half-moon. Once it reached the other side, the path swerved off to the south.

Some fifty metres farther on, Tero beheld a nicely decorated little house, built in the shade of a clump of broad black birches. Here, as around the pond earlier, the air was saturated with fine, bright, radiant dust. It was as though a comet had fallen to earth, breaking apart in these very woods.

Tuomas had barely brought the cart to a halt in front of the cabin when a man wearing a blacksmith's apron came out to welcome the travellers. The alchemist hopped down from the vehicle, better to embrace his old companion.

"Elijah! My dear, my good Elijah!"

"Tuomas! You old snake! I should tan your hide for not coming to see me for so long!"

The eyes of the two men filled with tears as they hugged each other. Elijah had spent the day hammering out horseshoes upon which he had inscribed his signature; his apron was covered with iron filings. As he grasped the frail Tuomas in his heavy smith's arms, he covered the alchemist's fine suit with grime. Elijah turned to Zora. The young woman curtsied.

"Elijah Saariaho."

"Zora Korteniemi. More beautiful than a doe at dusk."

Zora laughed.

"Ah, how well you know how to speak to the ladies, Elijah! But after all these years, do you really believe I am one of those women whose head can be turned by flattery?"

They spent a time laughing and exchanging the most urgent news. Tero stood off to one side, observing Elijah. The smith was a hulk of man, nearly two metres tall and no less than 115 kilos, Tero estimated. He was not exactly young, but his bushy beard was still a fine, light auburn colour, matching his curly hair, and tiny wrinkles were barely visible at the corners of his eyes.

"Let me introduce you to Tero Sihvonen," Tuomas finally said.

"A young physician from the capital who would like to discuss certain subjects of great interest to him."

"A doctor? Ah! Couldn't have come at a better time. My eyesight has been blurred the past several weeks. I may need a pomade."

"We have not come empty-handed," added Tuomas.

After pulling back the tarpaulin, the four of them unloaded the crates and sacks of gifts that the Korteniemis had brought the blacksmith. There was flour, bottles of wine, medicines, various kinds of sausage, canned fruit and a few pieces of fresh fruit as well, bread, pastries, butter, and utensils of all kinds. There was also a brand-new teakettle, so new the label had not yet been removed. It goes without saying that Tuomas also brought their host several sachets of tobacco in a variety of bright colours.

In front of the house, Elijah set up a small table on which he placed a bottle of iced vodka. Stepping inside, he produced a handsome hand-carved wooden chair and invited Zora to take a seat. Tero, Tuomas, and the blacksmith each took their places on sawed-off logs. As he poured vodka into wooden cups, the blacksmith eyed the crates of gifts lined up along the outside wall of the cottage. Did he need money? asked Tuomas.

"Not whatsoever! I've got all the fodder I need. Last summer, on my way through Iisalmi, an old geezer asked me to brass-plate his trumpet. No telling what was on his mind. Anyway ... he was so pleased he gave me twice the asking price and, what's more, I can assure you the asking price was more than ... don't ask! Next winter I intend to spend two months in those parts. The Laakso Corporation won a contract to build six hundred coal-mine wagons and sent out a call to blacksmiths from the region prepared to lend a hand. They pay very well ... No, my dear Tuomas, I've got all the wherewithal I need. I can even lend you some if you like."

He burst out laughing, hands folded over his ample belly, then tossed back a slug of vodka and let out a long "Ahhhh!" of satisfaction.

"You can spend the night here, in the cabin."

"Don't overdo it, my friend," Tuomas replied with a smile.

"There's hardly enough room in your little house for your outsized carcass. With your permission, we'll pitch our tent and fall asleep to the hooting of the owls."

The two men chattered on a few minutes more, trading news and reminiscing over old memories. By the time dinner hour had come, stomachs were growling.

"Rest easy," said Elijah. "I'll go wring the necks of two or three partridges and cook up a stew. With the fresh bread you brought, some mulberry wine, pastries, and creamy butter, we'll have more than enough to eat. And you and me, we can make our acquaintance," he added, tapping Tero on the shoulder.

Tero, Tuomas, and Zora had made a long trip; what they needed now was to stretch their legs. While the blacksmith was cooking his stew, they went for a walk through the woods that surrounded the house.

As they strolled among the birches, Tuomas noticed a change in Tero's physiognomy. The young physician seemed to be waning with the dying of the day. His handsome face, highlighted, glimmering, and shimmering with a thousand hues thanks to the sublime beauty of the Misty Woods, had turned grave and inert. The dark circles beneath his eyes were brown and wrinkled like dried dates. Tuomas slapped his forehead, as if in self-reproach. "That's what's been bothering me the past two days," the elderly gentleman said to himself. "He still has those enormous dark circles under his eyes, as if he hasn't slept for weeks."

Meanwhile, Zora's majestic presence held such sway over these woods that Tuomas would not have been surprised if the huge silver willows bowed low as she passed. He was moved by the sight of two such handsome young people, both of whom inhabited by deep darkness, evanescent young gods whose mystery was of a piece with the forest around them.

Zora moved with quick steps, stooping now and then to observe the mushrooms sprouting at the base of a tree. Tero watched her, curious.

"They say that here in the Misty Woods there are enchanted

mushrooms that transform anyone who eats them into a mushroom," she explained. She ended her sentence with a comical expression, almost clown-like, like someone trying to make a child laugh. "Can you imagine? I've been exploring these woods for the past six years, and for six years I've been trying to find those mushrooms. They are said to be violet with large mauve spots."

For the rest of their walk, Tero watched Zora discreetly. Whenever the young woman spied mushrooms at the base of a tree, she bent low to examine them. Her expression was serious, like a veteran naturalist irritated at not finding what she sought. When she was convinced that the specimen was innocuous, she stood up and moved on. At one point, with an acorn she picked up from the ground, she managed to attract a squirrel that had been observing her from a nearby branch. The rodent stuffed the acorn into its cheek and then – for no good reason – bit the tip of the young woman's finger before scurrying away. "Shit!" she swore.

When they returned to Elijah's, the table was set, and the stew was steaming in a clay pot on the checkered tablecloth. The blacksmith was waiting for his guests, pipe in mouth, feet propped up on a log. They all sat down to eat. Elijah and Tuomas, in high spirits, began to chatter. Smiling, Tero and Zora listened to the noisy babble of the two old friends.

Soon the mulberry wine had gone to everyone's heads, and they laughed for no reason at all. Tuomas related a funny story (the one about the man who walked into a chemist's with reindeer antlers on his head and a big bulge in his pants; no way you don't know that one), and Elijah laughed so hard he fell off his log. He got up, caught his breath, and laid his massive paw on young Tero's shoulder. His face was flushed with drink.

"Come on now, down the hatch and loosen up!"

But Tero did not touch his wine, and he said nothing. Tuomas, whom the young man's silence was beginning to bother, drew a portrait of Tero for the blacksmith.

"Our young friend here has just recently graduated from the Imperial Alexander University. But he has vowed to place his knowledge at the service of the country's peasants and pioneers. He left the big city about a year ago to work for the Lake Ladoga Company as a travelling doctor in our region. But the lad has an idea in his head, which might interest you more than his skills as a bone setter or pustule pricker, so lend an ear."

Tuomas recounted to Elijah Tero's passion for the imaginary world of the Finns, and of his great undertaking, to transcribe the folktales and poems of days gone by.

"And after a series of adventures that he'll relate to you himself – if he so desires – Tero Sihvonen has honoured us, Zora and me, by spending the past two days in our company. As you can imagine, Elijah, my old friend, we are more than delighted to offer him lodging, for opportunities to converse with literary figures are rare indeed in these parts. So, in the two days that we have come to know him, Tero has taught us many fascinating things. And when he told us of the ancient folktales that he has written down, I immediately thought of you. Imagine, though, that for all his peregrinations in the region, never once had our young friend Tero heard your name spoken!"

When he heard those words, the bear-like Elijah erupted in laughter so loud that two owls perched in the tree branches near the house took flight.

"Think nothing of it! It's hardly surprising that you've never heard my name. This absurd friendship with which Tuomas has honoured me for more than forty years makes him exaggerate my talents and reputation. Today I live far from men and worldly affairs, Mr. Tero. Those who remember me are few and far between. But it is true that, in my youth, I knew more than a few folktales, and I needed little incentive to recite them on those long winter evenings by the hearth. But that was long, long ago ..."

Tero focused his black eyes on the blacksmith. In the young man's gaze there was a troubling hint of nothingness.

"I know who you are," he said simply. "I've heard of you. I am here because I have been looking for you."

Tuomas was startled.

"You've heard about him? How … But no later than the day before yesterday you assured me that –"

"I lied to you," said Tero Sihvonen. "What I have to tell, I didn't want to relate to anyone until I had Elijah Saariaho before me."

Whatever the case, Tero Sihvonen's grave mien disturbed Elijah not in the least. The blacksmith pulled a partridge foot from his pocket and began to clean his teeth with its claws.

"You make it all sound so mysterious," he said to Tero. "I'm a poor old lonely blacksmith. What could you possibly want from me that could justify such a solemn tone?"

"I am looking for someone."

"Who?"

"I am looking for Gladd the Argus."

The reaction was immediate. Tuomas brought his fist down on the table, shouting, "That will be enough of that!" Elijah, his great bear's eyes on Tero, made a throat-cutting motion with his hand, a movement that said: "Never play that trick on me again!" A moment of silent astonishment ensued.

"And just what do you want from Gladd the Argus?" Elijah finally asked.

From one of his jacket pockets, Tero drew the pipe that Tuomas had given him two days before.

"I have a pipe, but no tobacco."

With his eyes Elijah invited the young man to help himself from his pouch that lay wide open on the table.

Tero stuffed the pipe and lighted it. Then, breathing a long trail of smoke into the air, he re-narrated the story of his adventures of the past few months, the same ones he had told Tuomas and Zora two days earlier, but this time adding a series of events he had concealed from his hosts on the Plains of Archelle.

"For over a year I've been criss-crossing the region. I visit lumber camps, treating the sick and the injured. But my true and abiding passion, as Tuomas has told you, is folktales and legends. For months now I have spent my evening hours, and sometimes whole nights, listening to the ancient airs of the land, and I don't mind telling you that this activity satisfies me far more than does my profession. Here is the sum total of all I have heard and written down in the past year and a half. I would be so bold as to say that even you, Elijah Saariaho, whose knowledge of these matters is immense, will find songs and stories of your own region that you never knew existed, or that you had long forgotten. And, undoubtedly, should you agree to devote a few hours of your time to me, you could help me discover some of the old songs I have never heard before. Some say that of all the bards of Karelia, you are the master."

Tero gently nudged the notebooks in Elijah's direction, the ones in which he had transcribed the tales. In the quiet of the night, the friction of leather against the rough-hewn wood of the table sounded like an invitation.

"The folktales, the legends and poems, the songs and riddles … they're all there, pell-mell, without regard for order or chronology. When I've accumulated enough material, I will try to put this mess in order. My objective is to find a publisher in Helsinki who would be prepared to publish these ancient stories."

And to Elijah, who was reaching his hand toward the notebooks, Tero declared, "I will gladly show you what I have accumulated to date, but please first allow me to finish my story."

Elijah nodded. Tuomas filled everyone's glass with wine.

"Last fall," the young man continued, "the Lake Ladoga Company dispatched me for several weeks to Kajaani, where it operates a lumber mill. I was in Nurmes when I received my assignment. I was happy to take the mission, for the journey would let me stop off at Bull Creek where, I'd been told, an old bookseller sold copies of an unpublished book of fables by Jermu Agricola. A bibliophile like me could not have hoped for better. Off I set on horseback. Two weeks exactly, that's the time it took me. When finally I reached the village, night had fallen. I had no choice but to put off my search for the bookseller until the next day. I took a room at the Menninkäinen Patachon inn. You are known there."

"That's true," said Elijah Saariaho. "When I was young, I would go there to eat oysters and drink beer. The innkeeper was called Leena Neminen. She was enormous, and had a moustache. Does she still mind the bar?"

"Yes," said Tero. "On my last visit, the inn was full of young people from the environs who were eating, talking, reciting poetry, singing. Madame Neminen ... I don't know, she's getting on in years, for sure ... but she's still lively, and most of all, kindly. All the young customers seem to know her personally. They call her by her first name, as if she were their grandmother. To tell the truth, she was the first to speak of you. Later on, your name came up often, but she was certainly the first to mention it. I told her about my interest in the stories and legends of the region, and she said that I must absolutely seek you out and meet you, and that you used to live in the Fredavian Forest, but she did not know if you were still alive. But she made me promise to remember her to you if one day I were to cross your path. And now, lo and behold, consider it done."

So saying, Tero raised his goblet to Elijah, who replied in kind. On the blacksmith's lips was a slightly sad smile. Tuomas also raised his glass, and they drank to Leena Neminen, the fat moustachioed lady innkeeper of Bull Creek.

"I spent an entire week at the Menninkäinen Patachon inn. Madame Neminen and her husband introduced me to three bards from their village, and they taught me several charming songs. But that is not what I wish to discuss with you."

Tero paused and looked at Elijah. The massive bard had finished picking his teeth with his partridge claw, and now he was amusing himself by pulling on the nerve that protruded from the stump, causing the claw to clench and release.

"Something happened to me that week ... an incident that troubled me – no, terrified me. That incident is the reason I am here, before you, today. In truth, our paths would surely never have crossed but for this strange adventure ..."

Their curiosity piqued, Elijah, Tuomas, and Zora leaned forward, in Tero's direction. They cleared their throats, spat, and burped discreetly to avoid doing so during the young physician's story.

"The morning after I arrived in Bull Creek," he began, "Madame Neminen and her husband suggested that I visit the market. It was the thing to see in the town, so it seemed. I stepped outside to check the weather. The air was effervescent, a bit cool, it was a splendid day. I set off toward the marketplace. In the main square of the village a fair was in progress. The square was filled with tents, shelters, kiosks, and stalls. At the four corners of the square troupes of travelling players were reciting rhymes. Troubadours and acrobats blocked the streets with their cartwheels and somersaults, forcing people to stop and throw them loose change. Merchants sold vegetables, hot rolls stuffed with meat, furniture and farm equipment, wrought iron, and even livestock ... Everywhere children were scurrying hither and thither. I spent a pleasant hour. No one knew me, yet many greeted me. They seemed to know I had come from the south. Because of my clothing, perhaps?"

Tero lowered his head and examined the clothes he was wearing with a look of incredulity, as though he were seeing them for the first time. It took him a few seconds to understand that he was no longer wearing his own clothing, but the garments that Zora had purchased for him the day before. His eyes were as big as saucers, a blank expression on his face, but the story he was telling was as clear as could be.

"I strolled through the busy streets around the square," he went on. "Then I wandered away, and reached the edge of the village, where the houses give way to the fields. I spotted a man and a woman who seemed particularly poor, standing behind a dilapidated wheelbarrow filled with carrots. They were wearing rags, and dirty ... With them were two children – a boy, who must have been around seven or eight, and a younger girl. The children were playing in a manure pile. The girl was singing something. She had an enchanting, high-pitched voice, so I went over to listen. She was singing a simple melody, but there was something incredibly captivating about it. And her words ... It was a complete story, as you will see ..."

Tero's gaze was lost in the dark woods that surrounded Elijah the blacksmith's house. In a soft voice, the young doctor sang the song he had heard in Bull Creek. His voice was broken, tuneless, almost a croak: how exhausted Tero Sihvonen seemed! Yet the little song enthralled the others. Its beauty transcended the weakness of the voice singing it; in fact, the delicacy of the melody and the daintiness of the words seemed to magnify the young man's cracked delivery:

In the feline realm, every night is Sabbath
In the ancient graveyard, O pussy, take my claws
Our one hundred and one friends slide from the grave
One hundred and one stars stab the dying day.

See the cats from below, spewed up by the catacombs
Never singly do they come, march they only in pairs
Three dozen this night, thirty-six zombie cats!
For the zombie cats, let us kill the gravedigger!

O see the cats from high above, banquets they have prepared
Of sardines, sewer water, and dead rats
Five times thirteen tomcats, altogether sixty-five
Wearing tailcoats, bearing trays and tureens.

Cats above and cats below, and all have come for her
Black roses they cause to bloom, ravens they eviscerate
One hundred refined souls call out to the sovereign
Let the dusky moon spit upon the world.

Would you then not be mine?
Think how high my heart would leap ...

Tero fell silent, as did those gathered around the table. An enigmatic smile played on Zora's cherry lips.

"What a curious ditty!" she whispered, closing her eyes.

"Yes," said Tero. "My heart was torn, and the effect on me was all the stronger, for the little girl had a plangent and melancholy voice ... like a purling rivulet trickling across a dungheap. How touching it was ... I approached the little girl to speak to her. It was only then that I noticed her face. It was – how can I put it? – disfigured by fatigue. Her eyelids were black and swollen, so swollen that her right eyelid had burst open like an overripe fruit. A tiny hole had formed just below her eye, and drops of blood oozed from it when she attempted to speak. Her eyes! If only you could have seen her eyes ... as if they had been injected with blood! I went up to her parents, told them I was a doctor, and that their daughter needed care, they should allow me to examine her. They told me she hadn't slept for seventeen nights. She was not in pain, nor was she suffering, she assured me – it was only that she couldn't sleep. I insisted. I wouldn't ask them a single penny, I promised them. 'All you have to do,' I told them, 'is wait for me here while I get my doctor's bag at the inn where I'm lodging. It's quite close by.' They thanked me and said they would not budge. But when I returned, they had disappeared. I asked the people tending the nearby stalls what direction the couple and their children had taken, but nobody seemed to have the faintest idea what I was talking about. 'But of course you do!' I told them. 'The man and woman who were here less than a half-hour ago! Their children were playing in the manure by the roadside ...' Nothing. Disappointed, I returned to the centre of the village, to the main square. For the rest of the day I looked for them, up and down, in vain. Come sunset I returned to the inn and jotted down on a scrap of paper the few verses of the little girl's song that I remembered, the ones that had been running through my mind all that afternoon."

Tero took another sip of wine and puffed on his pipe.

"I spent a few more days in Bull Creek," he continued, "where I was treated like a prince by Neminen the innkeeper, a vivacious and high-spirited woman. On the morning of the ninth day I packed my bags and set off toward Kajaani."

As he spoke, Tero's gaze flitted here and there, never coming to rest, as though letting his pupils follow the rhythm of a tiny flame dancing in his mind. Between sentences he would pause, sometimes at length, and it was then that, observing him closely, Zora noticed the young man's lips were moving ever so slightly.

"The little ditty ... haunted me. I forgot some passages, but the parts I did remember, I kept repeating. This was no ordinary reflex, you know, like playing a catchy tune in one's head over and over again, then forgetting it a few hours later. No ... I'd reached a much higher degree of obsession. It was as if I'd fallen under a spell."

Then Zora began to hum the ditty Tero had just sung for them. On her face was that expression of curiosity mingled with hesitation that you often see on people who are sampling a dish for the first time. She wanted to see if the magic would work for her. Tero interrupted by tapping her on the wrist.

"Don't waste your time, it won't be the same for you. You'll understand why later. In any event, a few days after my departure, I reached a tiny hamlet at the foot of a mountain. Not more than fifteen families lived there. I was making my way through the hamlet on horseback when I encountered three children playing beside a stream. I listened carefully – and all but fell off my horse. Two of the children were singing the same tune that had been running through my head for the past ten days! This time, I decided to take no chances. I stopped, pulled out my notebooks and my pen, and asked the children to sing me the song again so I could write it down. But when, at the end, I asked them where they learned it, they looked at me in fear and took off running. In the days that followed I continued my journey, up hill and down dale, and on at least three other occasions I encountered children singing that very same song. I found the words to be very mysterious. To begin with, as a poem it's rather morbid. Not a single one of the children I met could recite the last two lines of the last verse. The ending was missing. But was there really an ending? How strange it would be if in this world there existed a song that left us hanging like that. Who wrote it? If we accept that the missing part really exists, what does the portion I possess represent? Half the song? Less? A quarter? A third perhaps? Maybe it was the prologue to a much longer song, maybe even an entire tale? I showed the text to the bards and minstrels I met to see if they recognized it. Each time they shrugged their shoulders and shook their heads. To this day I have not encountered a single adult familiar with the song."

Tero put his goblet on the table and went on with his story, gesticulating like a professor in front of his class. Zora noted he had single-handedly drunk an entire bottle.

"And yet," he continued, "my fascination with that song would not go away. Quite the contrary. As you know, I travel alone. When I am on the road, I seldom have the opportunity to speak with people. But I had that song, burrowing into my head like a worm ... Finally, there came a point when it was all I could think about. At first, it was far from unpleasant to spend my days with the song lodged between my ears. At night, before turning in, I would recite the words without the melody. I found them so pleasing I would light the candle again and bring out the notebooks where I'd written them down for the sole pleasure of seeing them in front of me, on paper, as though they were at my mercy. I perused them with the same pleasure we experience when we look at a bird in a cage. Other times I did just the opposite. I would whistle the melody without thinking of the words. And when I did, the music seemed so moving that tears came to my eyes. Then, very quickly, I began to feel ill at ease, as if something were missing. Not knowing the end of the song began to make me suffer. Slowly but surely, the other songs and folktales I'd collected from the bards began to lose their interest for me. It was around that time that I began to have trouble sleeping."

From all appearances, Tero was about to begin a particularly painful part of his story. When he spoke the word *sleeping*, with a casual movement, he indicated the dark circles around his eyes.

"At first, I wasn't overly concerned. Just irritated to be having bad nights. But soon things went from bad to worse. My sleep time began to shrink. The most I could get was two hours. During the day fatigue dogged me, and around noon I would get headaches that lasted the rest of the day. I felt like I was on a raft paddling through a sea of tar."

Zora listened in silence to Tero's tale. The young physician was a fascinating blend of lost innocence and dark determination. She watched the deliberate movements of his pale hands as he spoke; they were like two doves sadly fluttering their wings, as if to provide rhythm for his tired voice.

"I reached Kajaani," Tero continued. "One evening after dinner – I had been there a little more than a week – I went out for a stroll. At the end of an alleyway I came out onto the square in front of the church. There, near a fountain, a crowd was watching a family of antipodists performing their tricks. A father and four children, the mother was passing the hat. The children were truly skillful. A little girl was balancing a large barrel in the air with her feet, and next to her, her little brother – he couldn't have been more than six – sent a café table high into the air on leg power alone, and caught it on the way down. The other two were boys who were a bit older. Alongside their father, they kept pieces of furniture and large balls aloft with their legs. I suppose they were good, but I couldn't say, as I know nothing of that particular practice. But what interested me was the little girl, not because of her skill, but her face. The three boys had reasonably happy expressions as they sent objects up into the air and caught them before they hit the ground. They looked not at all like the small slaves you occasionally see in public squares amusing the passersby. But unlike her brothers, the little girl seemed to be in pain. Her face was livid and tense. It was hard to look at. I thought to myself, 'Maybe she's had enough of this. When you're seven years old, you have other dreams, I imagine.' Her mother came up to me, hat outstretched, and as I was about to pull a few coins from my pocket, I heard the crowd cry out. The little girl had missed a movement and the big wooden barrel had dropped right onto her head. I rushed over to her, pushing people aside, telling them I was a doctor. She was unconscious. I feared that her skull was broken. Immediately I asked that she be carried to the dispensary where I worked; it was close by. The men around me devised an impromptu stretcher from tent stakes and clothing. They placed her on it and headed to the dispensary. She died on the way."

There was no wine left in the bottle, so Tero poured himself a glass of vodka. His head nodded from side to side in a slow, irregular motion.

"Over the following days, I had occasion to speak with the girl's parents. They told me that at the time of the accident, she hadn't slept for more than ten days. 'She was always singing a nursery rhyme, something about cats in a graveyard ...' The parents were worried, but the relationship they established between their daughter's insomnia and the song was exactly the opposite of what I concluded later: they believed the morbid fatigue from which the child was suffering caused her to hum the same tune, over and over, like some misadjusted cuckoo clock. The little girl was fixated on the song, but it could have been any song, they thought. As they went from town to town, performing along the way, they had visited herbalists, apothecaries, and patent medicine makers of all kinds, looking for someone who could help the little girl find sleep. Without success."

Tuomas put his hand on Tero's shoulder. The young doctor looked as though he would slump over onto the table.

"Shouldn't you get some sleep?" Tuomas asked. "We can continue our conversation tomorrow ..."

"Sleep? You jest. I will sleep no more tonight than I have for the previous nights. Sleep, you say? I'll go and stretch out in the tent, eyes half-closed as if I'd inhaled vapours, and so I will remain all night long. At dawn, if I'm lucky, I'll be able to grab one or two hours of light sleep, more like a catnap. I'll wake up with a migraine and nausea. Such have been my nights for the past eight months! This afternoon, in the cart, I don't know how long I drifted off, it must have amounted to four or five hours of sleep. The last time I slept so long, my friends, was well before last Christmas."

As if to shake himself from his stupor, Tero downed another shot of vodka and slammed his goblet on the table.

"As I was saying. The little girl's parents could not tell me where their daughter learned that song. I stayed on in Kajaani a few weeks longer. To the best of my knowledge, during my stay, two other children also died from lack of sleep. The daughter of a bicycle-made-for-three manufacturer whose shop was located right next to city hall passed away after forty sleepless days. She was ten years old. And then there was a little boy, the son of a garbageman, whose body was discovered on the church steps, his bones broken. Apparently he'd thrown himself from the steeple ... He was seven years old, and had not slept for seventy-two days, according to his father. In the dispensary where I worked, lack of sleep made me completely useless."

"You were with two other physicians, weren't you?" asked Zora. "They could have examined you."

"There was one physician in Kajaani at the time, a Dr. Laakso. I knew him vaguely from the early years of my studies at the university hospital in Helsinki. He is a very serious man, someone who is neither startled nor bothered by the bizarre happenings of this world. And he is, above all, an excellent physician. Like me, he works for the Company. He examined me thoroughly, asked me probing questions about my habits, my diet, and the like. He prescribed medication, with relatively gentle properties to begin with. Then, a few days later, when he saw I still could not sleep, he suggested stronger chemical compounds. But I declined."

"Why," asked Tuomas.

"Because ... how can I put it? It's difficult to explain, but from the very beginning I've had the feeling that sorcery is involved in this outbreak of insomnia. I'm not suffering from any of the fashionable psychosomatic problems they talk about so much these days. I am an extremely well-balanced person, though I may not look it right now, with these circles under my eyes and my bilious complexion, but nothing could be truer. Only sorcery could explain how a man like me suddenly finds himself unable to sleep. May I have a bit of tea?"

With his thoughts elsewhere, Tero pushed his goblet of vodka aside. Elijah picked it up, emptied its contents on the ground, rinsed it, and filled it with tea. Tero immediately took a sip.

"I couldn't work in the dispensary anymore, but it was impossible to continue my travels. I was in a weakened state, close to death. I stayed on in Kajaani. Every day, at midday, I would leave my room and go walking through the city streets. I watched the children, and listened to what they said. I looked at their faces: were they fresh and bright, or drawn by fatigue? Were they singing the little song that had driven me to madness? I questioned everyone. For the first few days, I discovered nothing. More often than not, when people saw me approaching, my cadaverous face frightened them. And even when someone agreed to hear me out, that person was unable to help. No one had heard about this tale of cats and graveyards. But finally, by dint of diligent searching, I finally found what I sought. On the fifth day after abandoning my work at the dispensary, I finally gleaned some interesting information. It happened in a tavern on the outskirts of Kajaani, in a tiny district bordering the potato fields that surrounded the town. Two elderly drinkers who were playing cards advised me to go see the owner of a brothel located not too far from town, in a forest to the west. The madam was a sorceress and a brothel keeper all in one. It sounds funny, but when you think about it, the two occupations suit each other. In any event, the old men assured me that the procuress had been a folk poet in her youth but, in old age, she had switched over to the cathouse trade. It paid more than telling tall tales to beggars, she reasoned."

"Asta Ruodemäki," said Elijah.

"That's it. Asta Ruodemäki. On that day I went to the dispensary, I was feeling too weak to venture into the forest straightaway. But on the following day, I took my horse and travelled into the woods. Dunnock Woods, they were called. A pretty name, is it not? But the forest itself was horrifying, dark, and suffocating. I quickly found the house of ill repute. It was only a few minutes' ride from the edge. The place was full of woodcutters, labourers, and ladies of easy virtue. Asta Ruodemäki was totally daft, and nasty to boot. She invited me to peruse the merchandise, as you can imagine. I explained to her that I hadn't come to sleep with her girls, and showed her the sheet of paper on which I'd written down the words to the little rhyme. She couldn't read, she told me. I don't know whether she was telling the truth or not, but in any event I recited the song to her. She listened carefully. Then, her behaviour became truly strange. She sang the song for me ten times, twenty times, scolding the clients and the prostitutes who came to talk to her. But in the end, she reached the same impasse I had. She, like me, could not remember the last two lines of the last verse. I was at my wits' end – all this way, only to leave empty-handed. I told her how disappointed I was. She burst out laughing and informed me loudly that if I wanted to learn the rest, I would have to travel to the Fredavian Forest and there seek out Gladd the Argus, the sole custodian of the secret of those magical and miscreant rhymes."

On hearing the name of Gladd the Argus, a silver lynx that was fishing for brown bullhead in the pond close to the house fled with a whimper.

"I tried to learn more from the brothel keeper about Gladd the Argus and the Fredavian Forest, since I'd never heard of one or the other. The old lady clammed up and refused to tell me anything whatsoever. I insisted. After so many weeks, this was the first time that a path seemed to be opening up before me. I was so tired, and about to lose my temper ... I threatened to slap her if she refused to provide me with more information. 'Just try and touch me, you little bed shitter!' she hissed, and beckoned to three husky loggers seated nearby. I left before they could bust me in the chops."

"At least you didn't make the trip for nothing," said Zora.

"Indeed. Once I returned to Kajaani, I spent the entire evening looking for the Fredavian Forest on the map. It was nowhere to be found. I hoped that people in Grigol might give me directions. The following day, right after breakfast, I departed Kajaani and headed southwest. It took me almost two weeks to reach Grigol. On my way, in cities and towns, I asked the people I encountered about the Fredavian Forest. They responded with a thousand terrifying tales, but I could see it was a subject that people enjoyed talking about. That particular forest clearly stimulated the imagination of everybody in the region. I heard unbelievable stories about tiny dwarfs with immense heads ... The inhabitants of the forest fed on raw meat, people said, they were half-man, half-beast ... But when I uttered the name Gladd the Argus, people would turn pale. Change the subject. Put on angry looks. When I finally understood that the name Gladd the Argus turned everyone I met against me, I stopped mentioning him. The day after I arrived in Grigol, I went into a small bakery for some bread, and the baker and his wife invited me to spend the evening with them. The two of them were avid readers, and lovingly maintained a library stocked with collections of Danish and Polish folktales. I spoke to them of my passion for the ancient lays of Karelia, which utterly fascinated them. They plied me with questions and asked to see my notebooks. We spent a charming evening together. At the end, emboldened by alcohol, I took a chance and spoke the name of Gladd the Argus. The atmosphere took a frigid turn, as always, but I insisted they tell me what they knew. The baker's wife – Päivi by name – finally admitted she knew little about the Black Bard – that was the expression she used, I recall, and it made my blood run cold. Then she told me about you."

Tero looked Elijah Saariaho in the eye. The mighty blacksmith seemed dejected.

"When I was a young man, I did everything to make a name for myself," said Elijah, shrugging his shoulders. "How it has all come back to haunt me!"

"The baker's wife assured me I would find no one else in Finland to tell me about Gladd the Argus, and even then, she was not certain you would agree to meet me, let alone discuss the subject. She did not even know if you were alive. All she could tell me was that you once lived in the Fredavian Forest. Doubting as I did that there were signposts pointing to the Fredavian Forest along the Grigol road, I asked her for directions. I departed Grigol the next day, early in the morning. As I crossed the Ritva Swamp, I thought it would be a good idea to leave the trail and cut through an opening that seemed secure, but I ended up trapped in the swamp. My horse drowned there. Night had fallen by the time I reached the outskirts of the Fredavian Forest. I entered it by a narrow pathway. There I was, walking beneath dense foliage that blocked out the moonlight, beginning to wonder if it was really a good idea to keep moving deeper and deeper into that strange grove. But my clothing was soaked and I could see no place where I could spend the night, so I kept to the trail for a good four or five hours, perhaps longer, I don't know. It was after midnight when I reached the Inn at the Sign of the Farting Bear."

For the benefit of Elijah, Tero summed up in a few sentences his adventures at the inn, and the manner in which our plucky Zora had rescued him from Mustard's axe, and brought him to her and Tuomas's home.

"There you have it," Tero said by way of conclusion. "I've been nattering on like an unwelcome guest for more than an hour. I pray you forgive me. I'm not in the habit of *telling tales,* and I do not do it well. I prefer people to tell me stories, but I never open my mouth because I lack the gift of concision, which you have just learned at your cost."

Tero leaned his elbows on the table, keeping his eyes on the smith.

"Your knowledge is great, Elijah Saariaho, and your name is known throughout Karelia. You could hand down to me a large number of ancient tales if you agreed. I will transcribe them in my book and make them known to people, and ensure the stories will never die. But above all else, I want to learn from you what it is about Gladd the Argus and that curious little song. Can you tell me why I have not been able to sleep for eight months? Does it have something to do with that nursery rhyme?"

"Of course!" exclaimed the smith. "How could you possibly think otherwise?"

"Do you know that song yourself?"

"No."

"Then what is going on?" snapped Tero. "It strikes you as normal that a nursery rhyme can keep a grown man from sleeping for weeks on end?"

Zora had kept quiet as Tero described his misadventures. But now she was losing patience as she watched the smith trying to wriggle out of the question. She pounded her hand on the table.

"This is madness, Elijah Saariaho! Tell us what you know about Gladd the Argus and his magic spells, and tell us now!"

Tuomas, a meditative look on his face, was the only one to remain calm. He knew Elijah, and knew he would say what he had to say at the speed it must be said. Finally, the mighty blacksmith drew a hand across his forehead and pushed aside the goblet of vodka that stood before him.

"Gladd the Argus..."

He turned the name over on his tongue as though he derived a curious pleasure from it.

"Gladd the Argus... no one knows when he was born. I was still a little boy, and already my parents, my grandparents, and my great-grandparents spoke of him as though he had always been there, like a mountain. He is a black bard, and there is none other in the entire land. I know that others exist in the world. Among the Swedes, most certainly. Or far off to the south, among the French... It is a tiny confraternity that has existed for millennia. And a terrible breed it is, my lad! If you must know only one thing, it is this: Gladd the Argus and the other specimens of his race know songs that can rot your gums and cause you to shit out your intestines. They know magic that can drive the sanest of men to cannibalism, murder, and rapine. They have transformed the noble art of storytellers and bards into its opposite. As for Gladd the Argus, he is the last in the lineage of miscreant bards that hark back to the depths of time. It is through him that two millennia of songs of the damned, evil spells, and poems of vengeance are perpetuated!"

The call of a croaking raven sliced through the night. Elijah shuddered. He glanced up at the sky, as though fearing the bird was spying on him. The bird's raucous croaking finally subsided in the distance. He gathered himself, and continued his account.

"The Fredavian Forest, how can I describe it? The entire forest is, in a sense, the natural cage of a large community of the damned. The fates of those miserable characters are captives within the forest perimeter, and by some curious spell, cannot escape. How beautifully does nature work sometimes! You might say that it has drawn into itself the meanest, the stupidest, and the most dangerous elements from the farthest reaches of our country, and left them there, forever stranded. So it is that these dregs of humanity reproduce and kill one another without their perfidy ever contaminating the rest of the land. Thus it has been for centuries, and thus it will remain until the sun drops from the heavens and falls upon our heads."

Elijah gulped the alcohol that remained in his goblet.

"But Gladd ... Gladd the Argus is not one of them. He *lives* among them, but he is not of them. He has a mountain of his own, Mount Bolochel. It suits him perfectly – from the heights of his hill of the damned he looks down upon the world, loathes it, and devises sordid plots against its inhabitants. There are a thousand rumours about him, and I could not hope to distinguish those that are true from those that are not, but one thing is certain: if even one-hundredth of everything said about him is to be accredited, we are most certainly dealing with the vilest personage that the lands of the north have known for these many centuries!"

"But that song," stammered Tero. "The song that keeps children from sleeping? What's the connection with Gladd the Argus?"

"What's the connection?" exclaimed the smith with a growl that combined laughter and despair. "What's the connection? Can't you see it, staring you in the face? Such is Gladd the Argus! He composes magic songs that he sows like seeds among the inhabitants of the forest, and they in turn spread them throughout the region, and those damned ditties lead to harvests of death and suffering. Listen to me ... I can still remember a little fable that circulated among the children of the region when I myself was still a child. The tale was about a cricket, a butterfly, and a swarm of dragonflies, something on that order. At first glance, it was an innocent children's tale. But there was something ... how can I put it, something in the spirit of the words, something hidden in the invisible connections of the fable, an undetectable dark magic that made children see things, and caused them to hang themselves from trees or leap from cliffs!"

"Yes, yes, I remember it well," Tuomas interrupted. "Over a single summer, there were more than a hundred child suicides in Karelia. It all stopped in September. I think the suicides ended when the little rhyme vanished with the last death."

"They say," Elijah continued, looking straight at Tero, "that Gladd the Argus has no heart, but only an enormous spleen that oozes viscous, black liquid, like oil, into his body. No one dares go near Mount Bolochel, and he rarely leaves his den, and never mingles with the other forest dwellers. The destiny of Gladd the Argus encounters no other."

"It will have to encounter mine," said Tero, "if he is indeed the one behind this song that keeps me awake. If he truly is the only one who can cure me of my affliction, I shall climb to the top of Mount Bolochel and demand a full account. And it would be of enormous help were you to accompany me, for it is said that you know many magical spells. If there is still someone able to stand up to Gladd the Argus, you are that person."

"Accompany you? Never! Take a look at yourself!" Elijah would hardly have been more revolted had he been asked to throw himself head first into a dry well. "You turn up here, bright eyed in your naïveté, thinking that everyone is going to lend you a helping hand in your fatal quest! I can't believe it! Truly, you haven't understood a thing! Gladd the Argus's path will never cross mine, young man, nor that of anyone of sound mind you might meet in these parts. Gladd the Argus lives alone on Mount Bolochel, but he is on close terms with people … how can I put it, people who live far, far away from our verdant Finland, some of whom are even more knowledgeable and powerful than he is. He's nothing to look at, in fact, he's something of a midget, but as you know, you can't judge a book by its cover! He'll rip off the top of your head with one incantation! It's pure madness to go looking for him. Do I know magical spells? Of course I do! All the bards in the region know two or three! We hum an old refrain and make sparks appear, or we melt down a penny or two! But with my three miserable little jingles high atop Mount Bolochel confronting the Black Bard, I'd look like a hedgehog attacking the tsar's army with a peashooter. I'm a blacksmith and a storyteller, my lad, not a sorcerer. Neither are you. Abandon this mad notion."

Tero turned to Tuomas. The elderly alchemist had listened to Elijah's words in silence, nodding his head from time to time to indicate agreement. When the blacksmith finished, Tuomas placed his hand on the young physician's wrist and squeezed it gently.

"He is right, Tero. Forget this plan of yours. There are, in the depths of the Fredavian Forest, secrets more blood-curdling than the human mind can bear."

The discussion was over. Tero said no more.

*
* *

When they had drunk all the vodka, they made ready to go off to bed. Tuomas vanished for a quarter of an hour, returning from the woods with curious-looking plants, some mushrooms, and beads of pine pitch. He boiled water in Elijah's hut and prepared a decoction that he urged Tero to drink. That night, the physician slept just over five hours.

In the depths of the night, while Tero and Tuomas were lost in deep sleep, Zora crept out of the tent they had pitched close to the cabin and walked down to the pond. There she found Elijah Saariaho, who had lighted a campfire behind a thicket of cattails. She sat down on a log beside the smith. And for the rest of the night, Elijah, the singer of magic songs and the teller of magic tales, taught her secret rhymes, profane chants powerful enough to lay waste to harvests and awaken volcanoes. And, as he had done at least a hundred times in the past, during Zora's clandestine visits to the Misty Woods, he taught the youthful sorceress the innermost secrets of the ancient language, the tongue spoken by the fathers of the fathers of the first Finns.

*
* *

Over breakfast they discussed Tero's sleep problem. The young man had tried several of the insomnia cures offered by the European pharmacopoeia. Not a single one had worked. No one was terribly surprised. If, as events appeared to indicate, Tero's insomnia was the diabolical doing of Gladd the Argus, the entire arsenal of modern chemistry would be of no avail. Nor could Tuomas do a thing. Alchemy takes as its subject the transformation of vulgar metals into gold, the quest for the elixir of longevity, the art of creating homunculi, and the resuscitation of the dead. Alchemists wasted not so much as a second of their time on the prosaic problems that afflict mere mortals, such as insomnia, carbuncles, or twisted testicles. The previous evening, before going off to bed, Tuomas had drawn on two or three elements of the science of herbs that he'd acquired in the course of his lengthy lifetime. But in the long run, much more would be necessary for Tero to enjoy normal sleep. Since it was clearly out of the question to confront Gladd the Argus to demand a counter-spell that would cure him, another solution had to be found. Tuomas had a suggestion.

"I have an apothecary friend in Lapinlahti. Believe me when I tell you he is a master in his field. People come from all over Finland to seek his advice and purchase his decoctions. His daughter works with him, keeping the books and doing the typing. She and Zora are close friends. We often visit them in the springtime, when the snow has melted. I will write to inform him that you will soon be calling. You must leave as soon as possible. In my opinion, if there exists in Finland someone who can suggest a sleep cure, he is that person."

The three travellers made ready to depart. At the moment of farewell, Elijah Saariaho came up to Tero and shook his hand.

"Keep up the good work, young man. Travel through the land and write down the old stories before time sweeps them away like dust in the wind. It is a great comfort, for an old blacksmith like me, to behold your efforts to safeguard the tales and poems of the ancient Finns. But do not go up against the dark powers that dwell high on Mount Bolochel. Finland has too great a need of young men like you for you to be bewitched by Gladd the Argus. You still have so much to do, so much to learn. How old are you, by the way?"

"Twenty-seven."

"Twenty-seven!"

Elijah placed his immense bear paws on Tero's shoulders and looked him straight in the eye. His words were full of warmth, but his tone was more that of injunction than pleasantry.

"At twenty-seven, you do what you must to stay alive. And not tug the tiger by the tail, as the Chinese say."

Tero lowered his head slightly, as if to say, "I have heard your message."

Then Elijah bowed low before Zora. Coming close, he whispered a few intimate words in her ear. The young woman was visibly moved, for the water of the heart flowed from her eyes. She embraced the mighty blacksmith and hugged him close.

"That will be enough, my friend Elijah," Tuomas said with a laugh. With those tree-trunk biceps of yours, you'll smother my sweetheart. It would be unfortunate if she could no longer make those jams of hers – tasty enough to dispatch a saint to hell!"

"We shall meet again, my friends," said Elijah. "We shall meet again, and that's a promise."

So it was that the three travellers, with heavy hearts, climbed into the cart. Tuomas took the reins and shouted, "Whoa!" Yatagan lurched forward, turning onto the trail that would lead Tero, Tuomas, and Zora back to the Plains of Archelle. The Korteniemis, sadness in their eyes, stopped waving to Elijah only when he had vanished from sight.

A number of hours later, when the cart came to a halt in front of the couple's home, the sun had almost entirely vanished below the horizon. After unloading their baggage, they dined on sliced sausage and buttered bread washed down with herbal tea. Tero shared his plans with his hosts.

"Never could I repay you for all you have done for me, Zora Korteniemi. You saved my life! And you, Tuomas! I thank my lucky stars for having placed a friend of such wisdom on my path. I will never forget your kindness, and hope to see you again as soon as possible. I shall call on your friend the apothecary in Lapinlahti, and spend a few days there. If I can sleep again, I shall write to the Lake Ladoga Company to ask for a new mission. But I will need a horse to make the trip."

"We shall drive you to Grigol," said Tuomas. "You can purchase a horse there. No hurry, though. Stay as long as you wish. Our home is your home, my friend."

"I am very touched, Tuomas. But how am I to rest if I cannot close my eyes for more than one or two hours a night? No, really, the faster I get to Lapinlahti, the better. With a bit of luck, your apothecary friend will stun me properly with one of his potions. If we could travel to Grigol tomorrow, I would be –"

To the surprise of the two men, Zora interrupted Tero.

"No, not tomorrow," she said. "It's not reasonable. We've travelled a considerable distance over the past two days. Take at least one more day to rest. Stay in bed until late tomorrow morning. If you can't sleep, at least remain in a prone position, as if you were sleeping. *Pretend* to sleep, attempt to relax. You haven't slept for several weeks? Will another day or two worsen your condition? Tomorrow afternoon, you'll take the air in the shade of the sunflowers, in the garden. I'll serve you orange juice, and you'll make small talk with my gossipy husband. I'll cook up a nice meal for the two of you. We'll drink the Alexandras that Tuomas will prepare as we gaze at the stars, seated around the campfire, then you'll look forward to another restful night. Which means that when you awake the day after tomorrow, you may be more rested, and better disposed to undertake the long journey to Lapinlahti."

Tuomas, who had become fond of Tero, found his wife's arguments eminently sensible. Tero himself admitted that after the events of recent days, a few more spent in the fresh air of the garden would do him a world of good. He agreed to delay his departure for the day after tomorrow.

*

* *

That night, Tero could sleep no more than an hour and a half. At five o'clock in the morning, discouraged, he got out of bed and went outside for a stroll in the fields. When he returned to the house around six-thirty, Zora was awake and preparing French toast. Tuomas got up a little later. They took breakfast in the kitchen garden, in the sunlight, between two rows of sunflowers. Following which Tero asked permission to browse through Tuomas's library. The two men finally withdrew for a good part of the day to the laboratory, where they discussed literature, medicine, and astronomy. At midday, Zora served them sandwiches and beer. Tero plied Tuomas with questions about his research and his experiments in alchemy. Each man discovered in the other a humble and curious interlocutor. The gentleman was surprised by Tero's great sensitivity; he would not have thought that a lad educated according to the immutable laws of the pure sciences could possess such a poetic soul. Tero, for his part, found Tuomas to be as fine as amber. The two men who entered into the laboratory around ten o'clock that morning hardly knew each other, and more than sixty years separated them. When they emerged from the tiny room late that afternoon, they were friends for life.

At dinnertime, Tero was the recipient of a fine gift. Zora had made good use of the afternoon to travel to a breeder in the Drunkard Hills and there purchased for him a powerful yet docile stallion.

The next morning, as Tero had not been able to sleep at all and felt as lively as a mollusc, Zora tried to persuade him to postpone his departure. Tero refused. He was eager to reach Lapinlahti and meet the apothecary Tuomas had spoken of. The glorious sunlight of that September morn wreathed his sleep-starved countenance with a blinding halo, and it was a curious sight indeed to see this tall, thin, despondent young man hunched like a spectre, standing there beneath the blue sky next to such a dashing steed.

"I have already thanked you a thousand times over," he told Zora. "Today, at the hour of parting, I repeat all I have said, my dear friend. Thank you for saving my life."

Despite his fatigue, a look of boundless gratitude suffused his handsome face.

Then, with a suddenness that caused Tero and Tuomas to start, Zora grasped Tero by the sleeve of his riding jacket and pulled him toward her! She brought her rosy face close to that of the young man.

"If I were you," she confided to Tero, "I would make for the southwest via the woodsmen's route rather than the main road. At the Pesonen family hamlet, which you should reach by late afternoon, spend the night at the Inn of the Wriggling Whitefish. Ask the inhabitants to direct you to the road that leads to the old abbey, to the east of the village. From there, take the road that heads westward, and follow it until you reach the Forest of the Three Wonders. There, the road becomes a narrow path that will take you through the forest to the outskirts of Lapinlahti. You will have a pleasant journey. The forest is safe and full of respectable inns that serve excellent local food. And you can drink your fill of excellent vegetable juices."

"Fine. I'll see –"

"No, for the love of God! Make for the Pesonen family hamlet this very day, and spend the night there. Trust me."

Tero and Tuomas pointed out to Zora that it would be faster and less dangerous to take the main road, but so vehemently did the young lady insist that Tero finally gave in. Then Tuomas gave Tero his final recommendations.

"You have my letter to my friend Tommi? Don't lose it! If you do, he may not believe that it is I who sent you. He can be narrow-minded at times."

As a parting gift, Tuomas handed his newfound friend a pouch full of the exceptional tobacco he had given him to smoke a few days before. The two men hugged each other, then Tero mounted his new horse and went off. The horse, so lively when Zora had led it to the house the preceding day, now moved sway-backed across the plain, as though it had assumed a portion of its rider's affliction.

CHAPTER
11

The First of Her Race

T ero rode across the Plains of Archelle for the entire afternoon.
His extreme fatigue inclined him to melancholy. The blue
sky and puffy clouds, instead of delighting him, cast him into
tearful nostalgia.

When he arrived at the Pesonen family hamlet, all that remained
of the solar disc was an orange swelling. The hamlet, which numbered perhaps a hundred dwellings, was charming and prosperous.
Doughty, good-natured peasants bade him welcome and directed
him to the Wriggling Whitefish. He easily located the inn, whose
main entrance opened onto a spacious dining room in which men
were eating and drinking in silence. At the back, a handful of card
players were chattering away while waiting for the musicians to
appear and the evening's customers to arrive. At the bar, a plump
lady innkeeper welcomed Tero with great courtesy. The young
man paid in advance for a night's lodging.

"Is there anything you'd like to eat?" the innkeeper asked.

"Well, I never ..."

"Not to boast, but our homemade stew is the best in the region.
And if you're tired, we can bring it to your room."

"If only you knew ... By all means!"

"We know how to look after our customers here. A fine pint of
beer – brewed on the premises – to go with the stew?"

By now the innkeeper was babbling away to the displeasure

of Tero, who was exhausted and longed only to be left alone. The chatterbox had been going at it for a good fifteen minutes when finally, and with all due regard for the niceties, the young man was able to extract himself from the conversation and retire to his room. A large bowl of ragout and a tankard of beer were waiting on a small table next to the bed. The stew had cooled, and the beer was potent and gave Tero a headache. He ate without relish. After finishing the beer, he forced himself to go for a walk in the village before bed.

The hamlet seemed quite different than it had a few hours earlier, in the afternoon sunlight. The houses were just as pretty, and the large fieldstones that formed the foundations and walls were smooth and glistening. But beneath the streetlights, Tero could now see the children's inexpressive, chalky faces. The little ones with strained features were often seated against the walls of the cottages, legs drawn up to their chests and arms folded around their knees. Others wandered aimlessly, like ghosts. The streets were alive with adults as well: farmers returning home after a day's work; portly matrons in twos and threes, carrying baskets of carrots and commenting noisily on this or that shocking piece of gossip; labourers, bricklayers, and notables out for a breath of fresh air before retiring for the night. No one seemed even remotely concerned by the hordes of emaciated and enfeebled children wandering the streets, dark circles under their eyes and backs bent from fatigue.

Discouraged, Tero made his way back to the inn. He lay down on his bed and attempted to read, but the fatigue-ravished faces of the village's children loomed before his eyes. It was not long before he threw his book to the floor with an angry sigh. For a long while he lay there, stretched out on his bed, staring at the ceiling and thinking dark thoughts.

A few weeks before, when the cat ditty first began to make it impossible for him to sleep, he discovered with astonishment that the disease from which he was suffering had seemingly spared all other adults. Try as he might, he could not find anyone else who displayed the same symptoms. Not only were the parents of the spellbound children totally impervious to the magic of the little nursery rhyme, more often than not they found it idiotic and devoid of interest. That was why he had not hesitated to share the song with Elijah, Tuomas, and Zora: it never occurred to him that it could spellbind the three adults. As far as he knew, Tuomas and Zora had slept like babes the following nights. And so the question arose with greater urgency: what had made him, Tero Sihvonen, twenty-seven years old, vulnerable to the spell of a nonsense rhyme against which everyone else seemed to be immune? He had discussed the problem with Elijah and Tuomas on the morning they left the Misty Woods. No one could provide him with a logical explanation.

Now, lying on his bed in this clean and charming little room, he tried once more to fathom the mystery. The noises of the inn had ceased. The Wriggling Whitefish was hardly a place for merry-making, and Tero felt relief. He needed silence.

A few hours later, Tero began to relax. Just as he was about to drop off into an unhoped-for sleep, an irritating noise made him jump. He sat bolt upright in his bed.

Someone was scratching at the window.

Tero was close to panic. Thieves? Cutthroats? Succubi?

Driven by that curious reflex that impels us to seek out the sources of our deepest fears, better to reveal their true dimensions, so true is it that the unknown has a far more powerful effect on our imagination than does reality, Tero leaped to his feet and rushed to the window! With any luck, he would come upon a large cat or a bird. But before he could cover the distance that separated the bed from the window, it opened with a *clack!* A large black figure bounded cat-like through the opening and threw itself on our poor insomniac.

"AHHH!"

Tero screamed as he fell to the floor. His assailant pounced on him, neutralized him, and covered his mouth with a gloved hand, pressing down hard. Tero was about to suffocate! He felt himself fainting, less due to lack of oxygen than to fright. Colours whirled around in his head ... His attacker leaned close to his head. The assailant ... well, I'll be damned ... he smelled of vanilla, the low-life! And his warm breath in Tero's ear ... and the muffled voice that whispered ...

"Calm down, for God's sake! It's me, Zora Korteniemi! You'll awaken the whole inn!"

The young woman straightened up. What a relief for Tero! And what a surprise as well!

"Zora Korteniemi? What are you doing here?"

"Get your things together. I am taking you to Gladd the Argus."

Zora was not smiling. On the contrary, her face was a disquieting blend of obstinacy and ferocity. Tero began to shake like a leaf in the wind. The tall slender girl stood up, took a step backwards, and inspected the room. She seemed to avoid Tero's gaze by design. Tero got to his feet in turn. He sat down on the edge of his bed; breathing deeply, he tried to recover his wits.

"But ... Elijah and Tuomas ... the other day, in the Misty Woods ..."

"I know what Elijah and Tuomas think. They tried to befuddle us with learned arguments about the Black Bard on his mountaintop. I don't claim that it's perfectly safe to visit him. But unlike Tuomas and Elijah, I have already ventured into Gladd the Argus's lair. That place ... I don't know how to explain it ... I must return there. That place is in debt to me. And to you as well. You have not had a proper night's sleep for months now, you have ashes under your eyes, and you can barely stand upright. Look at yourself, for God's sake! Your face would terrify a bear! You must find sleep, Tero, my friend. Come and reclaim it from Gladd the Argus. I shall help you."

"Have you been to Mount Bolochel?" Tero exclaimed.

"Yes. I will tell you everything on the way ... if I so choose. For the time being, we must hurry. The two of us will ride Yatagan. One of his paces is worth five of the nag's I gave you this morning."

Zora began striding through the room now, touching nothing but examining everything from every angle. She seemed to be taking inventory of the items Tero would need to pack before their departure, and was growing more agitated by the minute.

"But won't Tuomas come looking for you?"

"He won't. He's used to my nighttime outings. He'll think I've gone off to gallop around the outskirts of the Misty Woods. I often go there at night."

Zora's impatience was growing.

"Come on! Pack up everything!" she said, pointing with a sweep of her arm to Tero's personal effects on the night table. "But hurry, we don't have a minute to waste! If we leave now, we can reach the Fredavian Forest before dawn."

"You exaggerate! We are at least one day's journey from the forest!"

"Not with Yatagan."

Tero stood and looked at himself in the mirror. His eyelids were puffy, and his face drawn and discoloured. He had lost twenty-five kilos in eight months. "Enough!" he thought, clenching fists and teeth.

"Then let's be gone," he whispered.

*
* *

And so it came to pass that Tero Sihvonen ventured forth to rescue his sleep from the incantations of Gladd the Argus. It was a frigid autumn night. At first he hardly noticed the bitter cold. Zora held the reins and he, seated behind her, attempted to make sense of what was happening to him. "Indeed, I was surprised to see Zora slip into my room like a thief – who wouldn't have been?" he reflected. "And I am concerned by her obstinacy regarding Gladd the Argus. Could it be that she is mad? Could it be that she, in some fit of aberration, is leading both of us straight to our doom?" Then Tero, rejecting his first impression, tried to piece together all that the young woman had said and done over the past several days. He searched for a unifying thread, for an argument that would lend coherence to the diverse guises by which Zora appeared to him since he had first made her acquaintance. Only then was he forced to acknowledge how strange she seemed from the very first hour he had spent with her and Tuomas.

Once they had reached the Plains of Archelle, Zora spurred on Yatagan to maximum speed. Tero could not hold back a cry of surprise; the horse devoured the distance at supernatural speed! The cold brought tears to the corners of our young physician's eyes. Yatagan was an immense gelding, a mount that more resembled the steed of some god of war than the earthly creatures of the kind encountered on the high roads or working the fields. Zora, with her long legs, had no difficulty in sitting astride the animal's broad back. But Tero was having increasing trouble maintaining his balance. His hands that clutched the back of the saddle (he dared not take hold of Zora's hips or shoulders, and neither had she invited him to) were cramped and red.

Zora guided Yatagan through hidden vales, to bypass her house at the greatest possible distance.

Thus they travelled for two hours before the Fredavian Forest hove into sight. The moon was full and the night, clear. Tero saw the shadowy fringe of the woods emerge, a thin black ribbon slowly unfurling just above the horizon. He shivered.

*

* *

Rather than head directly into the forest, Tero and Zora held to the plain, skirting the edge for a good half-hour. In the spectral brilliance of the moonlight, Tero watched as the overpowering silhouette of Mount Bolochel swung into view. Mysteriously, though they swept through the darkness on their magical steed, the peak seemed to grow no nearer. Then, though Tero could not tell at what exact point, Zora cut suddenly to the left and dove into the dark woods. There was no trail. The horse and its two riders were swallowed up by the great spruce seemingly woven from immateriality. With astonishing grace and fluidity, Yatagan made his way through the narrow openings between the trees.

It was not long before they came onto a beaten path that followed a north-south axis. Zora, who apparently knew exactly where she was going, turned southward. Less than fifteen minutes later they halted in front of a large log cabin. A handwritten sign hanging from the door read The Amber Jowl. At the foot of the stairs that led to the entrance, an old donkey was sniffing at the ground with its muzzle. Zora dismounted and went slowly toward the animal, a look of surprise on her face.

"Well, I'll be! It's Ermentaire!"

Slowly, she stroked the donkey's coarse coat. The beast was covered with round scars, as though it had been burned in various places by the bowl of a burning pipe.

"I know this donkey," said Zora. "It belongs to Sagadat Leino and Jarkko Saarinen, two inverts who hung around my father's inn when I was a little girl. I wonder if..."

The young woman fell silent for a moment, pensive.

"Are you all right?" asked Tero.

"Yes. But I have a debt to settle with Sagadat Leino. Let me see if he's inside. Are you hungry? If you wait here quietly, I will bring you a bustard wing with green sauce that you can eat on the way."

"I prefer to go inside with you."

Zora clicked her tongue in irritation. She looked haughtily at the physician.

"If you insist," she said sharply. "But don't play the fool. Speak to no one and keep silent. You are a stranger in these woods."

They climbed the four steps that led to the threshold and went through the door. Inside, only one of the eight tables was occupied. Four muscular bearded men were playing dice. Behind a bar made of knotty pine, a surly type was wiping beer steins. Zora went up to him.

"Do you know Sagadat Leino and Jarkko Saarinen?"

The innkeeper looked Zora up and down quite impolitely for several moments too long.

"What are you doing here, my fine young dandies? Aren't you worried you'll dirty your shoes in my joint?"

"Sagadat Leino and Jarkko Saarinen?" Zora repeated, insistent.

"Looking for work, my pretty? There's no lack of men to satisfy around here. Brew is fine for an hour or two, but afterwards, they want something more, get it? You're big and strong. It's one hell of a pleasure to see a strapping girl who doesn't have ham hands like a peasant and skin cracked by the cold. I'll pay you plenty, if you –"

Zora shut the blabbermouth up by drawing two banknotes from her pocket and throwing them onto the bar. The innkeeper stared at the money as he continued to dry the steins.

"Who did you say you were looking for?"

"Sagadat Leino and Jarkko Saarinen."

"Jarkko who?"

"Jarkko Saa – You know, Little Lulu."

"Ah, Little Lulu ... he's over there." He motioned with his chin toward a door at the rear of the dining room. "On his knees, as usual. He'll siphon you off for two pennies. That's the kind of work he likes, the little creep. And me, I get half of the take, so ... you can ask him to shine up your button if that's what you're looking for, but you don't seem to be his type, if you see what I mean."

The barkeep burst into laughter, such violent laughter that he choked on his own spittle. After he'd spat up a gob to clear his throat, he continued.

"As for Sagadat Leino, he used to lick out the pots but I haven't seen hide nor hair of him for quite some time. I don't have the faintest idea what became of him. Neither does Little Lulu."

Zora turned to Tero and instructed him bluntly, "Wait here, or outside if you prefer."

She turned her back on him and strode to the back of the room. She did not notice that Tero was following her, despite her injunction. As she passed by their table, the card-playing lumberjacks whistled and burst out with catcalls.

Reaching the back of the room, Zora opened the door without knocking. There was revealed a tiny storeroom in which dust-covered plates, cups, and saucers were stacked on mouldering shelves. Jarkko Saarinen, ass bare, was in the process of being sucked off by a blond, smooth-faced woodcutter who couldn't have been more than sixteen. The lad was startled to see a tall blond girl in riding breeches standing in the doorway.

"Get out," hissed Zora, without so much as a glance at the young fellow, who rapidly pulled on his pants and rushed out, red as a tomato.

Jarkko Saarinen plopped down on the floor. How old he'd grown! How ugly! He still insisted on braiding his thinning grey hair into two ridiculous plaits. He wore a tattered old dress. His legs were covered with hair, scars, and burn marks. In his drunkenness he'd slobbered on his chest. His chapped lips were studded with dried yellow secretions. As he stepped into the little room, Tero was sickened by the pervasive, rancid stench of piss, alcohol, and vomit. It took him no more than a few seconds to grasp that the stink emanated from Jarkko himself.

Zora had dispatched his customer, but Jarkko did not seem to understand what was happening. He looked neither at Tero nor at Zora. Instead his vitreous eyes were focused on the stack of plates in front of him.

Tero found the poor man pitiable, and his heart constricted. How startled he was to see Zora knee the poor man violently in the face! Jarkko's head struck the floorboards with the thud of a battering ram breaking down a wooden door. The shock brought the transvestite to his senses. He scrambled to his feet, wiping the sleeve of his dress across his mouth, which drooled blood and saliva.

"So, Little Lulu! You're looking fine, I should say," Zora shot at Jarkko. "Does it pay, drinking straight from the bottle?"

"Oh, not at all! It's not for money, really, just for fun."

"For fun?"

Zora clicked her tongue and wagged her finger in Jarkko's face to indicate her disapproval.

"Jarkko, sweetie, you like playing the kazoo for a living, nothing to be ashamed of! But just look at me a second! Come on! Look at me! What a nasty face you're getting from this work of yours ... Look, your lips are cracked in ten places, and you've got a crust all around your mouth. You're a discredit to the profession, letting yourself go like that!"

Zora was admonishing him softly now, her tone like a mother tenderly scolding her children, but in her attitude and in her voice lay so much irony, so much contempt, and so much hatred that Tero, standing behind her, was paralyzed. Then Zora, unable to restrain herself any longer, slapped Jarkko so hard the poor devil spat out a tooth. Now he was bleeding profusely as Zora raised his chin with a gloved hand.

"Feeling better now? Stop looking at me with those eyes like a dog that's just shit on the floor. Tell me, Little Lulu... does my face remind you of anything?"

For the first time, Jarkko looked at Zora. He shook his head no.

"The Farting Bear? Seppo Petteri Lavanko? You'd pass the days at a table near the window with your little friend Sagadat Leino. You'd stuff down rabbit kidneys with mustard sauce, and guzzle gallons of patantine, wouldn't you?"

"Sagadat..."

"Yes, Sagadat, your husband. It's all coming back to you now? There was this little girl who went scurrying through the inn now and then, a skinny little girl with blond hair. Seppo's daughter. One time, when he was drunk, Sagadat crushed the little girl's hand with the heel of his boot. Remember that?"

Zora raised her leg and, slowly, drew the toe of her boot across Jarkko's face.

"The little girl was crawling on all fours under the tables, in between the customers' legs. It must have been, oh, midnight or one o'clock in the morning! The inn was filled to overflowing, and the poor little girl was trying to make her way through the drinkers' shins to her straw pallet in the kitchen. When she got to where Sagadat was sitting, she jostled his leg with her tiny behind, and that made Sagadat jump and spill a few drops of ale on his trousers. In a fit, he leaned over to see what was under the table. I'll give it to you straight, what was under the table: it was me. I was maybe five years old. So to give everybody a laugh, Sagadat

Leino, your pretty boy, your husband, crushed my hand with the heel of his boot. I screamed and everyone in the room burst out laughing when they saw me dash out from under the table with tears pouring from my eyes. You, Little Lulu, you were laughing so hard I'm surprised you didn't piss in that shitty dress of yours. Now do you remember?"

Jarkko Saarinen was drunk enough to have forgotten his mother's name. He looked as though he were trying to remember, then shrugged his shoulders as if to say no, and exhaled through closed lips, making a farting sound.

Tero could see the blow coming but could do nothing to stop it. Zora lifted her left knee, and with the heel of her boot she crushed Jarkko's hand as it lay spread on the floor. Then came the sound of cracking bones, and Jarkko let out a shriek. He thrust his hand into his armpit and rolled across the floor, whimpering.

Tero was speechless. So Zora Korteniemi was the daughter of that cheating, stinking innkeeper who had so shabbily treated him the night he was attacked? That educated young woman, who carried out experiments in alchemy in her husband's laboratory, who spoke French, played Chopin on the piano, and who was an accomplished horsewoman, had grown up among the drunkards of the Fredavian Forest? Had she not, before his very eyes, crushed under her heel the hand of a sodomite dressed as a woman in the china cupboard of a sordid country inn? It was too much for Tero; he took Zora by the elbow.

"Enough! Let us be gone."

Zora allowed herself to be led away. But before exiting the little room, she turned around and spat on Jarkko.

"Give my best to Sagadat," she hissed.

No sooner had she spoken those words than Jarkko Saarinen began to sob piteously. Zora stopped.

"What is it?"

"He'll never return, Sagadat. He's gone for good. Booooooohooo!"

Zora waved her hand dismissively in the transvestite's direction.

"Well," she muttered, "may he go to the Devil!"

She was about to step out of the china cupboard, following Tero, when Jarkko added, "Gladd the Argus ... it was him! He ate him! Ouugghh!"

And Jarkko collapsed to the floor, squealing. He began tearing his hair and beating his temple with his one remaining functional hairy fist.

Tero and Zora glanced at each other. They stepped back into the cupboard and closed the door behind them.

*

* *

Tero and Zora emerged from the Amber Jowl three-quarters of an hour later. Jarkko, after Zora promised not to bother him any further, had related to them the events of recent days, confused though they were.

It happened that Sagadat, a few weeks earlier, had travelled to Grigol to perform an abortion on a society matron who'd been knocked up by the neighbourhood rag picker. The aristocrat wanted to be rid of the fetus before her husband got wind of it. Having practised his art to the best of his ability and received the agreed-upon emolument, Sagadat left the fine lady's home without bidding goodbye and went off to a dive in the Aveline district where he regularly hung out. There he forked over all his money to the barwoman. In exchange, she let him enjoy himself with her two little boys for several hours.

Sagadat admitted to Jarkko later that after lavishing love and caresses on the barwoman's children, he'd spent a number of hours chewing the fat with them. One of the lads, he said, a nipper of seven called Markus, had sung him a curious little ditty about cats and graveyards. "Poor little puppy dog, he was wobbling on his feet he was so tired," Sagadat had told him. But when he got back home to the Fredavian Forest, Sagadat found himself spellbound by the same ditty. Rapidly, obsession turned to madness, then delirium. He couldn't sleep, and spent all his time humming the song, for he wanted to know how it ended. At the Amber Jowl, where he and

Jarkko had been working for several months (Sagadat washing dishes, Jarkko grazing the livestock), the two men learned from the mouth of a crayfish shucker from Pudasjärvi that, to get to the bottom of things, they would have to go see Gladd the Argus, and in that event it would be "better to slit your wrists yourself and go peacefully." Sagadat was terrified to learn that Gladd the Argus held the secret to the last verses of that troublesome tune.

In the days that followed, he twisted and turned in his bed, trying desperately to find sleep. Nothing worked. Day and night, he could not close his eyes. According to Jarkko, after two weeks without sleep, Sagadat was overwhelmed by a kind of fury. One evening, around the post-prandial hour, he grabbed a shovel and shouted that he was going to slay Gladd the Argus. He would kill anyone who stood in his way with blows from that same shovel, he threatened. Jarkko had not been at the inn at the time of Sagadat's outburst; he learned of it second-hand. At the time, Jarkko was in the woods gathering mushrooms with which he intended to make compresses to soothe the pustules that had formed around his mouth. Had he been on the premises, he surely would have stopped Sagadat, his little cutie-pie, from climbing the summit of Mount Bolochel. Getting mixed up with Gladd the Argus? Better think twice … Gladd the Argus, the child killer. Gladd the Argus, the hyper-alchemist. Gladd the Argus, the arch-magus – the Black Bard himself!

"No one comes back from Gladd the Argus," sobbed Jarkko, kneeling before Zora and Tero.

He was right. No one had ever returned. Jarkko knew he would never again see his lover alive.

Outside, as they were about to mount Yatagan and resume their journey, Zora looked long and hard at Tero, her eyes inquiring. "Ready to go on?" Tero nodded silently. "Yes. Ready."

So it was that they journeyed ever deeper into the forest. The trees, which grew much closer together than had been the case before they reached the Amber Jowl, hampered their progress. It was growing ever colder. Their night ride seemed endless. Tero had held on as long as he could, it was a matter of pride, but now, two hours after they left the inn, he had had enough. He was about to tap Zora on the shoulder and let her know how impossible his position was when Yatagan, of his own accord, came to an abrupt halt. The sound of horseshoes on the trail stopped. The silence that followed seemed so unreal that Tero feared for a moment that the thundering gait of the horse had deafened him. Zora dismounted and breathed on her hands to warm them.

"We are here," she said, looking at a point straight ahead. "This is Mount Bolochel."

Tero dismounted in turn. He could see nothing, so dark was the night. Slowly he stepped forward, breathing deeply. The blood began to flow again in his numb limbs, much to his great relief. He noticed that some fifteen metres ahead of them, the ground began sloping gently upward. The night was clear, but the foliage above their heads was so dense it was impossible to see what awaited them.

Then, suddenly, Tero noticed that he wasn't cold anymore! With good reason: here, at the foot of the mountain, the air was damp, heavy, and sickening. The young man made a face, leaned forward, and emptied his nostrils.

"What is it?" asked Zora.

"The stench! I don't feel very well."

"From here on, we walk," she said coldly. "We have a ways to go before we reach the summit. As for the smell, better get used to it. But most of all, be as quiet as a fox."

They set off slowly, making their way upward. Zora guided Yatagan by the bridle, and the gelding, though as heavy as an elephant, made less noise than Tero.

They had not been climbing for more than twenty minutes when Tero began to puff and wheeze like a pig. The slope was gentle, to be sure, but the air … there was something about the air … Tero felt he had suddenly been carried off to a hostile star, the composition of whose atmosphere was unlike that of the earth. The darkness, the shadows, the threatening silence … the mountain … It seemed to breathe, as if possessed of life and the will to terrify any innocent person foolish enough to challenge it. Tero could not speak. Gasping for breath, he walked on like an automaton, in lockstep with Zora.

For two hours, the two young people climbed. They had to stop frequently for Tero to urinate, catch his breath, and drink some water. The fellow was sweating like a pig; he had taken off his greatcoat and knotted it around his waist by the sleeves. He had removed his vest too, and tossed it into the underbrush. Only the shirt on his back was left, and it was soaked through.

As they neared the summit, the slope turned much steeper. Zora knew the crest could be reached on foot without resorting to risky rock-climbing manoeuvres. There was a trail, full of twists and turns, but it was well marked. After an anxious moment spent clambering up a series of precipitous, slippery rock ledges, Tero, Zora, and Yatagan emerged onto forested level ground. At one point the trail seemed to end, and the three travellers encountered a dense thicket. Zora, with a vigorous sweep of her arm, pushed the branches aside, and Tero got a glimpse of what lay before them. He cried out in surprise.

For the trail opened onto a rocky headland that formed a natural observation post from which they could see the entire western flank of the mountain and its environs. Just by lifting his head, he could see the summit, a bare crest that stretched for three or four kilometres. They were almost there. That much was clear.

Tero turned to the forest far below. The slope hid a good two-thirds of it, but the visible portion – a broad black swath extending from the base of the mountain, stretching some thirty kilometres northward, as far as the comforting roundness of the Drunkard Hills – formed a majestic canvas in the full moonlight. Far to the west, the forest faded on the Plains of Archelle. When he lifted his eyes to the sky, he had the dizzying feeling he could actually touch the heavenly vault. Zora turned to Tero.

"Look," she said, pointing to the western slope.

A row of great crystalline arches marched across the mountain-side, like the abandoned skeleton of some forgotten serpent god.

The first arches, smaller in size, were visible in a nest of green hills that thrust upward through the forest growth; these were the Pisan Hills. The higher the arches progressed up the slope, the taller they became, until they stood several metres high, halfway between the foot and the peak of Mount Bolochel. From there, they diminished in height before reaching the summit. From where they stood, Tero and Zora could not make out the last of the arches. It was a fairy-tale spectacle. The stars threw moving columns of white light on this strange construction, then spread through the immense crystalline structures as they swung graciously back and forth, like the multi-coloured gasses encountered in the retorts of metaphysicians. The arches seemed animated by supra-human life, that higher life that orders the movements of heavenly bodies and galaxies.

"Everybody in the forest talks about these arches," said Zora, "but no one has ever seen them. What I mean is ... do you see the first ones, lower down, the smallest ones? Come autumn, the men of the Fredavian Forest hunt duck in the hills. Not a single one of them has ever seen the slightest trace of a crystal structure. They can only be seen from here. Even more extraordinary, they exist only when observed from this place. Should you make your way down to the hills to reach their base, or attempt to reach the largest ones, you will find nothing. They say in bygone days, when Gladd the Argus selected Mount Bolochel as his place of residence, he enslaved the Fredavians who inhabited the forest and forced them to build these great vaults of light for the sole pleasure of his eyes. Then, once they'd been built, he cast a spell on them that made them invisible to the inhabitants of the forest."

The two young people were silent, in contemplation of the dizzying bridge of light that seemed to draw this mortal earth toward a secret and threatening realm. Finally, Zora reached out and took Yatagan's bridle. The clink of hard iron awakened Tero from his dream.

He begged his friend, "Just a few more minutes, Zora. It is all so beautiful ... Who knows if we will ever again have the opportunity to contemplate such a spectacle?"

The young woman granted him not a glance.

"Definitely not. Time is of the essence."

Anyone else would have been irritated by her reply. But Tero was not one of those impetuous young bloods quick to take offence at the irreverence of ladies. He gazed upon Zora, this mixture of snobbish society lady and Amazon, a subject of interest. Though it did pain him to desert the promontory and leave the arches and their light.

It took them another full hour to reach the summit. There, on high, the woods were thicker still and the odour, more revolting. Tero turned up the collar of his greatcoat to cover his nostrils. Zora marched before him like a soldier. If the stench disturbed her, she let none of it show.

The trail they were following finally opened onto a wide clearing. Up until then, they had been able to only glimpse the night sky, lighter blue swaths through the black foliage, but now it stood revealed. The moonlight presented Tero with the most horrifying spectacle he had ever beheld in his life.

"My God, what is this ..."

On the flatland stood a succession of icy menhirs, each enclosing a human limb. Tero felt moved to grasp Zora by the sleeve and compel her, by force if necessary, to turn back and abandon her senseless plan. But the young woman, insensitive to the display, continued on her way without stopping, and headed toward a round object in the centre of the clearing.

It was too much for Tero. Part of him wanted to flee in the face of this dreadful display of ice and meat, yet his legs answered a much darker, more sinister part of his soul. To his surprise, he found himself moving slowly across the clearing, and stopping in front of each block of ice set atop a pedestal of dead wood.

Without pausing to count, he estimated that the clearing contained at least twenty of these macabre sculptures. At first, the sight of torn flesh horrified him. But after a time, his mind seemed to turn numb. What the ice encased troubled him less than the ice itself, a bluish-white liquor, an accretion that distorted the image of the limb imprisoned within it. Fascinated despite his revulsion, Tero found something comforting in those blurred forms.

He shook off the subjugation of what lay before his eyes. "Zora!"

His voice was muffled by fear, and his friend did not hear him. He called her name again, once, twice. She continued to ignore him, and he set out begrudgingly after her. She was striding straight toward the centre of the clearing, indifferent to the blocks of ice.

As he drew nearer, Tero saw that the object in the centre – a vaguely spherical black mass – was moving. It shivered slowly toward the ground, rose, then sank once more, slowly, weakly, but with a steady rhythm. Tero drew closer. Beneath the sphere appeared a form: two tiny legs, arms as skinny as drinking straws at the end of which hands that could barely be distinguished held a small shovel ... Yes, the creature – for it appeared to be something living – was shovelling, and this produced the oscillation he had observed. Beside the dwarf lay a tiny cradle. He would have sworn it was an infant's cradle had it not been fashioned from a material of great brilliance that scintillated in the night. It appeared, in fact, to be made of gold.

Zora stopped three metres from the object. Tero came up beside her. Perhaps you can imagine the abomination he now cast his eyes on ...

An elf with a minuscule body but an enormous head, as large as an elephant's! The little stump of a being was wearing dark-blue trousers, a threadbare white shirt, and a red sailor's sweater. The clothing would have suited a child; below the collar, the troll had the build of a boy of three. But that head ... that gigantic head ...

Tero would have given anything to know how a neck no thicker than a chicken's could support such a huge head. He would have loved to know how long it took the gnome to shave that grey, spiky beard of his that must have been a good metre across, so broad were the cheeks it covered. He would have also loved to know how it was that he had never heard of this type of anomaly, why in none of the three hundred medical texts he had read, the "cup-and-ball syndrome" was ever mentioned.

As well, he wouldn't have minded knowing how a living being could survive without a skull, for this one's brain was completely exposed to the air.

Nausea overwhelmed the young man. He pressed the palm of his hands against the frozen grass, then brought them to his face and rubbed his cheeks and forehead. The surge of revulsion passed, he contrived not to vomit, but remained bent over, eyes trained on the ground, not daring to lift them. His mind was racing, words and images rushing through his head at a dizzying rate.

It was true: the creature's cranial cap was missing. It had a face, a beard, hair, but the top of his noggin had been skillfully sliced off, and it had been a fine job. The cut was perfect.

Suddenly Tero felt intensely cold. He crossed his arms over his chest and hunched his shoulders, then went to Zora, who seemed caught up in deep conversation with the gnome.

"It was bitter cold," she was saying. "I was just a little girl, five or six years old. You chased me with your hatchet, I think you wanted to chop my head off. I'd lost my little hare … As I was running from the small clearing, I found it sitting on a stump of scrub pine. Stuck in a block of ice, like the other animals there. He was dead, and for a long time I wondered how it was that he ended up like that, in ice, when only a few minutes before, he was bounding about. I wanted to free him, but you were coming at me, very fast …"

"I'd just as soon shit on that hare of yours! And on you too, you little slut!"

The gnome spat out the words in a bullying tone. He had a high falsetto voice and stared at Zora with an expression of indignation that might have been funny had it not been topped by a brain as desiccated as overbaked puff pastry.

Zora took a step toward the gnome, and it immediately froze. It stopped shovelling, thrust its shovel into the ground, and leaned on the handle. Its wide, dull-witted eyes turned toward her.

"I ran as fast as I could toward the woods," Zora continued. "I looked behind me before crossing the clearing to see how far behind you were. I saw you pass by the hare and strike the block of ice with your axe. The block split open. You decapitated the hare. Do you remember that? Do you remember?"

"What a *twerrible* thing," the gnome answered, displaying his speech defect.

"What?" said Zora, irritated.

"*Twuly twerrible!*"

Then the gnome returned to his shovelling, paying no heed to his two visitors. Just then Tero noticed that the creature, as if by some poetic magic, was shovelling not earth, but moonlight! With each movement of his spade, the tool sliced through the moonlight that illuminated the clearing and filled it with a powdery cloud made up of tiny whirlpools of light. Then, as it would have done with sand, the Fredavian dumped the light into the cradle, which was slowly filling up…

"*Twerrible…*" repeated the Fredavian. "Look at this moon-light, *dwipping* all over the forest, *wunning* all over the ground, I've got to pick it up. Our master, Gladd, he can't stand it, you see. So we gather it up on nights when the moon is full, we gather up the moonlight and dump it into the Vandal Swamp… What a job! Oof! I'm stiff as a board."

It was then that Zora erupted in fury, and so great was her cry of rage that Tero recoiled and nearly fell to the ground! She jumped on the Fredavian, and with a galactic drop kick, smashed it right in the face. The gnome, carried by the disproportionate mass of its head, flipped over, and its head rolled for a good three metres, carrying the tiny body along with it.

"DO YOU REMEMBER NOW, YOU LITTLE STINKPOT?"

Zora did not give her victim a chance to get up. She charged it instead. The evil leprechaun was lying on its back, which seemed to be the cause of immense distress, for its massive head was so heavy its minuscule body was unable, in one movement, to sit or stand upright.

Zora picked up the Fredavian's shovel and pressed its blade against the creature's throat. She hissed like a serpent.

"Gladd the Argus," she said. "His house … is it far from here?"

The Fredavian seemed to be mired in suffering. His face was tense and red and he emitted a curious moan – "Oyoyoyoyo" – not unlike the cry of some tropical fowl. She pressed the shovel blade into the crepe-like flesh of his neck.

"Gladd the Argus," said Zora, "lives here, farther down the road. What must we know before we appear before him? He knows many dangerous incantations. What does he do to strangers who disturb him in his dominion?"

"Zora …" said Tero in a low voice.

The young man was staring at the creature lying before him on the ground, its brain like an old, dried-out sponge exposed to the air. Having rolled on the ground, the organ was covered in spots with dry mud and pine needles. The Fredavian's expression was one of mindless stupor and physical pain. Tero Sihvonen, kind-hearted and also a physician, was overcome with pity.

That was not how Zora saw it. At the sight of the inelegant gnome writhing on the ground, no longer listening to her, she became seriously angered – she delivered a violent shovel blow to its brain! Tero felt he would faint; he collapsed to his knees. Once punctured, the brain rapidly deflated *pffffftttt!* and grey powder issued from the cranial cavity.

The gnome was dead.

Zora kicked the cradle in fury. It toppled over, and moonlight poured out in a swirling flood. The brilliant dust formed a great spiral around Zora. The ascension was as magnificent as it was short-lived. When all the brilliance had dispersed through the heavens, the clearing, so brightly illuminated when Tero and Zora had first set foot there a few moments before, was suddenly plunged into the same deep darkness as the rest of the forest.

All the time she had been in the eye of the hurricane, Zora maintained her sullen expression. But once the light dissipated, she grabbed Tero by the sleeve of his greatcoat and pulled him along on the run toward the opposite side of the clearing from which they had arrived. There, the path through the trees lay open. Zora forced him to run for a distance, as though fleeing something. After some twenty metres she stopped and whistled for Yatagan, who was still in the clearing. Then she gripped Tero's shirt with both hands and shook the young man vigorously.

"Don't you see?" she cried. "Don't you see who we are dealing with? Gladd the Argus is mad! All around him he has created a tiny, infernal world. He finds it beautiful, understand? Which we find disgusting, you and I, those perverse gnomes, those protruding brains, those … those disgusting people who live down below … Did you see the dead animals in the blocks of ice?"

"Dead animals?" muttered Tero, in surprise. "Just a minute, those weren't animals, they were –"

"For him, it's a museum, don't you see? We can't allow this degenerate to go on any longer!"

Zora's eyes gleamed like burning coals. For the first time since the beginning of their night ride, Tero was convinced she was not altogether sane.

She set off down the path, with Tero close behind. Tiny slivers of light pierced the darkness on the horizon. It was already dawn …

At the end of the trail, Tero and Zora emerged onto a broad and barren expanse. The irregular surface was made of rocky outcroppings here, and sparse yellowed grass there. They had well and truly reached the summit. This was where the long, bare crest of Mount Bolochel began, and they could easily trace its gentle curve. A good fifty metres in front of Tero and Zora stood a ghastly-looking, decrepit, mouldering shack. Its windows were covered over with boards. The place looked long abandoned. The planks were rotting and the entire structure exuded the pungent stench of humidity and plant life. A tall stone chimney protruded from the roof. The creamy sky now cast a feeble light on the environs.

Never in his life had Tero seen a landscape so bleak, so

desolate. Here, sadness was a ubiquitous substance that found its way through the pores of the skin, clogged the organs, and thickened the blood.

"O Gladd the Argus!" shouted Zora.

Tero halted two paces behind her. No answer. The little house was abandoned, and the earth around it littered with stumps, rusted tools, and piles of green, mossy planks. In the early morning silence, so far removed from the world of men, Tero felt a new wave of fright engulf him.

Zora took several steps toward the shack. She could go no farther, for Tero snatched her by the arm and implored her, "Enough, Zora, my friend! We will never leave here alive! This place is the vestibule of hell. Look around, everything stinks of death! We'll never escape from such a place! Come to your senses, Zora, make an effort with me to rescue what remains of our souls."

Tero clasped Zora's frigid white hand in his two fine warm hands, and the young woman looked at him, her eyes welling with tears. She murmured her distress, and her grief rent Tero's heart. She fell to her knees. Tero kneeled beside her, took her head in his hands, and drew her to his shoulder. Zora was crying now, her howling incoherent like an animal's pain, and in the end, it was the name of Gladd the Argus she was calling. From inside the shack, a window creaked open, and the shutters clattered ajar. The sun had finally risen, but Tero would have preferred darkness, for the light revealed to them a world of death and devastation.

"You have come to pick a fight with me, my little ones?"

Tero and Zora were a good thirty metres from the hut, but the voice seemed to come from the far distance. "As if," Tero thought, "it was under water." In his life, he had often experienced nightmares in which macabre individuals called out in voices muffled by the same acoustic effect. Tero Sihvonen, for whom the border between nightmare and reality had all but dissolved in that dawn of suffering, had reached the limits of what his reason could endure.

Zora rose to her feet. She clenched her fists as she stared at the window where the silhouette of Gladd the Argus appeared.

The shutters opened, revealing wooden latticework. Behind it the blurry shape of a tiny being, like a baby: Gladd the Argus.

"Zora, no! Let's run!" said Tero.

But Zora was striding toward the cabin, and the little creature at the window, seeing her draw near, snapped the shutters closed. A few seconds elapsed before the door of the shack opened and Gladd the Argus emerged to meet Zora Korteniemi.

He was a thousand years old but looked six. From head to toe he was clad in animal pelts smeared with dried blood and shit. The furs seethed with worms. He wore pelts on his head as well. Only his face was visible, the face of a child, riddled with pockmarks and gouged by two eyes as black as a raven's plumage. In his right hand he gripped a bone, a femur fifty centimetres long. He stopped at some distance from the two young people, then excoriated Zora, brandishing his bone.

"You can come to Gladd the Argus, my little sow, but you cannot leave."

This was not the voice of a child. It was a pinched, nasal voice; a rasping, bantering voice. The voice of the beggar who accosts passersby for small change in the streets of Espoo, the voice of the drunkard who importunes handsome ladies with coarse talk.

"We will soon be on our way," said Zora. "Don't you worry."

"Whatever has brought you here, my lovers?"

"The song of the cats and the graveyard."

Gladd the Argus burst into hearty, theatrical laughter, and Tero felt the earth shaking beneath his feet.

"Ha ha! Ho ho! Cats! Cats! Cats! *In the feline realm, every night is Sabbath. In the graveyard, O pussy, take my claws. Our one hundred and one friends slide from the grave. One hundred and one stars stab the dying day.* Ha ha! Ho ho!"

The Black Bard launched into a primitive dance. He hopped and skipped, arms akimbo, his child-demon's face turned toward the rising sun, a tiny shit-encrusted prophet issuing commands to the dying stars. Tero was paralyzed with fear, but Zora regained her composure and gazed scornfully at the childlike figure. When he had pirouetted a dozen times, howling the words of his poem, he stopped abruptly and sized up Zora from head to toe. The young woman spat on the ground.

"Oyoyoyoyoy," gurgled Gladd the Argus and raised his bone higher.

"A Fredavian bone," he said, as though the words were weighty with unspoken implications. "You think it might hurt if I stuck it up your –"

He did not have time to complete his sentence. Zora began to vociferate.

It was not common Finnish she spoke, the speech of her country. She was speaking the ancient tongue, the Finno-Ugric of ten thousand years before, spoken before the great dislocation. She spoke the very roots of the language, the speech of the first of her race. Tero stared in disbelief. He understood nothing of what she was declaiming, barely could he recognize a few words, rare expressions that had made their way across the ages. Was Zora possessed by the gods? Had she fallen under some mysterious spell? Yet her face was calm and resolute.

Gladd the Argus also knew the old tongue, and was not at all surprised to hear ancient words in the mouth of the young woman haranguing him. He understood she was challenging him to a duel of erudition, a contest of ancient knowledge. Hoarse laughter laid bare his mouth to reveal stubby, crooked teeth.

Of the exchange between Zora and Gladd the Argus, Tero understood nothing. As for us, we will limit ourselves to the bare essentials of what was said.

Fully respectful of the formalities, Zora stepped forward to challenge her adversary.

"Gladd the Argus, seed of the broken slats of a whorehouse bed, I shall make you swallow your haughty ways. When I have finished with you, you will be lying face down on my thighs, and I shall scrape your ass by main force, flay your buttocks with a spruce branch, ram your rotten teeth down your throat with a fieldstone,

262

and you will be only too happy to reveal the end of your cursed song, the one that bewitches children and keeps them from sleep. Prepare for a fight, you wretched clump of snot!"

Then it was Gladd the Argus's turn to step forward.

"So that's it, you she-camel! While I'm lying across your thighs, I shall take the opportunity to polish up your cunny. That will loosen you up."

Far from being offended by the dwarf's insolence, Zora was calmer now. She climbed onto a small rocky mound and launched the first assault.

All that was perceivable in this world, she declared, would cease to be so for all while she slept.

Gladd the Argus interrupted her, rudely at that, and asked her to leave while he excreted the remains of a quartermaster whose gallbladder and meaty thighs he had devoured the previous evening.

Zora Korteniemi then explained how the ancient alchemists, by replacing saltpetre with foot juice in the fabrication of gunpowder, could propel cannonballs as far as the gaseous stratosphere of Jupiter.

At the young virgin's words, Gladd the Argus's bile began to bubble.

He proclaimed that he knew the difference between the smile of a cow, a dog, and an artist of fellatio, and he mimicked the three kinds of smiles while dancing disjointedly like a puppet.

Zora experienced sudden pressure on her bladder. "Oof," she remarked.

She proclaimed to whomever would listen how a Christian could be transformed into a Chinaman by feeding him a stew made of chicken feet and moon sputum.

Gladd the Argus began to hurt below the belt. He feared a torsion of the testicles (who does not fear testicular torsion?), but the pain quickly subsided. To his great relief.

He went on to relate how, to tame their horses, women of the days of yore would fill their troughs with north wind and plunge their heads into them.

Struggling mightily, Zora rose from the ground, not unlike the yogis of India. It pleased her not at all! She closed her eyes, concentrated fully, and managed to return to earth.

Then she described how to cause a toboggan to fly, using American tobacco and a pinch of sulphur. Gladd the Argus burst into mirth.

He needed neither tobacco nor sulphur, he replied, nor did he need a toboggan to fly, and confessed to having, with his own hands, removed the crystalline buoys that formerly marked the navigable channels for flying toboggans and armies of dragonflies.

Zora felt her liver itch, and she began to wobble. Contrary to popular belief, she asserted, it was possible to *quantify* good intentions, and even extract them from the body of an individual and with them fill a wineskin or a tankard, but that a container filled with good intentions was slightly less weighty than the same container filled with goodwill.

On hearing those words, Gladd the Argus sunk into the earth up to his hips. "Whatthehellisthat?"

Legs trapped in black soil, he told the story of a woman of the Fredavian Forest who had borne ten and a half children and who, finding them too numerous, decided to eliminate the sixth one by cutting its throat.

So it was that both protagonists attempted to scuttle their adversary with obscure erudition, and the expostulation of one was like a battering ram on the soul of the other. The heavens thundered with the words of bygone ages. Tero understood nothing of the exchange and covered his ears with his hands, so deafening was the duel of incantations.

But the declaimers were rapidly becoming unsteady on the tenpins. Gladd the Argus had extracted himself from the hole into which Zora's last outburst had thrust him. As for the young woman, she was white as marble. Gladd the Argus knew well many ancient words, and Zora's legs pained her. She put up a brave front and resumed the assault.

She described in fine detail the discombobulation of the old clock on the Nurmes public square. The words *foliot, verge, ballast,* and *moment of inertia* rained down on Gladd the Argus's head like cudgel blows!

This time, the Black Bard's legs were quaking visibly. The child sorcerer lost his temper, and began to insult Zora.

"Gibberish! Nothing but gibberish! You can stuff your childish knowledge back in your pocket, you young bitch. I shall teach you what suffering is!"

Then Gladd the Argus related how the Princess of the Nematodes, daughter of King Ostrichchick V, born with only half a thorax, survived until age thirteen, suffering atrociously, the right half of her torso collapsed and flaccid, and forced to excrete through a golden tube implanted in her body, until her parents, moved by pity, had her decapitated.

This time, the bard's words cut Zora Korteniemi's legs down to size. The young woman fell to her knees. She had forced her knowledge too far, and was running short of tall tales to tell.

For better or for worse, she narrated how, in a pasture in far-off Lapland, reindeer grazed around a narrow staircase that linked the earth with the moon. When the sun expired on the horizon, the herdsmen would climb high beyond the clouds, where they would sing lullabies the wind carried to their wives and children who had stayed behind in the villages.

Gladd the Argus did not flinch.

He struck back with the tale of a Moorish king who soothed his toothaches by forcing children to roll in thorn bushes.

Zora asserted that a spirit level was more accurate if one placed a toenail in the bubble.

Gladd the Argus affirmed that, by some mysterious compensatory effect, the crucifixion of suckling infants helped ease the pain of a case of the clap from which he had been suffering for exactly 487 years.

Zora Korteniemi swore she had visited a valley in Egypt where, for millennia, glass-makers blended liquid glass in pots made of moonstone and shaped their pieces by recruiting the prettiest young girls of the village to puff into the glass-blowing tubes. Thus were created the finest works of glass ever shaped by human hand.

Gladd the Argus boasted of using the little finger of a virgin that had been stuffed as a message spike, and her shrewish index finger to seal his mail to the Ministry of Water and Forests of the Grand Duchy of Finland. He invited Zora into his house so she might see the two appendices for herself.

Zora Korteniemi paid his proposal no heed and confirmed that once she had met, on the shores of the Black Sea, a man who could swivel his head 360 degrees.

Gladd the Argus, once again, proved insensitive to her claims. He thrust one of his hands beneath the animal furs that covered his body and began to scratch his prick as groundhogs often do. Raising his eyes, he narrated the following anecdote.

"As recently as a hundred years ago, I had the brilliant idea of casting a spell on some twenty distaffs that my friends the Fredavians had given me. I artfully bewitched the sticks and ordered my elves to distribute them throughout the township. And what do you know? What a fine time we had for the months that followed! All the spinsters that used my distaffs became pregnant – and there was a fine package of pretty little virgins among them. An excellent scandal, let me assure you! But the funniest thing is that they all bore brats uglified by an aggravated case of pachydermia! Ah, what charming little monsters soon filled the orphanages and the charnel houses!"

Gladd the Argus spit out everything at once in the ancient tongue, and with the same assurance as if he had been speaking everyday Finnish. That was too much for Zora, who gave in. Exhausted, she lay upon the ground, unable to raise even a little finger. The Black Bard was still standing. The joust had shaken him, but he had remained erect and was now taunting the young woman.

"You did not recite your verses properly, you nasty gash! All over again, da capo!"

But Zora lay motionless. Then the arch-magus, the hyper-alchemist of Mount Bolochel, smiled.

"So! That's how it ends, eh?"

And he thrust his hand into the animal skin that covered his diminutive torso and pulled out a penknife.

"Look, you little snipe, at the thumb slot of my penknife ... I've broken my nails opening it so often that there's dried blood on it."

He slid the tip of his finger into the slot and unfolded the knife as he moved on Zora.

Tero gathered her up, wrapped his arms around her, and began dragging her toward the forest. But he hadn't gone more than three metres when she raised her head and uttered her last pronouncement, the spell that was her final hope.

It was the recipe for rib-breaker tripe she learned from her father when she was a little girl. Of all she had read in her life as a woman, of all the learned words and poems, the scientific knowledge and other practices with which she had cultivated her spirit, nothing remained. Where had it come, when all knowledge seemed lost, how could something as prosaic and disgusting as the recipe from her childhood have resurfaced in her memory? She recited it in the ancient Finno-Ugric language. If Tero understood nothing, Gladd the Argus had no difficulty grasping every nuance.

From the first words, he stopped short, perplexed. As the successive steps of the recipe resounded, he blanched white. His two arms hung limply at his sides; he was so short the point of the penknife he held in his left hand almost grazed the ground. The words of the recipe became harsher, the images more shocking, until –

Crack!

Gladd the Argus shook with the convulsions of a trout that has been cast into the bottom of a canoe.

Crack!

Another crack, like a breaking branch! Gladd writhed in agony. He dropped his knife and clutched his sides, hands crossed over his stomach, face crimson. Not surprisingly, two of his ribs had just cracked.

Zora recovered her aplomb. Her voice became more assured,

and she mustered enough strength to prop herself up on two elbows. Now the words poured from her mouth.

Crack!

Yet another snapped rib, on the left side this time. Gladd the Argus, for the first time, uttered a cry of pain. But his cry was not that of some infernal creature; he whimpered and bawled like a snot-nosed seven-year-old calling for his mama.

Soon the snapping of two more ribs was heard, a few seconds apart. Convulsions wracked Gladd's face, and Zora, who was struggling to her feet, spared no detail of the recipe, stretching out the spell for as long as possible. The cracks were coming thick and fast now, nearly one rib a sentence.

Gladd the Argus let out a last scream. He could endure no more. Dropping his weapons, he turned tail and dashed toward the door of his hut. But Zora continued declaiming her recipe. She had enough time to break three more of his ribs before the dwarfish being could open the door and disappear inside.

Only then did she stop. She studied Gladd the Argus's lair. The once-fearful malefactor had lost the duel of declamation to which Zora Korteniemi had challenged him, and now he would have to pay the price.

Boom!

A deafening sound rent the morning stillness. The chimney of the hut spat a plume of black smoke like an explosion. High into the sky the smoke rose ... As they traced its ascension, Tero and Zora observed that an object had been ejected along with it. Tero watched the thing rise into the air, rapidly at first, then slowing as it gained altitude. There was something comical about the scene, the young man thought. Yet he was not laughing. The object began its descent. Though he did not know why, Tero was seized by an overpowering sense of panic.

"Oh, my God, no ..."

The inert mass crashed to earth with a hollow thud only a few metres from the house. Tero shook himself and rushed over to the morbid package the Black Bard had fired into the air.

Despite his fall of nearly two hundred metres, Sagadat Leino was still alive. His arms and legs and been sawed off, and the wounds crudely cauterized by direct flame. His skull had been opened, like the Fredavian they had encountered earlier. The insolent invert from the salad days at the Farting Bear was no more than a torso, bones shattered by the fall, topped with a feverish countenance beneath a denuded brain. Lying on the ground, he moaned as he stared at the sky.

Tero was filled with infinite pity for the fellow – whom, by the way, he was seeing for the first time – and he kneeled beside him. Blood was flowing from the seven orifices of Sagadat's face. The abortionist sucked in tiny gasps of air that he could not release. Nothing could be done for him. Tero smiled at him sadly, placed a hand on his forehead, and spoke to him in a soft voice.

"There, there … don't breathe so hard. Try to calm yourself. Let yourself go, don't resist. Let the bobbin unwind slowly, gently … Don't hold fast to the thread, you will only suffer more."

Standing behind him, Zora looked on in silence.

The dying man opened his eyes and looked at Tero. He tried to stir; he wanted to speak. His lips trembled, but made no sound. Tero leaned over, ear close to the doomed man's face. Sagadat moved his stumps, swallowed half a mouthful of air, and held it in his lungs a few seconds. His limbs relaxed ever so slightly. He started to speak again, and as he did, his chest gradually collapsed. His final words were lost in his death rattle, but Tero struggled to capture them. Memorize them, above all! Write them down, if necessary!

"Will you not stay with me? Now my heart is swept away, the cesspit of my heart; Charlotte has filled it with her black honeydew; how she terrifies me, the princess of the cats!"

When he had finished, Sagadat Leino, the last messenger of the great Black Bard, stared at Tero as he spat up scraps of blood-soaked lung tissue. His eyes stared wide and his face puffed up. Before dying he opened his mouth, as though someone had thrust an invisible branch into his trachea. Perhaps he was howling. Then his mouth snapped shut, his stupefied visage turned toward the piss-yellow sky.

Tero took his pulse, then closed his eyes with his thumb and index finger. For a moment he kneeled beside the expiring invert.

For the first time since she had come to know him, Zora found Tero handsome, handsome in a Christ-like way, magnified by the desolate open ground and the putrid sky above their heads.

Tero slipped his arms beneath the cadaver and raised it up. As he stepped past her, he cast Zora a vacant glance, then turned back down the trail by which they had come. Zora hesitated, looked back one last time at the little hut. Gladd was not dead – would he ever die? – he was tending to his wounds and sulking. There was nothing remarkable about his tiny dwelling. Someone even more powerful had built it expressly for Gladd; it was impregnable, and there was no point in trying to extract him from it. He would remain in hiding for a year, a decade, a century. One day, he would venture forth again to resume his troublemaking, and when that day came, someone other than Zora would have to force him to swallow his wickedness, for she would have been dead for many years. Gladd was eternal; she was not. She carried her death within her.

She set off down the path, following Tero.

*
* *

When Tero and Zora arrived at the Amber Jowl, it was almost midday. They had lashed the lifeless body of Sagadat Leino to Yatagan's flank. Over the four hours of the journey, the bindings loosened and the cadaver now dangled like a quarter of meat from the horse's flank. Tero went into the inn alone and found Jarkko Saarinen asleep under a table. Thugs had stolen his takings from the previous night as well as his dress, and the poor man wore nothing but a pair of long johns and a tattered undershirt. Tero splashed cold water on his face to revive him, and led him outside so he could kiss the cold cheeks of his lover.

Tero and Zora, numbed by the events of the night before, waited until Jarkko's lingering plaint finally faded. When his cry had been reduced to no more than a thin dribble of a voice, Tero went to the griever, placed his hand on his shoulder, and remained several minutes beside him. Then he asked Jarkko what he wished to do with the body of his friend. As Jarkko said nothing, Tero turned to Zora and asked if there were a graveyard somewhere in the Fredavian Forest. Each family buried its dead behind their dwelling, she replied. Between sobs, Jarkko finally declared he would look after the body himself. He picked up the corpse and dragged it into the inn, without so much as a fare-thee-well.

The sun was setting as the two young people came within view of the Korteniemi home. They had not slept for two days, and were so exhausted they cared little for what Tuomas might say when he saw them. The old man was sitting in the garden. He was smoking and drinking tea, and wore a serious expression. Yatagan halted in front of the house, and Tero and Zora, dirty and pallid, dismounted. Tuomas did not so much as glance at them. His head was half-bent over his chest, his gaze focused on the ground. Tero and Zora entered the house without a word. Zora went straight to her room; she would emerge eighteen hours later, after a dreamless sleep. Tero headed for the guest room. The comforter and sheets in which he had slept during his first days at the Korteniemi house had not been changed. He lay down without bothering to undress.

> In the feline realm, every night is Sabbath
> In the ancient graveyard, O pussy, take my claws

Tero knew that night he would sleep like a log. The last two verses of the ditty, which Zora had torn from Sagadat's mouth, unlocked the gates that had closed off the path to sleep. His mission was over.

> Cats above and cats below, and all had come for her

Now he could resume his life as before. He could continue to gather together the songs and tales of yore from the bards of

Karelia. When he thought about it, had not the whole affair turned out favourably? He had made two most excellent friends.

Black roses they cause to bloom, ravens they eviscerate

His eyelids were heavy as lead ... To sleep at last ... And that little song ... One last time before forgetting ...

Will you not stay with me?
Now my heart is swept away, the cesspit of my heart
Charlotte has filled it with her black honeydew
How she terrifies me, the princess of the cats!

*
* *

It was still dark when Tero awoke. He made his way downstairs on tiptoe. In the living room he glanced at the cuckoo clock hanging on the wall: twelve minutes past three ... His haversack was lying on the table. He picked it up and stepped outside.

There, millions of stars lit up the sky. Old Tuomas was leaning with his elbows on the fence that surrounded the kitchen garden. With one foot resting on a crossbeam, he was gazing at the heavens, seemingly more amenable than he had been the previous day.

To announce his presence, Tero closed the door with a gentle click. Tuomas did not budge an inch. When he came over to the elderly gentleman, Tero in like manner propped his elbows on the fence and lifted his head to admire the great dark void strewn with tiny flecks of flight.

"She would have caught up with you somewhere along the woodsmen's road," said Tuomas without turning his head toward Tero, "and would have obliged you –"

"I swear to you, Tuomas, it never once occurred to me she would have even dreamed of such folly. I would never have contemplated such a thing without having spoken to you first. She met up with me at the Pesonen family hamlet and exhorted me to follow her into the Fredavian Forest. I should have refused, I suppose."

"She would have gone without you, in any event."

"Yes, she would have gone without me."

The two men were silent for a lengthy interlude. Tero was the first to speak. His voice was soft, and his eyes were fixed on the edge of the Misty Woods, which emanated a magnificent, moss-green light.

"At the summit of Mount Bolochel, before we arrived at the abode of Gladd the Argus, we came to a clearing. Perhaps I should call it an open-air museum. Huge blocks were set here and there on top of stumps. In the darkness, I could not immediately see what they were. We moved forward a few steps, Zora ahead of me, with no hesitation. I took pains not to stray too far from her, so terrified was I … But I was curious as well. I had no idea what we had discovered. I went over to one of the blocks, and only when I had drawn close enough did I realize they were not stones that had been placed upright, but blocks of ice. Just then, the clouds parted and unveiled the moon, and the clearing was bathed in light. And I saw that those blocks … that in each one there was a limb … a human limb. Arms, torsos, legs … sometimes almost whole, or almost whole bodies, with horrified faces. The place was a charnel house of ice! But the most revolting thing was that a diseased mind had found in that exposition of ice and human remains something … something artistic! The spectacle itself was terrifying, and I will never forget it, never. But it is the very idea that there can exist in this world a spirit malignant enough to *imagine* such a place, to wish it, then to bring it about, that preys upon my mind!"

"Gladd the Argus!"

"Yes … As if all the cruelty in the world had found its expression through him. In that place, I had the impression that evil was a *force* in and of itself, and that deep down, Gladd was nothing but its incarnation, its instrument."

Tero paused. Earlier, when he awoke, he felt well rested. But now, the events of the past days had caught up with him. His brow

273

was burning hot and every muscle in his body was exhausted, parched, distended.

"In the middle of the clearing we found a frightening gnome, a kind of leprechaun with a huge head."

"A Fredavian," said Tuomas. "One of the evil angels of Gladd the Argus."

"So that was a Fredavian?"

Tero described the exchange between the Fredavian and Zora to Tuomas. But he chose not to relate how the powerful young woman had decapitated the creature and splattered its brains with a shovel, fearing it would be too painful for Tuomas to learn that his wife was capable of such unchained violence. He said only that the Fredavian, after having been scalped, had died in front of them.

"Zora then took me by the arm and guided me some distance from the clearing. She looked me straight in the eye and told me things that surprised me immensely. Ever since the beginning of our journey, in fact, since the moment she pulled me from my room at the Wriggling Whitefish, she had barely spoken to me. But suddenly, she was excited, I could tell from her voice. She spoke quickly, she was short of breath, and her cheeks were flushed. 'Did you see that? Did you see?' she said. 'All those animals imprisoned in blocks of ice ... Can't you see what sort of monster we're up against?' I asked her to repeat what she said, I thought I had not heard correctly. She was insistent. 'I came here when I was a little girl, I've seen it before. A monster is what Gladd the Argus is, a monster!' The more she spoke, the more animated she became ... She had really seen dead animals in blocks of ice. And I, I saw torn-off limbs, hands, arms, and eyes of human beings ... Which one of us was seeing things? Or in that place was there some kind of magic that made us see different things?"

From the pocket of his greatcoat, Tero pulled the pipe and the tobacco pouch that Tuomas had given him.

"No," he went on. "There was nothing magical about it. I would have preferred to be wrong, believe me. I would have preferred there to be nothing in those blocks of ice but dead game displayed for some morbid aesthete's pleasure. But I have full confidence in my five senses, Tuomas Juhani Korteniemi. There were well and truly pieces of human flesh in those blocks of ice."

The two men fell silent for several moments.

"I believe you, Tero Sihvonen."

And then, since he had developed a sincere affection for the fellow and come to trust him, Tuomas related the lengthy story of Zora's infancy and childhood to him. He described how he had come to marry her, and did not conceal that his relationship with Zora partook more of the bond that linked a father to his daughter than the one that binds lovers.

The two men talked on until the first cries of the ravens, proclaiming the arrival of the day. Tero turned to Tuomas Juhani Korteniemi and took his elbow in a gesture of brotherhood.

"Tuomas, my friend … I must go. I thank you for all you have done for me. Please bid Zora farewell for me."

Tero no longer had a horse, since he had left the one Tuomas and Zora had given him two days before at the Wriggling Whitefish. Tuomas suggested that he take Yatagan and return to the Pesonen family hamlet, where he could recover his mount. There, he could simply give Yatagan his freedom. The great black gelding would easily find his way back to the Plains of Archelle, for he was an animal unlike all others.

"Come back and pay us a visit, Tero, do come back," said Tuomas before letting the young physician go. "I have grown old, and I have few true friends. Zora and I have a great liking for you. Do not abandon an old man, and do me the honour of including me among your friends."

"I promise you, Tuomas Juhani Korteniemi."

"And write often, if you can!"

Tuomas went off to fetch Yatagan from the stable, then the two men embraced one last time. Tero climbed into the saddle and, after waving farewell to Tuomas, rode off to the southwest, into the dawning morn. Tuomas watched him go until he became a tiny dot on the far horizon. Then he sat down on a wicker chair in the garden and watched the sunrise, puffing on his pipe.

Zora awakened around midday. Contrary to her habits, she emerged from her bedroom in her peignoir, having neither washed nor prepared her face. She quickly made a cup of coffee – so quickly she splashed coffee everywhere – and stepped outside. She looked around, then spotted Tuomas sitting in his wicker chair.

Without turning toward her, Tuomas said, "Our friend left last night."

"Really? He left? Like that, without saying goodbye?"

Troubled, the young woman went back into the house. She sought refuge in the attic and spent the day knitting, sketching, and casting unclear looks through the skylight.

CHAPTER
12

The Entrails of the Monkey God

From mid-September, Tuomas and Zora spent three months in the capital, as they had every year since they wed. They first travelled to Grigol by horse cart and, from there, took the southbound train. The trip to Helsinki lasted a little over thirty hours, and for Tuomas and Zora, it was always a pleasure to journey through the southern reaches of the Duchy by train. The area was quickly becoming urbanized with the growth of the logging industry, which seemed more active to them with each passing year. After leaving the forests, the train made its way across the broad fields of the agricultural zone that surrounded the capital.

Until that year, their autumns in Helsinki had always been an inexhaustible source of enchantment for Zora. Tuomas's prestige among the capital's loftiest nobility never ceased to impress her. In these wealthy, precious, and rationalist circles where bluebloods rubbed shoulders with academics, scientists, industrialists, and prominent artists, how could an elderly alchemist who lived like a hermit in the uninhabited wasteland of the north be welcomed with such high consideration? Wherever they went, Tuomas was treated with sincere affection; few other visitors to the capital could make such a claim. Zora observed how this or that pretentious parasite who, two minutes earlier, before a small group of fawning yes-men and lapdogs, would deprecate an illustrious absentee, would lose all trace of haughtiness in Tuomas's presence. Instead, he would let out a cry of delight – "Ah! Look! You are here? Yes, indeed, here you are! And in September, what's more, when last year we had to wait until October to clasp you to our bosom!" – and frenetically grasp the elderly gentleman's hand, or even be so familiar as to take him in his arms, better to inundate him with questions, trying to keep him at his side for as long as possible.

"Charisma such as yours truly makes a person giddy!" Zora would tease her husband. "Why, you could reconvert Rome to paganism!"

And so they would spend their evenings in the most *recherché* salons of Helsinki. Zora had a few friends, young women for the most part, but also some well-behaved and spirited young men whose company she had come to appreciate. She chatted and played cards with them while Tuomas discussed the question of *habeas corpus* with a British gentleman, tea with the Japanese ambassador, or misandry with a French dress designer.

But what Zora preferred most in the course of their travels were her husband's "clandestine" meetings, as she called them. For Tuomas, whose past work had gained him renown in the secret inner circle of European alchemists, met furtively with members of the chemistry department at the Imperial Alexander University, and with geologists, physicians, and biologists, all old friends of his. They provided him with mercury, with sulphur and cinnabar, with stibnite and galena, and with the other substances he needed to carry out his experiments. In return Tuomas would bring them living insects or specimens of parasites from the Plains of Archelle. From the botanists of his acquaintance, he purchased balms that Zora insisted on placing in her luggage and which, upon their return home, infused the young woman's clothing with invigorating fragrance.

But above all, truly above all, Zora loved to accompany Tuomas to the port. Each year, she would beg her husband to allow her to join him. Tuomas was hard to convince for he feared for their safety: on the docks you could well encounter gallows birds. There were hulking sailors with tattoos, hard liquor, and brawls. Tuomas was not a young man of twenty anymore (and even at twenty, he had been something of a weakling); how would he have found the strength to protect his wife? But Zora was tall and robust, and most of all, resourceful. Tuomas invariably ended up letting her join him.

On the docks, Tuomas met merchants from faraway lands. He purchased jaborandi leaves from Brazilian traders. Zora heard him lose his temper once in Chinese with a broker connected with the Qing court who sought an unreasonable price for three swallows' nests. She saw him kiss both cheeks of a hairy Iberian who had sold him some bismuth. On the quays, or in the greasy cafés where Tuomas conducted his business, outsized Russians, Swedes, Asians, and Saxons with oily moustaches drank alcohol, rolled dice, bemoaned their misfortune, and stared at Zora with their animal eyes. While Tuomas was bargaining, Zora drank bergamot tea and listened to the talk of the travellers. To make themselves understood, the traders (most of whom were meeting for the first time) would exchange a raft of hellos in a multitude of tongues until one or another of his interlocutors' faces would light up. "Yes! I know that language a little! Do you by any chance have what I need to caulk the keel of a small whaler?" "You there, do you know where I can find a deck entry plug?" "Yeah, you see that fat legless guy at the bar who sells cod line and prick bags? He sells plugs too." In this way merchants from India and America could strike a bargain in a rudimentary pidgin composed of five or six different tongues. At the bar, amid the smoke and shouting of drunken sailors, a Nippon and an African Bedouin could carry out their transactions in a mutually understood argot. The Babelian nature of their dealings brought a smile to Zora's face, not because she found it attractive – it was all, in truth, one deafening din – but because the thirst for money that drove this community of men from every possible place tore down the barriers of language.

When he had completed his negotiations and purchased all he had sought, Tuomas placed his orders for the following year, and then he and Zora left the port with rare and exotic substances and products in great quantities. Among his numerous acquisitions,

Tuomas always included a gift for Zora: a porcelain China plate decorated with pastoral scenes, a small bag of caramel candies from Nantes, a bouquet of evergreen candytuft, macadamia nuts ... Arms laden with gifts, Zora was as excited as a young girl. She grasped her husband's hand, covered his aging cheeks with kisses, and led him outside for a walk along the pier for a breath of sea air. She appreciated the spectacle of the mighty waves as they broke against the hulls of the great ships. She and Tuomas cast admiring glances at the proud and sharply attired barge men who, in their natty uniforms, strode briskly up and down the jetties. One year they took a short cruise in the harbour, but Zora suffered from seasickness and never set foot on a boat again. "I don't have my sea legs," she said with a smile. "I'm a girl of the plains." And Tuomas, without knowing why, was moved that she did not say "of the forest." Zora could not get enough of the life of the harbour. Her two eyes were hardly wide enough to take in its fallen and licentious creatures and its majestic seagoing cathedrals, the material expression of human genius that, curiously, was not to be found in a single one of the beings who frequented them. Zora felt as though she were strolling through an immense, strange, and forbidden zoo, and that brought her the most powerful of pleasures.

When she had had enough, when her feet began to ache from too much walking, she and Tuomas would sit on a bench, and she would lay her head on the old alchemist's shoulder. Indefatigable, he would go on pointing out ships or groups of seamen, and tell her funny or fantastic stories. Zora blessed her good fortune to have a husband who, to an already pleasing theme, never failed to add an extra touch of poetry. For Tuomas, Zora's happiness transformed their outings to the docks into moments of pure grace. The memory of those promenades would sustain him until the following year.

This year, for the first time in her life, Zora found their stay in Helsinki execrable. Her friends, whom she had not seen since her last trip, seemed crude and vulgar. Their hosts she found mortally boring. At whatever salon they were invited to, Zora took refuge in a corner, and did not budge until the evening was over. She ridiculed the perfumed coupon clippers who feigned delight at the hors d'oeuvres, heaped scorn on the pretentious tailcoats who disparaged those not present while stuffing their mouths with *babas au rhum*. Pompous erudites, the corners of their mouths flecked with foam, approached her to chat. Repulsive bluestockings, with their strange and secretive manners, likewise attempted to strike up conversations. Zora received them so frigidly that they scurried away in embarrassment, muttering goodbyes. Zora was introduced to a cortège of eccentrics of indeterminate provenance: princes from overseas, pashas, American businessmen, African kinglets, and, worst of all, Frenchmen insupportable in their prolixity and vanity. "My dear," they addressed her, "allow me to introduce you to Grigor Bristov, the young prodigy of the piano who has brought tears to Moscow's eyes!" "Ah, have you met the duchess of Balanite? Few are more … *Parisienne*. And comely as well!" "Here, young lady, is Monsieur Mustafa Egoyan, a pamphleteer from Constantinople. He may still be young, but keep your eyes on him: he will secularize Turkey!" "What an odd bunch," Zora thought as she suppressed a yawn. "But I couldn't give a plugged nickel!"

One evening, a light-haired fellow who had exchanged pleasantries with her over a glass of wine touched her elbow. She slapped him so hard that the other guests stopped talking and turned. A woman muttered, "What impudence!" Deeply embarrassed, Tuomas who, up until then had been engaged in an enjoyable discussion of Kabbalah interpretation with an Italian authoress, had no alternative but to return precipitously to his hotel with his young spouse of feline comportment.

During the trip, Zora spoke hardly at all. And when she opened her mouth, it was to utter caprices that threw Tuomas into consternation. It may well have been raining cats and dogs, but the young lady preferred to stroll along the pebbled shore and admire the venerable French three-master that had anchored in the port for a few days. And not infrequently, though the hour was late, she demanded to stop for a piece of cake in one of the chic cafés in front of which they had passed during their stroll earlier that day or, worse still, she insisted on exploring the poor districts of the city, as though some improbable poetry might conceivably be born of the marriage of poverty and night.

On the final day before their return home, at the Sewer Rats' Café, she was sipping insufficiently sweetened lemonade as Tuomas bargained with an Ethiopian sailor over the price of a sack of khat leaves. An aged beggar woman came over to the table to ask for two pennies, but Zora dismissed her with an irritated wave of her hand. Fifteen minutes later, four dark-skinned musicians clambered onto a makeshift stage and began to play exotic, entrancing music. Three dancing women undulated before them. The spectacle amused Zora no end, and at one point she got to her feet to smile at the dancers and execute a few dance steps. One of the dancers called out to her, "*¡Hola, guapa! ¿Te apetece venir a bailar une habañera?*" The show lasted twenty minutes, then the artists, who were about to leave for Germany, departed the café lest they miss their ship. Zora returned to her seat. Tuomas was still busy. This time, he was bargaining with a French merchant, in the language of Molière, over the price of a statuette representing a Spanish warrior. The discussion dragged on and on; the Frenchman appeared to have taken a liking to Tuomas, and was prolonging the negotiations for the simple pleasure of conversing with a gentleman for once. After a while, irked and impatient, Zora began drumming both feet on the cement floor so loudly that the proprietor came over to warn Tuomas to get his "cutie" out of the establishment, failing which he would "grate the little lady's butt with a surgeonfish." In the cab back to the hotel, to distract his wife whom he could tell was in a rage, Tuomas showed her a vial in which two tiny worms were crawling.

"Look!" he told her in a falsely upbeat tone. "Grain zabrus! I bought them for next to nothing from a French wine merchant."

Zora turned her head aside with a look of disgust.

"What hideous things! Put that back in your pocket. People are staring."

The sight of his young wife in such an insolent mood first saddened, then angered Tuomas. For several more minutes, the cab made its way along the quays. Head turned seaward, Zora watched the ships weigh anchor for faraway lands of which she no longer dreamed.

At long last they set out for home. On the train between Helsinki and Grigol, Zora grew irritated at Tuomas's continuous presence, and she burst out of their compartment to stride up and down the corridor. In the bar car, she spent an hour chatting with a young assistant conductor who could not believe his luck at such a happy encounter, though he was not amused to see the young woman detrain at Grigol without so much as a fare-thee-well.

Once they returned to the house on the Plains of Archelle, Zora developed new habits that Tuomas found displeasing. Instead of tending to her sewing in the living room on the ground floor, as she had been accustomed to doing, she withdrew to the attic that was illuminated only by the rays filtering obliquely through the skylights. She spent hours by the scratched window glass, sewing and drinking tea, but most of all staring outside, a vacant expression on her face. It soon became apparent that her affliction had affected her appetite: she was growing visibly thinner.

When she did venture downstairs for meals or to take a bit of sun, she stopped showering Tuomas with the charming chit-chat that once delighted him. Quite the opposite: should he, by some ill-considered pleasantry, attempt to make Zora laugh, his words would echo coldly in the vacant pupils of his beloved. This so disturbed him that he would be discountenanced for the remainder of the day, and would retire earlier than usual, often without drinking the glass of hot milk with honey that he had been taking every night for the past eighty years. He went off to sleep saying, "Everything will be better tomorrow. It will be a fine day, and the sun will disperse the clouds hanging over her heart." But things did not get better. In the morning, Zora treated him coldly, deepening Tuomas's despair.

Some days, though, she came down from the attic and offered Tuomas a small piece of passementerie, a hanky, or some knitted item she had made for him during those long hours in the attic.

One afternoon, she embroidered a pretty purple cushion for the large French armchair where Tuomas would sit and read in the evening. At dinnertime, when she emerged from her garret, she came slowly to her husband's side. He was reading in front of the fire. After serving him coffee and stoking the fire, she handed him the cushion with feigned indifference. Surprised, the old man studied the piece of handiwork for several seconds, then broke into sobs. A long, awkward silence ensued. Zora returned to her attic. Tuomas wept long afterwards. Later, when the evening was well advanced, he made a sandwich and ate it alone in the garden.

At the beginning of their union, Tuomas and Zora developed a capacity for dialogue and openness whose equal would have been difficult to find, even among the most forward-looking couples in the great cities of the south. What had happened so suddenly that after six years of happiness they were no longer able to speak to each other?

Zora rode off less frequently, but when she did she was absent for a longer period. Each time, Tuomas watched her apprehensively as she disappeared in the distance, and anxiously awaited her return. Every two or three days, Matias Nissien, a little boy from the plain whose parents raised cows, came by mule to deliver milk to Tuomas's house. On one occasion, when Zora had been gone with Yatagan for two whole days, the little boy came to pay his usual visit. As Tuomas handed him payment for the milk, the lad piped up.

"Mr. Tuomas, is it true your wife is in Crankbill?"

"In Crankbill?"

"Sure enough! My father was there yesterday to sell some extra milk at the fair, and he said he saw your wife on her horse. She was talking with some people, that's all I know. She was looking for someone, I think."

Once the lad had gone off, Tuomas stood several moments on the doorstep, the two full pots of milk at his feet.

That night he slept not at all, and sat in the armchair in front of the fireplace. Zora returned at dawn. She and Tuomas exchanged brief glances. Then she retired to her room, where she slept soundly for nearly fourteen hours.

Some days later, when Zora had once again gone off God-knows-where, Tuomas, in a depressed state, went up to the attic. He hoped to find a hint of the scent of vanilla that trailed behind his wife like the tail of a comet, and that he loved so well. He rummaged through her refuge and came upon, on a small table next to the skylight, a copy of Olli Koivisto's *Folktales*, which he had purchased for Zora two years before as a birthday gift. On another table in the middle of the room, he found an old sailor's sweater of his. So there it was, the holey old pullover! He had been looking for it for the past three weeks. Zora always insisted it was a horrible, scratchy, dull old garment, but she knew Tuomas was deeply attached to it, and she was mending it as a surprise.

Then Tuomas opened the doors of an old commode. Behind the dresses and the wimples that Zora no longer wore, on the rear shelves he came upon sheets and pillowcases carefully folded. Under the bedding, he was only half-surprised to discover a poorly drawn charcoal portrait of Tero Sihvonen. "How clumsily she draws, the dear little one," said Tuomas, drawing his fingers over the places that Zora had cross-hatched in an attempt to reproduce the dark circles under the physician's eyes. When Tuomas thought of his wife, he forbade himself the use of possessive pronouns. He never thought of "my little wife" or "my dear" or "my spouse," as though, deep inside, he had from the very beginning understood that the person who had joined with him in holy matrimony would never be his.

Tuomas lingered in front of the commode, confused. Then he replaced the portrait of Tero, made his way downstairs, took his frock coat and cane, and stepped out for a brisk walk.

It was autumn, his favourite season. The late afternoon was grey, and a light but invigorating wind was blowing across the plain. His whole life long, Tuomas loved wandering beneath the metallic October skies, when the air had a bite and he had to walk with his coat collar upturned. But on that afternoon, nature summoned morbid thoughts rather than pretty figures of speech. He tried to clear his mind. Five minutes later, he concluded that was a particularly foolish exercise. "Stop thinking ... Why should I do that?" For another five minutes he ruminated, then came to an abrupt halt and spoke in a loud voice.

"Devil take it! Could it be that I'm jealous?"

He resumed his walk, but at a slower pace.

At age eighty-nine (he looked no more than sixty), Tuomas, for the first time in his life, was afflicted by lovesickness. He loved Zora, that much was certain. The events from which their lives were woven had created between him and the young women bonds worth more than a world of pledges and promises. By saving Zora's life and her honour with their chaste marriage, Tuomas had sacrificed the peace and quiet of his last years, but how much had he gained in exchange! Her arrival in his life had happily given relief to his smooth and predictable existence. He had won the love of a young woman of uncommon intelligence, of playful and happy temperament. Zora herself could be good-hearted even though, as we have seen, she was quick to adopt a hostile demeanour in her relations with others. When, six years before, on the day following their marriage, Zora the beggar girl first crossed the threshold of the house on the Plains of Archelle, she was half-dead of soul. It would be too late, Tuomas feared, to teach her to read and write and give her a taste for the finer things. Over the first few days, he set out to fathom the conscience of his wife, hoping to find a spark of curiosity that he could fan into flames. He watched Zora explore the house, scrutinize the decoration and the books, and prowl through the laboratory with eyes at first fearful, then amused, then fascinated. It was then that he discerned in his young wife the beginnings of a process of imprinting through which her mind began to absorb the colours, the movements, and the concepts that would constitute the setting for the new theatre in which her life would be played out.

Six years had passed since their wedding day, six years during which the old gentleman, fully recognizant of the new happiness life had bestowed upon him in his final years, had slowly given himself over to deeper sentiments toward his spouse.

Tuomas returned to the house with a sigh.

In the ensuing weeks, the pendulum swings of his heart combined to cast him into a state close to madness. One moment, he luxuriated in the fullness of his fatherly affection for Zora, and the next, he experienced the furies of amorous passion, so jealous of Tero as to wish him dead. Often, on awakening, even before he had opened his eyes, dark thoughts filled his heart and his mind, thoughts that were to haunt him for the rest of the day.

But Tuomas was far too wise and too well balanced a man for such disarray to undermine his morale indefinitely. He was a reasonable man, and knew his days were numbered, and did not want to depart this life on a note of sadness. He cured his wounded heart, and after balancing the selfishness of his amorous feelings against Zora's happiness, he resolved to let the young woman be the mistress of her fate.

But it was one thing for Tuomas to bask in his own magnanimity, and something else entirely for him to inform Zora of his resolution. Tuomas was an elderly gentleman, open-minded and liberal, but still! Where was he to find the words to explain to her that he, her husband before God and man, would not object should she give her love to another?

*

* *

So it came to be that, for the first time in her life, Zora was in love.

To explain the origin of musical instruments, the Kyrgyz tell the following tale. One day, a monkey god was swinging from tree to tree. Losing his grip, he also lost his life by slicing open his belly on a green sapling, leaving his entrails stretched between two branches. Months later, a passing hunter was struck by the sound of the tissues vibrating in the wind. To reproduce the sound, he undertook to create an object to imitate the configuration that hung before him. Thus, say the Kyrgyz, the first lute came to be.

Love, we would venture, borrows liberally from the tale of the monkey god. Its victims feel as though they have been eviscerated. He who observes the victim's affliction from afar will often find echoes of great lyrical beauty. In any event, the ache of love is an ever-flowing source of music. We who tell the tale could not care less about Zora's lovesickness, as the hunter of the legend was saddened not a whit by the death of the monkey. What obsessed him was the music. First there is pain; only later, music. Two distinct qualities. Pain. Music. Each man has his own pain. Music is for everyone. And like the hunter, what matters to us (to tell the truth, what we deserve) is to be the sounding board that issues forth the music that resonates in Zora's heart. So let us lend an ear.

The suddenness of her feelings for Tero surprised Zora herself. Hoping to understand the events of her heart, over and over she played the film of her relation with the young physician, from the very first moment. That was what occupied her over those long days of solitude in the attic.

First there had been their dramatic meeting in the Fredavian Forest, the unexpected rescue that made Tero beholden to her. She and Tuomas had then come to know the intelligent, well-mannered fellow. Zora had immediately appreciated his reserved manner and humility that was sadly lacking among the wealthy townsfolk she encountered in the salons of Grigol and Helsinki. But Tero spoke little, was frequently lost in thought, rarely smiled, and Zora had first seen in his placid nature the signs of a certain ponderousness. To be sure, he was well intentioned and well educated. But he was also rather indolent and thick-headed. Of course she found him good-looking, but – heavens! – she knew far better-looking ones in Grigol.

Then came that day in the Misty Woods, and the night with Gladd the Argus. At the end of her duel with the arch-magus, Zora looked on as Tero consoled Sagadat Leino in his death. She also saw him give succour to Jarkko Saarinen who had lost his lover. The young doctor shared the hurt of that man in whom Zora saw nothing but a worthless, filthy, obtuse invert. Only then did she recognize in the eyes of the physician the compassion, empathy, and humanity that Tuomas had taught her to seek out and venerate in others. Despite the revulsion he must have felt for Jarkko, or perhaps, for that very reason, Tero Sihvonen's gesture shone in her eyes in all its goodness, and Zora felt herself being swept up in boundless love for him.

And now, Tero was gone. He had stolen away in the darkness, like a thief. He had not tried to see her a final time. Had he been angered by what he had seen of Zora, there on Mount Bolochel? Before their adventure on the mountain, Zora had shown so little interest in him. How bitterly did she regret it now! How she castigated herself for not realizing how good-hearted and worthy of love Tero truly was! And now, he was far away. He said he would return, but who could believe him? Zora had been so cold and indifferent during his stay that it would have been surprising for him to consider returning. Of course there was Tuomas, with whom he had established the bonds of friendship ... To see Tuomas once more, he might well keep his word. Were that to happen, were heaven to grant her that chance, Zora promised herself to show Tero the respect and esteem due someone with such lofty qualities of heart.

But for now, she was terribly alone in her attic on the Plains of Archelle. Her hours were filled with memories, remorse, and boredom. Most of all, her hours were filled with Tero's absence.

The long months passed in this manner. Every day, fresh memories of time spent with Tero came to Zora's memory. Of each such memory, she made a tiny pearl that she placed in her breast, in that breeding ground of love her heart had become. Against the flow of time, she experienced love for a young man for whom – how bitterly she blamed herself now! – she had not been able to measure her feelings when he had been near.

In the weeks that followed their adventure on Mount Bolochel and Tero's departure, Zora lost her appetite and began to waste away. One day, as she was doing her hair in front of the mirror in the attic, she found herself emaciated and ugly. An unaccustomed surge of coquetry swept over her, and she made up her mind to eat properly once again. To put colour back in her complexion, she forced herself to go out three or four times a day with Yatagan, even if only for a quarter of an hour. It was the depth of winter, and the intense cold restored the colour to her cheeks.

And at long last, as if to reward her for her fine resolutions, spring brought Tero back to her.

It was a mild afternoon in April. As she had done every day for the past several months, Zora had taken up position in the attic, seated in front of the skylight. It opened to the west, and Zora heard the sound of galloping hooves in the distance. Someone was approaching from the south. She slipped her shoulders through the opening to see who was coming. The visitor was still far off, but she recognized him immediately.

He was seated bolt upright on the young black stallion she had purchased for him. His greatcoat was covered with dust, and his fine black curls undulated in the wind. Zora found him even more handsome than she remembered.

Reality shifted beneath her feet. Tero's imminent presence, the certainty that soon he would enter the house in the flesh, absorbed everything that had seemed so true to Zora a few moments earlier. Like that cup of herbal tea ... The languor of the spring afternoon she had been observing, head resting pensively on one hand, a scant instant before ... The click-clack coming from Tuomas's laboratory ("Just what kind of useless junk is he churning out today in that muddle of his?") ... The very idea of Tuomas, who spent his time running between two Bunsen burners, fiddling with vials of insect excrement – how could anyone possibly waste his time with such nonsense when, in this world, Tero existed? When, in this world, there existed the possibility, however remote, that Tero was coming to see you? Those were the tiny details that for nearly seven years had given shape and substance to Zora's daily routine, that lent order to her days, her every gesture, her movements, the very colours with which she had thoughtlessly wasted her youth – how well she understood! – all was now overthrown, uncreated by Tero's mere presence. Zora, who had always been less than half-aware of the people around her, glanced avidly at herself in the mirror on the closet door and rushed downstairs as though the attic was on fire. She did not even notice Tuomas, who was opening the door to his laboratory, intrigued by the sound of approaching hooves. She shot out of the house like a cannonball.

There was Tero, dismounting, smiling. Zora halted in front of him and made a half-curtsy. Great rosy blushes tinted the young woman's cheeks. In her joy she broke into giddy laughter that choked her, and she tried to stifle it so not to appear foolish in his eyes. The lad clasped her hands in his.

"Zora! My dear friend."

Tuomas came out of the house and gave Tero a heartfelt hug.

A pink complexion, a pleasant roundness of cheek and chin, his presence invigorated by sleep and the open air: the young man who had come galloping across the Plains of Archelle today was totally unlike the one of the previous year. To Tuomas, Tero looked a paragon of vitality; to Zora, he seemed slightly less handsome without the dark circles under his eyes, but no less desirable for that. The heavens had opened before her and revealed a thousand promises of happiness, and all the greater was her dissatisfaction when Tero announced he would be staying for only a few days.

"I was assigned to Kuhmo last Christmas. A month ago, I received a letter from my mother telling me my father had fallen ill. The company gave me a leave of absence and I returned to Parola. My father had a serious scare, but was on the mend. I was happy to see my folks. I hadn't been back home for more than a year. And now I'm heading north to take up my position again. Of course, I could not pass through the region without paying you a visit! Unfortunately, I can't stay for more than two or three days. In my absence, Dr. Pikkarinen, my supervisor, is alone in the dispensary at Kuhmo. An unjust state of affairs for him."

Zora's newfound happiness gave way to great distress. Two or three days? How was she to find the right moment in two or three days? How was she to find the words?

In late afternoon, before going down to dinner, Zora rinsed her mouth with vanilla-scented lemon juice. As they ate, Tero and Tuomas chattered like schoolboys. Zora was in no mood to talk. She was happy enough listening to Tero's fine voice, watching his hands slowly move through the air as he spoke, sitting close to him and smelling his sweet smell – "he has a faint scent of brown sugar," she thought. All she wanted was for the two men to ignore her so she could silently feast her eyes on Tero. But the young physician plied her with questions. How had she liked Helsinki this year? How was Yatagan doing? How had she spent the days since their last encounter?

When at last he turned his attention from her to enquire into Tuomas's alchemical experiments and recent reading, Zora rested her chin on her hand and, lost in contemplation of Tero, let her mind wander in sweet reverie. Even in the prosaic action of eating, Tero was a thing of beauty, a balanced composition in which the dark colours of his clothing were reflected in the subtle glow of his face. He wielded his utensils with deliberation, never a sudden movement, never a hint of excessive enthusiasm or irritation. And those fine, solid hands of his ... Zora could see the compact but powerful muscles that reached down to his fingertips as they rippled beneath his skin. By then, even had she wished to follow the discussion between the two men, she would have been unable to, so occupied was she with fanning her face with one hand and wiping her brow with the other.

At the end of the meal, having nibbled a piece of cake and taken tea, Zora felt a touch of weakness, and asked for permission to retire.

"That way, you will be able to pursue your discussions in peace," she said to the two men with a smile that convinced neither.

Concerned, Tuomas felt her forehead. He found her slightly feverish and enquired after her health.

"I am fine, my dear friend, do not be concerned. Merely the beginnings of a cold, it's nothing serious. Spring is here, you know ..."

Tero offered to examine her. "No!" she exclaimed before murmuring some excuses and going upstairs to her room, and to bed.

"Have I upset her?" Tero asked, turning to Tuomas.

"Come," said the elderly gentleman, taking him by the elbow. "Let us go for a walk."

*
* *

In the course of their stroll, Tuomas, who did not want to discuss the young woman's secret, did everything necessary to make sure the conversation never once turned to Zora. He spoke of alchemy, for he knew that each time he raised the subject of his experiments, he captured Tero Sihvonen's full attention.

When they returned to the house, Tero carried his rucksack up to the guest room, and then came back downstairs, carrying a package. Tuomas was awaiting him in his laboratory. Tero sat down, placed the package on a coffee table, and pushed it gently toward Tuomas.

"A little gift for you, Tuomas. The finest ambergris."

"Well, I'll be damned! How did you find it?"

"We should thank Dr. Pikkarinen. His daughter is married to a whaler from Kokkola. The couple comes to visit the doctor every spring and this year, at my request, the doctor wrote his son-in-law requesting that he bring some ambergris. I knew you had exhausted your supply and that you need it for your experiments."

Tuomas unwrapped the package; a pungent odour suffused the room.

"Well, look at that!" whispered Tuomas. "I haven't had a shred in more than a year. In our lands, ambergris is the alchemist's *rara avis*. During our annual autumn holidays in Helsinki, I always attempt to acquire some, but for the past three years its price has been exorbitant. I can never afford more than a tiny pouch. My reserves are exhausted in the blink of an eye, as you can imagine."

"How do you use ambergris?" asked Tero. "Some connection with your magnum opus?"

So saying, Tero pointed to a thick notebook open on the work table across from the armchair, between a penholder and a retort.

"That may well be!" answered Tuomas, rubbing his chin.

"Tuomas, what is so significant about this project that you have been working on for so many years that you will not even discuss it with me?"

Tuomas slapped his hands against his thighs to show his determination.

"I am preparing an elixir of longevity."

Tero said nothing, but nodded his head skeptically.

"It must seem curious to a physician, I wager?"

"How far have you progressed in your research?"

"I am almost there, young man, almost ... Have you any idea how long I have been working at it? For more than seventy years. Seventy years of continuous labours in this great book of spells. An interminable alchemical formula of more than eight hundred pages. I am almost there! Almost there!" Squinting, Tuomas held up his thumb and index finger, bringing the two so close together they almost touched. "Eight hundred pages of ingredients, steps and procedures, distillations and sublimations, of quintesseciations, cooking, even alcoholization ... How cautiously I must proceed! Validate and counter-validate the formula, avoid precipitation ... With absolute precision I have catalogued the 256 ingredients necessary to create my potion. It must contain ambergris, ambergris of the finest grade, as well as sulphur, mercury, and cinnabar ... It must contain stibium, galena, and nostoc ... hair and excrement of a virgin ... belladonna ... two or three rare specimens of legumes, plants that grow in those regions of the world where people live naked all day long ... Ah, yes! The pills of six virtues! They come from China, would you believe it? Shit! Where have my ... Ah! Here they are ... Dried *Zamia furfuracea* fronds. One is enough, two is too many."

Tuomas looked up. In the candlelight, Tero noticed the old gentleman was perspiring.

"Seventy years of work ... seventy years! Oh! Must not forget to number the pages of the last chapter!"

Unable to sit still, Tuomas got to his feet and lit his pipe, muttering to himself. In the kitchen the cuckoo clock sounded midnight.

"Mmmmmhh ... mhu ... mh? Oh ... Circulate ... must circulate ...

circulate the solution in a rain gutter ... Mnnn? Should I galvanize it before or after the summer solstice? Hmmm ... Ahh!"

The gentleman suddenly turned to Tero.

"What am I lacking?" Now Tuomas was speaking clearly, and addressed Tero, looking straight at him. "What could I possibly have forgotten?"

He went to the book of spells that lay open on the table and closed it carefully, stroking it with his hand.

"I am but a hair's breadth from success, Tero. A hair's breadth from saving my life – and yours – from the clutches of death. The only thing missing is ... the only thing still missing is a substance, a formula, a prayer, whatever it might be, the only thing missing is an ingredient, one single ingredient, and I cannot find it! I have accumulated 256 ingredients. All I need do is identify the 257th. And when I have identified it – for surely I will succeed, it is only a matter of time – I will cause gallon upon gallon of life-prolonging water to flow! I will make this precious knowledge universally known, and death will be forgotten!"

Tero wasn't laughing anymore. Distractedly, he drew his finger along the edge of the coffee table.

*
* *

Tero remained two days on the Plains of Archelle, two days that to Zora seemed like weeks. Yet for all that, she could not muster the courage to reveal to her friend the depth of her feelings toward him.

As he was about to leave, Tero grasped her hands in his and squeezed them.

"I hope to see you soon, my friend."

"Goodbye, Tero."

She searched the lad's grave countenance for some reflection of her own feelings, and found nothing that might give her reason to hope. Like the monkey of the legend, she felt as though a sharp branch had disembowelled her and that her entrails were twisting in the wind like a garland.

Tero and Tuomas shook hands and exchanged expressions of their emotions. When Tero and his mount were no more than a tiny dot on the distant horizon, Tuomas's face turned dark. He looked at Zora.

"He will return … He will return come autumn. He promised."

But Zora heard not a word he said. Her head, her body, her lungs, right down to the insides of her cheeks … her limbs and her organs were flooded with an acrid, stifling humour. She was drowning in an ocean of sorrow.

Without a word, she turned her back on Tuomas and went into the house. Slowly she made her way to the second floor, entered her room, lay down on her bed, and there she remained, too stunned even to cry. She felt as though her heart *vrrrrr!* was breaking apart, breaking apart like those islands near the poles that, so claim some explorers, are split by cyclopean earthquakes into two, then four, then broken down into a galaxy of tiny particles to be swallowed up by tsunamis and vanish forever. Such was Zora's heart: made fragile by a succession of telluric tremors, it now shattered and threatened to plummet to the girl's feet.

In the days that followed, Tuomas became so concerned by his wife's state that he decided to have a frank discussion with her about heartbreak. He could not bear seeing her face, at mealtimes, so drawn it reminded him of the collapsed features of a drunkard. Her eyes were puffy, and her cheeks and forehead red and coarse from constant wiping with a handkerchief. The liquor of her fine black eyes had turned into viscous sludge. For the first time, Tuomas was concerned for her physical health.

*

* *

One evening – eight days had passed since Tero's departure – Tuomas knocked on the door of her room to inform her that dinner was served. Inside, she muttered something he could not understand.

"Zora … I'm warning you, I'm coming in."

Tuomas opened the door. The drapes were drawn. Zora was lying on her wide Gustav III bed. She had brought the covers up to her nose and her back was turned.

"You must eat, dearie," he said. "Enough is enough."

"No ... not hungry ... got a cold," answered Zora, her voice muffled by the comforter.

Tuomas closed the door without another word. He had lost his appetite as well.

He forced himself to eat a bowl of vegetable soup, but every mouthful hit his stomach like a spoonful of mud. Suddenly beset by a migraine, he moistened a rag, slumped down in his chair, and placed the cloth on his burning forehead.

The cuckoo awakened him at midnight. Tuomas made his way upstairs to see whether Zora was sleeping. The door to her room yawned open; inside, the bed was empty, the covers cast aside.

Tuomas rushed down the stairs four steps at a time. Through lily-shaped apertures in the shutters he could hear his wife sobbing. He wanted to rush outside to comfort her, but as proof that in Tuomas's being the alchemist had overcome the man, his first reflex was to stop in his laboratory to pick up an empty flask. Then he stepped out into the garden to look for his wife.

When she awakened before midnight, Zora left the house, intending to go for a horseback ride. She found herself standing beside her immense steed, Yatagan, but lacked the strength to mount. Too high, too difficult ... Believing it was simply a case of fatigue, she decided to rest a few moments in the flower garden next to the vegetable patch. There she found the brown garden chair in which she loved to sit and sip lemonade during the warm summer days. She spent an hour studying the stars, and when she wanted something to occupy her hands, she went into the house to find her embroidery. She came back outside and embroidered for some time, distractedly, until her pain, which ebbed and flowed like the tide, once again flowed over her at midnight. Dejected, obsessed by Tero's face and hands, she began to weep, and cried so hard that spasms soon overcame her, and she fell to the ground. That was where Tuomas found her, kneeling on the moist earth of the garden, her hands, her nightgown, and her face crusted with mud.

Tuomas was so panic-stricken to see his beloved in such distress that he flung himself upon her and pressed her to his heart. From the depths of her pain, Zora embraced her old husband with all her strength. He rocked his wife gently, and the young woman, still a child, for the first time in her life feeling the pangs of unrequited love, wept copiously. Her face in Tuomas's arms, she understood that the old man knew, and understood, that there was no need to be ashamed or to explain anything to him, that he would support her where any other man might have become violent. She wept, but said nothing, for such things are not to be spoken, and Tuomas, comforted, his old, calloused hands in his wife's hair, also felt much relieved.

And while, out of pain and relief, Zora wept, Tuomas drew from his pocket the tiny flask he had taken from his laboratory and placed it delicately below the poor girl's eye, first the right eye, then the left, and so abundantly did her tears flow that the vial quickly filled to the brim. He then sealed the flask, held Zora's head close, kissed her on the forehead, and showed the vial to her.

"Come summer," he said, "we will water the azaleas around the house with these tears, and they will flower more abundantly and more colourfully than any flower in the world."

For the first time in months, Zora smiled, and it seemed to the elderly gentleman that he had spent his whole existence waiting for that smile, and that smile alone.

CHAPTER 13

A Pimp Never Forgives a Debt

Thirteen years had passed since Captain Gut's last visit to the Inn at the Sign of the Farting Bear. For the first ten of those years, the white slaver had embarked on lengthy business trips that had taken him to the farthest reaches of the empire, there where people's eyes turn to slits and their skins become brownish. In Manchuria, after a Mongol fondue prepared from a very mature joint of mutton, he all but succumbed to food poisoning. In Korea he fathered children with at least two women. One delivered a stillborn child, while the other gave birth to Siamese twins joined at the hip. The villagers, out of respect for an obscure superstition, abducted the infants, cooked them, and devoured them. None of this, in any event, did the Captain ever know. He had fled precipitously after planting his seed, and went off to make one of his fondest boyhood dreams come true: to piss in the cold waters of the Strait of Tartary, which he accomplished on the morning of June 17, 1904, in the small port city of Vanino. He remained for several months in Vanino, not that he liked the place, but his incessant travel and his excesses had rendered him penniless. The Russian Empire was at war with Japan, and for a man in good health and of fortitude, it was possible to earn a living honourably and patriotically. But contrary to his pretensions, turnip juice was what flowed in Captain Gut's veins, and he much preferred to pick on those weaker than himself. The whole idea of war displeased him. He offered his services to a gang of Russian smugglers who, despite the ban on such traffic, sailed between Sikhote-Alin and Hokkaido, selling tiger skins and the notorious bile of the black bear to the Japanese, for Asians attribute aphrodisiac qualities to it. For three years he travelled much but earned little, for his partners in crime were men of ravenous appetites, and left him only a few crumbs because he was a Finn. But it was better than getting ventilated by a Japanese sharpshooter in a Mukden suburb.

One evening he and his partners were enjoying themselves in a pricey Sapporo hotel when the Captain tipped over the expensive vase that was the centrepiece of the ballroom. The administration insisted he reimburse the cost of the damage, but the sum exceeded his ability to pay by a thousand times. He was thrown into prison. It was wartime and he was a subject of the great Russian Empire. The authorities were suspicious, and left him to moulder in the emperor's jails for the duration of hostilities, and long after.

So it was that on Zora's fifteenth birthday, when ownership of Seppo's daughter reverted to him under the terms of the pact he'd concluded with the innkeeper six years before, the Captain was still languishing in the Mutsuhito jail. When he was finally set free, after a lengthy incarceration, he was ruined. For a time, he considered staying on in Japan. "I am industrious," he told himself. "I should be able to make a living here." He survived on petty scams. One year later, he'd had enough of subsisting on raw fish and taking off his shoes every time he called on someone; he decided to return to his homeland.

A pimp never forgives a debt. The Captain had certainly not forgotten the one he could call in from Seppo Petteri Lavanko. He figured that, once he returned to Finland, he would re-establish his once-flourishing business, and that a good way to get started would be to go straight to Karelia, to that corpulent jerk of a tripe butcher, and claim his daughter.

In the end, things worked out much better than anticipated. On arrival in Helsinki, he took up with his former henchmen. Together they carried out a few quick and easy kidnappings, and it wasn't long before the arch-pimp had assembled a respectable herd of five females, four of whom were not at all ugly. But he had not forgotten Seppo's debt. On his way to Ostrobothnia, with his girls and his dogs, he did not fail to stop off at the Farting Bear. Seppo's daughter must be more than twenty by now. "Just as long as she's worth the trouble," reasoned the old mongrel.

Of a mid-September afternoon, Captain Gut swaggered into the Farting Bear. He looked around for Seppo. Three tables in the middle of the dining room were occupied by a troupe of travelling minstrels. Seppo, behind the bar, was bent over, filling glasses with vodka.

"You old groundhog!" shouted the Captain, bursting into guffaws. "With an ass like that, you should have croaked years ago! How come you're still here, serving up slop to these dim-wits?"

Seppo stood bolt upright and stared at the white slaver. To tell the truth, he turned pale so fast that one of the minstrels, worried, offered him a glass of white vinegar.

Meanwhile, the Captain laughed.

"Well, get a load of that! Now I've got you scared of me? Well, well, you're getting old, Seppo! All flabby and ugly! And what's left of your hair, it's grey! Even white in places!"

Seeing Seppo freeze, the Captain quickly understood that something was wrong. Instinctively, he brought his hand to his heavy belt.

"So, Seppo? How long has it been? Twelve, fifteen years since we last met? I've got plenty to tell you, lard-ass! But first, hustle into your kitchen and whip me up some fox-bladder cabbage rolls, and bring me a big bottle of cold vodka. But before I eat ... where is my little partridge, eh? You know, the little sausage end you promised me fifteen years ago? Because when you promise the Captain something, you big pile of manure, you know very well you can never un-promise, right?"

Since Seppo said nothing, Captain Gut turned to the travelling players who had already begun to soft-pedal their high-pitched peeping when they saw him come swaggering in. The white slaver approached the nearest of the minstrels, a scrawny young man with a beard, wearing a ridiculous scarf with a stem of pink cowherd stuck in his hair.

"Get out," the Captain ordered.

"What?"

"Out. Get out of here. All of you. I need the dining room to myself."

There was grumbling around the table, but they were artists, and semi-emaciated; they wouldn't dare take on the Captain. The bearded lad spoke with an effeminate voice, which contrasted with his beard.

"But, sir, we've already paid! We're just sitting here and –"

He didn't have time to finish his sentence. Faster than you could say "Jack Robinson," the Captain grabbed him by the ears, lifted him from his chair, and propelled him out the window.

Outside, the dogs began to bark. Within, the minstrel's pals got to their feet as one, picked up their haversacks, and rushed out without asking for their change.

The other customers, accustomed to incidents of this kind, took their time getting up, taking care to bring their bowls and plates to continue their meal outside. They streamed out single file, cursing under their breath, but taking care not to look the Captain in the eye.

Six years before, as we know, Seppo sold Zora to Tuomas Juhani Korteniemi. Years had gone by since the Captain's last visit to the inn, and Seppo had no way of knowing if he would ever reappear. But Seppo had been clever enough to use a portion of Zora's sale price to purchase a poor girl for next to nothing from a brothel in Grigol. Should the big shot turn up one fine day, he could always pass her off as Zora. But five years later, as he'd seen neither hide nor hair of his creditor, Seppo traded the poor youngster from Grigol to a pastry chef from Aveline in exchange for a huge chocolate cake in the shape of an octopus, and a balthazar of lemonade.

You can well imagine the fear that seized our poor innkeeper when he heard the voice of the white slaver call his name that fine mid-September afternoon.

"So, Seppo, that wench you promised me, how long ago was it? Half a century? Where is she, so I can give her rump a good working over?"

Seppo was obliged to confess that Zora was no longer his to give.

"She was kidnapped by a blueblood," he recounted. "An old dandy who lives somewhere up north, I don't know where. Tuomas Juhani Korteniemi, by name."

The Captain pulled his long fish-filleting knife from its sheath.

"You're talking shit, you eater of broken meats."

"Not at all! Not at all! Ask around, you'll see!"

Seppo begged his tormentor and offered to indemnify him richly. Unfortunately for him, in the underground industries that sustained men like the Captain, it was generally impossible to redeem with money the dishonour inflicted by the failure to back up one's word.

"What's the name of the guy you gave my girl to?"

"Tu ... Tu ... Tuomas Juhani Korteniemi!"

"So I'll have to claim what's mine by right from him."

"Oh! Definitely, commander! And don't hold back one bit, because the old magician is a schemer."

"What you're telling me is that you're totally useless to me now, is that it?"

"Me?" babbled Seppo. "What I mean is –"

The Captain's arm described a theatrical U, and the fish knife came to rest up to its hilt in the soft area just below Seppo's sternum. Then the white slaver pulled out the knife and wiped it on the innkeeper's apron.

Instinctively, Seppo brought his two hands to his chest. A large red stain had begun to spread across his filthy shirt and apron.

He turned tail and staggered, dying, toward the exit, hands pressed to his chest. Before pushing the door open he gasped, croaking, as if he wanted to say something, but all that issued from his mouth were small bubbles of blood. His mocking adversary called out after him.

"Hard to talk when your squawk box is sliced through, eh?"

With his shoulder, Seppo pushed open the door and went out. The Captain poured himself a tankard of ale and filled his pipe. He was in no great hurry, and sipped his beer slowly, and only then did he step outside to see what had become of Seppo.

The innkeeper laid there, face down on the ground, a few metres from the stairs that led to the main entrance, not far from the women and dogs. The prisoners looked on indifferently. The customers, who had stepped outside to wait in the hope of returning when things had calmed down, scattered like so many frightened rabbits when they saw Seppo stagger out, intestines dangling from his belly. Except for the chirping of birds, everything around the inn was totally silent.

The assailant walked up to his victim. With the tip of his boot, he rolled him over onto his back. Seppo was still breathing, though weakly.

In the knacker's shed behind the inn, the Captain found a machete with a dull blade and a large sharpening wheel. He rubbed the former against the latter, energetically, touching his index finger to the cutting edge to test for sharpness. When he emerged from the knacker's shed he was whistling.

He didn't bother killing Seppo before dismembering him, so that the innkeeper, who had spent his life disembowelling forest animals to sell their innards, was the dismayed spectator to a good part of his own butchering, which was – how could you not agree? – amusing enough when you thought about it.

*
* *

Thus did Seppo Petteri Lavanko die a cruel and violent death. The Captain threw the pieces of his body to his dogs, but the massive animals, though they had not eaten for a day and a half, would not touch the meat. The tripe butcher's head was set upright on the grass. His wide, dull-witted eyes stared in an amusing expression of open incomprehension. Then, most curiously, as the dogs were sniffing at the chunks of cadaver, and Captain Gut's back was turned, from the innkeeper's left ear issued a tiny man no taller than a tangerine! A homunculus. He wore red coveralls and had a long white beard.

"In by the right, out by the left!" said the tiny being in a shrill voice. Then he vanished into the woods without either the dogs or the Captain noticing his presence.

Angry because his dogs refused to eat Seppo, the big fiend unleashed an avalanche of blows upon them. When, out of breath and out of curses, he lay his stick down on the ground, he heard the sound of suspicious footfalls in the woods, just to the south of the inn. Someone hidden in the brush had observed the scene and was now making a run for it – surely to recount all he had seen! Furious, the Captain dove into the forest in pursuit of the mysterious witness. He quickly caught sight of a form some twenty metres ahead. A brief chase ensued, at the end of which Gut leaped upon the fugitive like a tiger, crushing the victim under his body and forcing him to turn over.

"Well, I'll be damned!" thought the Captain, and he laughed aloud.

He had pinned down a skinny individual of some thirty years old, with a perfectly round head and an empty stare. Around his lips were flaky yellow scabs.

"Ah, so it's you!" the Captain cried out. "You wouldn't be the little snot I gave the Captain in trade for his girl, would you? Now look at you, a fine imbecile! You had that pig's asshole look when you were a child too."

The Captain got to his feet and brushed the twigs from his pants. He ordered Mustard to stand as well.

"Can you talk, or not?"

Mustard answered with an ambiguous "huh," and nodded his head.

"Can you talk, or not?"

"Yes."

"Yes what?"

"Yes, I talk."

"Fine. Seppo's girl, the one he promised me in exchange for you, do you know where she is?"

Mustard shook his head no, but his eyes said yes. He was terrified, and the Captain immediately concluded he was lying. It was the second time that day that someone had tried to fool him. "Enough!" he thought. Furious, he delivered a sharp elbow to Mustard's temple. The lad dropped like a fallen tree.

*
* *

When Mustard came to, the Captain was brandishing his long filleting knife in front of his face. The miscreant began by chopping off small parts: first his nose, then his ears, then three centimetres of tongue and the fleshy part of his chin … Finally he lopped off a hand. Mustard lost consciousness again, but the Captain revived him with violent slaps and cold water, then cut off the first joint of his little finger on his remaining hand. But it was only when the Captain brought his knife blade just below Mustard's left eye that the hapless lad gave up and revealed the place where Zora and her husband lived. The Captain pried his eye out all the same and then, satiated, slammed him hard in the head and left him for dead in the underbrush. Mustard waited until the rattling of chains and the panting of dogs had vanished in the distance.

For hours he ran like a crazed animal. It had taken him some time to decide what route to follow to reach the Korteniemi household. It was a dilemma. On one hand, he had to reach the Plains of Archelle before the Captain; on the other, the shortest route was the one that the Captain and his cortège of women and dogs were travelling. Mustard could have set out after them and, once he drew within sight, tried to sneak past them in the woods. But it was a dangerous plan. Mustard would be bound to make noise, and the dogs would catch his scent for sure. So there was no choice. He would have to make a detour to avoid the bloody white slaver. The best thing was to take the southern route, follow the shady slope of Mount Bolochel, and then, at the western edge of the forest, head north under the cover of the trees.

Mustard ran on and on, moaning and weeping, for he knew he was all alone in the woods. He had little chance of arriving before the Captain, but he held fast to the hope that the corpulent fellow, who rarely visited the forest, might lose his way, or even decide to take a nap under a tree, and so be delayed.

He was squirting from ten wounds, and his shirt was stained with blood. Yet how curious it was! His concern over what the Captain might do to Zora so absorbed him that he felt pain only in brief, irritating pangs.

By the time he emerged from the forest, the sun had begun its long descent toward the western horizon. Exhausted now, Mustard could run for short stretches only. He ventured from the comforting safety of the woods to attack the open Plains of Archelle. As he loped across the wild grass, he considered what to do next. Mustard knew every stone on the bumpy plain that surrounded the Korteniemi residence. Thousands of times he had come to hide in the tall grass and spy on Zora, watching her live her life, without the young woman or her husband ever suspecting his presence. He had kept a safe distance, of course. Today he would have to be cautious. If he were to get there first, he would go directly to the house and alert Zora to the coming danger. But if Captain Gut had arrived first, it would be dangerous. The dogs could catch his scent from afar.

Desperate, he made up his mind to risk everything and approach the house in the open, but deliberately. He followed a broad circular path across the plain to avoid the direct route. The Captain might already be there.

When he drew near to the hedge that surrounded the Korteniemi house, it was dark, making it easier to see, from some distance, the flames devouring their home. In a panic, he dashed toward the blaze until he could make out dancing silhouettes.

Lying on his stomach he observed the scene, protected by the night. The house was an immense pyre. In the light of the flames he spotted Zora. She was wearing a heavy iron collar with a ring, and five other women were similarly shackled. Zora was passive, beaten down. She showed no resistance to the Captain, who was testing the strength of the links. "And the old fellow?" thought Mustard. "Zora's old husband, the man with the fine white hair? Where is he?"

Mustard lay hidden in the grass until the procession had gotten well underway. With slow steps, the captives and their master headed north. Mustard, feverish and weak, rolled onto his back. He stayed there for some time in the cool grass, gazing at the stars.

CHAPTER
14

Zora's Journey

When the Captain showed up to capture Zora in her little dwelling on the Plains of Archelle, Tuomas Juhani Korteniemi had been in Grigol for the past week. The old alchemist was attempting to lay his hands on Fredavian bone powder for his great experiment. To the best of his knowledge, there was only one place in the world where he could obtain such a substance: the Grigol Municipal Museum, where for the past half-century a Fredavian tibia and shoulder blade had been on display. It goes without saying that Tuomas himself, on several occasions during his lifetime, had encountered *living* Fredavians. Each time, the experience had been funereal, and his recollections haunted him to this day. But he would have dearly loved to have the body of a dead Fredavian in his laboratory to work with. No doubt he could find happy uses for all the creature's organs – the lungs for a new, experimental alkahest, the bile to distill a superhuman syrup, the intestines for a particularly efficacious paregoric elixir, the liver … the liver, with onions and raven bullion for a tasty repast; there was no lack of good ideas – but in this world, no one knew where Fredavians went to die.

The museum's curator, Toni Järvikivi, was an old friend of Tuomas. All his life he had followed the alchemist's work with interest. He was a paunchy, short-legged, good-natured man who had little love lost for his profession. Then again, the Grigol Museum was anything but interesting. The galleries were crammed with old prows of rotten boats, broken ceramic plates, and ugly still lifes that had accumulated a thick layer of dust. No one ever visited the place.

It was indeed the most boring museum one could possibly imagine, except for two things: the Fredavian tibia and the shoulder blade that graced a particularly elegant display case positioned along the southern wall of the gallery. The display itself lay atop red velvet and was protected by a thick glass bell. Tuomas knew that Toni, even though he was completely indifferent to the contents of his institution, had a near-mystical attachment to those bones, for nothing like them could be found in any other place on the planet. Think about it: the bones of a fabulous creature, drawn directly from a fairy tale! The bones had been there for a half-century and never – it goes without saying – had anyone been allowed so much as to touch them. Without some extraordinary compensation, Tuomas knew that Toni would never let him remove some scrapings from either the tibia or the shoulder blade.

Before going to Grigol, Tuomas had deliberated at length over the question. It just so happened that Toni had become enamoured in recent months of a lady of questionable morals thirty years his junior, the stuck-up and badly spoiled daughter of one of the town's more prosperous vest makers. Tuomas selected a handsome (and expensive) medallion that the Countess of Benzodiazepine (whose name, in the mid-twentieth century, due to the scientific accomplishments of a representative of the next generation, would be given to a chemical compound) had given him ten years before on one of his voyages to France. The white cameo representing Courtine Zépherin, the celebrated vinegar seller whom, it is said, Louis XIV was wildly in love with, was mounted on a fantastically beautiful and calming oval incarnadine stone, ringed with 240 tiny diamonds. When the medallion was shifted in one's fingers, the crown gave off bursts of dazzling blue. The piece was worth several thousand marks. All for a bit of bone dust … "Toni is not crazy enough to refuse this," Tuomas thought. "And with so valuable a piece, he should be able to extract at least a kiss from his heart's desire."

Toni Järvikivi hemmed and hawed. He turned the magnificent medallion over and over; the conflict between his professional conscience and his passion for the lass pained him. Finally, won over by the extraordinary piece, his face puffed and purple with love, he agreed to allow Tuomas to remove a bit of powder and four tiny fragments of Fredavian bone. It was not much. Tuomas would have to use the precious product parsimoniously.

Altogether, the alchemist spent seven days in Grigol. He read for hours in the bookstores and the town library, and bought several items for the house, as well as groceries, utensils, and some small household furnishings. He spent many hours in the company of Madame Makinen. On the morning of the eighth day he set off for home with Yatagan and a fully loaded cart. In the Fredavian Forest he made a long detour, as was his custom, to avoid the Farting Bear.

In the early evening, when he reached the Plains of Archelle, the sky was striped with long ribbons of fire. As he drew nearer to his home, Tuomas first thought old age had won out and that his eyes were deceiving him. What was that formless heap in the distance where his house should have been?

His stomach knotted. With a snap of the whip, he sought to urge Yatagan to gallop, but the horse seemed to have understood the emergency on his own. He flew forward in such agitation that the cart he was pulling nearly tipped.

When he finally gazed upon the cold ruins of his home, Tuomas felt such a surge of horror that he feared he would go mad. He dashed to the house and searched through the ruins for traces of Zora. For a half-hour he looked, turning over boards, stones, and beams, calling out the name of his beloved until his voice grew hoarse. He walked to the bathhouse behind the main dwelling. It too had been reduced to ashes. A good twenty metres farther stood a tall birch tree. From one of its branches a man was hanging from a rope.

Tuomas recognized Mustard. He had grown since the last time he had seen the lad, but his head was still shaped like a coconut. The poor child had been horribly mutilated: one of his eyes pried out of its socket, one of his hands cut off, his ears as well ... As he drew nearer, Tuomas noticed, directly under the feet of the hanged man, two small branches driven into the ground to form an X. Bending over for a closer look, he realized that someone – Mustard, it could have been no one else – had drawn a line of stick figures on the earth. The first, to the left, was tall and wore a hat. The others had triangular torsos and were linked to one another with a horizontal line. The one at the far right was taller by a head than the others: Zora. "The harness," Tuomas understood. "The dog harness."

The old man's concern was now joined by profound fury. On the plain, a powerful northwest wind had arisen. Tuomas stood amid the ruins of what had been his home, and his happy life with Zora. The wind whipped his face and pulled at his fine white hair. A murderous desire swept over him. His heart oozed thick, dark liquid into his veins. He hurried off to locate Yatagan, freed him from the cart, mounted the horse, and galloped off toward the north.

*

* *

Twenty minutes later, Tuomas, galloped up to the home of Ville Kaartinen, a miller who lived with his family in a large stone house close to a crossroads. The miller was not at home, but Tuomas found his wife weeding the garden behind the house. She greeted the visitor, whom she had known for a good forty years, with great delight. Tuomas paid no heed to her affable words and, without dismounting, asked her impatiently if the team had passed by.

"Well, yes! It would have been what ... three or four days?"

"Did you see the procession? Did you see the prisoners?"

"No way! Captain Ball-Buster hasn't passed through these parts for quite some time, but we heard him coming from afar, with the clanking chains and the dogs. So me and Ville, we tell the children, 'Come on, children! Time to leave! Captain Gut is coming, he steals children that have misbehaved.' We battened down the shutters and left by the back door, hitched up the mare and disappeared into the fields! Just a second, that reminds me, it must have been fifteen years ago ..."

To the astonishment of the miller's wife, Tuomas uttered a resounding oath and cut her off.

"Are you sure? You didn't see anything? You didn't see my wife among the captives?"

"What? Zora? God protect us! But what can you possibly ..."

The miller's wife, who finally understood Tuomas's abrupt manner, froze in horror. She shook her head no. Tuomas Juhani Korteniemi spurred Yatagan on. At the crossroads he headed northeast. The team was three or four days ahead of him, but the Captain was travelling on foot. Tuomas, though, had Yatagan.

*
* *

Zora was sitting on the ground, on a carpet of spruce needles. Her four companions in distress were close by. When they had begun their journey three days earlier, they had been six, but one of the girls flung herself into a rushing river and drowned. To make good her escape, she used the fact that, at night, the Captain would sometimes unchain the girls so they could lie down and sleep, relying on the dogs to keep watch. That night, as the camp was some hundred metres from the rapids (you couldn't see them, but you could hear the roar of the water), the girl paid the dogs no heed and ran as fast as her legs could carry her toward the falls. One of the mastiffs caught up with her. She lashed out with her feet and managed to break free and leap into the swirling waters. Had she planned to kill herself, or did she hope to avoid the whirlpools, make it to the other side, and escape? No way of knowing; she had not breathed a word of her intentions to a soul. The Captain forced the others to contemplate the corpse from the cliffs that overlooked the river. For endless minutes, the captives stared at the twisted white body of the poor girl, whose downstream progress was obstructed by boulders near the bank.

That day, there were only five of them, seated together for their noon meal. Zora looked around. They were sitting beside a rutted, muddy road. The sky was grey; it had been raining heavily for the past few days. The showers had stopped the day before, just after nightfall, but the air was still damp and the earth on which the captives sat was sodden. That afternoon they would be hiking with bladders full of lemonade. But they had far more serious problems to worry about.

The road the Captain and his captives had taken was bounded on the west by a sparse forest. Autumn was already well advanced, and the trees had lost a good half of their leaves. On the other side of the road, stretching off to the east as far as the eye could see, was black stubble that had been plowed into furrows so deep it would have been exhausting to walk among them. Every ten metres, huge uprooted stumps appeared to have been strewn there by some giant. Even more than the meagre forest to the west, that broad deserted expanse that seemed to mark the limits of the land known to men, the final terrestrial boundary, gave rise to an unfathomable sadness in the hearts of Captain Gut's prisoners.

In her bosom Zora had hidden a tiny partridge leg. Captain Gut had killed the bird with a stone a little earlier, cooked it, and shared the meat among the women. Zora had eaten almost nothing for the past three days. She was so exhausted she was nauseous. She forced herself to try a mouthful but immediately felt like vomiting. The meat was spongy and still soggy with the bird's salty blood. Zora laid the partridge leg on her dress, the fabric stretched by her crossed legs, and stared at the meat blankly for several minutes.

The girl seated beside her and bound to her by the hateful chain, laid her head on Zora's arm.

"Do you want my meat, Hanna?"

"Aren't you going to eat it?"

"No. I'm feeling queasy."

314

"Then sure, I'll take it."

Zora and Hanna were, respectively, last and next to last in the chain gang, always side by side or one after the other. When the Captain moved away, they could talk. After Zora was captured, a few hours later they were acquaintances, then friends. Of the three other girls, two were Russians who understood not a word of Finnish. The third was from the south of the country, near Porvoo. She was pretty and well turned out, but it was difficult to talk with her because she was the first in the gang, and walked directly behind the Captain. In any case, she never spoke a word. As she was good-looking, she was the one Captain Gut raped repeatedly. Hanna, on the other hand, was skinny and ugly, and the Captain was extremely harsh with her. He called her "the buzzard" and beat her with his staff after he finished eating or once he'd amused himself with the Porvoo girl.

When she was abducted, Hanna worked in a brothel in Kotka. Before becoming a prostitute, she had worked as a linen heckler in one of the capital's textile factories. She was a hardened young woman, and of the five, the one who best withstood the tribulations of the road. During the rare moments of rest the Captain would grant them, Hanna would tell her newfound companion in misfortune amusing stories. In the first hours after Zora was abducted, she was the one who informed the new prisoner where their journey would most likely lead them.

"In Lappeenranta, we stopped not far from a lumber camp. The Captain played cards with the men there for half a day. I could hear what they were talking about. Apparently, we were being taken to Kuhmo. The two Russians aren't bad looking. The Captain wants to sell them to settlers over that way. And the settlers, they're ready to pay because they're looking for wives, and they're pretty demanding. You'll be sold to one, for sure! You've got an odd face but you've got nice eyes, your skin is white like a cloud, you've got full breasts, and you're tall and strong! You'll be working in the fields, that's understood. But I don't have much in the way of tits and my teeth are rotten, so the cap's likely to sell me off as a cheapie in some lumber camp, or maybe to some pimp up north, for sure. Here, look at my teeth, see how rotten they are?"

Maybe because she wanted to make Zora laugh, she opened her mouth wide to show her teeth. But Zora did not laugh.

Kuhmo … Isn't that where Tero is working? Assuredly, if she were to make her entry into the village with an iron collar around her neck, beaten and dressed in rags, Tero would waste no time rescuing her and avenging the outrage she had suffered. And when he'd disposed of the Captain, when he'd beaten him within an inch of his life, he would take Zora, trembling, in his arms, brush the hair from her forehead and there deposit a kiss, and whisper those words that console and bring relief. "My poor Zora, how you have suffered." And perhaps he would even weep and she, her nose deep in his shirt collar, would answer, "Oh, you know, the blows, the hurt, the hunger, nothing was too high a price to pay to come and bid you good day. This journey, for your fingers in my hair, and the tears that bathe my face, I would repeat a hundred times over." And Tero, moved, would hold her tightly in his arms, and thus pressed close one against the other, they would live happily ever after.

Ah, love! Love can drive you to distraction. And the pain of love can drive you to desperate measures.

One day you become enamoured of a beautiful girl. You shower her with candies and flowers and tender words. She smiles at you and treats you as if you were her Prince Charming. You spend money, large sums of money, and you cast your friends aside. What could it possibly matter? The future has smiled upon you. And then, one fine day, you learn that your little fancy has left you for a pastry chef-cum-lemon squeezer from the next street over. You go wild. On the day of her wedding you burst into the church and pour a full jerry can of lemonade on the bride's head, shouting, "Take that, you worthless nobody! See what you get for choosing some scullery boy over me!"

You have climbed to the summit of love, but your beloved is

not there to meet you, which sends you tumbling down love's precipitous far slope.

For long afterwards, you regret that moment of jealous brutality. In letters, you bow and scrape – "My fairest Dulcinea, one thousand pardons, I wish you happiness with your cookie maker" – but certain failings are unforgivable.

Such are the crimes that, for love, you commit against yourself.

We who pen these lines feel no shame in confessing that, one day, tormented by a broken heart, we sliced off our left nipple and sent it to the fishwife with whom we were smitten. What did we achieve? The slut remained with her lover, and as for us, to this day it is difficult to sling our haversack over our left shoulder to go duck hunting.

Caught up in the madness of love, Zora, feverish with hunger and privation, convinced herself that Tero would be awaiting her on the mountaintop. In truth, she was abusing herself, a painful deception if there ever was one, for the inventions of her imagination made it impossible for her to draw up an escape plan when there was still time.

The clucking of her tongue and the sucking sounds Hanna made with her bad teeth as she gnawed laboriously on the partridge leg snapped Zora out of her reverie.

"Look," said Hanna, her voice low with astonishment, as she pointed to Captain Gut.

Some two hundred metres south of the bivouac, their captor was standing at the roadside, surrounded by a chain of lynx. From where she was sitting, Zora could count seven creatures, but there may well have been others in the underbrush, it was hard to say. The Captain, pipe in mouth, was *talking* to the lynx with hand signs! And even though there was nothing particularly strange about it (in Finland in that day and age, you could find people who would talk to anything. Confound it! Zora knew a peasant woman from the Grigol countryside who complimented her tomatoes to make them redder!), what truly disturbed her was that the lynx were *listening*. They lifted their heads toward him, attentive, and on occasion nodded and emitted whistling sounds.

After a few minutes of this strange confab, which the chain-gang girls watched with fear and fascination, the Captain returned smartly. The lynx, which appeared to be expecting something, stood motionless.

"So what are you staring at, you bunch of rustics?" said the Captain with a grin. "Haven't you ever seen a man talk to animals?"

Then he turned to Zora.

"The lynx told me that your old husband is after us. He's hot on our trail. That bothers me to some small degree ... We could wait for him here, nice and easy. I could settle his hash with no trouble. But then we'd waste time, and with the damp ground and rain on the way, it wouldn't be a very comfortable camp. Luckily for us, the lynx agreed to look after your old shit eater. All they want in exchange is a girl to eat. So for you, buzzard" – and here the Captain looked straight at Hanna – "the trip ends here."

Zora felt she was going mad. She jumped to her feet, intending to punch the Captain in the stomach. But the poor girl had become feeble, and her chains held her back; her white fist only ruffled the fabric of the heavy man's shirt. Laughing, he grabbed Zora by the hair, bent her over, and kneed her in the face. *Smack!* For several seconds Zora lost contact with the world of the senses. Behind her closed eyelids, hundreds of tiny vibrating coloured particles made her head spin. Neither her eyes nor the rest of her body obeyed her will. When she regained consciousness, she found herself lying flat on the ground. A piercing pain was drilling into her brain, and her mouth was full of blood.

Zora heard Hanna screaming next to her, and she opened her eyes: the Captain was thrashing the little harlot from Kotka. When he'd knocked her fully unconscious, the whoremonger unchained Hanna, picked her up, and threw her over his shoulder. He strode off toward the lynx and cast Hanna in their direction without so much as a fare-thee-well. The beasts leaped upon the girl, sunk their claws into her arms and legs, and dragged her into the bush.

The pain snapped Hanna into consciousness. She shrieked, and her death rattle reached the chain gang, though faintly. The Captain followed the lynx into the underbrush and disappeared from his prisoners' sight for a minute. Zora covered her face with her hands and sobbed; it was the first time she had wept since her capture. Hanna! Tuomas! Her husband, her infinitely kind husband! Zora's mind raced from one to the other: Hanna, whom no one could help now, was being torn to pieces by the lynx, and Tuomas was in great danger, Zora knew it. She absolutely had to help him.

Not a sound came from the underbrush. The Captain returned to his captives, gnawing on something. Zora felt the disgust rising in her throat and clapped her hand over her mouth.

"On your feet, strumpets! No loafing if we want to get to the village of Toppinen before nightfall. I guarantee one hell of a beating to anyone I see dragging her feet."

The two Russian girls understood nothing, so the Captain kicked them to their feet. The prisoners – there were only four now – stood painfully. Zora's head was aching so badly she feared she would faint. Yet she managed to continue her march. A moment later, she was startled to see that something had shifted in her field of vision. In front of her, instead of Hanna's bony shoulders and straw-dry hair, one of the two Russians now walked, a blond only slightly smaller than her, and who once would have been shapely of form, but who had become gaunt from the privations of the journey.

The small column moved slowly along the rocky path, the Captain and his hounds walking beside them. After the swaggering bully had torn what he could from the bone, to amuse himself he spat what remained in his mouth in Zora's face. The young woman wiped her cheek and gazed at what her fingers had raked up: a shred of white and pink cartilage.

*
* *

Tuomas paused only to eat and drink a little and to piss. He travelled from hamlet to hamlet, everywhere inquiring whether the chain gang had passed that way. At Crankbill he was informed that the Captain had moved through the village thirty-six hours earlier. The news encouraged the old gentleman. He had hoped that by maintaining a rapid pace he could make up the lag of kilometres in a few hours, but at the western edge of the village, he began to feel queasy, and he dismounted from Yatagan. He stretched out in the tall grass. Since his wild pursuit began, he had not allowed himself more than a few uncomfortable naps, two or three hours of relief at most. He slept in the woods or in the fields, never at an inn. He would awaken in a confused state, bones and muscles aching. Devil take it! Our man was ninety years old! On the third day he began to suffer bouts of dizziness. Five times during that day, he had to halt and stay completely still for fifteen minutes; it was the only way to recover his wits.

On the sixth day, a bit before midday, he suffered another dizzy spell, the worst yet. It happened in a tiny village. Some curious peasants who'd earlier provided him information, and who had accompanied him to the outskirts of the hamlet, saw him topple from his mount. A fat woman, feeling pity for him, caught him by the arm and insisted he come and sleep at her house. Tuomas, more dead than alive, babbled a few words of thanks, then lost consciousness. They laid him on a tarpaulin. Four husky villagers, each grasping one corner, carried the poor man off.

The fat woman was the village baker. She and her husband laid Tuomas in the children's bed, where he slept for eleven straight hours without interruption, but when he awoke, he could ill conceal his anger at having wasted so much time. He would have preferred his hosts rouse him earlier. He thanked them quickly and asked for directions to the nearest forest path. They explained that after making his way through the woods that bordered the village to the north, he could reach the Karelian Track, the great forest highroad of Karelia, in a dozen hours or so.

"In any event, after you leave the forest, there are fields everywhere. Farmers are plowing this time of year, and they can show you the road."

They forced him to swallow down a big bowl of pea soup, some sausage, bread, and an onion. They also gave him a big loaf of black bread for the road.

Tuomas mounted Yatagan, who had been watered and fed his fill of hay. The peasants refused to accept payment, and the gentleman did not insist too vigorously, so pressed for time was he. Once more he set out northward. Standing in front of their house, the baker and his wife watched him ride off. When Tuomas's silhouette had finally disappeared in the distance, the husband turned to his wife.

"The geezer's got real balls, if you know what I mean ... Take after Captain Gut like that, and at his age! I mean ... he's at least sixty, the old guy, right?"

In the woods, a crystalline, liquid voice guided Tuomas to a creek. He dismounted, kneeled down, and took a deep draught of water. He pulled out his kerchief and shook it free of pine needles and twigs, then wiped his forehead and his cheeks.

At that moment, the lynx launched their attack.

It all happened very fast. Tuomas had no time to understand what hit him. He heard only the hissing of the big cats ... A split-second later, the compact mass of one of them was attacking him. He fell into the water.

The little stream was about a half-metre deep. Tuomas found himself stretched out in the water, his head submerged. He could not hear the roaring of the wild animals, but the ear-splitting neighing of Yatagan reached his ears as though in a nightmare. The wildcats had attacked the horse's legs and thighs. Tuomas felt a stabbing pain pierce his left shoulder like a gimlet. A rain of claws as sharp as scalpels fell upon his face. To throw off one of the beasts that was trying to climb onto his chest, he lashed out blindly with an elbow and struck the animal hard in the ribs. It dropped to the ground. But no sooner had he thrown off the first attacker than he felt other pairs of slathering jaws closing around his calves and his left arm.

Overwhelmed by panic and rage, Tuomas flailed his arms and legs, his main task being to get to his feet and out of the water.

Using his elbows and ignoring the pain, he managed to get his head above water and take in two good gulps of air. Those few seconds were enough for him to see that four furious lynx were attacking Yatagan. The horse had fallen onto his back, and the maddened hunters were gnawing his legs. Then one of the lynx, the one that had been clawing Tuomas's arm, leaped on the old man's face. Again he found himself head under water, spending what remained of his strength wildly flailing his limbs. The lynx that had been tearing at his face now crouched on his chest, intending to submerge him completely. Gasping for air, Tuomas felt his whole body sink deeper under water. When the lynx closed its mouth around his throat, Tuomas abandoned all hope. He closed his eyes and let himself sink.

But at the very moment when all was turning black in his mind, the weight of the lynx on his chest fell away. Gone was the choking feeling. Even the clamp of jaws on his legs eased. Tuomas felt as though he were departing his physical body to take on a more ethereal form, floating upward to become one with the galaxies. Then a strange and beautiful thing happened: just before losing consciousness, he saw the head of a great she-wolf. He closed his eyes, recited a prayer (you never know!), and bid this life farewell.

CHAPTER
15

At the Twilight Hour

The thought that Tuomas might meet a cruel death slaughtered by a pack of lynx in the dark forest was more than Zora could bear. When she felt reason deserting her, she forced herself to think of Tero, and so was able to calm herself, enough to begin hatching a plot to escape. She absolutely had to free herself to find Tuomas and protect him from harm.

But it was no easy matter to evade the vigilance of the Captain and his dogs. When, for whatever reason, he was unable to keep direct watch over his captives, he could count on his mastiffs to guard them. If Zora believed she could outrun the Captain, she would have not a hope against the dogs.

On the morning of the seventh day, the prisoners and the Captain awoke in an old abandoned stockade. The girls breakfasted on hot water and a loaf of mouldy green bread. As she ate, Zora observed the dogs. There were seven altogether, seven large Anatolian shepherds, filthy with festering skins, thin of flank but broad of chest. The Captain had bought them from the Turkmen breeders who set up shop in the port of Helsinki for a few weeks every summer, more often than not trading dogs for women. For a female in not half-bad condition, the Turkmens would offer three, sometimes four dogs.

The eyes of the dogs gleamed with terrifying savagery. Their daily pittance was no better than that of the prisoners. Clothed in the dignity that women never cast aside, even in the worst of indigence, the prisoners remained calm and avoided crises, despite their constant pangs of hunger. But the animals, catching the scent of game wafting from the forest, behaved like the caged carnivores they were, so much so that the Captain had to whip them to keep them in line so they would not devour the women outright. The blows from his whip explained the long, purulent scars that striated their caramel-coloured coats.

That morning, as she chewed on her bread, Zora carefully watched the dogs lying on the ground. A few of them were awake but, enfeebled, they could not rouse themselves to seek food and drink. Later, when the time came to set out again, the Captain had to lash them to force them to resume the journey. Zora felt such pity welling in her heart that she vowed to share her next meal with them.

Shortly after midday, after walking for the entire morning, they paused to rest near a lake. The Captain gave permission for the girls to wash while he brought out his fishing pole and went to try his luck. All he could catch were whitebait and ruffe; each time, he cursed loudly in dismay. An hour later, for twenty-one whitebait and a dozen ruffes, he had landed only three trout (of which one, truth to tell, was of good size). While the girls were drying themselves, he lit a fire. In the end, it was he who ate the trout, along with a raw onion. When his meal was over, he belched with dissatisfaction, and instructed the captives to gather small branches and grill the small fry while he bathed in the waters of the lake.

"The first one I hear complaining, I'll tear out her fingernails with my knife blade. The lakes in this region are not fish ponds. You have to settle for what they offer."

When the Captain had gone off some distance to bathe, the poor girls sighed in desperation. One of the Russians began to weep softly. Their daily diet consisted almost entirely of whitebait. Even when eaten with forest mushrooms, without salt and vegetables, the repast was a sorry one indeed. While one of the Russian girls – the one who was not sobbing – foraged for mushrooms in the underbrush, Zora gutted the fish and skewered them on the branch that the Captain had used to grill his trout. She turned them back and forth over the fire until they were crispy. The prisoners ate in silence, without appetite, huddled against one another.

As she chewed on a mushroom, Zora noticed that the Captain had left his pack on a large rock, a few metres from the fire. She knew the travelling pimp kept a large dry sausage in one of its pockets. When his stomach began to growl as they walked, he would pull it out of his pack and take a bite, gnawing away at the lump of meat for several minutes. It was his snack between meals.

Having swallowed their wretched fare, the captives remained seated on the ground. The blond Finnish girl who never spoke lay down to take a nap. The two Russians began talking to each other in low voices. No one paid attention to Zora, who crept over to the pack and stuck her hand into the left pocket. Her fingers could feel the sausage. It was oozing good fatty grease! Zora suddenly felt so ravenous that her stomach knotted in violent cramps.

She removed the sausage and looked it over. Gut had already eaten half of it; no more than a meagre fifteen centimetres remained. She turned her head toward her companions. The blond was still asleep, but the two Russians were staring at her with terrified eyes. The one who had been sobbing seemed worried by what might happen if the Captain were to discover the theft. The other girl's lips formed a small O of surprise and slight reproach, but her eyes were urging Zora on. The latter, meanwhile, was studying the dogs.

They were lying close to the fire. Four of them were asleep. The other three, apathetic, were nuzzling the earth with their snouts. Their last meal had been the previous evening when the Captain had let them devour two fat partridges. Zora, without moving, clucked her tongue and waved the sausage to attract their attention. The two sleeping dogs did not awaken, but the two others, emboldened by its greasy scent, approached the young woman, drooling. Zora let each of the dogs tear off a chunk of meat. One of the sleeping dogs awakened and came over, tail wagging, and devoured the last piece. They chewed hastily for they were near starving, and long rivulets of slobber slid down their jaws and dripped onto their paws. When they'd eaten everything, they turned back to Zora to see if the dispenser of meat had anything left over. They lay down at their benefactor's feet to lick the grease from her fingers, sniff her socks, and in the case of one animal, to thrust its muzzle into its provider's lap. Zora realized she had just won a small victory over the Captain.

The dogs paid dearly for their frugal feast. On his return from bathing in the lake, when he saw the mastiffs licking their chops and belching up gas that smelled of pig fat, the Captain immediately suspected they'd eaten his sausage. He checked the pocket of his pack and duly noted it was missing. He whipped the dogs, and the forest was filled with the yelps and whines of the poor creatures.

All of this saddened Zora, but the young woman was building a strategy that – she hoped – would make things easier for her when the time came to make her escape. From that day on, whenever she had the opportunity, she slipped a bit of food to the dogs, even if it meant forgoing her own starvation rations. Prudence was essential. Most of the time they ate together, with the Captain watching closely. When that was the case, she would slip food into the sleeve of her dress. In the evening, having eaten his fill, the Captain would smoke his pipe and sip a glass of eau-de-vie. Then he would go off to sleep in his tent, often taking the blond girl with him. Ever since that one prisoner had contrived to escape and run off to drown herself in a river, he did not unchain his captives for the night. Instead, he coiled the chain around a tree trunk and fastened it with a padlock, keeping the key in his pocket at all times. When, from the tent, the Captain's snoring became audible, Zora drew out her crusts of dry bread, partridge thighs, or hedgehog grease, and shared the food with the dogs as best she could. While they were eating at her feet, often she would urinate. The dogs sniffed the piss. Zora had no idea whether this would be of any use to her. But, in any event, it certainly couldn't hurt.

Three days later, she finally managed to actually *touch* one of the dogs. She gently laid her hand on the head of the smallest of the pack, the one who made the least noise. At her touch the dog froze for a few seconds, then shook its head slightly to shrug off her hand and walked away, indifferent but not aggressive. The next day, Zora repeated the experiment with three other dogs. Two of them allowed themselves to be patted for a few seconds before moving away. The third reacted violently, growling and attempting to bite Zora's hand. (A bit closer and it would have succeeded!) The day after, Zora managed to pat the first dog, the little one, for some time. Surprised at first, the animal appeared to take a liking to it. It now deigned to crouch at the girl's feet and allow her to scratch its throat, going so far as to roll over on its back to invite her to stroke its belly. Over the next few days, Zora managed to seduce half the dogs of the team with her affection. She would give them meat whenever it appeared, keeping the vegetables for herself. But her meagre rations of mushrooms, horse chestnuts, onions, and berries could not satisfy her hunger. She began to experience bouts of diarrhea and colic. Worse still, she was in a state of continuous weakness. Often she nearly fainted during the long days of walking. In the evening, famished, she lay down beside her companions in misfortune. She dreamed of Tero, and sometimes of Tuomas. A week and a half later, she was so ill that she had no choice: it was time to implement the next phase of her plan.

*

* *

Tuomas drifted for long hours through pain- and fever-wracked dreams. He knew he was alive (had he not been, how could he have been dreaming?), but for the present that was his sole certainty, and all his awareness could grasp were the fantastic swirls of blood mingled with water, the blades of night that sliced through the rosy heavens, and the great sharks pursuing him through acid seas that seeped through his clothing and burned his skin. There were moments when he felt he was sinking into toxic, burning liquid. When that happened, he tried to clutch at the splinters as big as fists that paraded past, from top to bottom, above him as he watched. There were other moments when he felt as though he had been cast into a chasm filled with runny, stinking lard, a tiny pebble dropped into a bucket filled with a meringue of droppings and rotten eggs. In this universe of feverish suffering, Tuomas danced like a condemned soul, trying to lend his conscience a coherent direction, and escape from the darkness that enveloped him. But each time he was about to realize who he was and what was happening to him, the fogs of delirium closed in on him once more. He panicked briefly, wracked with pain, then fainted. From farther and farther away, the sound of coarse, damp rubbing intruded violently into his nightmare state, but he could not tell if it was a contact from beyond his madness, a distant call of the world from meaning. All he knew was that the caress he felt, just like the warm, supple pressure from time to time on his arms and face, did not hurt, but neither did it bring him relief.

After what seemed to him an eternity, the hellish forms that thronged his dreams dispersed; everything turned dark. The screen of his awareness was now speckled with tiny pinpoints of light. His thoughts began to thread themselves in orderly fashion on the spool of consciousness. He now distinctly felt a large, soft tongue licking his face, and a warm breast of fur and odour covered his upper body.

He emerged fully from his state of limbo only after a long period of sleep haunted by acrimonious dreams. Eyes open now, he could make out, far above, the tops of tall, leafless willow trees. His sense of hearing returned. The wind was whispering in the branches, and nestlings were chirping. His arms and legs were stiff. He felt as though there was an anvil in his head, and waves of nausea swept over him, but he was well and truly alive.

At times the head of the she-wolf he had glimpsed before slipping into unconsciousness would reappear. The beast thrust its muzzle into his mouth – he could not resist – and she opened it to deposit a trickle of warm water.

She came to give him water five or six times, and when she

spoke to him for the first time, Tuomas, who in his life had seen many strange and wonderful things, was not as astonished as he thought he should be to hear an animal speak. Did his fever make him more readily accept things that normally would have astounded him? Far from being surprised, he was delighted. "Well, I never!" he thought. "A wolf that speaks! Unheard of! Imagine what I could have done with that long ago. But I am wrong to complain. What incredible good fortune to be able to speak with a she-wolf in the twilight of my life. How many men have had such luck?"

The she-wolf looked at Tuomas with her iridescent pupils, and spoke.

"I licked your woundsss. I gave you water. Now you mussst eat. But only raw food. Fire I cannot make."

So saying, one at a time, the beautiful she-wolf picked up the berries she had gathered and placed them on Tuomas's chest. But she did not remain to watch him eat; she vanished into the woods.

For the next two days, the she-wolf kept busy. From pine boughs she made a pallet for the old man. For him she caught two plump partridges, a hedgehog, and a hare. Tuomas's sack still lay where it had fallen, beside the disembowelled body of Yatagan, and the she-wolf brought it to him. Thanks to the matches he found in it, Tuomas lit a fire and cooked the meat.

At dusk on the second day, the alchemist managed to get to his feet with the aid of a willow branch. He took a few steps and then, exhausted, plopped to the ground. Earlier in the day, the she-wolf had brought two trout, and now the fish were grilling over the fire. Satisfied, Tuomas pulled his pipe and tobacco from his sack and smoked as he looked closely at the wolf seated as canines sit, two metres away from him. On the animal's grey forehead, white fur formed a motif of startling symmetry, something like a dome topped by a pointed crest, or the shape of a cheese bell.

The she-wolf looked right back at him.

"Do not ssstay here too long," she said, at last.

"I understand."

"Tomorrow. We mussst leave tomorrow. You hold on to my back."

"Tomorrow is too soon," said Tuomas. "I cannot even stand on my feet."

The she-wolf took two strides in his direction. "Your wife," she said in a confidential tone. "I alwaysss followed her. For her whole life long. I followed her, watched her live. Ssssometimesss I helped her."

"Is that so? But why?"

The she-wolf turned her head toward the south. In the ever-changing gleam of her eyes lay distances too great to be travelled, and secrets too terrible to tell, but also a great and deep kindness.

"Long ago, I had a lover. Long, long ago. We lived in hiding, in the Basssilian Woods. Men came, hunting for usss. Ssso we hid in the landsss of Arnuphle. For a long time. And then, in the Fredavian Forest. Other wolvesss lived there. Not too many. A few. We hid there along with them."

The lisp of her *S*'s seemed interminable, like a knife blade against a sharpening stone.

"We ssspent the sssummer in the forest, and the autumn too. And then the winter. That winter, for the firssst time, we sssaw your wife. She wasss ssstill a little girl."

Just then, as if she had heard something, the she-wolf pressed her muzzle against the cold ground and sniffed. A false alarm, perhaps. She lifted her head as quickly as she had lowered it.

"The sssnow melted. Ssspring had come. But there wasss no food. People were hungry. Men travelled through the foresssst. Along the way, sssometimesss, they would fall. Dead. When they did, we would eat them. But it wasssn't enough. One day, my friend and I ssscented a hare. He went off and did not return. I looked high and low. Until morning, I looked for him. There he wasss, lying at the foot of a willow tree. Hisss foot caught in one of thossse terrible thingsss men make ... thossse iron teeth!"

"A trap."

"Yesss. Close to him I ssstayed. I wanted to bite off hisss leg, to free him. He said no. He feared the pain. Then he fell asssleep, and I alssso."

Once more the she-wolf broke off her story to sniff the ground.

"With sssteel claws beneath my hide I awakened," she resumed after a short pause. "In a man'sss den. I turned my head and sssaw my friend. He alssso had long sssteel claws in his ssside. Dead. Half a day, no one came. At nightfall, two men came in, pulling behind them a third. Into boiling water they plunged him. They ssstuck sssteel claws into hisss sssides and hung him up beside usss. Then they left."

As the she-wolf told her story, her tone did not change, and her angular face never lost its lupine hardness. To communicate her pain she had nothing but the brute strength of her staccato narration made of coarse descriptions and ordinary enumerations. Yet at that point in her story, she hid her muzzle beneath her front paws that lay flat against the ground, and kept it there for a long time. Tuomas did not dare ask her to continue.

"Later, your friend came to sssave me," she said, finally raising her head. "It wasss night. She pulled the clawsss from my sssidesss. Bravery she had greatly. I ssspeak to you of a day when your wife wasss ssstill a little wisssp of a girl. She helped me essscape. And ssso I did. My friend, there he ssstayed."

That sudden incursion into the childhood of his beloved took Tuomas's breath away.

"And that man ... who was he? What happened to him?"

"What man?"

"The one they hung up on meat hooks beside you?"

"I don't know. Your wife, she sssaved me first."

Those last words startled Tuomas.

"My woundsss healed," the she-wolf continued. "And in hiding, I ssstayed close to your friend and kept watch over her asss she grew up. One day you came for her at her father'sss housssse to take her where men are asss numerousss asss the leavesss of the treesss are here: I wasss there. I followed you. That very night, you took her home by the foressst path. I wasss there, behind you. On the plain, you kept her in your houssse and she became your friend. All that time I wasss nearby, in the Misssty Woodsss. Even ssso … when the man with the dogsss came at the lassst full moon, I wasss hunting hare in the woodsss. I wasss not there to honour the sssecret promissse I made the day she delivered me from the sssteel clawsss. For that, old man, I ask your forgivenesssssss. My pain is as yoursss."

The she-wolf let out a long howl. Tuomas, overcome with unspeakable terror at the thought of the torments Zora must be suffering, joined his voice with that of the animal, so powerfully that in the end he was shaking with sorrow and rage.

"The path of the man who chainsss women," concluded the she-wolf, "leadsss to the Karelian Track, farther north. We shall take that route."

CHAPTER
16

The Koskela Gap

When Zora awoke on the morning of her tenth day of captivity, she felt as though the pounding in her head that had plagued her since the start of the journey had doubled in intensity, and that all her strength had abandoned her. She staggered to her feet, almost collapsed, then stood up once more. Her heart was throbbing as if it were about to burst.

As there was nothing to eat that morning, the Captain forced the four captives to take to the road immediately. Around midday they came to the edge of a wretched hamlet. At a good distance from the village, the Captain attached the chain to a tree, left the dogs to guard the women, and set out to purchase provisions and have a drink at the local tavern. When he came back, he stank of eau-de-vie, but he was carrying a basket of sour apples in one hand. He fed them to the girls along with a big slice of cheese. But before he allowed her to eat, he uncoupled the first girl on the line, the pretty blond, and led her off to the village. There, in a room in a hovel, he humped her until the blood flowed.

When the Captain brought her back to the chain gang, the girl's eye was swollen, and she was walking strangely, rolling her pelvis as if her hip pained her. Her face was as blank as it always was. She was not crying.

The whoremonger insisted on starting up right away, even though he'd had his fill. They walked for two hours. Over the past several days, the scenery had changed. Broad wooded plains, covered with green and yellow dying grass, alternated with forestland. So it was that the chain gang, come evening, emerged from the woods and ventured onto an empty expanse, bereft of vegetation and water. Here and there, the flatness was broken by towering hummocks of such an abrupt pitch that they might well have been sculpted by human hands: great rocky massifs that sloped gently upward, only to end in precipitous cliffs, often striated by deep crevices ... At first burnt thickets dotted the cold brown earth, monstrous trees like long, black, rotten teeth. Then, soon enough, the trees vanished completely. Nothing remained to break the monotony of the landscape but tiny lakes, craters filled with water, really. The prisoners and their captor slogged on across this lunar vastness until the sun had half-disappeared to the west. The land was ugly, but the cold-beaten earth made walking easier than on the woodland trails they had been following before. Just before nightfall, as they halted to set up camp, far to the northeast Zora caught sight of giant twin mountains rubbing the sky with their round summits. They nestled together, the right flank of one merging with the left flank of the other, but only at one point, so that each mountain conserved its individuality. The opening between the two mountains was the Koskela Gap. Zora had never seen the place with her own eyes, but had often heard tell of it. There was a tale about these two mountains that the venerable Karelian storytellers all knew. It was said that on these flat lands, when the world was created, only two mountains thrust up, each at the farthest extremity of the land, and in the centuries that followed, the distance that separated them had slowly been absorbed, a kilometre at a time, until they ended up as two loving mountains that desired to spend eternity side by side. The local inhabitants called the passage between them the Koskela Gap, though no one knew why. About this passage, as about the mountains themselves, extraordinary things were told.

Zora was moved by the spectacle, but soon much more calculating thoughts pushed emotion aside. She tried to determine the distance that separated them from the gap. A dozen kilometres, perhaps? She turned toward the Captain. Alcohol had made him heavy footed. Zora's nerves twisted painful knots in her stomach and breast.

When darkness fell, they stopped at the shore of a small lake, no more than a large puddle covered with pond scum. The Captain put down his rucksack, then did something that Zora, in the course of planning her escape, had not foreseen, but that turned out to be a veritable blessing. Seeing as alcohol had heated his organism and he was sweating profusely, the Captain took off his cloak and laid it flat on the ground. Then he pitched the small tent where he spent his nights. This done, he turned to Zora.

"I'm going to see if there's any fish in this lake. Make sure you sweep the earth in my tent before I get back. And start a fire too. Dilly-dally and I'll slice you in two."

The Captain snapped his fingers; immediately, the dogs gathered around the girls. He unchained Zora with a look in his hard eyes that said, "Just try to escape and you'll see. If I don't catch you, the dogs will, and they'll tear you to pieces." Then he pulled from his pack a glass jar full of partridge offal, which he tossed to the beasts. The dogs' task was to keep watch over the captives, but they were tired, hungry, and indifferent. Most of them flopped to the ground, ate without appetite, and dropped off to sleep. They would have feasted on the partridge livers and hearts, but the Captain kept them for himself, leaving the mastiffs only the bones, the feet, the heads, and the shitty rear ends.

The three other prisoners were seated on the ground. The two Russian girls were massaging their feet and calves. After making sure that the Captain was out of earshot, they began talking in low voices. The blond rubbed her feet for a time, then lay down on her back. She stared silently at the sky, her face emotionless. Zora did not take her eyes off the Captain: he had stopped at the shore of the lake, some thirty metres from the bivouac, and was tying a hook to his line.

She opened the Captain's rucksack and removed the matches and the big raffia mat on which he slept. Apprehensive, she decided it was better to forget the fire and proceed with her plan. She hid the matches in her sleeve and walked purposefully toward the cloak lying on the ground, a few metres from the tent. The key to the chain was in its right pocket. She pulled it out and clasped it in her fist. Then she lifted her dress, lowered her drawers, squatted over the cloak, and pissed. Once finished, she picked up the cloak and put it on. Then she hurried over to the other three girls. As she went, she glanced in the Captain's direction; his eyes were riveted on the cork bobbing at the end of his line. Some of the dogs, however, had caught a whiff of urine. Not enough for them to get to their feet, but four raised their heads and their ears. They watched the actions of the tall woman who had fed them so often.

Only at the last minute did the two Russian girls and the blond realize that Zora had come to free them from their chains. When they understood she was about to unlock their iron collars, they were dumbstruck. One of the Russians, at the very moment her bonds fell to the ground, was overcome by an uncontrollable surge of panic. She grabbed her compatriot by the hand and headed south on the run, paying no heed to Zora's silent exhortations to keep quiet and sneak away!

Their movements alerted the dogs. The pack got to its feet and began to howl. Three of them set out after the fugitives. The other four stayed where they were, barking at the top of their voices. The Captain turned around, spotted the two escaping Russian girls, and exploded.

"AH, THE SOWS!"

In the time it took him to fling his fishing rod to the ground and make for the bivouac, the blond girl, the one he'd raped so often, had set off on the run, but not in the same direction as the Russians; she headed west instead. A man in full possession of his faculties would have needed no more than ten seconds to cover the distance that separated the lake from the camp. But the Captain, still reeling, took twenty. When he reached the chain, three of the prisoners had made good their escape. But Zora was still there, standing motionless, the Captain's cloak over her shoulders and the key to the chain in her hand. With all his strength he punched the insolent girl in the jaw.

Zora felt her jawbone crack in at least twenty places. She did not feel the pain for long, as she lost consciousness almost immediately. When she came to, she found herself on the ground, the taste of blood in her mouth and a feeling that a train had run her over. A cutting pain sliced through her face. Lying face up on the ground, she saw nothing but the starry black sky, but from the deafening din, she could imagine the scene being played out around her.

The dogs.

She had not expected they would bark that way, like puppies, as they attacked their master. Such big dogs, she had heard them howl, growl, bay, and yelp, but now, as they settled accounts with the man who had beaten them time and time again, they sounded as though they were crying, in their own way, as dogs do when they cry. Despite the piercing pain she felt in her face and shoulder blades, Zora got to her feet. Two of the mastiffs had locked their jaws around the calves of the whoremonger, while a third worked to tear a chunk out of his scrotum. The others, which had dashed off in pursuit of the captives, abandoned the girls and turned back at full speed, better to attack the Captain.

There you have it. The hour had come. Zora took off as fast as her anemic legs would carry her.

Before continuing with our story, we should note that Zora would never again see her companions in misery, as the three girls fled in different directions. But for those among you who would like to know what happened to the two Russian girls and the pretty Finnish blond, such, told with admirable verbal economy, is the fate life held in store for them.

The two Russian girls, after many hours of wandering across the cold fields, finally reached the miserable hamlet near which they had halted earlier. For half the year they worked as domestics in the household of the sheriff. With the money they earned and a gift in coin given them by the sheriff's wife (who took pity on them when she heard their story), one of them returned to her family in Russia. The other, quite unexpectedly, married a young baker from the hamlet, a fine, strong young lad who lavished gifts upon her and cared for her her whole life through. She gave birth to four plump, good-natured little boys.

The blond walked all night. In the morning she came upon a lake. She drank deeply and the icy water revived her. After slaking her thirst, she entered the water and slowly immersed herself. Then, she slipped beneath the surface, never to reappear.

But let us return to Zora. Our heroine now headed toward the Koskela Gap, first at a trot, glancing behind in panic, then more slowly. After an hour of flight she spotted two hedgehogs making their way across a grassy patch. With a stone she broke the spine of one of the animals as the other dived into its burrow. Zora was nauseated with weakness and did not have the strength to extricate it from its hole. After stripping the animal of its quills she attempted to butcher it. But without a knife, the hedgehog being so difficult to skin, she ended up holding a small carcass of fur and pink, bloody flesh in her hands. She glanced behind her. There was no sign of the Captain, but that did little to comfort her, and she set off on the run once again with the meat of the dead animal in her hands. Perhaps a half-kilometre farther on, she came upon a small pond. There she washed the hedgehog meat, then bit into its still-warm fat, at first with disgust, and then, as her palate grew accustomed, with greater appetite. She gleaned a few extra calories by sucking the animal's vertebrae, but every bite caused her blinding pain, since the Captain's uppercut had shattered her jaw. In the end, she was still hungry. A flight of pochards passed overhead, and three of the birds came to rest on the placid surface of the pond. Zora looked at them hungrily. For some pochard meat she would have mustered the strength to make a fire with the matches she'd stolen from Gut. She picked up a small stone from the ground. In top form Zora had gunsight eyes and could knock a pigeon out of the air with a single throw. But on that day, in her feeble hand, the stone felt heavy. She put it back on the ground and with a heavy heart stared at the pochards.

Then she turned her head toward the mounts of Koskela, and for a brief moment forgot her fatigue and pain.

The two mountains presented a strange and captivating aspect, like two testicles sprung from the earth and covered with dense, dark woods. Each had an identical shape. Their summits were rounded and smooth, and their slopes described straight lines descending at identical angles. The twin mountains were irregular only at the exact spot where they joined, in the centre. In that place, a great protuberance of green vegetation seemed to emerge from each of the two mountainsides, joining the other. In the narrow V between the two rounded peaks lay the Koskela Gap.

Night had fallen, and the temperature had dropped. Zora shivered beneath her tattered clothing. Two or three hours of walking would bring her to the foot of the gap. Weak and tired, she wanted only to lie down and sleep, but whenever she stopped moving, her limbs stiffened.

About a half-kilometre from the slope, the hostile surface of the open fields gave way to soft, compliant pasture that was gentle beneath her feet. Now the gap lay before Zora, but to reach the passage, she would have to make a steep climb that, even were she in the best of shape, would have taken her no less than an hour. In current circumstances, the excursion became prohibitive. "Come what may," she thought. If she could reach the first outgrowths of spruce that she saw growing in quincunx on the slopes, she might find a hollow where she could curl up, sheltered from the wind, for the rest of the night.

She spent what remained of her strength on the gentle slope and finally found a clump of spruce in whose lap she nestled. She covered herself as best she could with her clothes and quickly fell asleep, but an hour later, shivering, she awoke. She understood that she would die of cold if she lay there without moving, beneath the stars; she would have to spend the night walking.

The thread of her thoughts began to slip away from her, and before her eyes, faint images of Tero's face took the place of the landscape. Then, in the girl's growing delirium, the beloved face with its princely features suddenly melted, as though subjected to intense heat. His flesh gradually took on the guise of horned demons, then transformed again to become the terrifying visage of Captain Gut.

It took Zora two hours to reach the top of the hills, the point where the passageway passed between the two peaks. The gap opened onto a dense and clammy grove of black spruce that emitted a warm, fetid odour of humus and sweat. Before venturing into these troubling woods, Zora cast a last glance behind her, over the path she had travelled. In the clear night, endless kilometres of bare land broken by tiny black lakes and pointed rocks stretched out at her feet. The moon shone like a shield. Zora advanced into the gap.

Her mind was vacant of all thought. Her legs moved forward as though on their own, with the mechanical regularity of a pendulum. She noticed that the air grew warmer as she advanced and was overlaid by a curious and disagreeable odour of rotting vegetation. On she walked, on and on, finally emerging into a clearing. The spectacle she beheld there was familiar.

Rectangular blocks of ice of different sizes had been placed atop tree stumps. The ice had turned to fine silvery powder, volatile dust scattered on the ground. Dazed by exhaustion and hunger, Zora wandered among the throng of dolmens. In the middle of the clearing she came to a halt.

These blocks of ice did not contain dead animals, but human parts. Some of the blocks, larger than the others, held the complete corpses of naked men and women, their crazed eyes gaping wide in expressions of horrified surprise, their ashen faces warped by pain.

Our plucky Zora felt herself drifting inexorably into madness. Her legs buckled under the dead weight of her body. There she remained, kneeling on the ground, eyes glazed over.

It was in that state that Captain Gut found her when he arrived in the clearing, just before dawn. As he strode through the necropolis, he glanced indifferently at the icy tombs. For a moment he stood there, above Zora. His plump red face was swollen, damp, and oozing, like an enormous abscess that had just burst. Finally, he rained blows down upon her, then grabbed her by the hair and forced her to look him in the eye.

"What a lovely place this is," he hissed. "Why don't we rest a while and enjoy the setting?"

When, much later, he returned Zora to the camp near the lake, the girl's face was so swollen she was unrecognizable. Worst of all, she had lost her necklace, the one that had been given to her on the day of her baptism, twenty years before, by an ancient madwoman at the Inn at the Sign of the Farting Bear.

CHAPTER
17

For Life

On that warm September Sunday morning in the Kuhmo marketplace, Tero Sihvonen was hovering over a stall that sold fresh eggs. Under his arm he held a leek, a loaf of black bread, and a bottle of vinegar. He was chatting with the egg merchant, a pretty woman who made eyes at him and offered her eggs for a good deal less than the asking price, considering that – no doubt about it – Tero was a fine-looking lad. The egg vendor's husband, who was unloading crates from a cart nearby, looked on with a smile as his wife giggled and flirted with the young physician.

"Give me ten pennies for a dozen," he said with a laugh, "and I'll throw in my wife."

"Oh, Sami!" clucked the farmer's wife with a blush.

Tero, who had purchased everything he needed, made his way toward the far end of the marketplace, where the worst of the merchants set up shop. The best cuts of meat, the freshest vegetables, and the most finely crafted teapots were to be found in the first aisles, those that gave directly onto the street. But the deeper you ventured, the less attractive became the merchandise on display: the fish was rapidly rotting, the vegetables, spoiling. When you reached the last stalls, you found yourself at the very depths of the market. There, flimsy vendors' shelters had been thrown up against the oozing masonry of the high wall that delineated its southern extremity. Tarpaulins thrown over wooden frames formed a broad ceiling of thick fabric, blocking the slightest ray of sunlight. Even at high noon this section of the market was shrouded in darkness. Above the counters hung the carcasses of skinned dogs. In one corner, on a grill over a fire of dried dung, an old woman was frying earthworms and ravioli. Almost no customers were to be found in these aisles where the melancholy silence contrasted with the lively atmosphere of the central section. Beyond the fishmongers' stalls, the passageways were strewn with fish guts, blood, and detritus. Here was the downward slope to oblivion, the dark and violent side of self-satisfied humanity disporting itself a few paces distant.

Each time Tero visited the market, having bought all he needed, he lingered for a while in the clandestine section. He never bought anything. It was enough to seek consolation, as we all do when given a chance, in the spectacle of other people's poverty.

On that particular day, as he made his way toward a corner along the stone wall, he noticed before him a man and a woman. Standing upright, motionless, obscured by deep shadow, they seemed to be waiting for something. There was no one around them, only empty stalls. The awnings were lowered, and the floor was covered with shit and fruit peelings. At first glance, Tero took them for a peasant and his wife, undoubtedly trying to sell something. But what could it be? There was no merchandise at their feet, no crates of onions or buckets of crayfish. Tero was about to turn away when he halted, paralyzed.

That tall, lean figure, that straight back, that blond hair ...

With each step he made in the couple's direction, he could not stop telling himself that the darkness must be playing tricks on him, that everything would come into focus once he drew closer. "What a case of mistaken identity! It's almost funny. Yes, funny, that's it. She'll get a laugh when I tell her about it the next time we meet: 'Just imagine, in the Kuhmo marketplace, I happened upon a farm girl who was your spitting image! To tell you the truth, she smiled at me, and that threw me into a tizzy!'" But when he came near the couple, when self-deception was no longer possible, Tero felt as though his heart was being shredded.

Zora's face was deformed by swelling; its left side was so bloated that her eye had all but vanished amid the reddened flesh. Her right cheek was laced with deep cuts encrusted with dried blood, as though her entire cheek had been harrowed by a huge clawed paw. When Zora smiled at Tero, he saw she was missing two incisors.

The man beside her was tall, husky, with several days' growth of beard. Both of his eyes were black.

"Want her?" he asked Tero in a low voice, his lips revealing the teeth of a shark. "Eight marks for a night. A hundred and fifty and she's yours for life."

"I ... I don't have any money on me," answered Tero, and waved his leek, his bread, and his bottle of vinegar in embarrassment, as if to prove that he'd come to the market with the intention of buying only small items. "I have enough at home. I'll go back home ... You can come with me, I'll pay you at my place."

"You buying or renting?"

"Buying."

"Oh yeah? Good. So go get the money, then come back and take her if I haven't sold her before. Make it fast, believe me, you're not the only stud who has eyes on her. She's one hell of a gal, and when her face gets back to normal –"

"Come with me to my house and I'll pay you on the spot."

"Nope. I don't deliver. You take me for a milkmaid, or what? Rustle up the cash, come back, and the strumpet is yours, and that's that."

"Listen! I'll pay more – how much did you say for life?"

"One fifty."

"One hundred and fifty. I'll throw in ten marks for delivery. Does that suit you?"

"Twenty."

"Very good, twenty marks. But I ... All things considered, let's do this. I'll return home first. I don't want to go through the market in your company, you understand ... I'm a physician here and I wouldn't want people to think ... I wouldn't want people to think that –"

"That you've got a taste for spoiled meat, is that it? I can understand. Whatever the case, I couldn't care less. All that interests me is the colour of your money. And to get rid of this wildcat. If you only knew what she's put me through, the she-ass. I'd have dumped her long ago, but she's all I've got to sell and I need money to go back south. But there's nothing like her for churning your butter, believe me. And if she starts to get on your nerves, just chop her up and feed those fine thighs of hers to the hogs."

A lengthy silence ensued. Tero seemed to have been dumbstruck.

"Hey! You still there?" said the big man, placing his hand on Tero's shoulder and shaking him.

The young physician snapped out of his stupor.

"Yes … yes, yes," he said, his voice self-assured. "Listen, I like the gash, but I'd rather complete the transaction in a more out-of-the-way place. There's an abandoned stable on the northern outskirts of the village. Let's meet there in a half-hour. That will give me time to go home and get the money. One hundred and seventy marks. I'm leaving now so people won't see us together. Wait ten minutes, then come and meet me there. If you can't find your way, ask someone."

The Captain was a lucky man, and he knew it. Ten minutes after Tero left, he grabbed Zora by the arm and pushed her through the market. Of a butter and egg merchant whose stand was located near the exit, he asked the way to the abandoned stable.

"Easy," answered the woman. "Just follow the main road and head north. You'll be there in twenty minutes. It's not like you're bound to get lost. Kuhmo is the size of a rabbit's ass."

The Captain and Zora turned onto the main road and walked north for a good half-hour. At the city limits, little brick dwellings held together with straw and mud mortar dotted the poorly maintained highway, and the intervals between them grew greater as they moved away from the market. Finally, there were no houses at all, just old farms whose fields stretched out as far as the eye could see. It was haying time, and broad swaths streaked the gently sloping fields like large, puffy scabs. It was an easy matter for the

Captain to locate the stable of which the physician had spoken. There, on his right, the decrepit structure stood in the middle of a pretty green meadow.

Gut and Zora crossed the grassy expanse toward the stable. When they reached the building, the whoremonger pushed his merchandise inside. Tero was there, waiting for them. He was standing in the middle of the empty space. If he had been able to read on faces the expressions written by extreme emotion, the Captain would have detected in the features of the man standing there such bottomless fury that he would undoubtedly have recoiled in horror. But Captain Gut was a hard, emotionless man who understood nothing of the human soul. He figured it was sexual desire, and not distress, that flooded Tero's twisted, sweat-stained face.

He walked up to the young physician, his hand extended. Tero, his forehead burning but his manner assured, also stepped forward, and with a rapid thrust of his forearm, plunged a scalpel into the Captain's chest. He paused a moment, then violently swept his arm downward. Beneath his ecru shirt the massive stomach of the white slaver gaped open like a wineskin, cleanly. Then Tero, crazed with grief, dropped his scalpel to the ground, thrust his forearm up to the elbow into the gaping wound, and pulled it out abruptly, his hand grasping the malefactor's viscera. He dropped the steaming intestines to the floor. The Captain appeared not to believe what was happening to him. He put his hands delicately to each side of the wound and for several seconds pondered his soft tripe dangling upon the earth. Finally he kneeled down, then lay upon on the ground, gurgling.

Only then did Tero notice that Zora was no longer in the stable. Slowly he started to make his way outside. The young woman was there, facing the fine green meadow that surrounded the structure, her back turned to him. He paused in the doorway to contemplate her. The acrid scent of the freshly cut hay, which Tero normally found pungent and displeasing, now seemed intoxicating and enchanting for no other reason than it accompanied the pastoral tableau that lay before his eyes. All nature seemed to sing the praises of Zora, to celebrate her beauty and liken it to that of the moon, whose earthy disc already gleamed against the still-blue late-afternoon sky. All nature seemed to say of Zora, "How much lovelier she is!"

*

* *

Tero entrusted Zora to the care of Dr. Pikkarinen. The older physician ordered that a bed be prepared for the young woman in a free room in the dispensary. The patient was given potage, bread, and plenty of water. It was difficult for Zora to eat because of her broken jaw. In the end, she brought everything up. She asked to be left to sleep, but Dr. Pikkarinen insisted on examining her first. Tero sought refuge in the kitchen. After a half-hour spent brooding over a cup of tea, feeling queasy, he stepped outside and sat down in a rocking chair on the dispensary veranda. He smoked three cigarettes. The nurses who hurried in and out, usually so prompt to flirt with the likeable young man, found his expression so glacial they dared not even greet him.

After he had examined Zora, and the young woman had fallen asleep, Dr. Pikkarinen joined Tero on the veranda.

"She is sleeping."

Tero could barely nod his head.

"Listen carefully, Tero. I won't beat around the bush, so you know what to expect. Your friend has a nasty wound on the back of her head, and I suspect she is suffering from a concussion. We will have to observe how her condition develops over the next few hours. She is also experiencing pain in her ribs, and that disturbs me, her jaw is damaged, and she is suffering from dehydration. But what worries me most is the fever. I cannot even imagine where she slept these past few days. The autumn nights are cold in these parts. Still, by tomorrow we should have a clearer idea of her situation. She has numerous facial contusions, and may end up with scars, but nothing that would disfigure her. She has lost two teeth, as I imagine you know."

The doctor lit his pipe and added in a weak voice, "She denies it, but I must tell you nonetheless, she –"

"I know," Tero cut him off.

The two men smoked in silence for a quarter-hour. Eventually, Dr. Pikkarinen shook out his pipe to empty it of the burned tobacco and returned to his patient's bedside.

*
* *

The next day when she awakened, Zora, in a feeble voice, insisted to a nurse who had come to help her wash herself that Tero be refused access to her room. She did, however, allow Dr. Pikkarinen to assess her state, after which she pecked at a bowl of porridge and a plate of toasted buns and hard-boiled eggs. Before noon struck, she slipped into a deep sleep, broken by cries the nurses found terrifying.

Nonetheless, two days later, the fever had almost entirely disappeared. That evening, Dr. Pikkarinen sought out Tero once more. He was in the backyard of the dispensary, in front of an open fire. Wrapped in a quilt, a book open on his thighs, Tero was staring into the flames. He noticed the doctor's presence only when he sat down beside him on the ground.

"No doubt about it," said the veteran diagnostician, "she's a strong girl, your friend. I wouldn't have thought as much when she arrived here two days ago, but it seems she is on the road to recovery. The fever is easing. Tonight she ate an entire omelette and baked beans that Mrs. Hämäläinen prepared for her. If she still won't see you, you can attribute it to coquetry. Her face is nastily swollen."

"I know. Was she sleeping when you left the room?"

"Yes."

"Fine. I would have dropped by to see her, but if she is sleeping …"

it can wait until tomorrow. I scoured the town to find a few books she might like. She must be bored, all alone in that room the whole day long."

"Mrs. Hämäläinen found some novels and left them with her, but she's suffering from a migraine and has difficulty concentrating. In a day or two, perhaps … Still, try to see her tomorrow. I believe that, deep down, she would like nothing better."

After a short pause, Dr. Pikkarinen took up where he left off. But now he was speaking in a soft voice, and his words, buffered by his hoarse yet caring voice, brought tears to Tero's eyes.

"She has made a long journey, this fine, fair slip of a woman. To reach you she has had to overcome great obstacles, and has foundered on life's most treacherous reefs. And yet, there she stands, bones shattered but still alive, tenacious … She makes me think of the salmon that so often end their lives as they make their way back upstream to the place they were born."

The older man lifted his eyes toward the heavens and looked at the moon.

"She loves you, my good Tero. I would not be so impudent as to tell you what to do. I am only an old bumbler. But I believe, for your own good, that you should hear the truth from a third party: she loves you, with a love that few of us could boast of receiving in our lives upon this earth. Believe what you hear from the mouth of an old widower who loved his wife infinitely, and who recognizes in his patient's devotion an abnegation that cannot be feigned."

Dr. Pikkarinen got up, patted Tero absent-mindedly on the shoulder, and went off.

*
* *

Next morning, Tero went into town to purchase flowers and fresh fruit. At noon, as was his custom, he lunched at the lumber-camp kitchen on the outskirts of the locality. He returned to the dispensary late that same afternoon, sought to visit Zora, but was restrained by a nurse who told him the young woman was sleeping, having spent an agitated night due to a sudden but minor rise in her fever. The nurse advised Tero to return in the evening, as she did not anticipate Zora would awaken much before then. Tero stepped onto the veranda to take the air. At four o'clock, a lumberjack who had sliced through his calf with a wayward axe blow was brought to the dispensary. As Dr. Pikkarinen had gone off to deliver a baby among the peasants, Tero was obliged to treat the wounded man. Just as well, as he sorely needed something to distract him.

Come suppertime, as he approached the canteen, he heard the nurses, the stretcher bearers, and the two cooks chattering away as they ate. Their gossip irritated him. He abandoned the idea of eating at the dispensary and decided to dine alone, at the Kuhmo tavern. There, he ate a partridge breast and salted turnip washed down with a coarse German wine, of which he drank only half the bottle before asking for an infusion of linden flowers. When he stepped onto the street, as it was still light and mild, he decided to walk off his sadness in the fields outside the town. There, he picked wildflowers and attempted to bunch them together. His efforts yielded a scraggly bouquet; all the same, he preferred it to the one he bought that morning. Back at the dispensary, he completed his rounds swiftly, then stepped outside once more to smoke several cigarettes and watch the night fall.

Finally, he had to admit to himself that by postponing his visit from hour to hour, he was counting on Zora being drowsy when he finally called on her, and that all he would have to do was sit by her bedside and gaze upon her as she slept. Feeling ashamed, he lit another cigarette. He finished it in two shakes, then tossed the butt to the ground with a sigh of irritation – "Ah!" – and strode quickly back into the dispensary. He picked up the flowers and fruit from the table and went into Zora's room.

The gleam of a candle on the bedside table, next to a pitcher of water and a glass, provided the room's only light. Zora lay bundled in her blankets. Contradictory images of sarcophagi and cocoons flashed through Tero's mind as he looked upon her. Only her head was visible, and her face was turned toward him. It was as though, throughout the four long days at the dispensary, she had not budged an iota as she waited for him. When she saw him enter the room, her face lit up.

For Tero the shock was enormous. He could barely recognize her. Her forehead and cheeks were covered with bruises and a purulent black eye decorated her left side. A deep scar slashed across her face; the cut was deep, red, and inflamed, began at her right eyebrow, swept downward on the diagonal across the bridge of her nose, cut like a plow through her lips, and disappeared from view somewhere below the left side of her chin. The mark left by Captain Gut's knife awakened in Tero hatred of such searing intensity that he would have killed him all over again had he been standing in front of him. He forced himself to look into Zora's eyes. The pity the poor girl's face awakened in him, that face once so round, so full, and today so waxen and sallow, slowly diluted the river of hatred that had shaken his heart, and he sat down on a stool close to her bed. After putting the basket of fruit on the bedside table, he handed the bouquet to Zora, who pressed it against her heart and did not let go.

Her voice was weak, but it had a sparkle that revealed the pure joy Tero's appearance brought her.

"Ah! At last you are here! My friend, my dear Tero! I knew it ... I heard you were here, in Kuhmo. I said to myself, 'Just imagine that! What a coincidence! Who would have believed it! And so, by purest chance, he and I will meet once more in the same town.' Life is funny that way, is it not?"

She seemed sincerely astonished, as if she and Tero had veritably met each other by accident. So massive was the outrage she had suffered that the survival mechanism allowed Zora's brain to erase, or at least consign to the most distant, inaccessible reaches of her thoughts, the torments inflicted on her by Captain Gut and the state of degradation in which she had been presented to Tero at the public market. On she went with her feverish invention.

"I kept saying to myself, 'He must come see me, otherwise I will be very angry with him!' But deep down, I never doubted for a moment. I knew you would come, sooner or later! And here you are! Still, I almost feel like scolding you. It's just that –"

A violent coughing fit swept over her. As she struggled for breath, Tero gave her water. She sat up in bed to drink. When at last she stopped coughing, she apologized.

"It's nothing, nothing at all. I must have caught cold during the journey. The last time we saw each other, had I mentioned to you that I intended to make a journey? Oh! Of course, Tuomas takes me to Helsinki every year. We meet people, go out to restaurants, stroll along the docks ... That's all very fine, but still, my little Tuomas, with his books, his appointments with the – what's her name – the lady poet, those snobbish dinners ... That can make any trip unpleasant!" And here, she frowned. "Oh, how well you know that I adore my little Tuomas, don't you? I would never allow you to doubt it a second! If I scold him sometimes, it's because deep down I see him as a son! How he needs to be looked after! A constant distraction!"

Zora laid her head back on the pillow. Smiling, she stared at the ceiling. In the dim candlelight, Tero could see her forehead was beaded with sweat.

"Did I ever tell you the story of how Tuomas swallowed a spoon one day? Oh, today I'm laughing, but the scare he gave me! He had that annoying habit of reading at the table. How many times did I ask him not to bring along his books at mealtime? That day he was reading – I can't say for sure ... *Pantagruel*, I think it was – and he was eating molasses and raisin pie. He had the spoon in his mouth and then he started to laugh and – *Glug glug!* One thoughtless second and he lets go the spoon, and in the blink of an eye the utensil slides down his gullet and into his stomach! Poor Tuomas! There he was, with a piece of metal as long as a hand in his tummy, and there I was berating him. We had to rush off to the hospital in Grigol. Dr. Marjamaki removed the spoon with a long pair of forceps, but it really hurt him, my dear old Tuomas! 'Let that be a lesson to you!' I kept telling him on the way back, and he was all red in the face and couldn't say a word his throat was so sore. How nasty he must have found me that day!"

She spoke those last words in a muffled voice; her eyes filled with tears and she was weeping softly. Tero felt heavy hearted too. Tuomas, whether he was your friend, your husband, your neighbour, or your accountant – or even your enemy! – was someone you could not help but love with overpowering and enthusiastic affection. In her divagations, Zora had only to conjure up his name for the memory of the old alchemist to fill the room with a near-palpable presence. Tuomas was a ubiquitous entity who, even when his physical body was absent, watched over and brought comfort to the people whom he knew and loved in their times of trial.

Tero edged his stool closer to the bed, took out his handkerchief, and dabbed the tears from Zora's eyes. He murmured words of consolation. "Come, come … it's nothing … everything will be fine …" But in truth he felt completely helpless.

Choked by her sobs, Zora broke into another fit of coughing, more violent than the one before. Tero was so concerned he leaped to his feet.

"I will call Dr. Pikkarinen."

"No," said Zora hoarsely, as she stretched out her arm and gripped the sleeve of his overcoat. "Please close the door, I see you left it ajar. I hear people walking by. Quiet, how much I would like a little quiet …"

Tero hastened to close the door. This time, Zora motioned to him with her chin that she wanted to drink.

"You can clearly see he needed a woman to look after him, that silly goose!" she said after calming her cough. "For all the little necessities of daily life, he's so distracted he doesn't seem to know what he wants! Ever since we married, I've had to mind him like a mother looks after her child so he won't get into mischief. But … a mother's love for her child is not the love that sets a heart afire, is that not so?"

Zora's livid cheeks grew flushed. She turned her head and continued to speak, staring at the far wall.

"Ah, so that was it! My good Tero, look at me! I have become like those old chatterboxes who burden their doctors with their gossip ... You will forgive me, I trust. I made the long journey from the Plains of Archelle to reach this place, and I am so tired! The time has come for me to stop talking."

To hear Zora speak of her ordeal as though it had been a voyage of pleasure, an excursion she had undertaken of her own volition, crushed Tero's heart. He wondered whether it was the partition deployed by a violated vestal to conceal her dishonour, or whether, to keep from going mad, she had come to believe in her own lies. So great was his pity for her that he wished with all his heart that the second hypothesis were true.

"And now, now that I have you at my side, may I tell you?" she continued. "It was a little bit for you that I have come this far. I found you cruel indeed to have left me as you did, without so much as a fare-thee-well, on your last visit to the plains. Would it have been so difficult for you to make small talk with me on the day of your departure? We could have gone for a leisurely ride to the edge of the Misty Woods ... Better yet, close to our house there is a lovely pond where the ducks come to feed in fine weather. How much I would have loved to go there with you that day! Instead, as you see, you forced me to pursue you this far. That's because I still have one thing to tell you ... do you know?"

Zora looked at Tero and spoke with her eyes the words her mouth could not pronounce. And he looked back at her, and in spite of himself his eyes spoke of the tenderness he felt for her, which he could not admit. Zora understood her journey had come to an end. She sighed a funeral sigh and closed her eyes. Tero leaped to his feet. Placed his hand on her cheek. Her eyes were half-open and she was struggling for breath.

"Dear, fine Tero ... how I tried to cure myself of you! It takes time, the books say. I tried, how hard I tried, but how much time would I have needed to forget the heavenly, deceitful horizons you had drawn upon my heart? And even if I had been able to return, at the snap of my fingers, to that state before you, I would have said no, so sweet was my pain. And if you ascended to the most distant glacier of the Himalayas to care for the homeless and the hungry, I would have found a way to seek you out and tell you of my torment, at least once."

She lowered her eyes.

"How filled with vanity is love," she murmured. "How could I have wanted you all to myself, when you do so much good for so many people as you travel over hill and dale? How could I have forced you to bend to the imperatives of my heart? Was it you I truly loved, my dear Tero? Or did I love the image that the love I hoped you felt for me would shine upon me?"

Then she waved her hand as if to dismiss a wild idea.

"In any case … you have caused us to undertake a fine journey indeed, my vanity and I."

It was immensely calming for Zora to speak those words and loosen the reins that kept her heart silent.

Tero sat down again. He held his head in his hands, and his tears fell hard upon the floor. Zora looked upon him and stretched a frail hand in his direction. He took her hand and squeezed it hard. She opened her eyes one last time. Tero stood and kissed her tenderly on the forehead.

"My heart is wanting, I fear," she murmured, smiling weakly.

Then she closed her eyes, never to open them again.

So it was … the great geyser that Tero's presence had opened in Zora Korteniemi's life became a fine mist. Then disappeared as the life of the poor child flickered out.

*
* *

The good doctor Pikkarinen was a poet. He undertook to draft the death certificate. After a rapid examination, as he was unable to pinpoint any apparent cause, he entered on the form, *Zora Marjanna Korteniemi, died of love.* Zora became the first woman in the history of humanity, and the only one to this day, to have surrendered her soul out of unrequited love.

*

* *

Shortly after midnight, Tuomas Juhani Korteniemi entered Kuhmo on horseback. At the outskirts of town, a sheriff's deputy instructed him to proceed to the dispensary. He arrived there in less than ten minutes. He tied his horse to a post and rushed inside.

Nearby, from the woods that lay close to the clinic, the endless howl of a she-wolf rose in the air.

PART THREE

CHAPTER
18

The Two-Hundred-and-Fifty-Seventh Ingredient

It was Kabuki Day at the Golden Spur Theatre. The presentation had begun at nine in the morning, and it was nearly one o'clock in the afternoon, and the Japanese actor who had been invited to Finland by the National Cultural Renewal Society was still onstage. Tero Sihvonen was standing outside in a narrow alley along the western wall of the theatre with Anelma Nöyränen. After four hours of kabuki in the suffocating heat of the auditorium, the young lady was feeling indisposed. Tero was playing the gallant gentleman, less because he found it pleasing than because convention demanded it. He had accompanied her outside to rub her back while she vomited an amalgam of bile and cherry porridge. He had come to the theatre that morning with a group of friends, fashionable young men and women, demimondes whose company he kept for lack of anything better. His had been the misfortune to be seated next to Anelma Nöyränen. When, nauseous and satiated by a kabuki performance of which she understood nothing, she felt herself about to retch, naturally enough it was Tero's sleeve she tugged on to obtain assistance. Tero turned in her direction and saw her livid complexion – how could he not have accompanied her outside?

So it was that he found himself in that narrow alley alongside the theatre, breathing in the brisk winter air while the spoiled daughter of some wealthy landowner vomited into the snow. "All things considered, I'm better off here than inside!" thought Tero as he lit a cigarette. He raised his head. Nothing pleased him as much as these cold winter skies, grey, melancholy, and peaceful. In the tavern next to the theatre, inebriated students were engaged in a moustache competition. It was hardly midday, and they were already three sheets to the wind … The walls muffled their raucous cries, but he could hear them singing "Ibidem," a popular drinking refrain.

Anelma Nöyränen finally stood upright.

"Are you feeling better now?" Tero asked, smiling.

She was as white as a sheet. How annoying, what had happened. She had a crush on Tero (as did several other birdies present in the theatre that day), and now that she'd puked at his feet, she was out of luck for sure.

"You should return home and get some rest," Tero advised. "I will see you this Monday for dinner at the Countess Of Vihko's."

As he accompanied Anelma Nöyränen toward the street to hail a cab, he noticed a few specks of vomit on his vicuna overcoat. "Shit!" he muttered to himself. "What a pain in the backside she is!" But Tero was a well-mannered young man and disclosed nothing of his irritation. He took the upchucker by the elbow as she climbed into the cab and offered a few vague promises. "I shall be the first to ask you to dance Monday at Madame … uh … at the countess's, that's it … yes, yes, I promise. But above all, take care of yourself." Then he smiled one last time, waving as the cab moved slowly off along Theatre Street.

Tero stood there for a moment. A plump, short student came running out of the tavern. Holding high a nebuchadnezzar, he shouted something that Tero did not understand, and smashed the empty bottle with all his strength on the pavement. Passersby looked on, indignant, but Tero burst out laughing. He tossed his cigarette butt in the gutter and lit another. Ah! This winter afternoon was far too poetic to waste on a kabuki performance! Let the social niceties fall where they may; Tero would not return to his seat. Instead, he would treat himself to a long walk through the streets of the town. He would stop off to see Henrika, who sold exotic fish, then he would visit the bookshops – now that's an idea! But first, he would tuck into a bowl of steaming stew and a thick slice of buttered bread at Your Mother's Breast.

Soon he reached Chimneysweeps' Way. A few steps later, his shoes and socks were completely soaked by slush. His feet were freezing, but no matter! He was dreaming of Henrika. She was a sassy little blond who owned a shop in a market not far from his house. When he dropped by her modest store to flirt with her, he justified his visits by pretending to be an aquariophiliac. To lend some credibility to his lies, each call he would buy one or two surgeonfish, which he would throw still alive into the nearest trash can as soon as he left the premises. His real ambition was to snuggle up to Henrika at his place, in his cold apartment on Spurned Street. Tero, in recent years, had become a redoubtable virtue depressor. His conscience troubled him not in the slightest. After all, he was a healthy unmarried lad and could do what he pleased.

Twenty paces from Your Mother's Breast he stopped to buy a newspaper from a newsboy. As he raised his head after counting his change, his gaze took in the street before him. It was empty except for a stoop-shouldered old man making his way slowly toward him. Tero froze.

He recognized Tuomas even before the man noticed he was there. The elderly alchemist had grown so old that at first Tero doubted it was his friend. His hair had turned yellow, that piss-coloured yellow that takes hold of even the finest silver manes after a certain age. His face was creased like a folded paper garland and his profile, once haughty, was bent and emaciated. His steps were less sure, but the look in his eyes had not changed. Striking blue-grey, one in a thousand.

Between the two men, the street described a slight dip, at the lowest point of which, on Tero's right, in the midst of shops, boutiques, and mansards crowded in at close quarters, stood Your Mother's Breast. Moved, Tero looked on as Tuomas descended the dip, then made his way up with short steps, until he stood before him. Only then did he raise his head to see where his steps were leading. His eyes came to rest on Tero.

"Tero Sihvonen."

"Tuomas Juhani Korteniemi."

The two men stood there for several minutes, looking at each other. Many years had passed since their last meeting. Tero stepped forward and took Tuomas's wrinkled hands in his.

"Where are you going?" Tero enquired.

"Well, to tell you the truth, I was on my way to visit a sick friend. But we should dine together this evening, if you are free!"

"Let us meet here at seven o'clock," said Tero, pointing to Your Mother's Breast. "The food is good, and it's quiet. We'll be able to talk."

Tuomas promised he would be there, and the two men went their separate ways, confounded by their extraordinary meeting. Tero completely forgot he had come to the neighbourhood for the purpose of having lunch, and he returned home on foot, his mind in a curious state of disorder.

His apartment was located on the second and topmost floor of a small house on Spurned Street, only five minutes from Your Mother's Breast. He hurried upstairs four at a time and rushed headlong into his ill-heated lodgings. He immediately went over to the fireplace. There, on the mantelpiece, between a Romanian crystal ball and a painted wooden figurine depicting a bearded hat maker stitching a headpiece, stood a curious little object. Tero closed his fist around it. It was a marble statuette, heavy and compact, and he could feel its smooth coldness as he squeezed it between his fingers. Then Tero sat down in an armchair near the window that looked over the street, set the statuette on a reading table in front of him, and remained there for nearly an hour, motionless, eyes focused on the curious effigy. From time to time he removed a cigarette from the pack in his coat pocket, lit it absent-mindedly, like an automaton, and smoked it slowly, letting the ash fall to the floor. He wanted to weep – it would have done him good, he reflected – but his heart was dry. Finally, his back aching from sitting stiffly for so long, he got to his feet, hesitated briefly, then poured himself a glass of Scotch. He spent the rest of the afternoon pacing up and down, talking to himself, and drinking whisky. Just before seven, head spinning, he put on his coat, slipped the statuette into his pocket, and stepped out.

At Your Mother's Breast, Tuomas was waiting for him at a table near the back, close to the fireplace.

Tero sat down. There was a lengthy, embarrassed silence during which each man wondered what path the other had taken since the last time they met.

From the innkeeper's wife, Tero ordered for himself and his guest two bowls of sage soup, sautéed seal steaks, Balkan rock-partridge cutlets, meatballs in cream, honey-roasted potatoes, beluga caviar, a plate of grilled *juustoleipä*, Finnish crusty rolls, and a pitcher of lemon water. He also asked to be served a linden-mint infusion immediately.

"What! You do not want wine?" exclaimed Tuomas.

"No. I feel a case of the grippe coming on," Tero lied. He had been guzzling whisky all afternoon and now had a nasty migraine.

"As you wish. But I," said Tuomas as he drew a bottle of French wine from his overcoat, "will drink *this*. In Grigol, all you can find is that raspy Russian stuff they ship in tank cars from St. Petersburg."

Since he had joined the old man, Tero caught himself wringing his hands painfully. Meanwhile, Tuomas maintained the dignified, inexpressive countenance he always displayed.

"Nine years," Tuomas muttered. "Already. How time flies! And what a man you have become! Just look at you! That full beard suits you well!"

"You seem well also, Tuomas."

It was a pathetic attempt at flattery. He did not look well at all, and surely knew it. He thanked Tero nonetheless.

"I am not dead yet," he said laconically.

"What are you doing in Helsinki? Do you live here now?"

"No, no ... I'm passing through, just a few days. A friend of mine is quite ill. Illka Ahtola. I've come to visit him."

"Ahtola ... the leading authority on the harmful effects of tobacco?"

"Yes. He and I know each other from the days when I taught at the Imperial Alexander University. You might as well call it an eternity."

"What is his problem?"

"Your guess is as good as mine. A blood ailment no one can identify. He spent the past several months in Paris being seen by a specialist, but nothing came of it, and he decided to return home to die. He is suffering terribly. I do not come often to Helsinki. By the time I visit again, he will surely have travelled down the River of Tuonela. To tell you the truth, I've always found him to be coarse and vulgar, and a hypochondriac to boot. We were never close, but I believe he thought highly of me, and often wrote me. When I came to visit him, he would take me to lunch and keep me the entire afternoon, bombarding me with questions about my alchemical research. Illka is a man who knows how to listen. I'll be one hundred this year, my dear Tero, and by that I mean to say I've met people, many, many people, in my lifetime. And of that number, I could count on the fingers of one hand those who know how to *listen*."

Tuomas pointed to the bottle on the table.

"He gave me this wine. 'Drink it, you old potion brewer!' is what he told me. 'Me, my mouth is as dry as an old stump ... You die first from the mouth, Tuomas, remember what I said next time you have bad breath!' We were never close, but we've known each other for sixty-six years ... I wanted to say goodbye for the last time."

"How much longer will you be in town?"

"I have decided to leave tonight."

To fill the awkward silence, the two men took out their tobacco, one his pipe, the other his cigarettes. Nine years ... How, over one dinner, could they untangle the skein of nearly a decade? Where would they start?

"Congratulations on your book," Tuomas began.

Several years earlier, Tero Sihvonen had published, under the title *Ancient Poems of the Finns*, the sum total of the legends he had

364

harvested during his peregrinations through Karelia. His compilation involved rigorous work of organization that demonstrated the existence of narrative coherence among the tales. True to his intuitions at the time, Tero had, during those years, assembled the scattered fragments of a fabulous lyrical epic. The book had met with considerable success, and he abandoned medicine to become a professor and researcher in the literature department at the Imperial Alexander University.

"I haven't worked for more than a year now," he explained to Tuomas. "In fact, I just returned to Helsinki a few weeks ago after a long trip to France and Italy. The English call it a sabbatical year."

Tuomas guffawed.

"At the university," continued Tero, "they granted me thirteen months' leave, on condition that in the course of my travels I write a short treatise on the *zanni* in the *commedia dell'arte*. I decided to take up residence in Turin, but first of all, I wanted to see France. From Paris to Brittany first, then working my way along the Loire I toured the literary faculties, met folklorists, drank wine, and visited old churches. I also perfected my French. After a time, I headed south toward the Mediterranean."

The innkeeper's wife served the meal. Instead of attacking the meat, Tero, eyes fixed on a point on the wall, thrust a fork into the wooden tabletop and twisted it back and forth on its axis.

"Before travelling to Italy, I spent several days in Marseille. Have you ever been to Marseille?" he asked Tuomas.

"Yes, three times."

"Did you ever go for a stroll in the market at the port?"

"Of course. There's nothing quite like it in these parts, is there?"

"No! Nothing quite like it. The day I visited, as I was strolling among the stalls, I came upon this."

Tero pulled the figurine from the pocket of his greatcoat and placed it delicately on the table. At the sight of it, the elderly alchemist displayed contrasting reactions. His lips sketched out the beginnings of a smile, but his eyes welled up with tears and his brows furrowed as though from sudden pain.

The statuette resembled a small marble monolith. With predominantly rectilinear chisel strokes, the sculptor had carved from a single block the rough forms of two figures locked in embrace, the lips of one joined with those of the other. So great was the economy of detail that it would have been impossible to distinguish the man from the woman had it not been for the roundness of her belly, which suggested she was the female, and pregnant. On either side of the block, each figure's arms, long, straight, horizontal planes, encircled the other, hands placed flat against the beloved's back in an inverted V. The forms seemed to emerge from the lines of the block: their heads were flat on top and curved behind. The sculptor had carved out hair with broad strokes. The block's asperities had been lightly rounded, so that no sharp edges remained. The sculpture seemed to summon the hand; you felt like stroking it, grasping it tight. It was a small but touching piece; the bond that united the man and the woman seemed to echo the subjection of the lovers to the block of stone that made them eternal prisoners.

Tuomas picked up the statuette between his thumb and index finger and raised it to eye level. All-conquering old age, which until only a few years before had been unable to breach his defences, now asserted itself with cruel ostentation. His arm moved slowly, and his hand was as crooked and misshapen as the talons of a dead partridge.

"To tell you the truth," muttered Tuomas in a wavering voice, "I'd just as soon stick your little statue up my ass!"

Tero realized he had committed a faux pas. How stupid to think Tuomas might have found this trinket amusing!

"You found it in the market in the port of Marseille?" the alchemist continued. "Well, that just gives me one more excellent reason to remain in Grigol. As it is, they come knocking at my door ten times a day with the same old story. Feh!"

A fine thread of saliva dripped from the old man's mouth and dribbled down his chin. Tero was troubled beyond all expectations.

"The rat catcher you bought it from, did he have many in stock?"

"Yes," Tero answered. "His stall was full of them."

"And was he selling them?"

"Plenty."

"Shit!" cursed Tuomas, a vague smile creeping over his lips.

"That's because the original sculpture was being exhibited at the Musée des Nations in Marseille, as part of an exposition on the art of the Carpathians."

"You don't say? And you attended that exposition?"

"Indeed. Corneliu Barna was present."

Why had the figurine touched off such a confrontation between the two men? Who was the mysterious Corneliu Barna? To understand why and how, we must retrace our steps, far back in time, to the very day of Zora Korteniemi's death.

Despite what good Dr. Pikkarinen had written on her death certificate, the actual cause of Zora's death was never elucidated, nor will it ever be. Still, in the weeks that followed the poor girl's demise, the report that a young woman from the Plains of Archelle had died of love in Kuhmo began to spread throughout the region. First the rumour reached the neighbouring villages, then the distant extremities of the township, before spreading through all of Karelia, from north to south, and to a good portion of Savonia and Ostrobothnia. The rumour rapidly became "fact," a news item, so to speak, that rapidly spread to every corner of the Grand Duchy before overflowing into Russia and then to the remotest corners of old Europe. One year after the event, the story of "Zora Korteniemi, who died of love" had touched a broad swath of European young people thirsting for grandeur and dreams.

In the months and years that followed, far from lessening, fascination with the story of the young Finnish girl was transformed from the status of an actual event to that of a legend. After her death, Zora was buried in the Grigol cemetery. Tuomas had erected a simple but gracious grave marker upon which the old man, every week for the first few months, laid a bouquet of fresh-cut flowers. Once the story of Zora had made the rounds of the continent, from Lapland to Italy by way of Turkey and Siberia, hordes of young travellers began to file past her grave. At first, two or three times a week, small groups of four or five young people would detrain at the Grigol station. The pilgrims would lodge at an inn for a few days, enquire as to the best way to reach the Jermu-Agricola Cemetery, then go off to pay tribute to the girl who now stood as the embodiment of the ideal of life lived poetically to the very end. Soon, in a matter of weeks, larger groups began to arrive. Two years after Zora's death, according to estimates provided by the Grigol railway station management, more than half of all passengers who disembarked at the town were Zora worshippers, driven to the farthest extremity of northern Europe by their veneration for the deceased and also, we might well add, by their dreams of journey and adventure. The young people brought flowers, letters, and gifts to the grave of their muse. In like manner, the merchants of Grigol began to pay homage to the dear departed. Some, moved well beyond what might be considered reasonable, collapsed upon the grave and wept bitter tears, invoking the name of her whose memory they venerated. Indeed, it was the least they could do. Zora had single-handedly quintupled the revenue of the tourist industry in a town that, until then, had been of no interest to anyone.

Nine years after Zora's death, the phenomenon continued unabated. The Jermu-Agricola Cemetery, once so quaint and deserted, a place where old philosophers would come to stroll, had become a sanctuary dedicated to Zora Korteniemi. A year and a half before Tero and Tuomas met in Helsinki, Corneliu Barna, inspired by Zora, created a sculpture entitled *The Embrace*; the figurine Tero had purchased in Marseille was a miniature reproduction. With *The Embrace*, a young Romanian sculptor whose reputation had barely moved beyond the confines of Bucharest café society suddenly found himself thrust to the forefront of the European art scene. There existed three versions of his sculpture. One toured through Europe and the United States for display at exhibitions. Barna conserved another in his Parisian studio. The third version, life size, was placed on Zora's tomb.

In the months that followed his wife's death, and in the depths into which it had cast him, Tuomas lived oblivious to the legend that had grown up around Zora's "heroic" death. About a year after her passing, when he began to look for an apartment in Grigol, and when his first health problems began to appear – nothing out of the ordinary for a man of well over ninety – he grew irritated by the raucous gaggle that interfered with his mourning. In public, he showed no hesitation about pouring scorn on the "cheap romanticism" displayed by a certain number of youthful cretins who robbed Zora's memory of the dignified silence it deserved.

Then Tuomas, experiencing the attraction of death and anger, came to hungrily embrace the universe's grand indifference toward worldly things. In the end, he cared no more about the uses made of Zora's memory, as long as her grave was respected (for though he did not know it, the mourners who came to pay their respects by depositing lilies displayed such devotion that, had anyone been so foolish as to transgress the security perimeter that had been erected around the gravestone, all those present would call him to order).

Then the years gradually overcame his indifference. Each day, worshippers attempted to contact him, and meet him. He too had become a figure of legend. He never agreed to meet the curious who came to prostrate themselves on Zora's grave. The most he could do was to become inured to the admiring glances and whispers that followed him whenever he ventured onto the street to buy a newspaper. And as for the sculpture that had journeyed from one end of the Western world to the other, it was far too modern for his taste. Worse, the very sight of it reminded him of the unbearable circus the great tragedy of his life had become.

"Did you speak to that famous Barna of yours?" he asked Tero. "Did you size him up?"

"Not at all, what do you think? What could I have possibly said to him?"

Tero took the figurine from the table and slipped it into his pocket. There was nothing more to say. Better that way.

As he no longer wished to talk about the absurd cult that had given birth here to sculptures, there to pilgrims and emulators,

Tuomas questioned Tero about his work and plans. It so happened that the *Ylioppilaslehti*, the Helsinki student newspaper, had offered the young man a grant to write a series of articles from China. Tero had travelled widely over the past nine years, but had never left Europe. It was one thing to make the rounds of the little hotels of Prague, Toulouse, or Madrid, and to rub elbows with southern European bluebloods; it was quite another to travel to the farthest reaches of the planet! All his life Tero had dreamed of discovering the Far East. But today he felt dispirited, fatigued. When he thought of his future, the horizon extended no further than Henrika, the exotic fish merchant, and his evening footbaths as he smoked. And so, he explained to Tuomas, he had decided to decline the offer from *Ylioppilaslehti* and stay put in Helsinki.

The innkeeper's wife continued loading the table with one steaming dish after another. The meal let the two men regain their composure, and their conversation, which until then had been curiously punctilious, took a more casual turn. Tero spoke of his work at the university, and his long research trips for the nation's folklore that he continued to make, in Finnish Karelia and around Lake Ladoga. He did not know whether Tuomas was really listening or not. With a sharp-eyed gaze the old man inspected the dishes arrayed before him, sampled everything, and drank more than he should have. His bottle of wine empty, he ordered beer, but would only relate the most prosaic details of his life. He was considering moving to Helsinki "for his research"; he "might have" located something in a private dwelling on Indulgence Avenue. For the time being, he had rented a house not far from Grigol, the summer residence of a Moscow author. It lay deep in the woods, and there was a little stream nearby – "a pretty thing indeed," he remarked in a flat voice. In winter, the place could be reached only by dogsled. When finally they turned to the cheese course, Tuomas's cheeks were flushed. Tero asked him what had come of his alchemical research. The centenarian sat up straight in his seat and wiped his mouth.

"Well," he said sententiously, "since you ask, it just so happens that I have recently made a remarkable breakthrough. Surely you remember the magister that I have been trying for years to concoct."

"The elixir of longevity?"

"The elixir of longevity, the panacea, the sovereign liquor, the ultimate cordial, call it what you will. I've made several interesting advances in the field. As I have been passing through Helsinki, I've shown my work to two colleagues, members of the Alchemists' Guild, for whom I have the greatest respect."

Tero was a child of the age, and much more in tune with the exact sciences. He did not believe it possible to prolong life, transform lead into gold, or dissolve diamonds. As he listened to his valetu-dinarian friend babble on about his obsession, he was overcome by an embarrassment mixed with pity, a sense of discomfiture identical to that which he felt nine years earlier when the alchemist first spoke to him of his research. The better to conceal his malaise, he stuffed a mixture of cheese, caviar, and bread into his mouth.

"It should be possible to find volunteers to test the potion," Tuomas continued, "but before letting someone drink an elixir made of 257 ingredients, including bismuth, excrement, whale sperm, and the ground tusks of the Malaysian deer-hog, the least I could do – surely you'll agree with me – is ask my colleagues who are as competent as I am, if not more so, to verify the formula. Tero ..."

Tuomas's tone, which had been pedantic, suddenly turned confidential. He leaned toward his friend, glanced behind him as though he feared being overheard, and said in low tones, "Tero, my friend ... there is one thing I would like you to keep for me. Under my overcoat is a notebook ... For the past forty years, on account of that notebook, I have been kept under surveillance, spied upon, followed ... Not for the notebook itself, of course, but for what it contains. In it, I have listed the ingredients, the steps to be followed, the precautions to be taken ... Everything. This notebook holds within it a great secret, *the greatest secret in the world*!"

"And you wish to give me the notebook?"

"Of course not! What could you possibly do with a formula that you do not understand?"

From the inner pocket of his overcoat, the alchemist withdrew a large leather notebook. He handed it to Tero.

The first six pages were given over to a preamble written in fine, closely spaced lines. The enumeration of the ingredients began on page seven and was quite simply interminable: 256 numbered ingredients, each accompanied by a description that could take up as many as ten lines.

"Followed," sighed Tero, holding the notebook open on his lap. "But by whom, and why?"

"Bah!" Here, Tuomas mimicked tossing something negligently over his shoulder as if to say, "Go figure." "Gladd the Argus, of course. Forty years ago, when the Fredavians informed him that on the outskirts of his forest lived an alchemist who had begun work on the magnum opus, he sounded the call to the hunt. But Gladd the Argus ... he is nothing but a pawn in the hands of much more powerful, much better organized forces. After you settled accounts with him ten years ago, he withdrew to his house and neither hide nor hair was seen of him. He is still there, for all I know, crouched in some dark corner, eating rodents and reciting for his solitary pleasure the millennial incantations and chants of the damned of bygone ages. If, for the time being at least, he has been rendered harmless, it is thanks to you and Zora. But Gladd the Argus is no more than one conspirator among the hundreds who haunt other regions of the world. In America they tell of an outsized man-child who hunts down scholars who seek the elixir of immortality. In the Balkans, it is an adolescent girl of spectral appearance who never appears but in the company of two gigantic undertakers ... In Asia, a fabulously beautiful woman who practises the tattler's trade ... There is nowhere in the world that does not possess its own alchemist hunter, and all of them are the flunkies of an immensely powerful coterie, with its own hierarchy and king!"

"Alchemist hunters? Really, Tuomas ... in our day and age? Aside from you, here, two or three spiritualists in Paris, and a handful of shamans in the Urals ... With all due respect, your clique appears to be quite inoffensive! Who could possibly so loathe and fear you as to persecute you from one generation to the next?"

"Death, Tero … death also has its forces, which find intolerable the idea that men might live forever."

Tuomas emptied his tankard of beer.

"I thought I had escaped their vigilance these past years – indeed, you performed a great service by neutralizing Gladd the Argus. But for the past eight months, everything indicates that they are circling me once more … Perhaps now you can see why all this chatter about Zora has so disturbed me. I have become a minor living myth, I who wished for nothing more than to relish my anonymity. It cannot have taken them long to find my tracks, Tero. That is the reason, in all honesty, why I must abandon my retreat near Grigol and vanish into the crowd here in the capital."

Tero lowered his head and skimmed the pages of the notebook. At the end of the list of ingredients, beside the number 257, was an empty space.

"And here?" asked Tero, pointing.

Tuomas pushed aside the collar of his overcoat and undid the first two buttons of his shirt, revealing a necklace made of simple blue silk ribbon. He pulled at the ribbon with two fingers and withdrew from his shirt a tiny glass vial that looked for all intents and purposes like a miniature milk bottle. A viscous liquid ebbed and flowed with each swing of the flask.

"Is that the 257th ingredient?" asked Tero.

"Yes."

"What is it?"

"Tears. Zora's tears."

*
* *

When the two men left Your Mother's Breast, the hour was well past eleven. Tero insisted on accompanying his friend to the railway station. They picked up Tuomas's luggage at the Imperial

Hotel. As a few minutes remained before the train's departure, they took a short stroll through the streets adjoining the station to digest their meal.

The area was deserted and silent. Tuomas took Tero's arm.

"It's none of my business, of course," said the elderly man, "but I think you should undertake the journey to China. It is another world, and a more poetic place on the planet would be hard to imagine, with the possible exception of Japan, which I encourage you to explore after you have feasted your eyes on the beauty of Peking, Nanking, and Canton. See things, Tero, see how men live. You do not like people. I know well that they are not your cup of tea. What's more, you are right. I do not like them either, the better part of the time. But you are an aesthete, my friend. Keep yourself far from the world if you so desire – who could hold it against you? Men are bothersome cretins. It's true in Grigol, true in Moscow, true in Africa, true everywhere. But the spectacle of humanity itself … it is one of the rare sources of distraction in this life. Observe the way they live. Look at their homes. See what is on their plates. Watch them open their shops in the morning and display their wares. See to what great lengths they go to make three pennies. Observe them as they drink and laugh, sing and chatter. The colours and movements of the world, of men and nature … you must ply yourself with them until your appetites are sated. And when you've had enough, lie down in the grass for a snooze. When you awaken, you will want still more. Don't stop filling yourself with the spectacle until old age makes it impossible to go on."

They walked in silence.

"Why did you not drink your elixir of longevity?" asked Tero. "Why do you not test it on yourself?"

"What makes you think I have not drunk it?"

"You look like an old monkey."

"I have not drunk it because … well, if you really must know, I do not want to live a long life."

The street was empty. Not a sound, save the puffing of a train entering the station. In the shadow of an overhanging cornice

Tuomas stopped, removed the silk ribbon, and slipped it into Tero's hand.

"Please keep Zora's tears," Tuomas implored him. "They are no longer secure in my old hands! I beg of you, Tero ... I know what you think of alchemy and the sons of art. I would certainly never speak ill of you ... I do not ask you to have faith. But I do ask you to protect these tears. You understand why I have confided this task to you, do you not?"

"Of course," said Tero, in a muffled voice.

"Try to grasp, if nothing else, what this vial represents for an alchemist. These tears are the key ingredient of an elixir the men of my calling have sought for centuries. Swear to me that you will protect them as you would your very life," exhorted Tuomas as he squeezed Tero's hands.

"Like my very life."

"You are a friend without equal, Tero Sihvonen."

"And you as well, Tuomas Juhani Korteniemi."

Tuomas pressed his forehead against Tero's. He was sobbing.

"How terribly I miss her, you know ... Not a day goes by, not an hour when I do not think of her."

And there in the Helsinki night, their two heads bent over the flask of tears, Tero and Tuomas wept together over the death of Zora Korteniemi.

At the moment of farewell, when the time came for them to separate in front of the station, Tuomas wiped his tears and paid the coachman to carry his luggage to the platform. Hurried but faltering, he turned one last time to Tero.

"Off with you, my lad! Go to the ends of the earth. It is in movement that man becomes man."

Then he strode off across the square without a look behind. Such was the last image of the alchemist that Tero was to keep: a hunched-over form in a fur coat and an ushanka, his stiff arms gesticulating impatiently to the coachman following him ... an old man who had to wiggle his way through the revolving doors to the station. As he watched Tuomas Juhani Korteniemi being swallowed up by the immense structure, Tero Sihvonen was struck with sudden certitude: he would never see him again.

*

* *

The time has now come to bring to a conclusion the tale of Zora, the young Karelian woman who died of love. But before writing *finis*, let us see what fate the great disposer of all things had reserved for Tuomas, for Tero, and, above all, for the precious tears of our heroine.

Let it first be said that Tuomas was correct: alchemist hunters did exist (and indeed they still do), and they were hot on his trail. They finally caught up with him on his return from Helsinki, just as he was nearing his country house by dogsled. They attacked at a bend in the trail. To dispatch Tuomas, the "forces of death" sent their "Black Corps," the elite perpetrators of evil deeds. Gladd the Argus had been called back from his splendid isolation. At his side, a marble-skinned teenage girl in a funereal gown commanded two undertakers and a tall, bald, one-armed man wearing a cape and carrying a valise. Around them was an entire colony of lynx and, should you be wondering what became of them, Fredavians in great number. Not to mention a host of other death-dealing figures. Poor Tuomas! You did not deserve to end your days disembowelled in the snow, on an obscure stretch of the Pelto-Pekka road! How unjust is life!

The assassins stole his precious notebook that contained the formula for the elixir of longevity, and searched at length for Zora's tears, but found nothing, and no doubt lost patience: beside themselves, they dragged the eviscerated body of the old alchemist to a nearby brook where they dumped it. We have no idea what became of the corpse. But at that very place, there stands a striking willow tree whose trunk is perpetually enveloped in mist, and whose leaves drip a fine trickle of silver. Every evening around midnight, an old she-wolf comes to curl up at its feet. It is there she sleeps until morning.

To this day, the notebook containing the interminable formula of youth has not been found.

Tero Sihvonen never married nor fathered a child. He did, however, cause many a tear to be shed by the fishwives, maidservants, and seamstresses of Helsinki. Though in his whole life he experienced nothing but passing infatuations, still he honoured his promise to his friend by religiously protecting Zora's tears. It proved to be the task of a lifetime, and a frequently perilous enterprise. After they eliminated Tuomas, the alchemist hunters quickly followed the trail of the tears to Tero. From that point on, and for the rest of his life, he was a hunted man, as Tuomas had been before him. But never once did he complain. Those tears had been wept for him. What could be more natural, he reasoned, than they fall under his protection? He carried out his mission with great courage.

One day, to help him carry out his apostolate, he enlisted the assistance of a group of young people inspired by Zora's story. The group set itself two objectives: to protect the tears from the alchemist hunters, and to retrieve from those who had stolen it the formula for the elixir of immortality. Over the years, the friendship of the co-conspirators would give rise to a body of rites, oaths, and prescriptions as the clique slowly turned into a fraternity. A few years later, it was decided that it would be better if the group's activities were carried out in secret, following which the singular conjuration took on a clandestine existence, without ceasing to win the devotion of new members from throughout Europe and beyond. The fraternity, wholly devoted to the defence of Zora's tears, has long been forgotten, yet it exists to this day. It continues to safeguard the tears, search for the formula of immortality, and combat alchemist hunters. Perhaps one day a full accounting of its exploits will see the light of day.

*

* *

At the end, as at the beginning of everything, stands Zora. Should you ever happen to pass by Grigol, show some consideration and pause briefly at the Jermu-Agricola Cemetery. You will easily locate the gravesite, for atop it stands a sculpture representing two roughly carved figures locked in embrace. Stoop to clean the grave. Push the rotting maple keys aside, sweep clean the caked-on earth, wash the accumulated grime from the letters incised on the stele. Then lay some flowers there. Lapland rosebays, the ones that grew in abundance around the little house on the Plains of Archelle. Zora truly adored them. And when everything is clean, sit down a few moments at the foot of the modest monument. The place is ideally suited for reading. Go ahead, don't be shy! Should you not feel like reading, lean your head against the cold stone, close your eyes, and listen closely to the strange metallic music that emanates from the forest encircling the graveyard.

End

AWARD-WINNING AUTHOR and literary translator David Homel also works as a journalist, editor, and screenwriter. He was born in Chicago in 1952 but left at the end of the tumultuous 1960s and continued his education in Europe and Toronto before settling in Montreal in 1980. He worked at a variety of industrial jobs before beginning to write fiction in the mid-1980s. His eleven novels to date have been translated into several languages and published around the world.

INTERNATIONAL JOURNALIST and award-winning literary translator Fred A. Reed is also a respected specialist on politics and religion in the Middle East. *Anatolia Junction*, his acclaimed work on the unacknowledged wars of the Ottoman succession, has been translated in Turkey, where it enjoys a wide following. *Shattered Images*, which explores the origins of contemporary fundamentalist movements in Islam, has also been translated into Turkish, and into French as *Images brisées* (VLB éditeur, Montreal).

After several years as a librarian and trade-union activist at the *Montreal Gazette*, Reed began reporting from Islamic Iran in 1984 and has visited the Islamic Republic thirty times since then. He has also reported extensively on Middle Eastern affairs for *La Presse*, CBC Radio-Canada, and *Le Devoir*.

A three-time winner of the Governor General's Literary Award for translation, plus a nomination in 2009 for his translation of Thierry Hentsch's *Le temps aboli, Empire of Desire*, Reed has translated works by many of Quebec's leading authors, several in collaboration with novelist David Homel, as well as by Nikos Kazantzakis and other modern Greek writers.

Reed worked with documentarist Jean-Daniel Lafond on two documentary films: *Salam Iran, a Persian Letter* and *American Fugitive*. The two later collaborated on *Conversations in Tehran* (Talonbooks, 2006). Fred A. Reed resides in Montreal.

PHILIPPE ARSENEAULT is a Canadian writer. A graduate in philosophy and law, he lived in China for many years. Since 2013, he has worked as part of the daily production team at *La Presse* as a copy editor. He won the Quebec Robert-Cliche Award in 2013 for *Zora, un conte cruel*, his first novel.